SONIC SELECT
BOOK THREE

W9-BNE-355

writers
MICHAEL GALLAGHER, KARL BOLLERS,
KEN PENDERS, TOM ROLSTON

cover by
PATRICK "SPAZ" SPAZIANTE

SPECIAL THANKS TO CINDY CHAU & JERRY CHU @ SEGA LICENSING

artists
PATRICK "SPAZ" SPAZIANTE, SAM MAXWELL,
DAVE MANAK, NELSON ORTEGA, JIM AMASH,
HARVEY MERCADOOCASIO, RICH KOSLOWSKI,
BARRY GROSSMAN & PAM EKLUND

ARCHIE COMIC PUBLICATIONS, INC.

JONATHAN GOLDWATER, co-ceo
NANCY SILBERKLEIT, co-ceo
MIKE PELLERITO, president
VICTOR GORELICK, co-president/e-i-c
BILL HORAN, director of circulation
HAROLD BUCHHOLZ, exec. director of publishing/operations
PAUL KAMINSKI, editor
STEPHEN OSWALD, production manager
ROSARIO "TITO" PEÑA, interior cover restoration
IAN FLYNN, DUNCAN MCLACHLAN,
VIN LOVALLO, production

SONIC SELECT
BOOK THREE

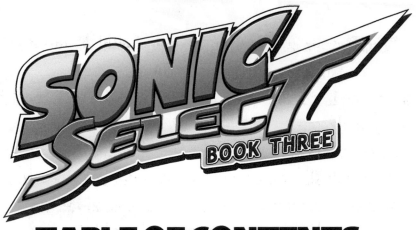

TABLE OF CONTENTS

"The Return of the King" (Sonic Super Special #4):
King Max may be back on his throne, but
something is definitely rotten in the Kingdom of Acorn! After
a royal decree to find the Robian (Roboticized Mobians)
population and dismantle them, the Freedom Fighters stand
in the middle of a virtual civil war! But are there more
sinister forces fueling this conflict behind the scenes?
Sonic had better figure it out quick, or his parents and
beloved Uncle Chuck'll be turned into spare
parts before you can say "chili dog"!

"Eel of Fortune" (Mecha Madness):
The Forty Fathom Freedom Fighters are back in
an all-new adventure under the high seas! A new
villain, EEL CAPONE, has slithered and slimed his
way to the top of the Underwater Underworld, and it's
up to the FFFF to stop him! Can our heroes save the
day without the help of FLUKE THE WHALE? Will Eel's
"hired mussel" capsize Bivalve's crew?
You gotta read this one to believe it!

"Bugged Bunny" (Sonic Blast):
Dr. Robotnik and his nephew Snively have planted
a secret device on Bunnie Rabbot! As the two villains
attempt to discover the secret location of Knothole
Village, Bunnie's skills prove to be a bigger
challenge than expected! It's a flashback
adventure you won't want to miss!

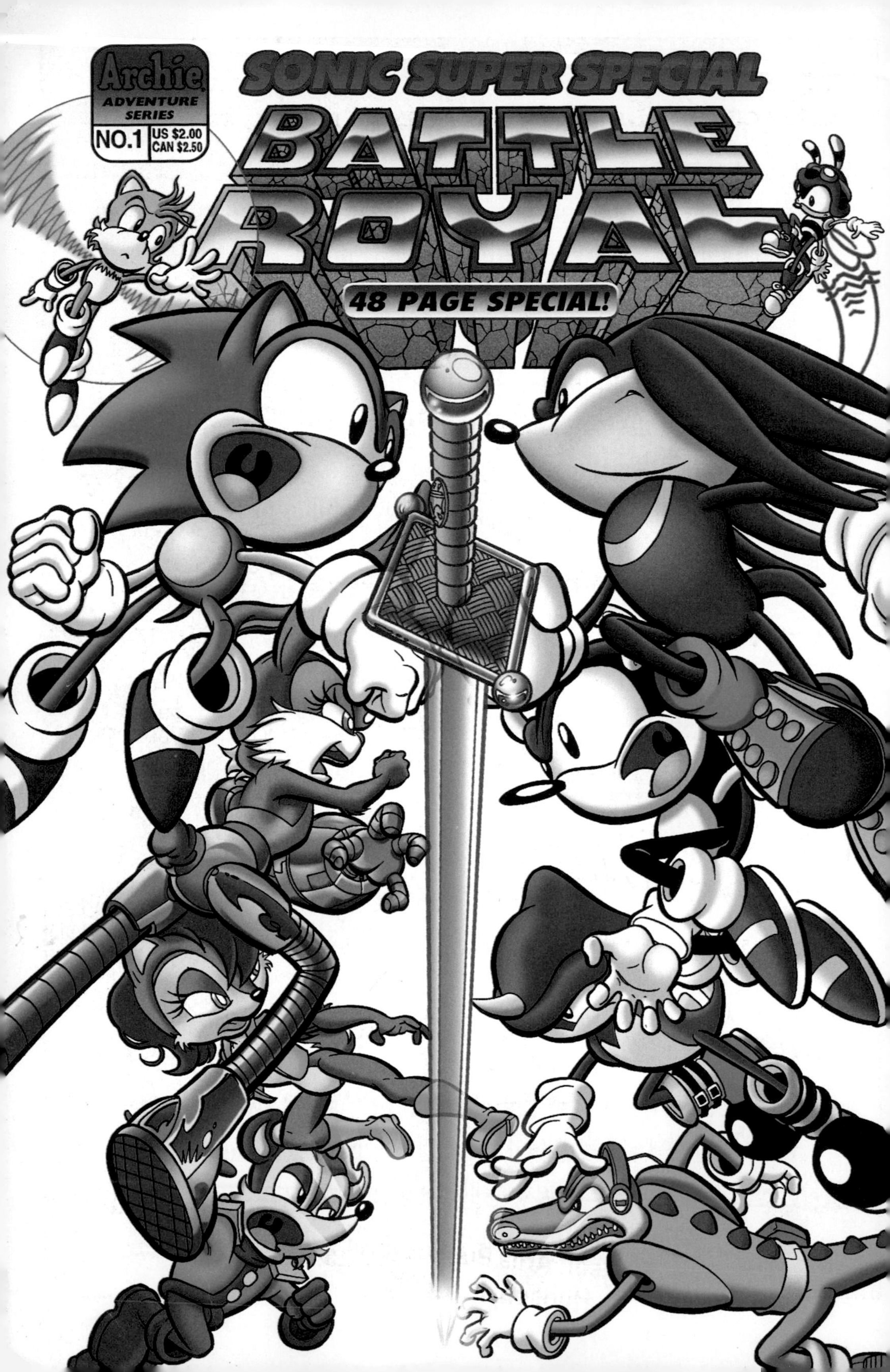
Archie
ADVENTURE SERIES
NO.1
US $2.00
CAN $2.50
SONIC SUPER SPECIAL
BATTLE ROYAL
48 PAGE SPECIAL!

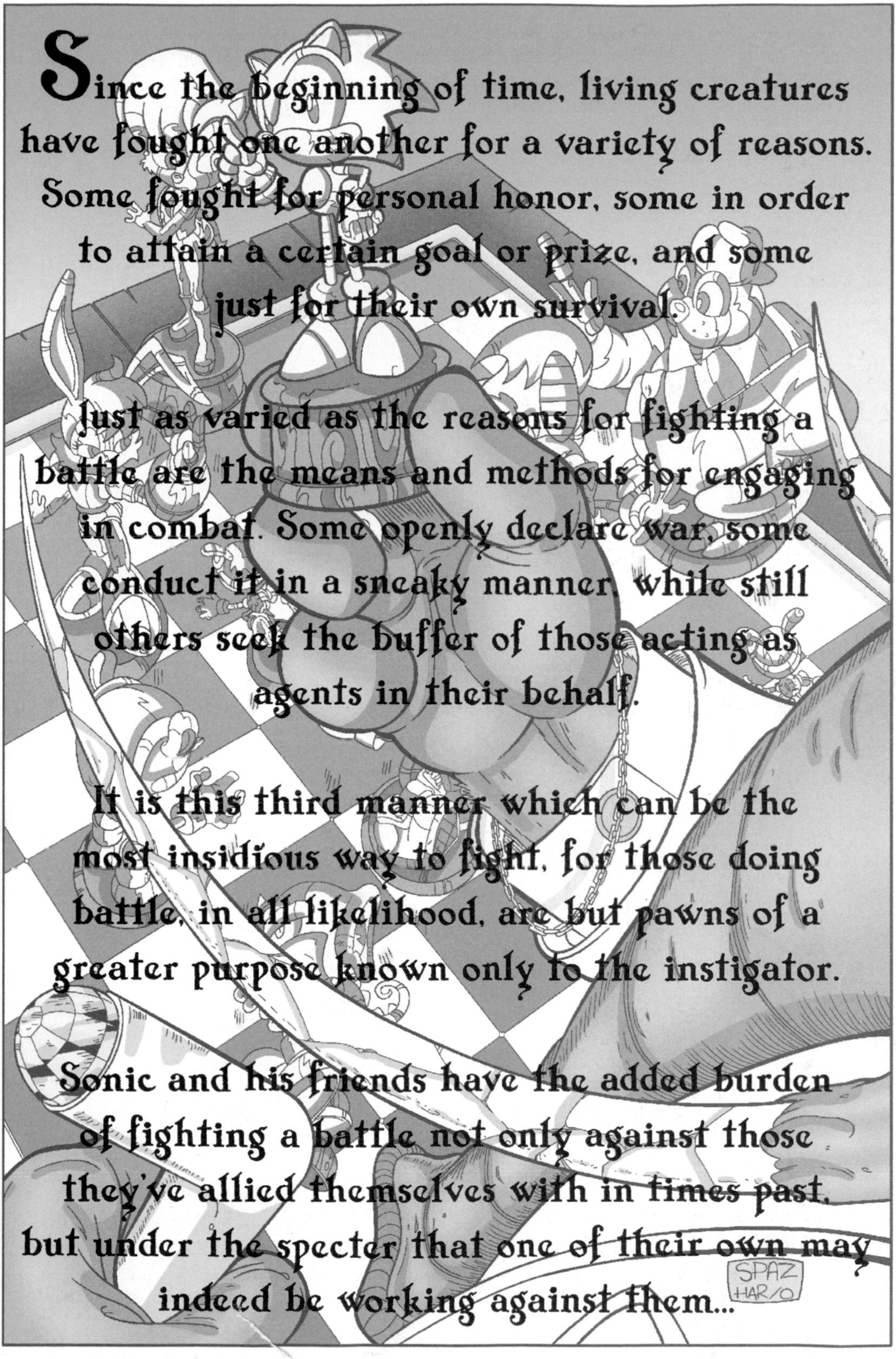
Since the beginning of time, living creatures have fought one another for a variety of reasons. Some fought for personal honor, some in order to attain a certain goal or prize, and some just for their own survival.
Just as varied as the reasons for fighting a battle are the means and methods for engaging in combat. Some openly declare war, some conduct it in a sneaky manner, while still others seek the buffer of those acting as agents in their behalf.
It is this third manner which can be the most insidious way to fight, for those doing battle, in all likelihood, are but pawns of a greater purpose known only to the instigator.
Sonic and his friends have the added burden of fighting a battle not only against those they've allied themselves with in times past, but under the specter that one of their own may indeed be working against them...
SPAZ
HAR/O

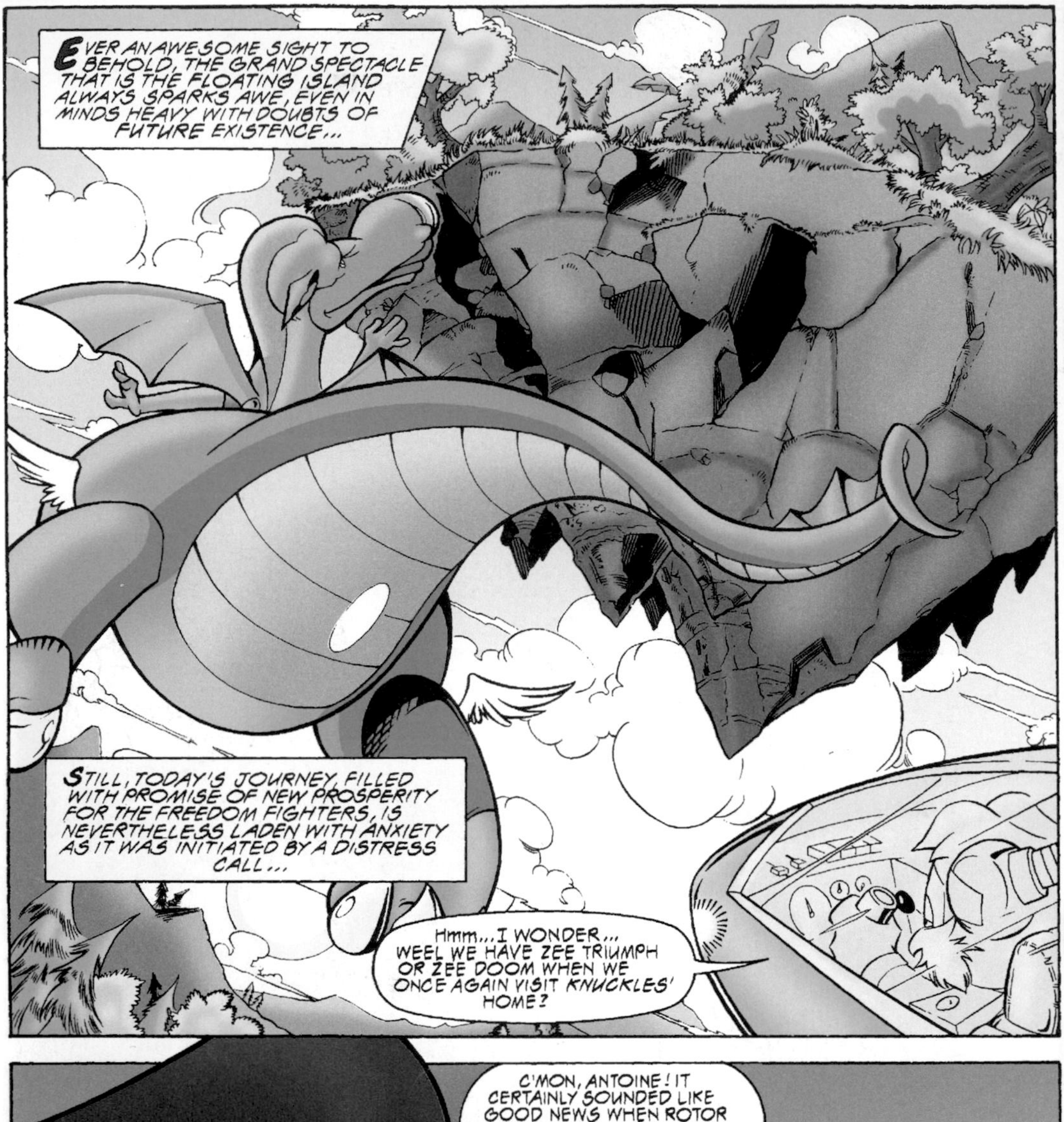
EVER AN AWESOME SIGHT TO BEHOLD, THE GRAND SPECTACLE THAT IS THE FLOATING ISLAND ALWAYS SPARKS AWE, EVEN IN MINDS HEAVY WITH DOUBTS OF FUTURE EXISTENCE...
STILL, TODAY'S JOURNEY, FILLED WITH PROMISE OF NEW PROSPERITY FOR THE FREEDOM FIGHTERS, IS NEVERTHELESS LADEN WITH ANXIETY AS IT WAS INITIATED BY A DISTRESS CALL...
Hmm... I WONDER... WEEL WE HAVE ZEE TRIUMPH OR ZEE DOOM WHEN WE ONCE AGAIN VISIT KNUCKLES' HOME?

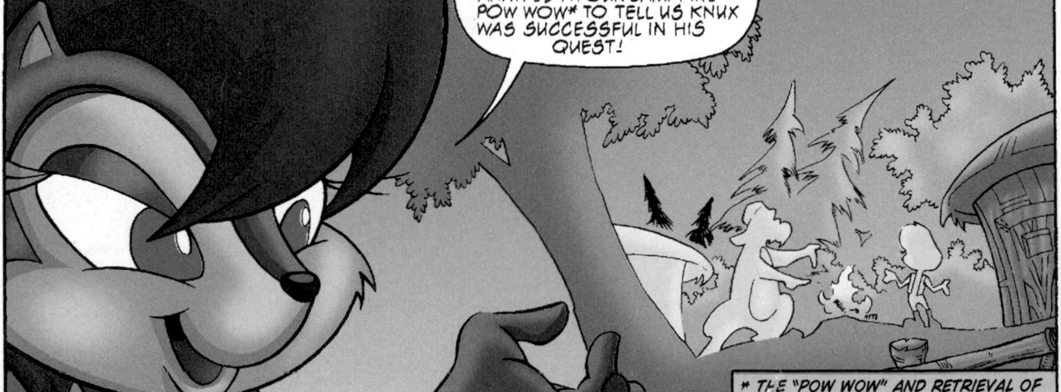
C'MON, ANTOINE! IT CERTAINLY SOUNDED LIKE GOOD NEWS WHEN ROTOR ARRIVED AT OUR CAMPFIRE POW WOW* TO TELL US KNUX WAS SUCCESSFUL IN HIS QUEST!
* THE "POW WOW" AND RETRIEVAL OF KING ACORN'S SWORD HAPPENED IN SONIC ARCHIVES VOL.12 - EDITOR

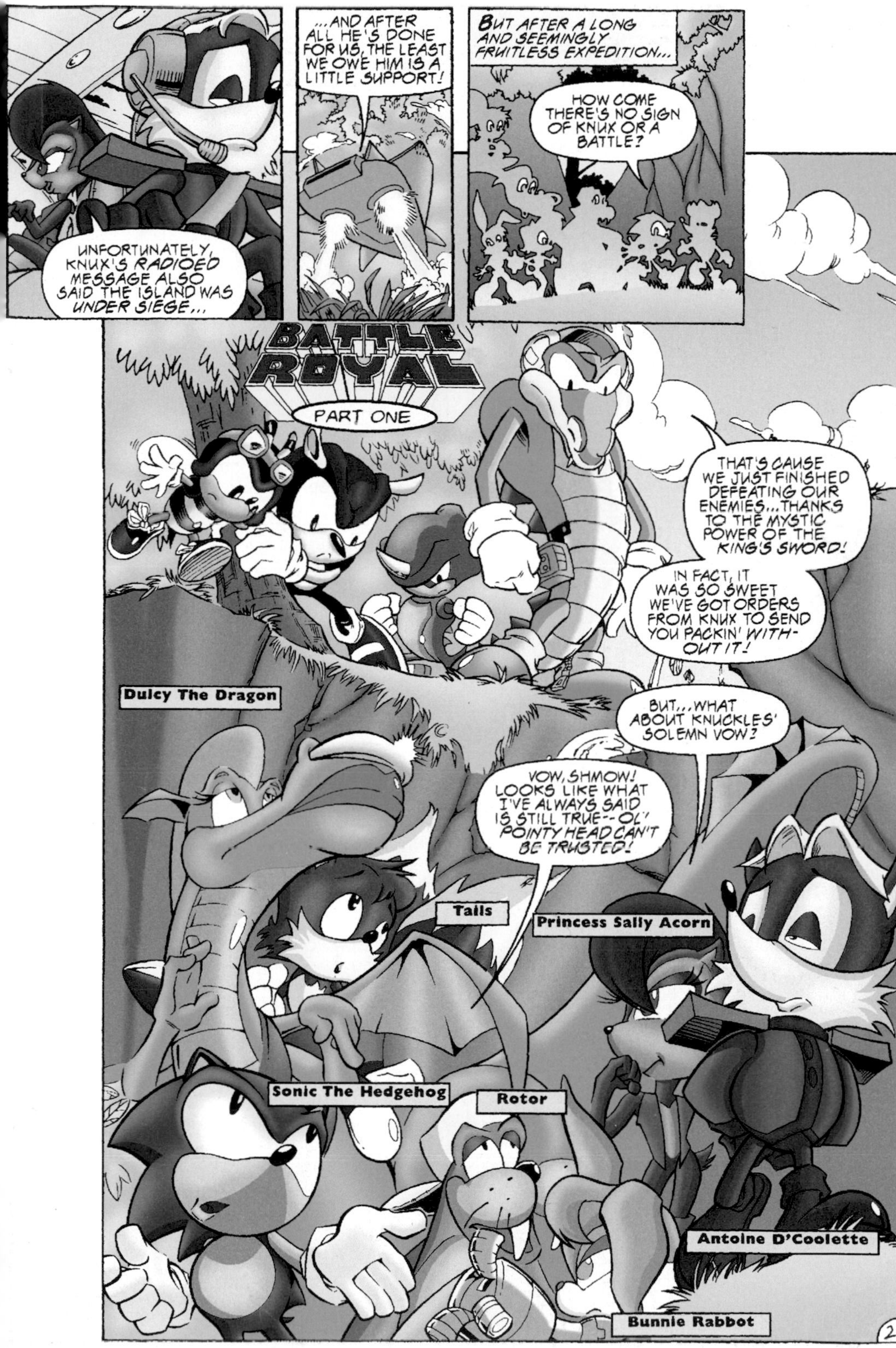
UNFORTUNATELY, KNUX'S RADIOED MESSAGE ALSO SAID THE ISLAND WAS UNDER SIEGE...
...AND AFTER ALL HE'S DONE FOR US, THE LEAST WE OWE HIM IS A LITTLE SUPPORT!
BUT AFTER A LONG AND SEEMINGLY FRUITLESS EXPEDITION...
HOW COME THERE'S NO SIGN OF KNUX OR A BATTLE?
BATTLE ROYAL
PART ONE
THAT'S CAUSE WE JUST FINISHED DEFEATING OUR ENEMIES...THANKS TO THE MYSTIC POWER OF THE KING'S SWORD!
IN FACT, IT WAS SO SWEET WE'VE GOT ORDERS FROM KNUX TO SEND YOU PACKIN' WITH-OUT IT!
BUT...WHAT ABOUT KNUCKLES' SOLEMN VOW?
VOW, SHMOW! LOOKS LIKE WHAT I'VE ALWAYS SAID IS STILL TRUE--OL' POINTY HEAD CAN'T BE TRUSTED!
Dulcy The Dragon
Tails
Princess Sally Acorn
Sonic The Hedgehog
Rotor
Antoine D'Coolette
Bunnie Rabbot
2

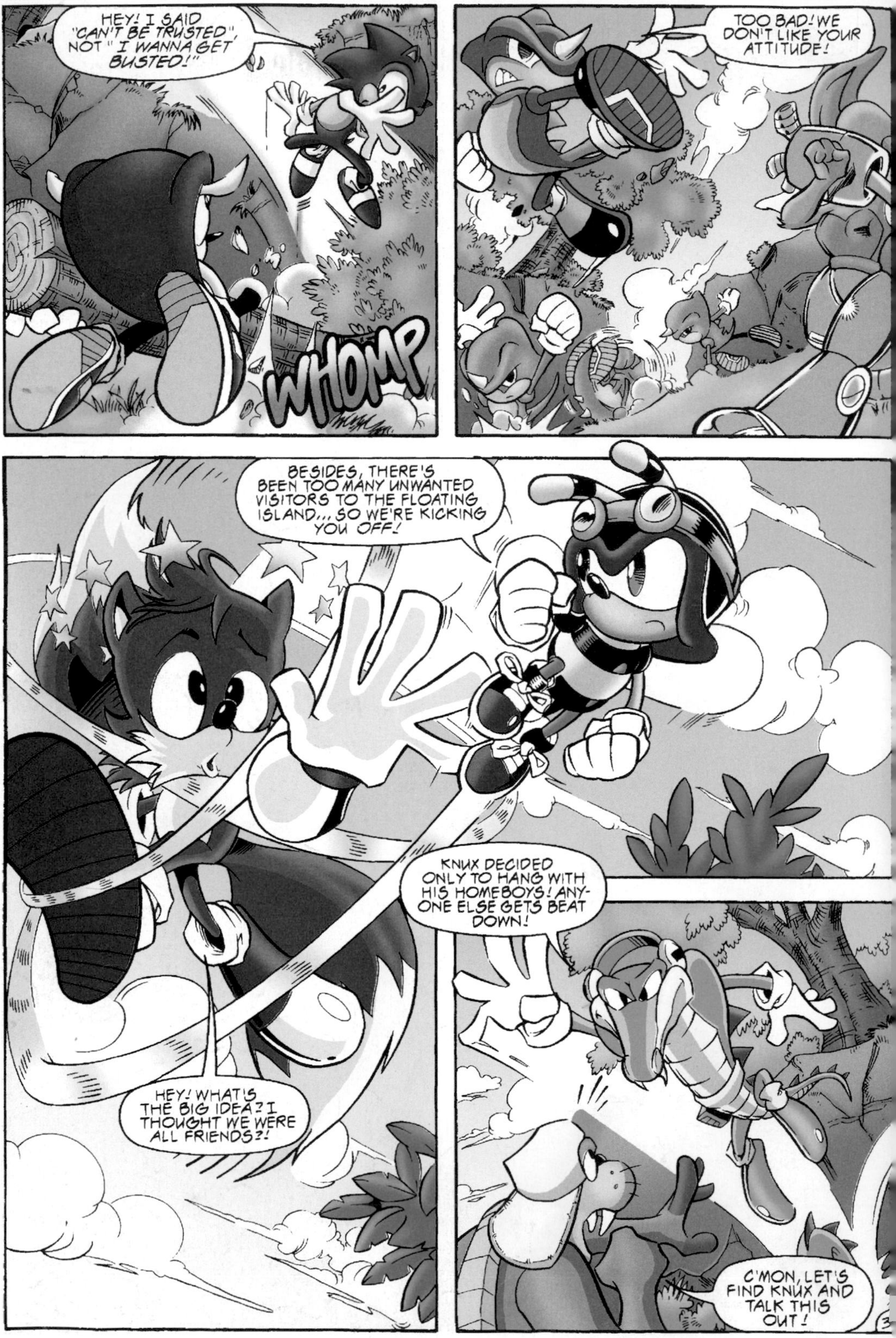
HEY! I SAID "CAN'T BE TRUSTED", NOT "I WANNA GET BUSTED!"
WHOMP
TOO BAD! WE DON'T LIKE YOUR ATTITUDE!
BESIDES, THERE'S BEEN TOO MANY UNWANTED VISITORS TO THE FLOATING ISLAND... SO WE'RE KICKING YOU OFF!
HEY! WHAT'S THE BIG IDEA? I THOUGHT WE WERE ALL FRIENDS?!
KNUX DECIDED ONLY TO HANG WITH HIS HOMEBOYS! ANY-ONE ELSE GETS BEAT DOWN!
C'MON, LET'S FIND KNUX AND TALK THIS OUT!

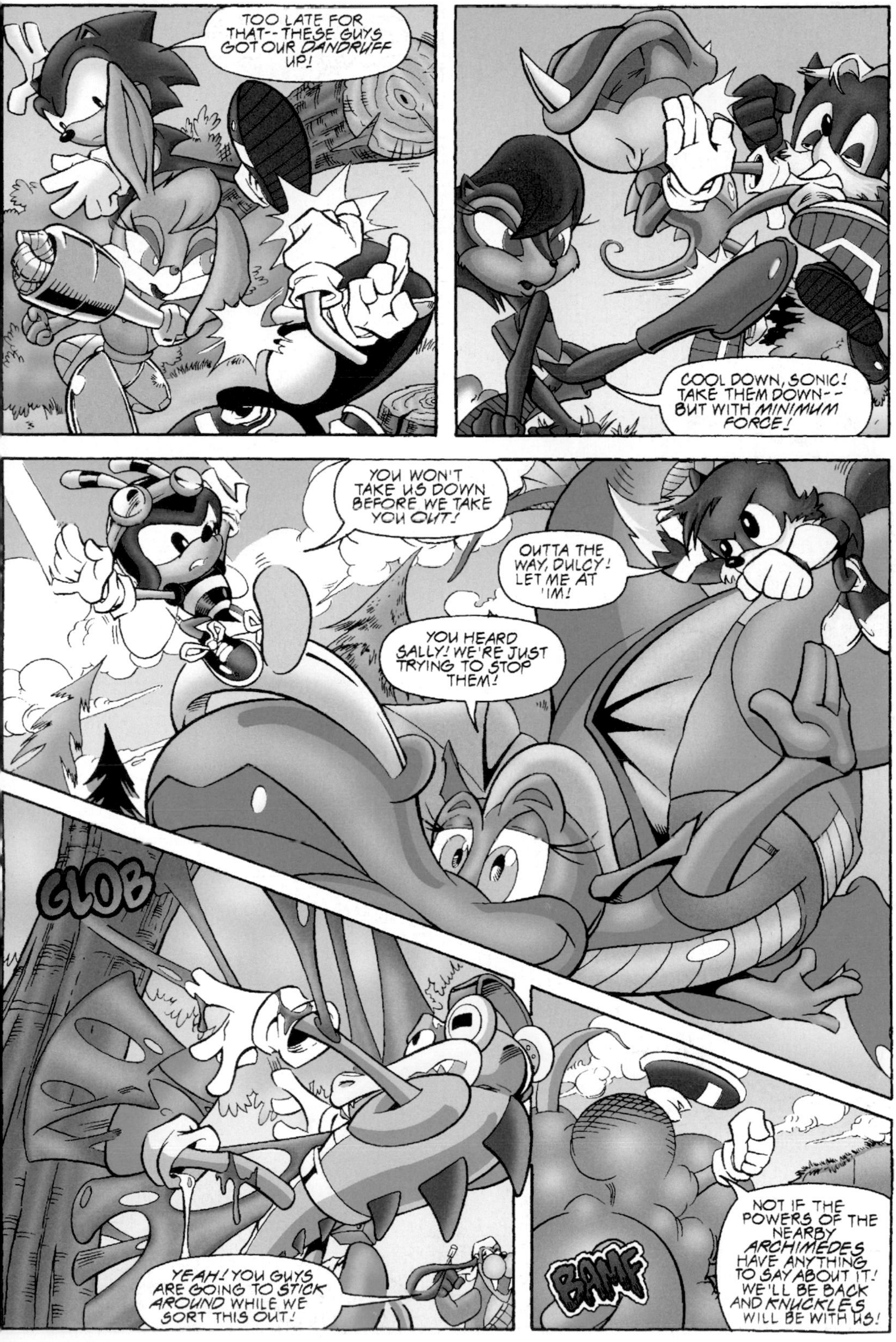
TOO LATE FOR THAT--THESE GUYS GOT OUR *DANDRUFF* UP!
COOL DOWN, SONIC! TAKE THEM DOWN--BUT WITH *MINIMUM FORCE!*
YOU WON'T TAKE US DOWN BEFORE WE TAKE YOU *OUT!*
OUTTA THE WAY, DULCY! LET ME AT 'IM!
YOU HEARD SALLY! WE'RE JUST TRYING TO STOP THEM!
GLOB
YEAH! YOU GUYS ARE GOING TO *STICK AROUND* WHILE WE SORT THIS OUT!
BAMF
NOT IF THE POWERS OF THE NEARBY *ARCHIMEDES* HAVE ANYTHING TO SAY ABOUT IT! WE'LL BE BACK AND *KNUCKLES* WILL BE WITH US!

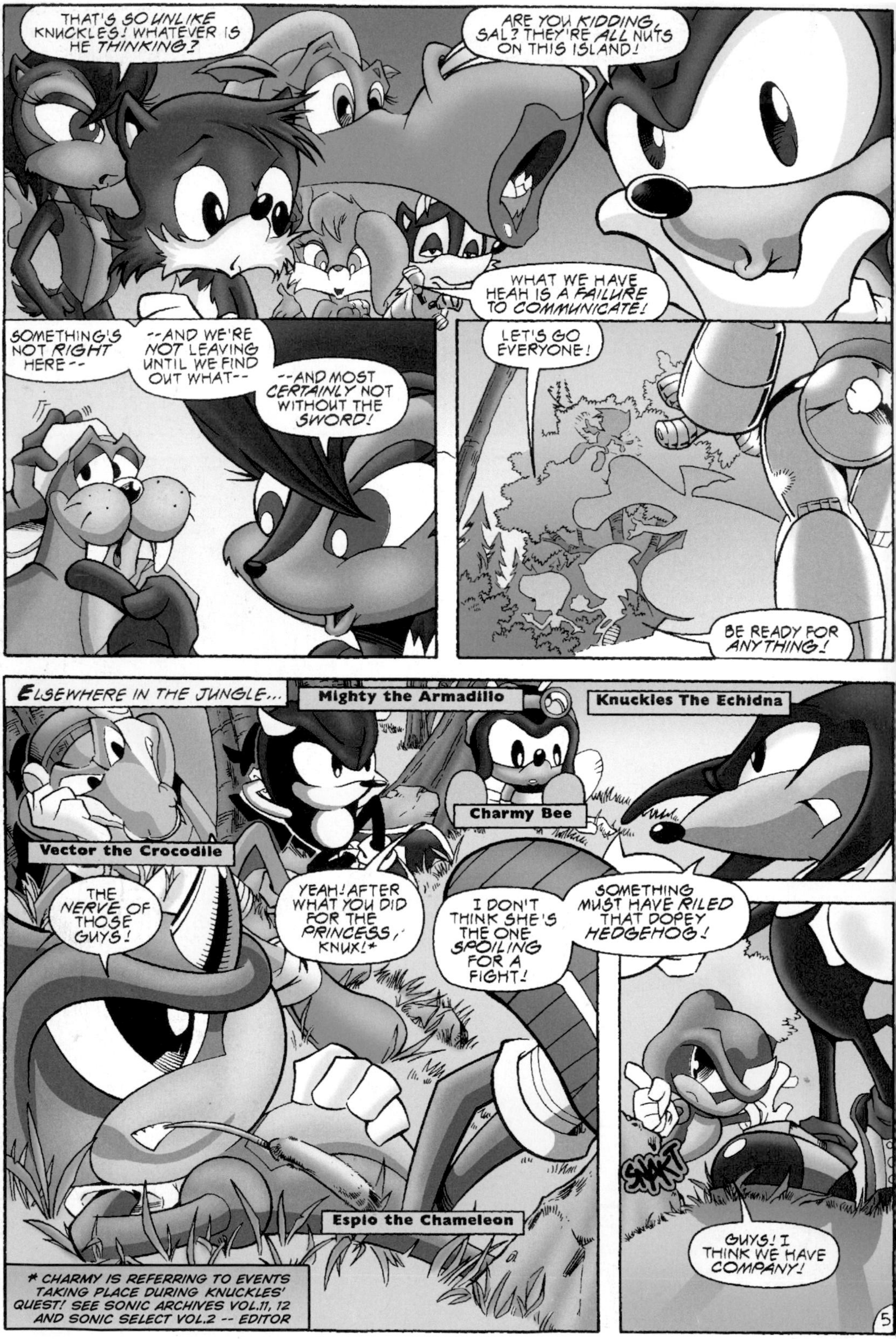
THAT'S SO UNLIKE KNUCKLES! WHATEVER IS HE THINKING?
ARE YOU KIDDING, SAL? THEY'RE ALL NUTS ON THIS ISLAND!
WHAT WE HAVE HEAH IS A FAILURE TO COMMUNICATE!
SOMETHING'S NOT RIGHT HERE--
--AND WE'RE NOT LEAVING UNTIL WE FIND OUT WHAT--
--AND MOST CERTAINLY NOT WITHOUT THE SWORD!
LET'S GO EVERYONE!
BE READY FOR ANYTHING!
ELSEWHERE IN THE JUNGLE...
Mighty the Armadillo
Knuckles The Echidna
Charmy Bee
Vector the Crocodile
THE NERVE OF THOSE GUYS!
YEAH! AFTER WHAT YOU DID FOR THE PRINCESS, KNUX!*
I DON'T THINK SHE'S THE ONE SPOILING FOR A FIGHT!
SOMETHING MUST HAVE RILED THAT DOPEY HEDGEHOG!
SNAKT
Espio the Chameleon
GUYS! I THINK WE HAVE COMPANY!
* CHARMY IS REFERRING TO EVENTS TAKING PLACE DURING KNUCKLES' QUEST! SEE SONIC ARCHIVES VOL.11, 12 AND SONIC SELECT VOL.2 -- EDITOR

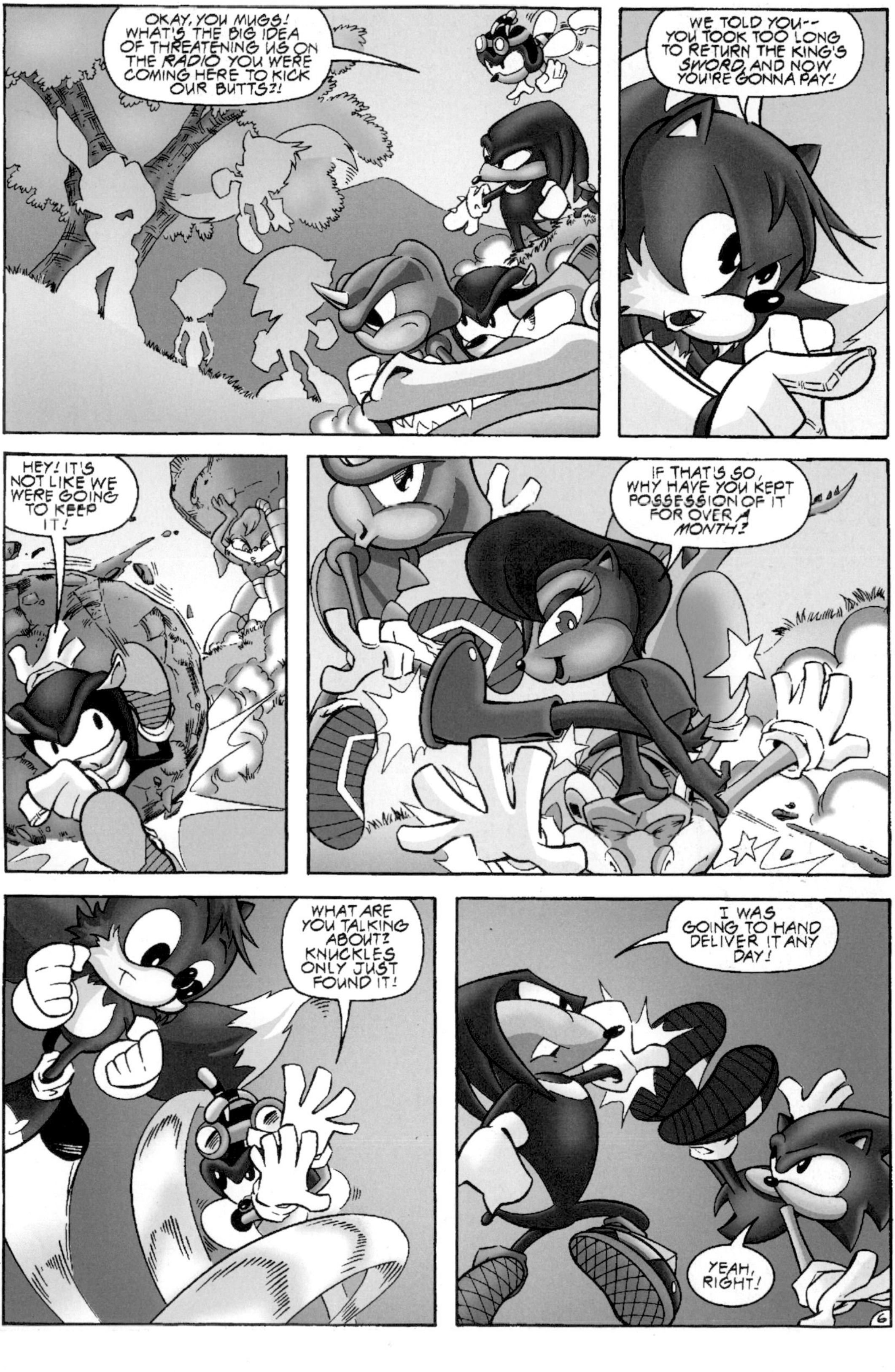
OKAY, YOU MUGS! WHAT'S THE BIG IDEA OF THREATENING US ON THE *RADIO* YOU WERE COMING HERE TO KICK OUR BUTTS?!
WE TOLD YOU-- YOU TOOK TOO LONG TO RETURN THE KING'S *SWORD*, AND NOW YOU'RE GONNA PAY!
HEY! IT'S NOT LIKE WE WERE GOING TO KEEP IT!
IF THAT'S SO, WHY HAVE YOU KEPT POSSESSION OF IT FOR OVER *A MONTH*?
WHAT ARE YOU TALKING ABOUT? KNUCKLES ONLY JUST FOUND IT!
I WAS GOING TO HAND DELIVER IT ANY DAY!
YEAH, RIGHT!
6

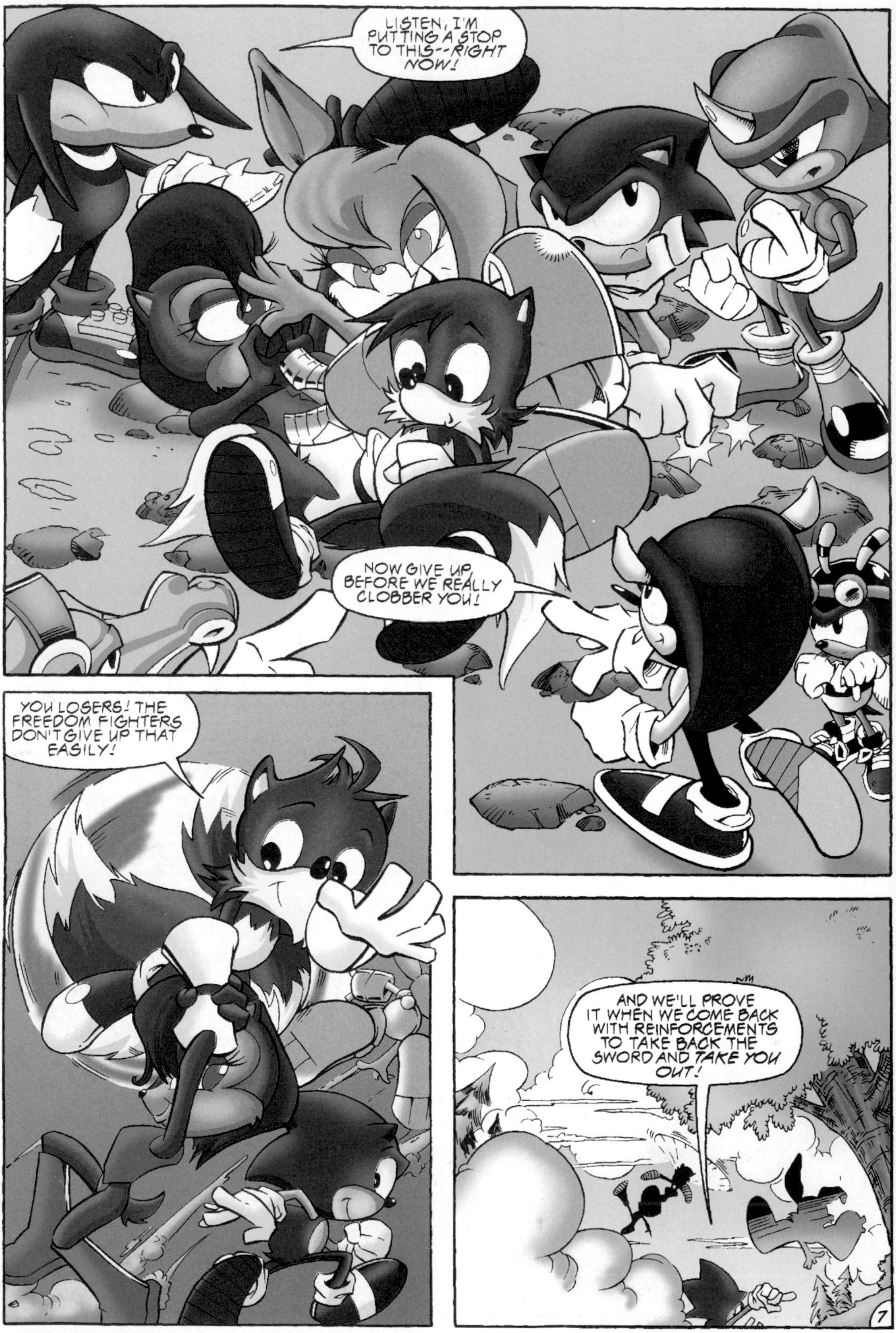
LISTEN, I'M PUTTING A STOP TO THIS--RIGHT NOW!
NOW GIVE UP, BEFORE WE REALLY CLOBBER YOU!
YOU LOSERS! THE FREEDOM FIGHTERS DON'T GIVE UP THAT EASILY!
AND WE'LL PROVE IT WHEN WE COME BACK WITH REINFORCEMENTS TO TAKE BACK THE SWORD AND TAKE YOU OUT!

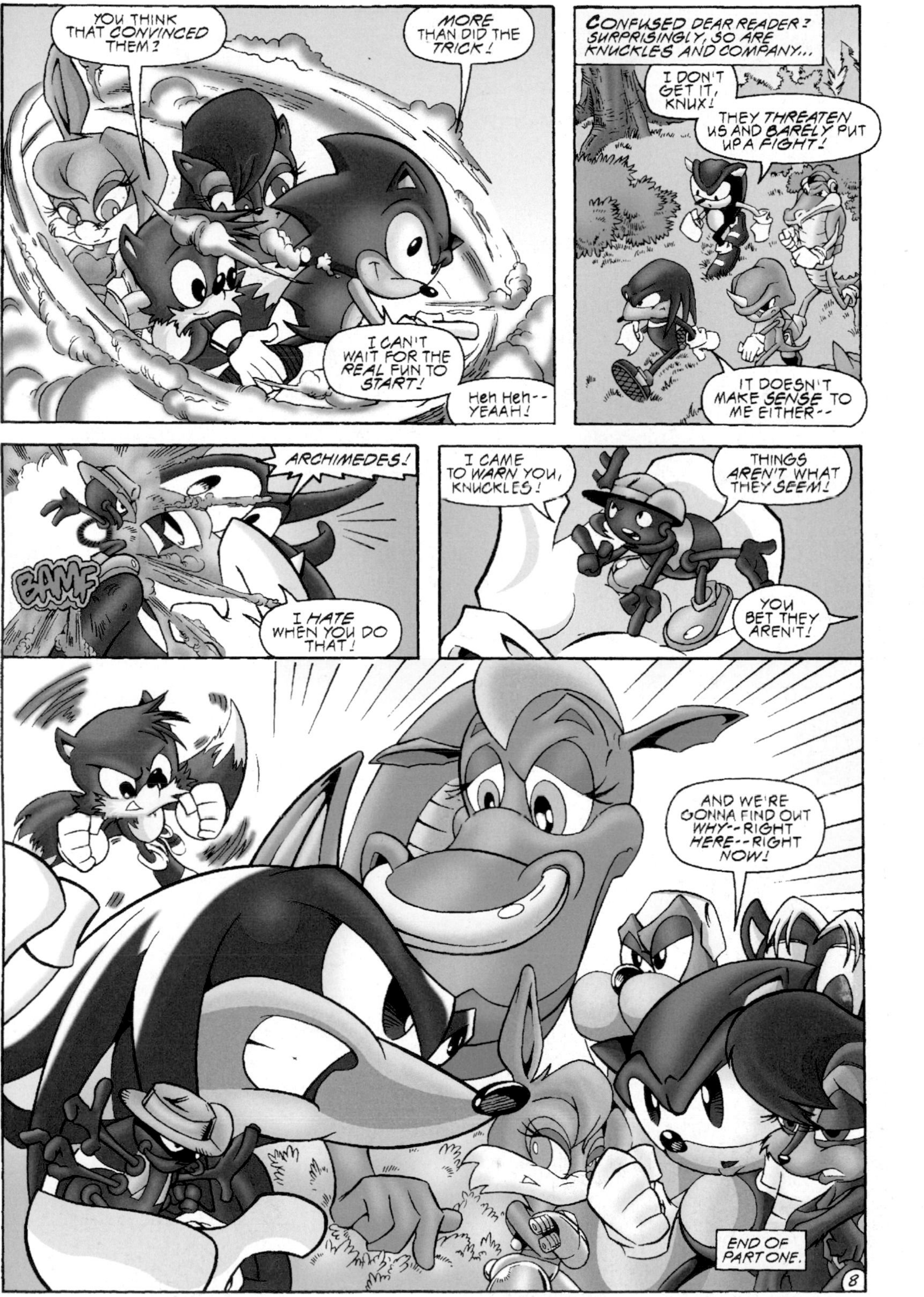
YOU THINK THAT CONVINCED THEM?
MORE THAN DID THE TRICK!
I CAN'T WAIT FOR THE REAL FUN TO START!
Heh Heh--YEAAH!
CONFUSED DEAR READER? SURPRISINGLY, SO ARE KNUCKLES AND COMPANY...
I DON'T GET IT, KNUX!
THEY THREATEN US AND BARELY PUT UP A FIGHT!
IT DOESN'T MAKE SENSE TO ME EITHER--
ARCHIMEDES!
BAMF
I HATE WHEN YOU DO THAT!
I CAME TO WARN YOU, KNUCKLES!
THINGS AREN'T WHAT THEY SEEM!
YOU BET THEY AREN'T!
AND WE'RE GONNA FIND OUT WHY--RIGHT HERE--RIGHT NOW!
END OF PART ONE.
8

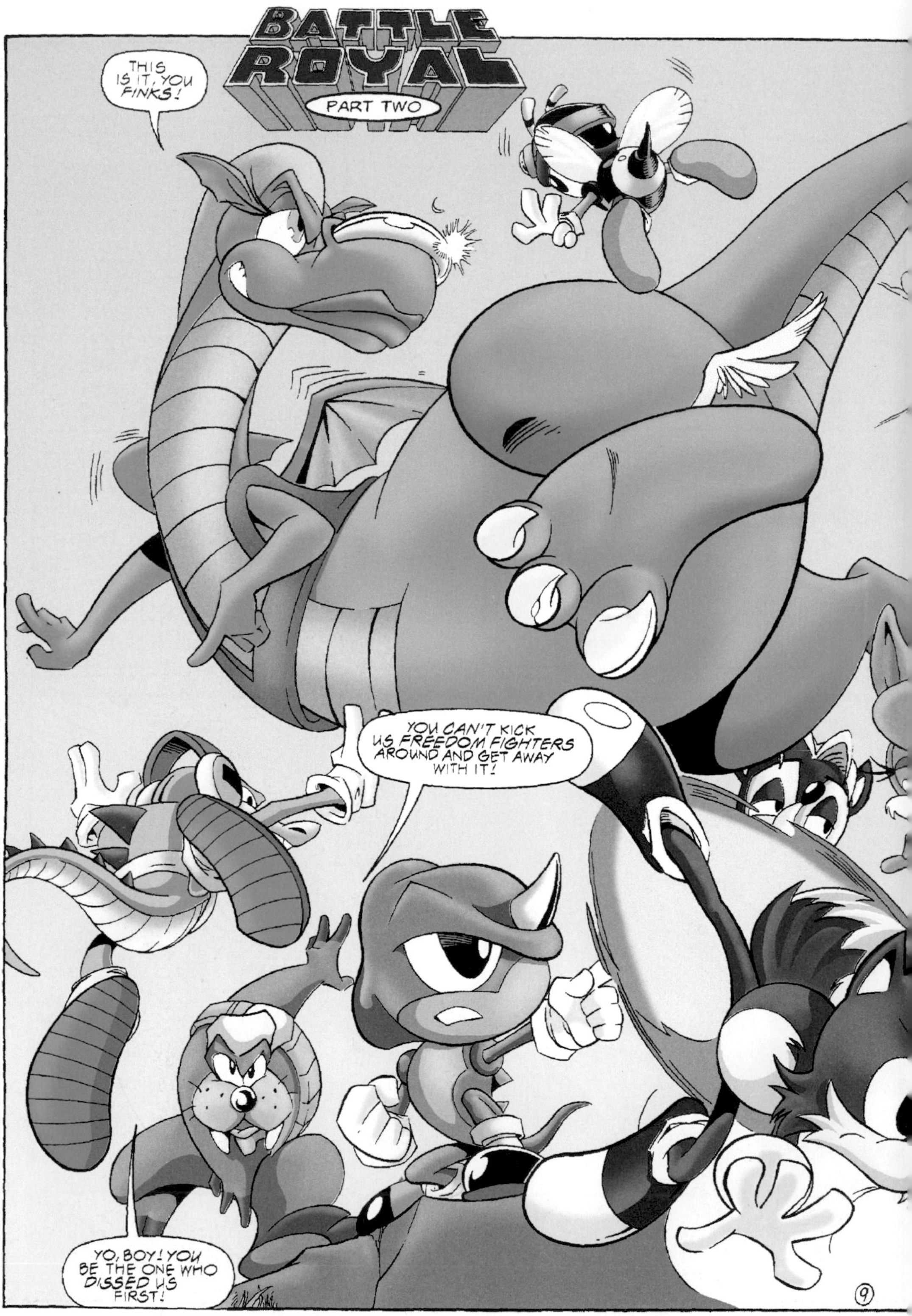
BATTLE ROYAL
PART TWO
THIS IS IT, YOU FINKS!
YOU CAN'T KICK US FREEDOM FIGHTERS AROUND AND GET AWAY WITH IT!
YO, BOY! YOU BE THE ONE WHO DISSED US FIRST!
9

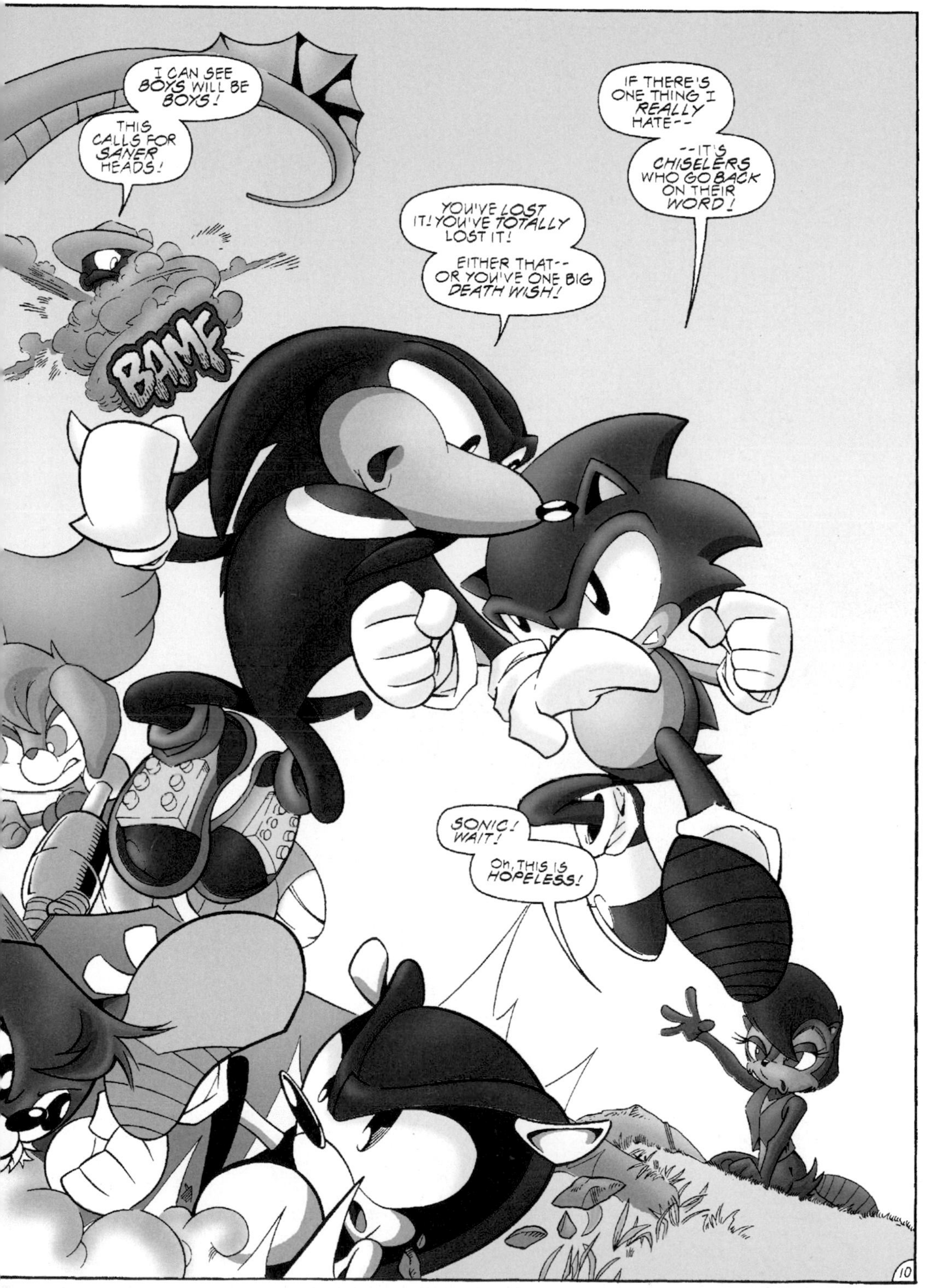

I CAN SEE BOYS WILL BE BOYS!
THIS CALLS FOR SANER HEADS!
IF THERE'S ONE THING I REALLY HATE--
--IT'S CHISELERS WHO GO BACK ON THEIR WORD!
YOU'VE LOST IT! YOU'VE TOTALLY LOST IT!
EITHER THAT--OR YOU'VE ONE BIG DEATH WISH!
BAMF
SONIC! WAIT!
Oh, THIS IS HOPELESS!
10

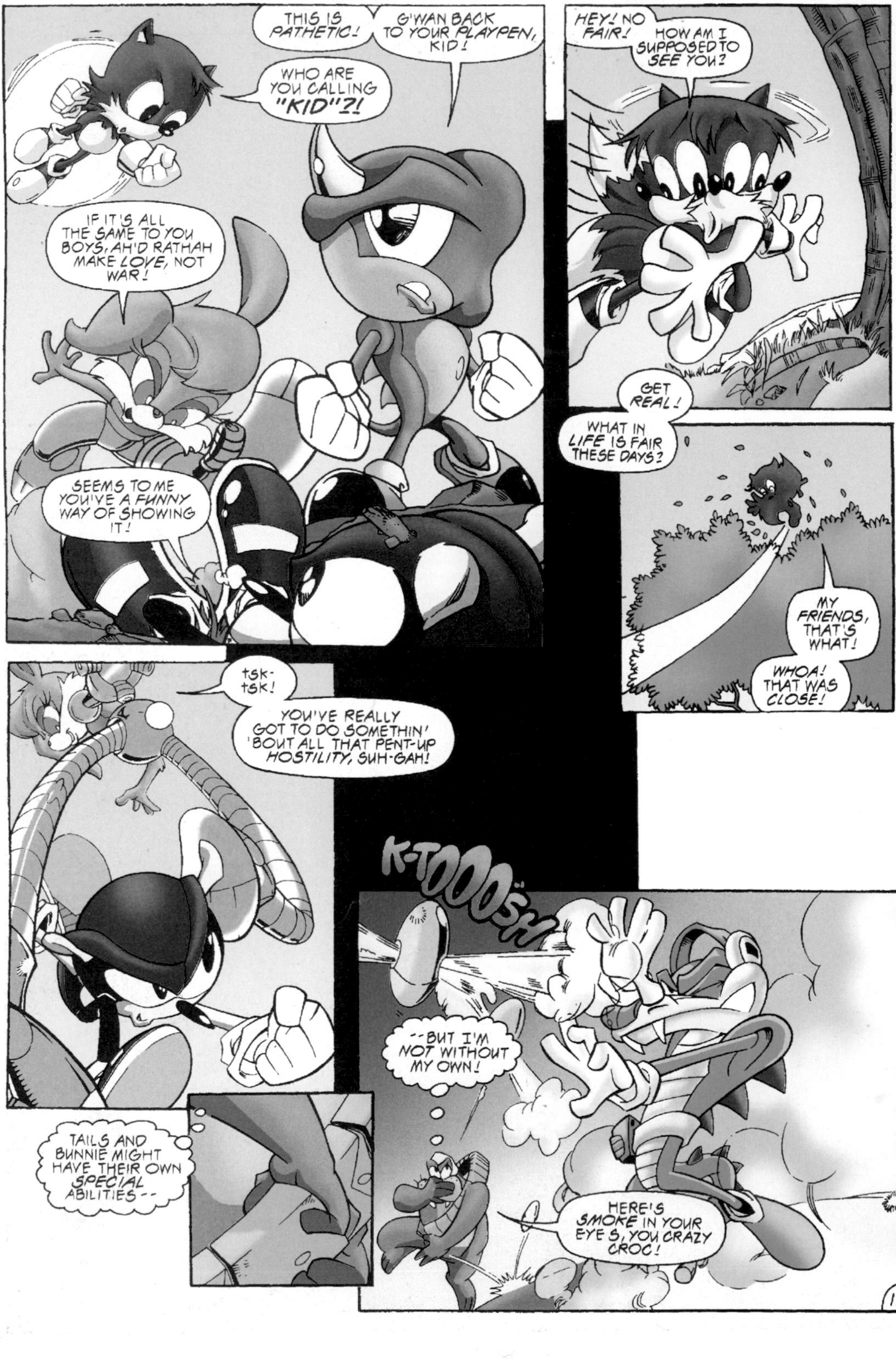
THIS IS PATHETIC!
G'WAN BACK TO YOUR PLAYPEN, KID!
WHO ARE YOU CALLING "KID"?!
IF IT'S ALL THE SAME TO YOU BOYS, AH'D RATHAH MAKE LOVE, NOT WAR!
SEEMS TO ME YOU'VE A FUNNY WAY OF SHOWING IT!
HEY! NO FAIR!
HOW AM I SUPPOSED TO SEE YOU?
GET REAL!
WHAT IN LIFE IS FAIR THESE DAYS?
MY FRIENDS, THAT'S WHAT!
WHOA! THAT WAS CLOSE!
tsk-tsk!
YOU'VE REALLY GOT TO DO SOMETHIN' 'BOUT ALL THAT PENT-UP HOSTILITY, SUH-GAH!
K-TOOOOSH
TAILS AND BUNNIE MIGHT HAVE THEIR OWN SPECIAL ABILITIES--
--BUT I'M NOT WITHOUT MY OWN!
HERE'S SMOKE IN YOUR EYES, YOU CRAZY CROC!
11

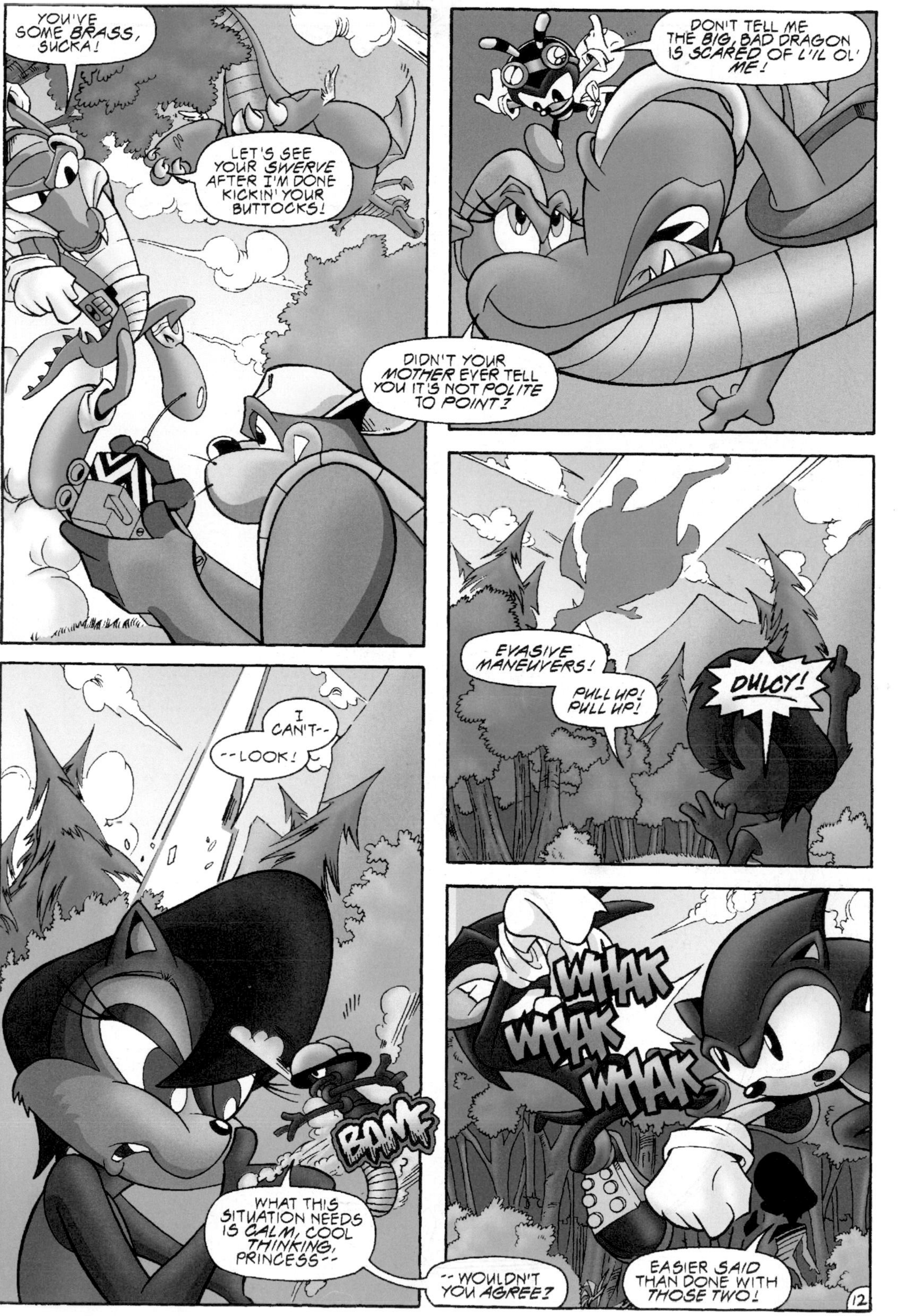
YOU'VE SOME BRASS, SUCKA!
LET'S SEE YOUR SWERVE AFTER I'M DONE KICKIN' YOUR BUTTOCKS!
DON'T TELL ME THE BIG, BAD DRAGON IS SCARED OF L'IL OL' ME!
DIDN'T YOUR MOTHER EVER TELL YOU IT'S NOT POLITE TO POINT?
EVASIVE MANEUVERS!
PULL UP! PULL UP!
DULCY!
I CAN'T--
--LOOK!
BAMF
WHAT THIS SITUATION NEEDS IS CALM, COOL THINKING, PRINCESS--
--WOULDN'T YOU AGREE?
WHAK
WHAK
WHAK
EASIER SAID THAN DONE WITH THOSE TWO!

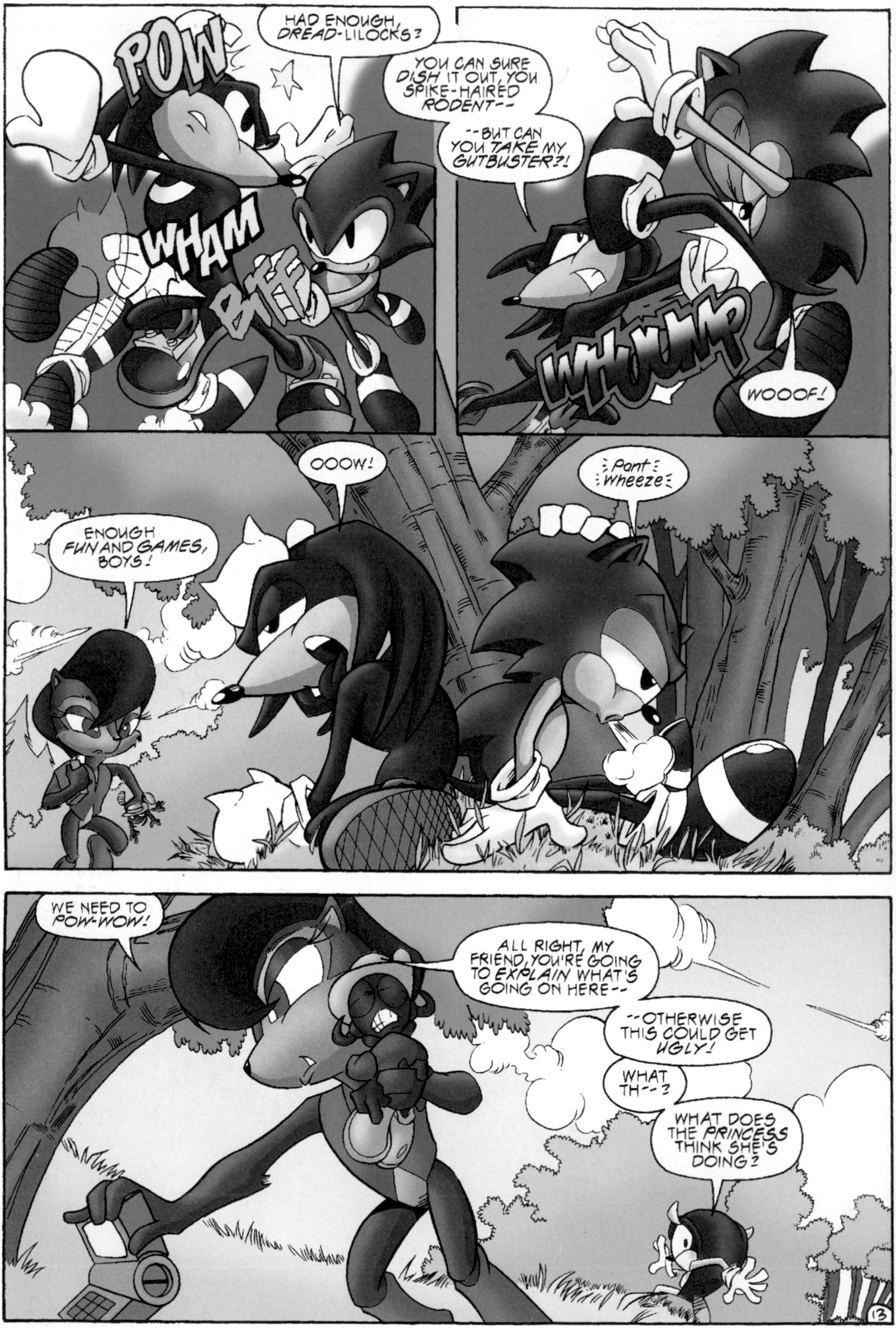
POW
HAD ENOUGH, DREAD-LILOCKS?
WHAM
BIFF
YOU CAN SURE DISH IT OUT, YOU SPIKE-HAIRED RODENT--
--BUT CAN YOU TAKE MY GUTBUSTER?!
WHUMP
WOOOF!
OOOW!
Pant Wheeze
ENOUGH FUN AND GAMES, BOYS!
WE NEED TO POW-WOW!
ALL RIGHT, MY FRIEND, YOU'RE GOING TO EXPLAIN WHAT'S GOING ON HERE--
--OTHERWISE THIS COULD GET UGLY!
WHAT TH--?
WHAT DOES THE PRINCESS THINK SHE'S DOING?
13

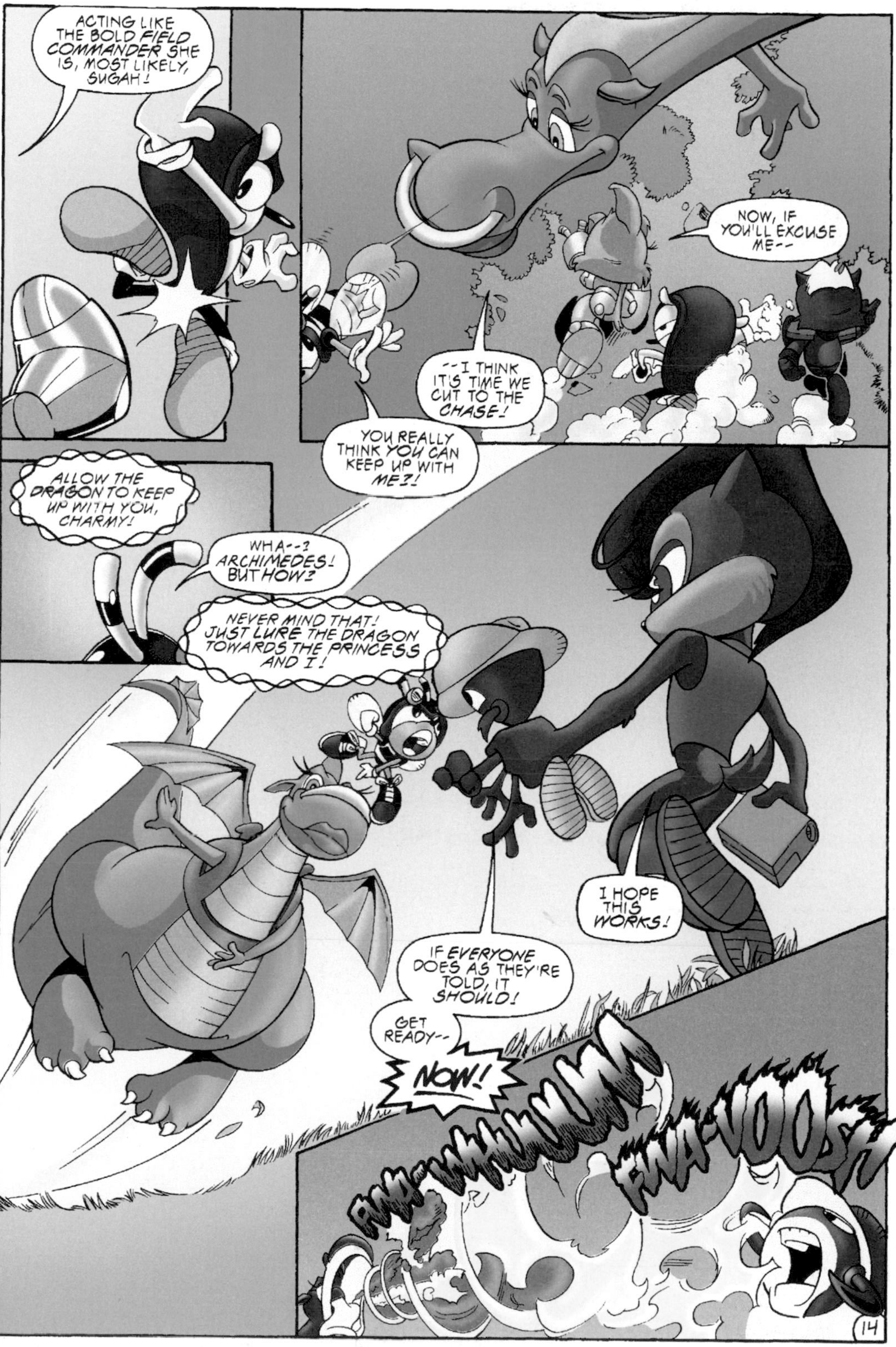

ACTING LIKE THE BOLD FIELD COMMANDER SHE IS, MOST LIKELY, SUGAH!
NOW, IF YOU'LL EXCUSE ME--
--I THINK IT'S TIME WE CUT TO THE CHASE!
YOU REALLY THINK YOU CAN KEEP UP WITH ME?!
ALLOW THE DRAGON TO KEEP UP WITH YOU, CHARMY!
WHA--? ARCHIMEDES! BUT HOW?
NEVER MIND THAT! JUST LURE THE DRAGON TOWARDS THE PRINCESS AND I!
I HOPE THIS WORKS!
IF EVERYONE DOES AS THEY'RE TOLD, IT SHOULD!
GET READY--
NOW!
FWA-VOOSH

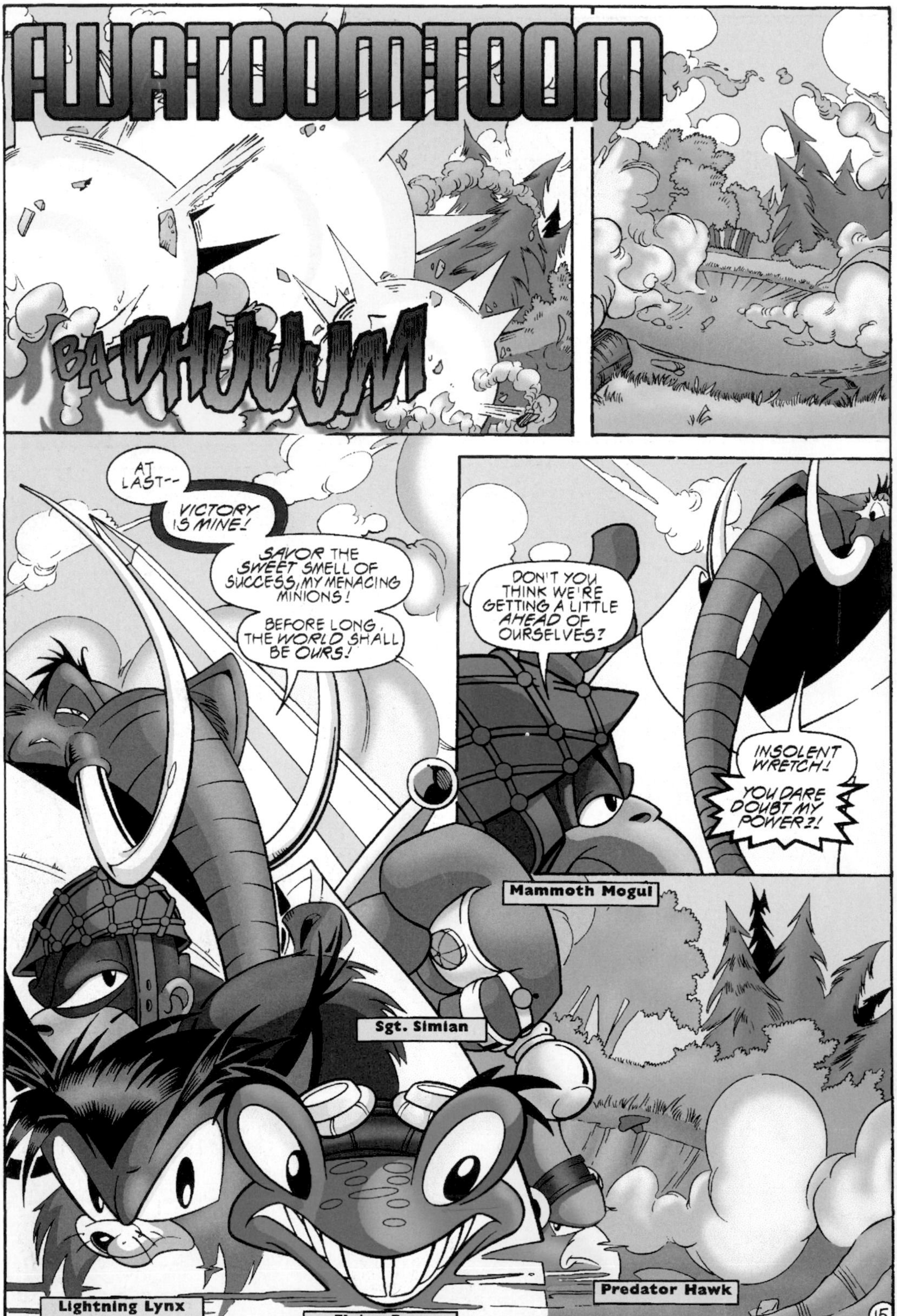
FWATOOMTOOM
BA-DHUUUM
AT LAST--
VICTORY IS MINE!
SAVOR THE SWEET SMELL OF SUCCESS, MY MENACING MINIONS!
BEFORE LONG, THE WORLD SHALL BE OURS!
DON'T YOU THINK WE'RE GETTING A LITTLE AHEAD OF OURSELVES?
INSOLENT WRETCH!
YOU DARE DOUBT MY POWER?!
Mammoth Mogul
Sgt. Simian
Predator Hawk
Lightning Lynx
Flying Frog

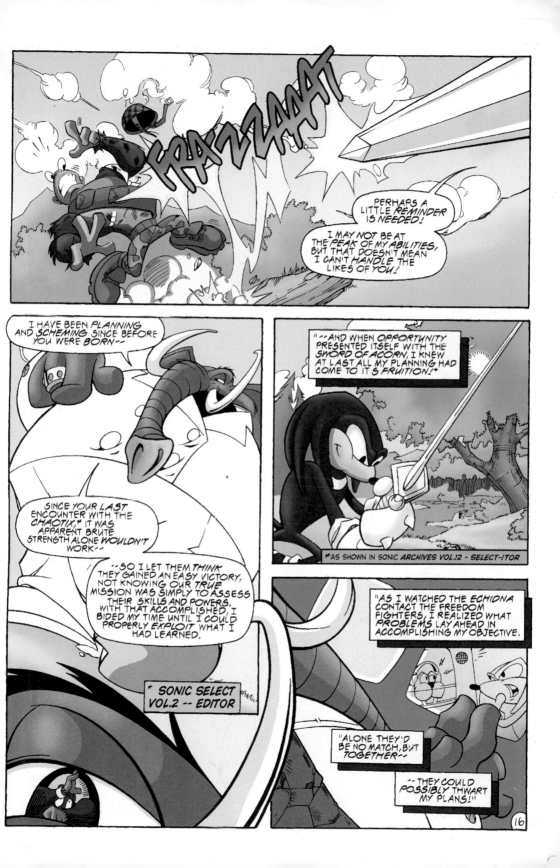

FRAZZAAAT

PERHAPS A LITTLE *REMINDER* IS *NEEDED!*

I MAY NOT BE AT THE *PEAK* OF MY *ABILITIES,* BUT THAT DOESN'T MEAN I CAN'T *HANDLE* THE LIKES OF *YOU!*

I HAVE BEEN *PLANNING* AND *SCHEMING* SINCE BEFORE YOU WERE *BORN--*

SINCE YOUR *LAST* ENCOUNTER WITH THE *CHAOTIX,** IT WAS APPARENT BRUTE STRENGTH ALONE *WOULDN'T* WORK--

--SO I LET THEM *THINK* THEY GAINED AN EASY VICTORY, NOT KNOWING OUR *TRUE* MISSION WAS SIMPLY TO ASSESS THEIR SKILLS AND POWERS. WITH THAT ACCOMPLISHED, I BIDED MY TIME UNTIL I COULD PROPERLY *EXPLOIT* WHAT I HAD LEARNED.

* SONIC SELECT VOL.2 -- EDITOR

"--AND WHEN *OPPORTUNITY* PRESENTED ITSELF WITH THE *SWORD OF ACORN,* I KNEW AT LAST ALL MY PLANNING HAD COME TO ITS *FRUITION!**

*AS SHOWN IN SONIC *ARCHIVES* VOL.12 - SELECT-1TOR

"AS I WATCHED THE *ECHIDNA* CONTACT THE FREEDOM FIGHTERS, I REALIZED WHAT *PROBLEMS* LAY AHEAD IN ACCOMPLISHING MY OBJECTIVE.

"ALONE THEY'D BE NO MATCH, BUT *TOGETHER--*

--THEY COULD *POSSIBLY* THWART MY PLANS!"

16

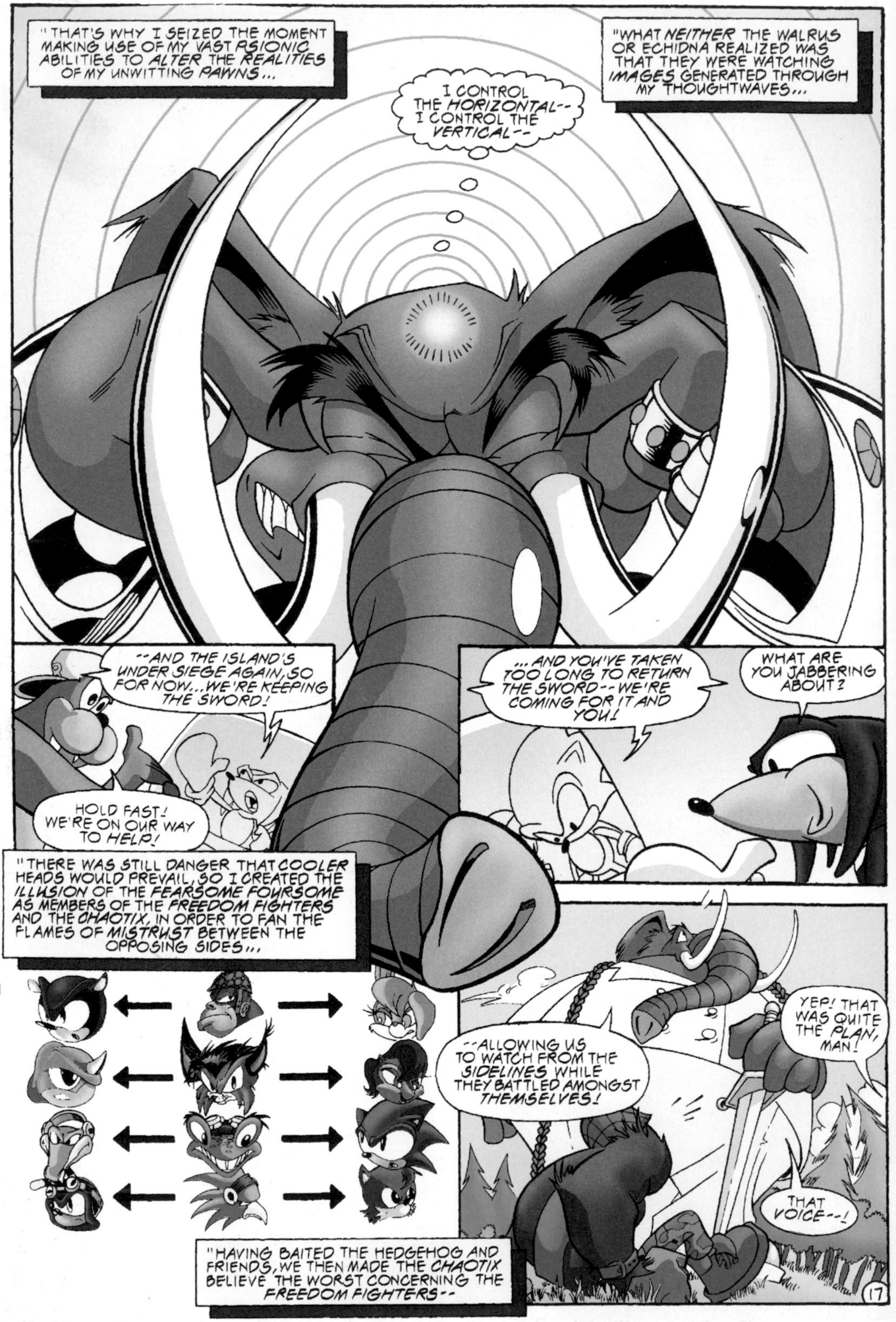

"THAT'S WHY I SEIZED THE MOMENT MAKING USE OF MY VAST PSIONIC ABILITIES TO ALTER THE REALITIES OF MY UNWITTING PAWNS...
"WHAT NEITHER THE WALRUS OR ECHIDNA REALIZED WAS THAT THEY WERE WATCHING IMAGES GENERATED THROUGH MY THOUGHTWAVES...
I CONTROL THE HORIZONTAL-- I CONTROL THE VERTICAL--
--AND THE ISLAND'S UNDER SIEGE AGAIN, SO FOR NOW... WE'RE KEEPING THE SWORD!
HOLD FAST! WE'RE ON OUR WAY TO HELP!
...AND YOU'VE TAKEN TOO LONG TO RETURN THE SWORD--WE'RE COMING FOR IT AND YOU!
WHAT ARE YOU JABBERING ABOUT?
"THERE WAS STILL DANGER THAT COOLER HEADS WOULD PREVAIL, SO I CREATED THE ILLUSION OF THE FEARSOME FOURSOME AS MEMBERS OF THE FREEDOM FIGHTERS AND THE CHAOTIX, IN ORDER TO FAN THE FLAMES OF MISTRUST BETWEEN THE OPPOSING SIDES...
--ALLOWING US TO WATCH FROM THE SIDELINES WHILE THEY BATTLED AMONGST THEMSELVES!
YEP! THAT WAS QUITE THE PLAN, MAN!
THAT VOICE--!
"HAVING BAITED THE HEDGEHOG AND FRIENDS, WE THEN MADE THE CHAOTIX BELIEVE THE WORST CONCERNING THE FREEDOM FIGHTERS--

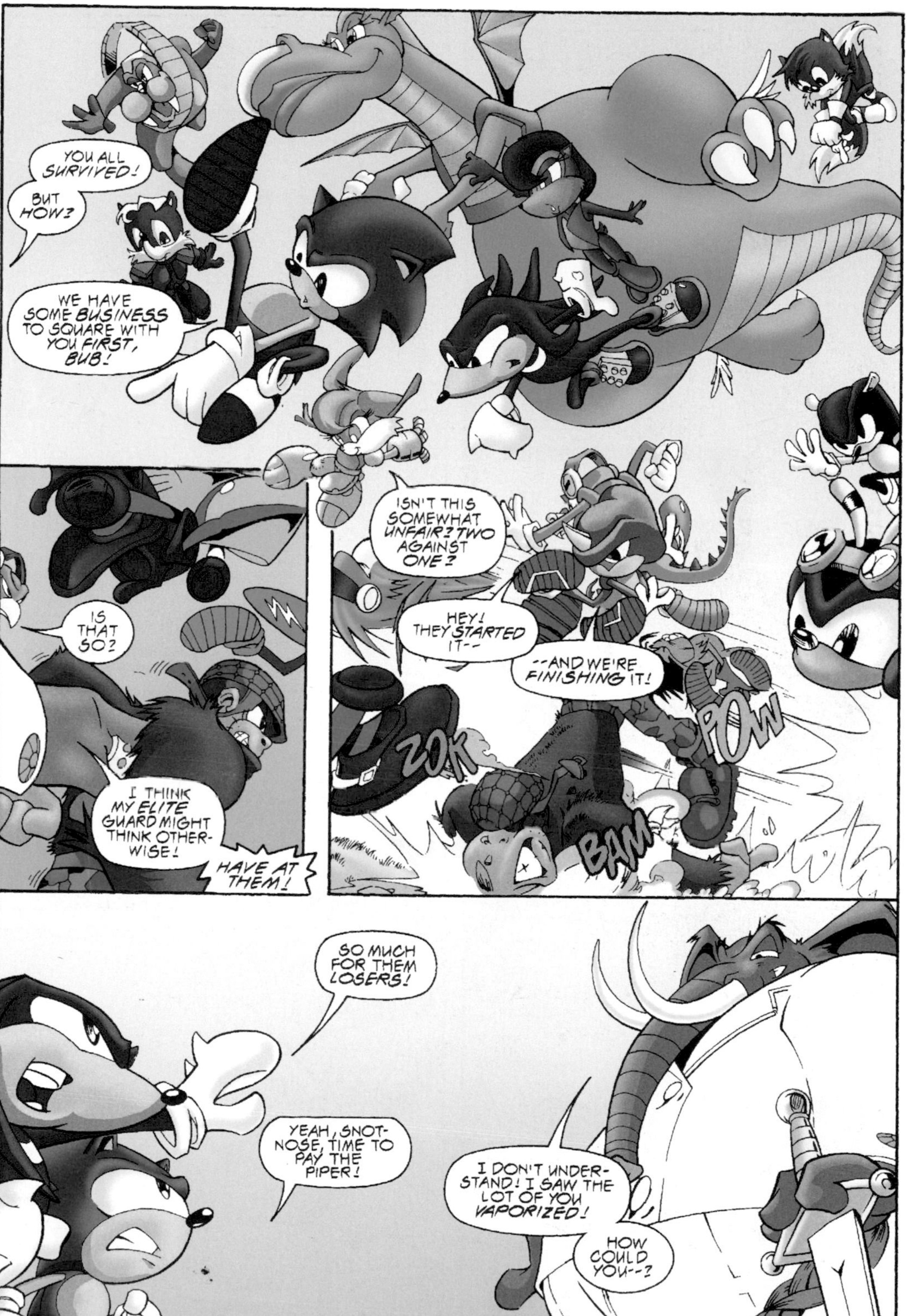
YOU ALL SURVIVED!
BUT HOW?
WE HAVE SOME BUSINESS TO SQUARE WITH YOU FIRST, BUB!
IS THAT SO?
I THINK MY ELITE GUARD MIGHT THINK OTHERWISE!
HAVE AT THEM!
ISN'T THIS SOMEWHAT UNFAIR? TWO AGAINST ONE?
HEY! THEY STARTED IT--
--AND WE'RE FINISHING IT!
ZOK
POW
BAM
SO MUCH FOR THEM LOSERS!
YEAH, SNOT-NOSE, TIME TO PAY THE PIPER!
I DON'T UNDERSTAND! I SAW THE LOT OF YOU VAPORIZED!
HOW COULD YOU--?

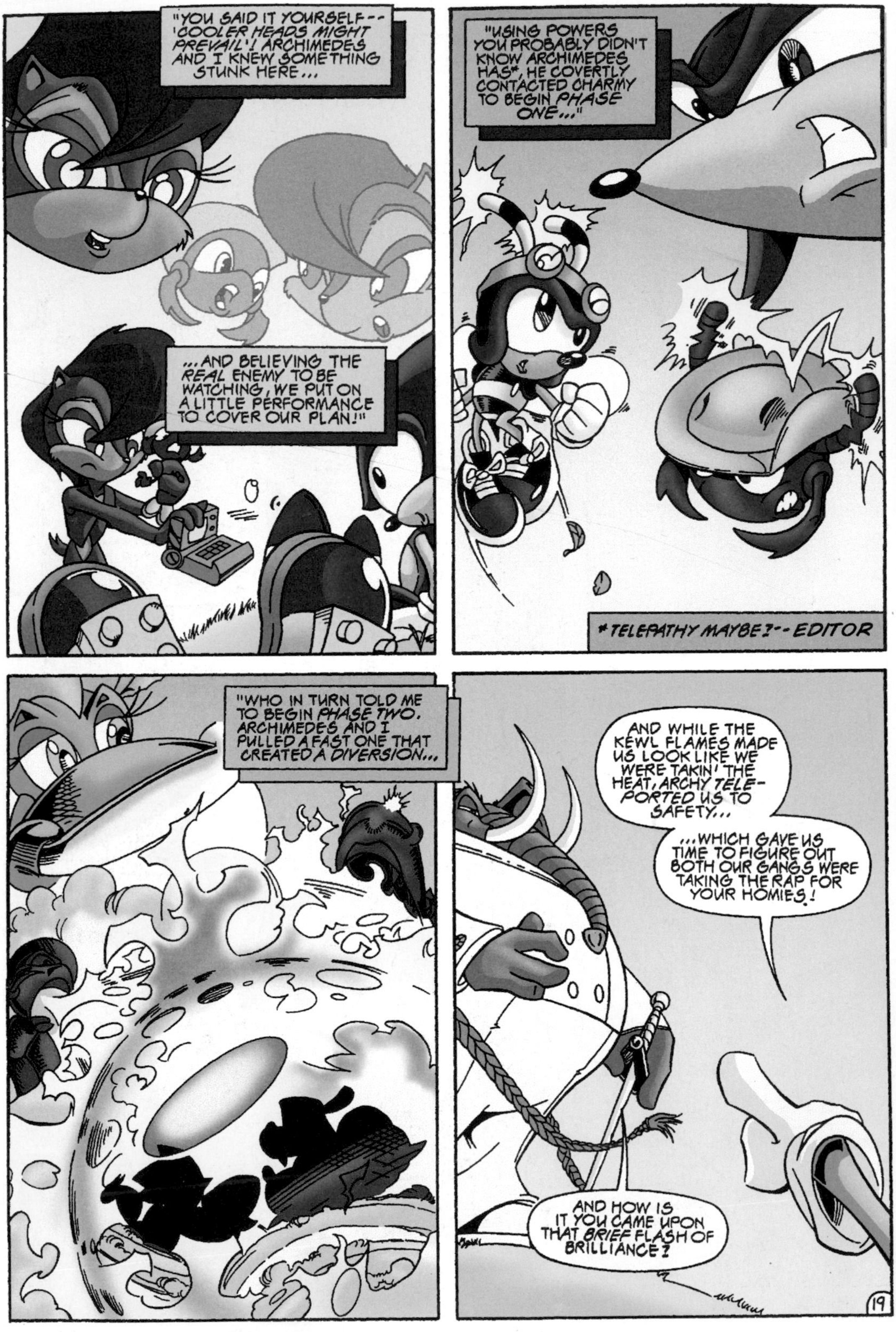
"YOU SAID IT YOURSELF-- 'COOLER HEADS MIGHT PREVAIL'! ARCHIMEDES AND I KNEW SOMETHING STUNK HERE...
...AND BELIEVING THE REAL ENEMY TO BE WATCHING, WE PUT ON A LITTLE PERFORMANCE TO COVER OUR PLAN!"
"USING POWERS YOU PROBABLY DIDN'T KNOW ARCHIMEDES HAS*, HE COVERTLY CONTACTED CHARMY TO BEGIN PHASE ONE..."
*TELEPATHY MAYBE?--EDITOR
"WHO IN TURN TOLD ME TO BEGIN PHASE TWO. ARCHIMEDES AND I PULLED A FAST ONE THAT CREATED A DIVERSION...
AND WHILE THE KEWL FLAMES MADE US LOOK LIKE WE WERE TAKIN' THE HEAT, ARCHY TELE-PORTED US TO SAFETY...
...WHICH GAVE US TIME TO FIGURE OUT BOTH OUR GANGS WERE TAKING THE RAP FOR YOUR HOMIES!
AND HOW IS IT YOU CAME UPON THAT BRIEF FLASH OF BRILLIANCE?

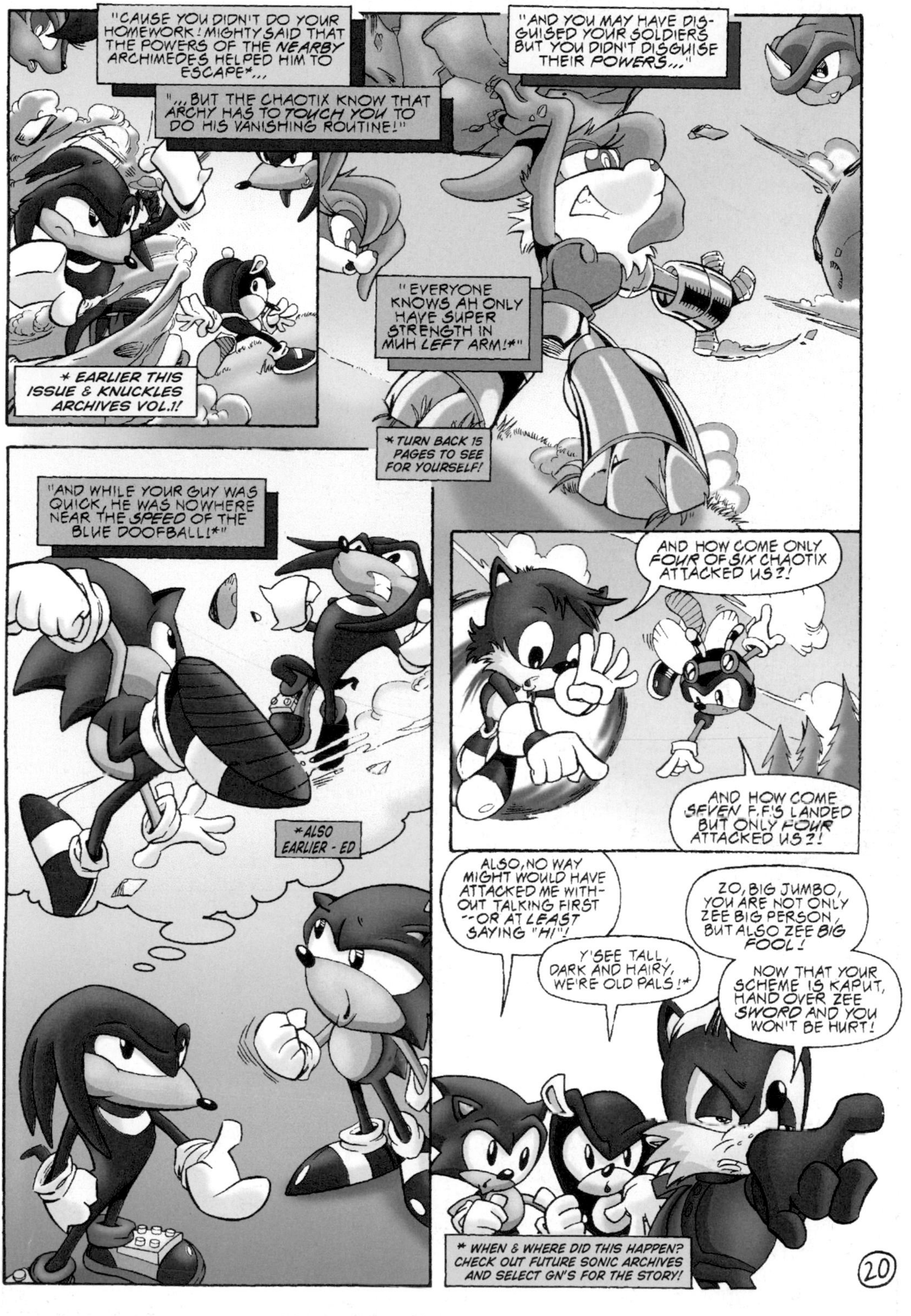
"CAUSE YOU DIDN'T DO YOUR HOMEWORK! MIGHTY SAID THAT THE POWERS OF THE NEARBY ARCHIMEDES HELPED HIM TO ESCAPE*...
"...BUT THE CHAOTIX KNOW THAT ARCHY HAS TO TOUCH YOU TO DO HIS VANISHING ROUTINE!"
* EARLIER THIS ISSUE & KNUCKLES ARCHIVES VOL.1!
"AND YOU MAY HAVE DISGUISED YOUR SOLDIERS BUT YOU DIDN'T DISGUISE THEIR POWERS..."
"EVERYONE KNOWS AH ONLY HAVE SUPER STRENGTH IN MUH LEFT ARM!*"
*TURN BACK 15 PAGES TO SEE FOR YOURSELF!
"AND WHILE YOUR GUY WAS QUICK, HE WAS NOWHERE NEAR THE SPEED OF THE BLUE DOOFBALL!*"
*ALSO EARLIER - ED
AND HOW COME ONLY FOUR OF SIX CHAOTIX ATTACKED US?!
AND HOW COME SEVEN F.F.'S LANDED BUT ONLY FOUR ATTACKED US?!
ALSO, NO WAY MIGHT WOULD HAVE ATTACKED ME WITHOUT TALKING FIRST --OR AT LEAST SAYING "HI"!
Y'SEE TALL, DARK AND HAIRY, WE'RE OLD PALS!*
ZO, BIG JUMBO, YOU ARE NOT ONLY ZEE BIG PERSON, BUT ALSO ZEE BIG FOOL!
NOW THAT YOUR SCHEME IS KAPUT, HAND OVER ZEE SWORD AND YOU WON'T BE HURT!
* WHEN & WHERE DID THIS HAPPEN? CHECK OUT FUTURE SONIC ARCHIVES AND SELECT GN'S FOR THE STORY!

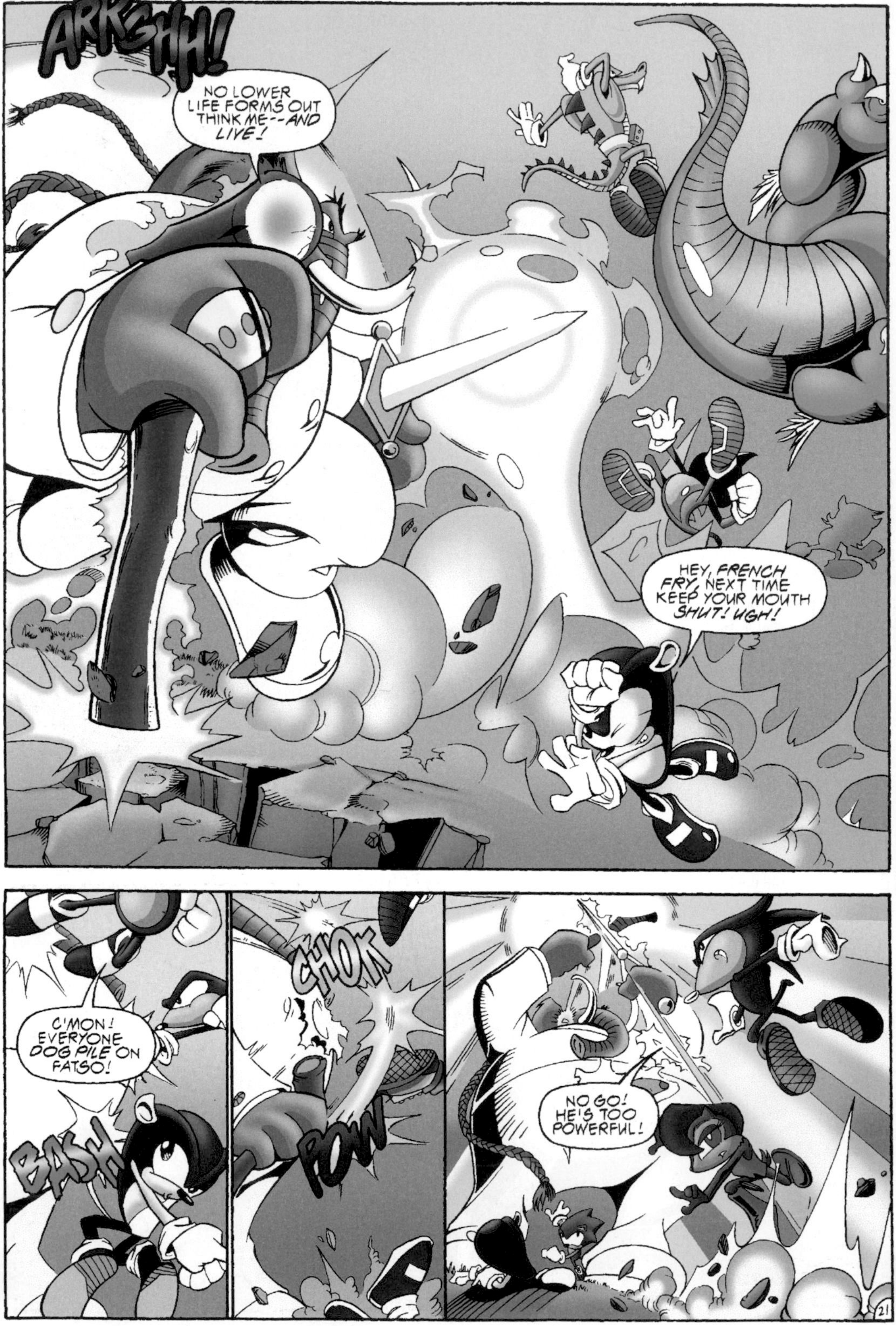
ARRGHH!
NO LOWER LIFE FORMS OUT THINK ME--AND LIVE!
HEY, FRENCH FRY, NEXT TIME KEEP YOUR MOUTH SHUT! UGH!
C'MON! EVERYONE DOG PILE ON FATSO!
BASH
CHOK
POW
NO GO! HE'S TOO POWERFUL!
21

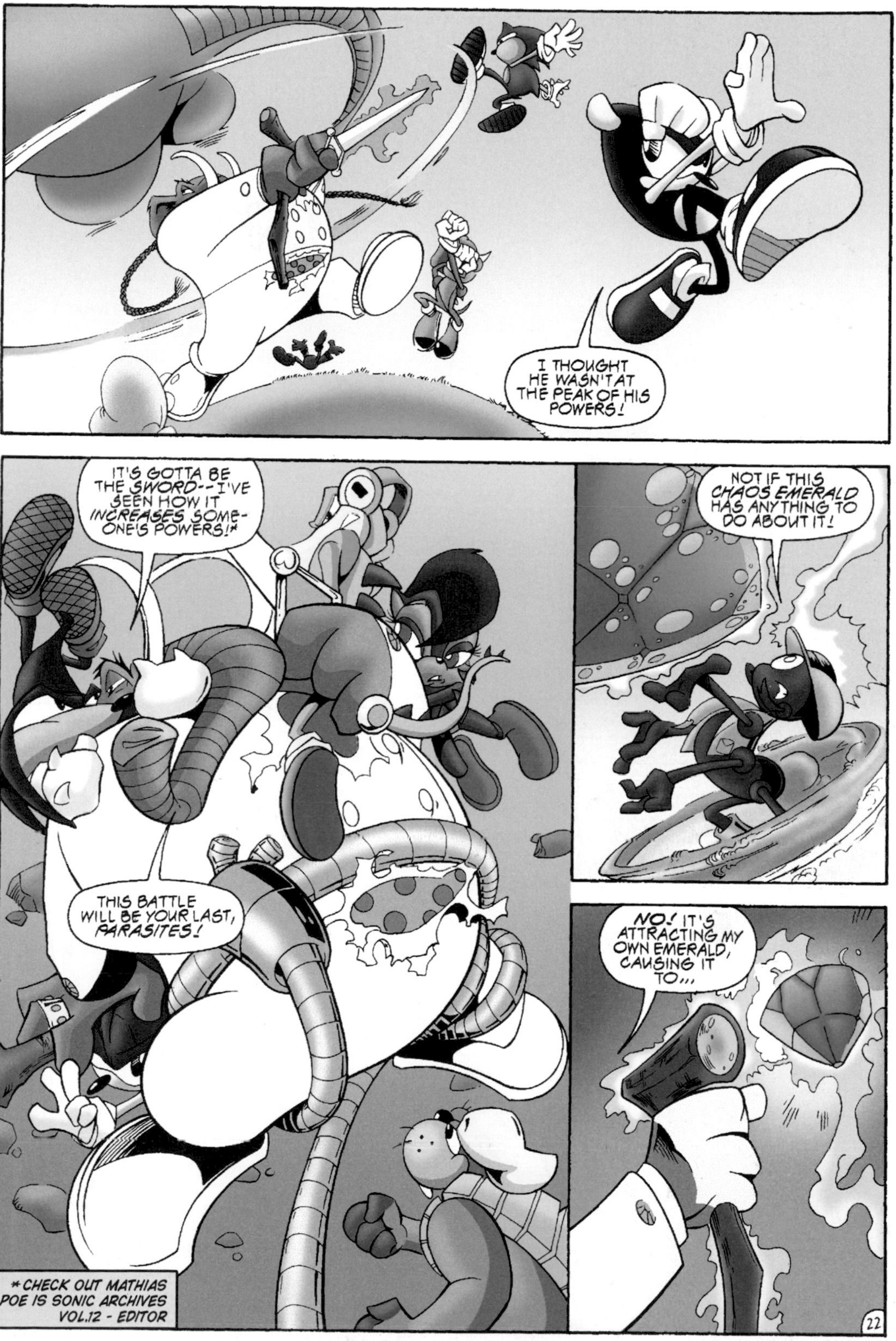
I THOUGHT HE WASN'T AT THE PEAK OF HIS POWERS!
IT'S GOTTA BE THE SWORD--I'VE SEEN HOW IT INCREASES SOME-ONE'S POWERS!*
THIS BATTLE WILL BE YOUR LAST, PARASITES!
NOT IF THIS CHAOS EMERALD HAS ANYTHING TO DO ABOUT IT!
NO! IT'S ATTRACTING MY OWN EMERALD, CAUSING IT TO...
* CHECK OUT MATHIAS POE IS SONIC ARCHIVES VOL.12 - EDITOR

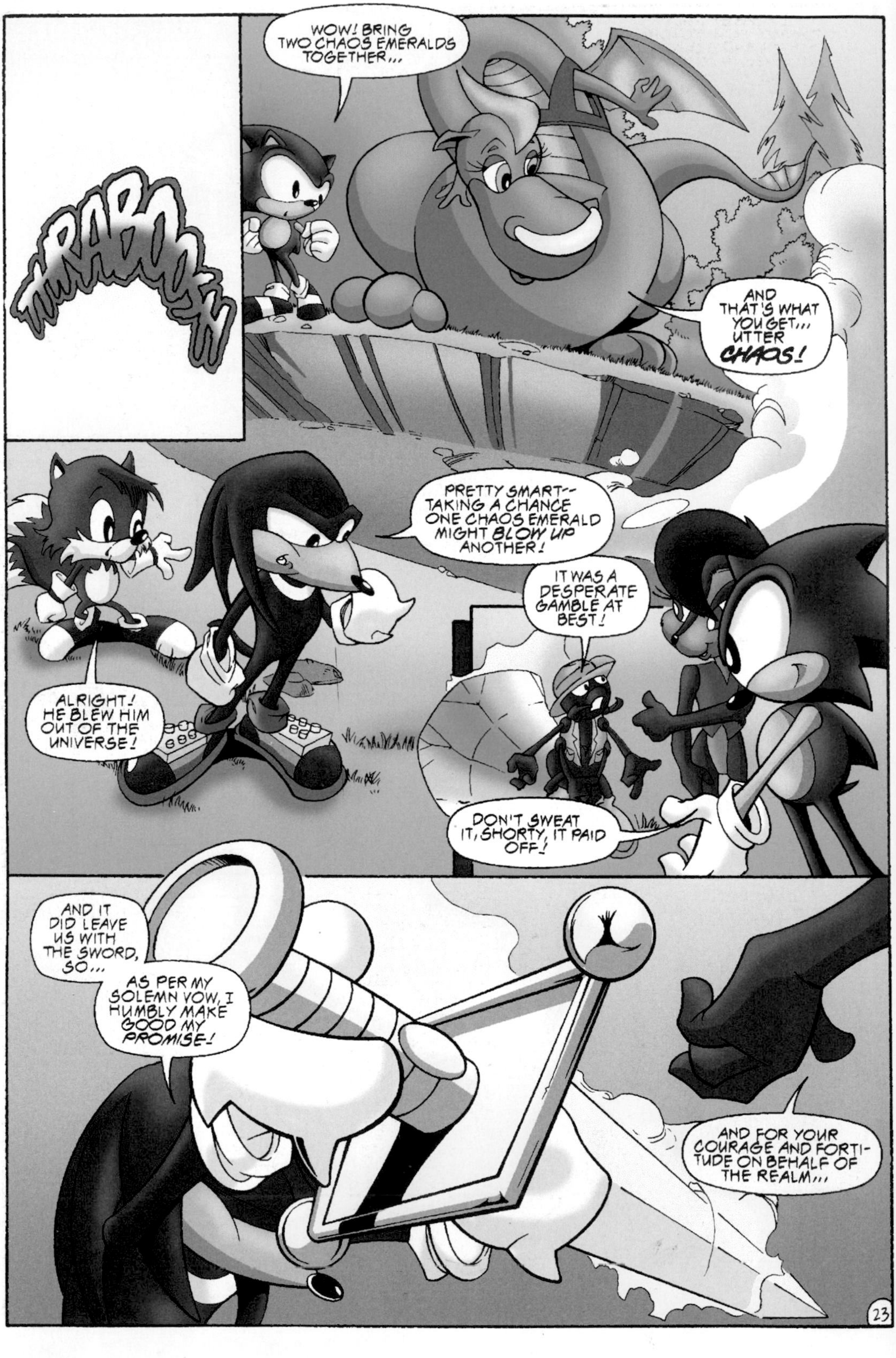
THRABOOOM
WOW! BRING TWO CHAOS EMERALDS TOGETHER...
AND THAT'S WHAT YOU GET... UTTER CHAOS!
PRETTY SMART-- TAKING A CHANCE ONE CHAOS EMERALD MIGHT BLOW UP ANOTHER!
ALRIGHT! HE BLEW HIM OUT OF THE UNIVERSE!
IT WAS A DESPERATE GAMBLE AT BEST!
DON'T SWEAT IT, SHORTY, IT PAID OFF!
AND IT DID LEAVE US WITH THE SWORD, SO...
AS PER MY SOLEMN VOW, I HUMBLY MAKE GOOD MY PROMISE!
AND FOR YOUR COURAGE AND FORTITUDE ON BEHALF OF THE REALM...
23

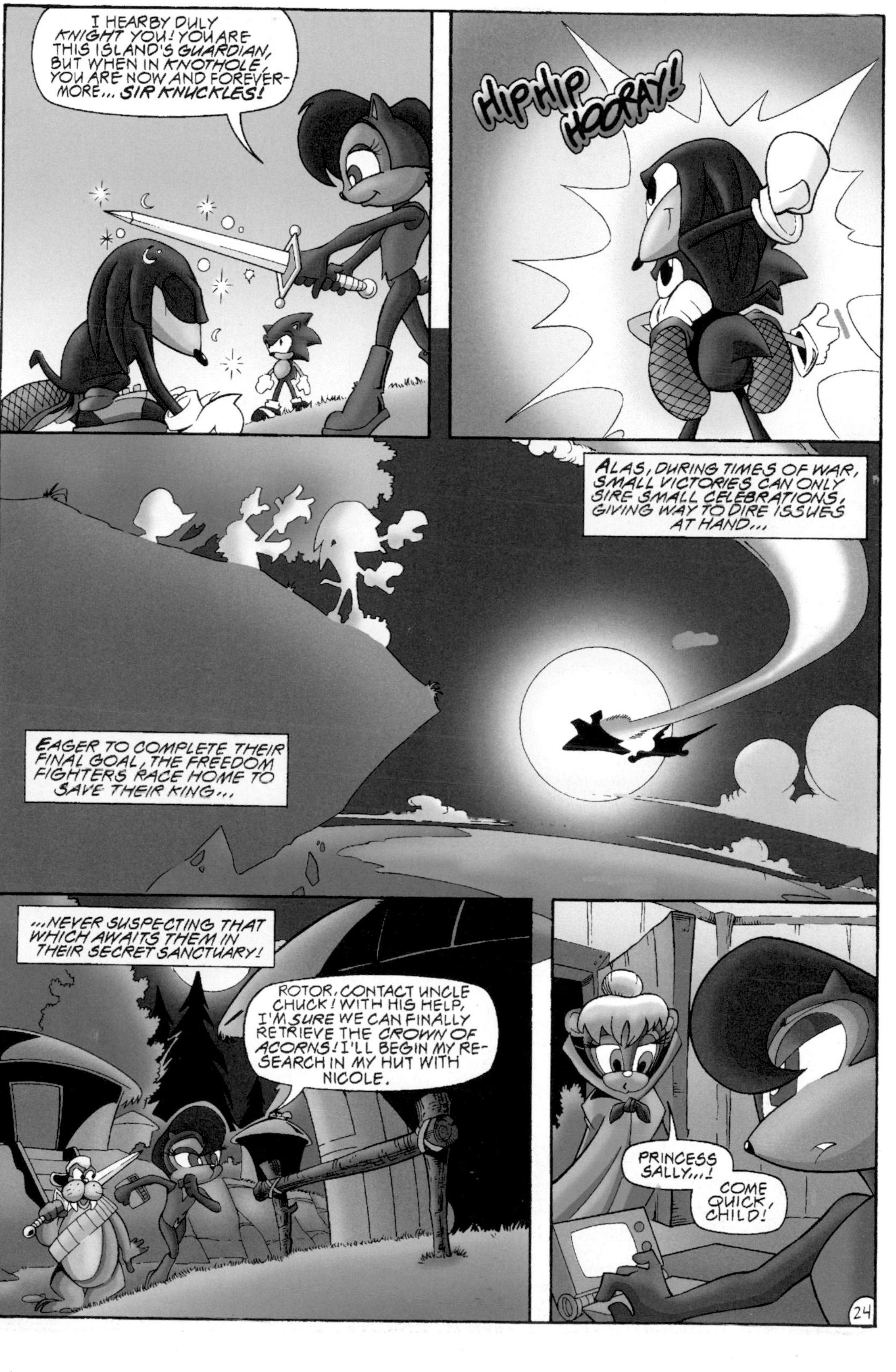

I HEARBY DULY KNIGHT YOU! YOU ARE THIS ISLAND'S GUARDIAN, BUT WHEN IN KNOTHOLE, YOU ARE NOW AND FOREVERMORE... SIR KNUCKLES!
HIP HIP HOORAY!
ALAS, DURING TIMES OF WAR, SMALL VICTORIES CAN ONLY SIRE SMALL CELEBRATIONS, GIVING WAY TO DIRE ISSUES AT HAND...
EAGER TO COMPLETE THEIR FINAL GOAL, THE FREEDOM FIGHTERS RACE HOME TO SAVE THEIR KING...
...NEVER SUSPECTING THAT WHICH AWAITS THEM IN THEIR SECRET SANCTUARY!
ROTOR, CONTACT UNCLE CHUCK! WITH HIS HELP, I'M SURE WE CAN FINALLY RETRIEVE THE CROWN OF ACORNS! I'LL BEGIN MY RESEARCH IN MY HUT WITH NICOLE.
PRINCESS SALLY...!
COME QUICK, CHILD!

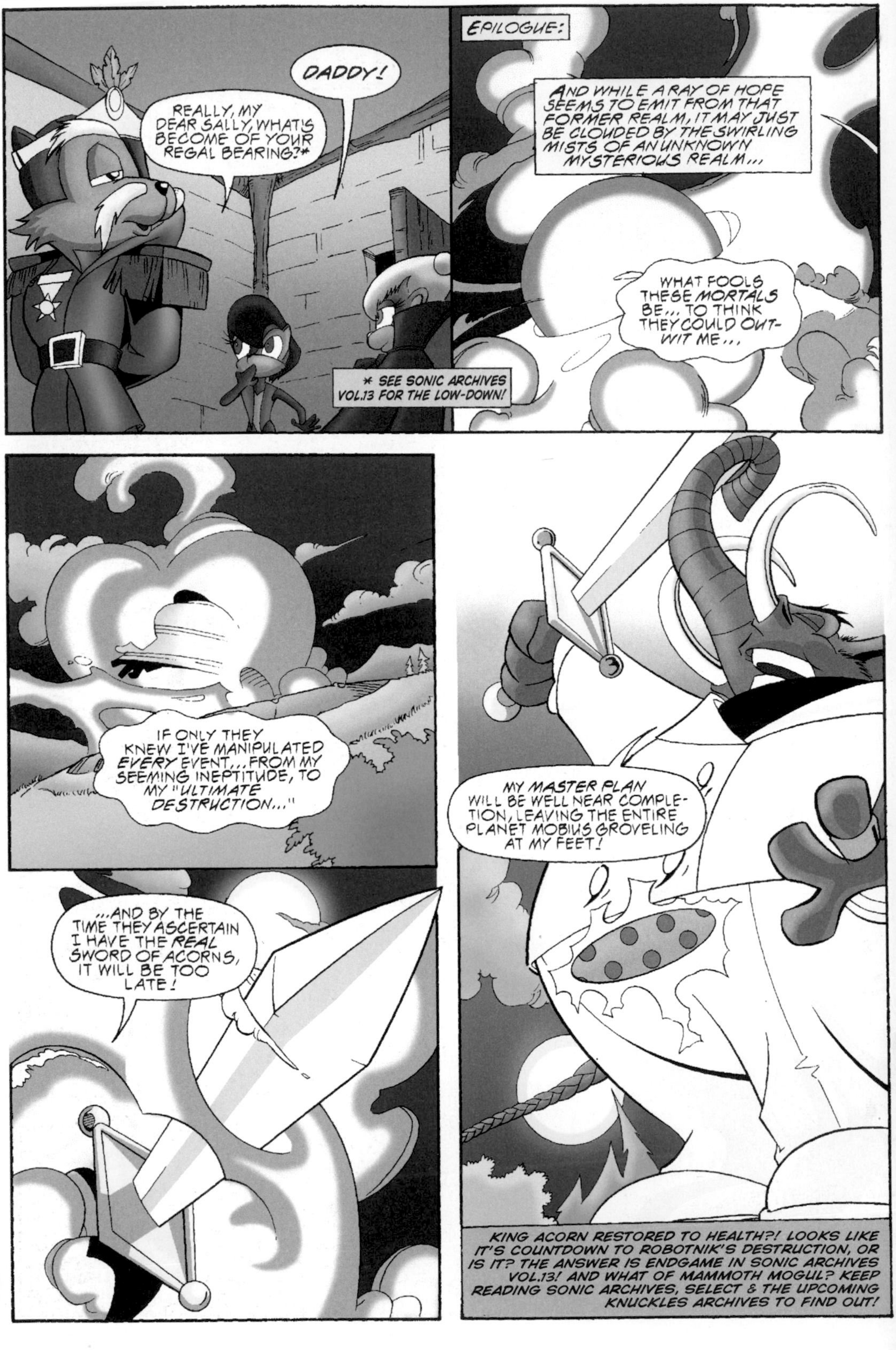
DADDY!
REALLY, MY DEAR SALLY, WHAT'S BECOME OF YOUR REGAL BEARING?*
* SEE SONIC ARCHIVES VOL.13 FOR THE LOW-DOWN!
EPILOGUE:
AND WHILE A RAY OF HOPE SEEMS TO EMIT FROM THAT FORMER REALM, IT MAY JUST BE CLOUDED BY THE SWIRLING MISTS OF AN UNKNOWN MYSTERIOUS REALM...
WHAT FOOLS THESE MORTALS BE... TO THINK THEY COULD OUT-WIT ME...
IF ONLY THEY KNEW I'VE MANIPULATED EVERY EVENT... FROM MY SEEMING INEPTITUDE, TO MY "ULTIMATE DESTRUCTION..."
...AND BY THE TIME THEY ASCERTAIN I HAVE THE REAL SWORD OF ACORNS, IT WILL BE TOO LATE!
MY MASTER PLAN WILL BE WELL NEAR COMPLE-TION, LEAVING THE ENTIRE PLANET MOBIUS GROVELING AT MY FEET!
KING ACORN RESTORED TO HEALTH?! LOOKS LIKE IT'S COUNTDOWN TO ROBOTNIK'S DESTRUCTION, OR IS IT? THE ANSWER IS ENDGAME IN SONIC ARCHIVES VOL.13! AND WHAT OF MAMMOTH MOGUL? KEEP READING SONIC ARCHIVES, SELECT & THE UPCOMING KNUCKLES ARCHIVES TO FIND OUT!

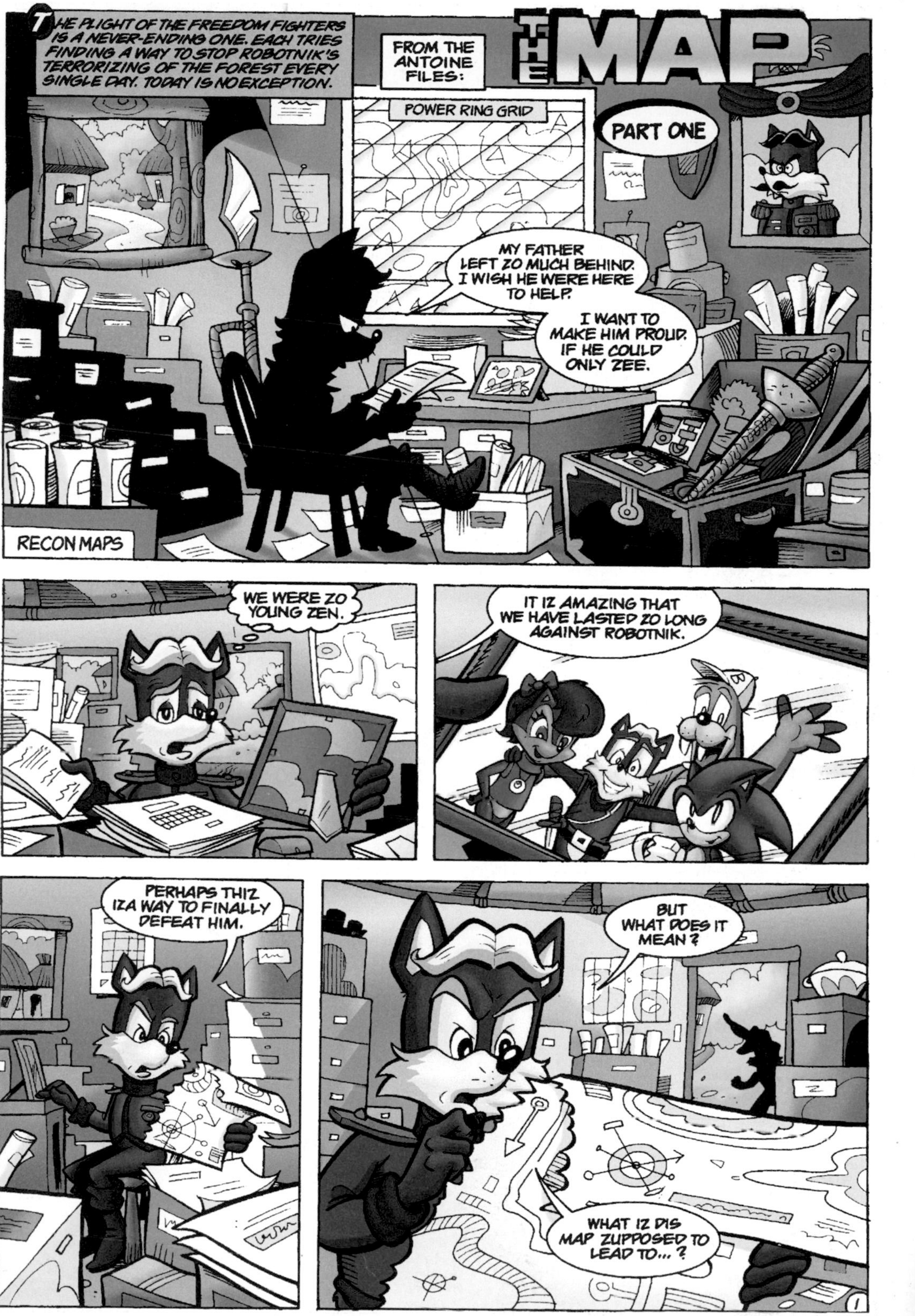
THE PLIGHT OF THE FREEDOM FIGHTERS IS A NEVER-ENDING ONE. EACH TRIES FINDING A WAY TO STOP ROBOTNIK'S TERRORIZING OF THE FOREST EVERY SINGLE DAY. TODAY IS NO EXCEPTION.
FROM THE ANTOINE FILES:
THE MAP
PART ONE
POWER RING GRID
MY FATHER LEFT ZO MUCH BEHIND. I WISH HE WERE HERE TO HELP.
I WANT TO MAKE HIM PROUD. IF HE COULD ONLY ZEE.
RECON MAPS
WE WERE ZO YOUNG ZEN.
IT IZ AMAZING THAT WE HAVE LASTED ZO LONG AGAINST ROBOTNIK.
PERHAPS THIZ IZA WAY TO FINALLY DEFEAT HIM.
BUT WHAT DOES IT MEAN ?
WHAT IZ DIS MAP ZUPPOSED TO LEAD TO... ?
1

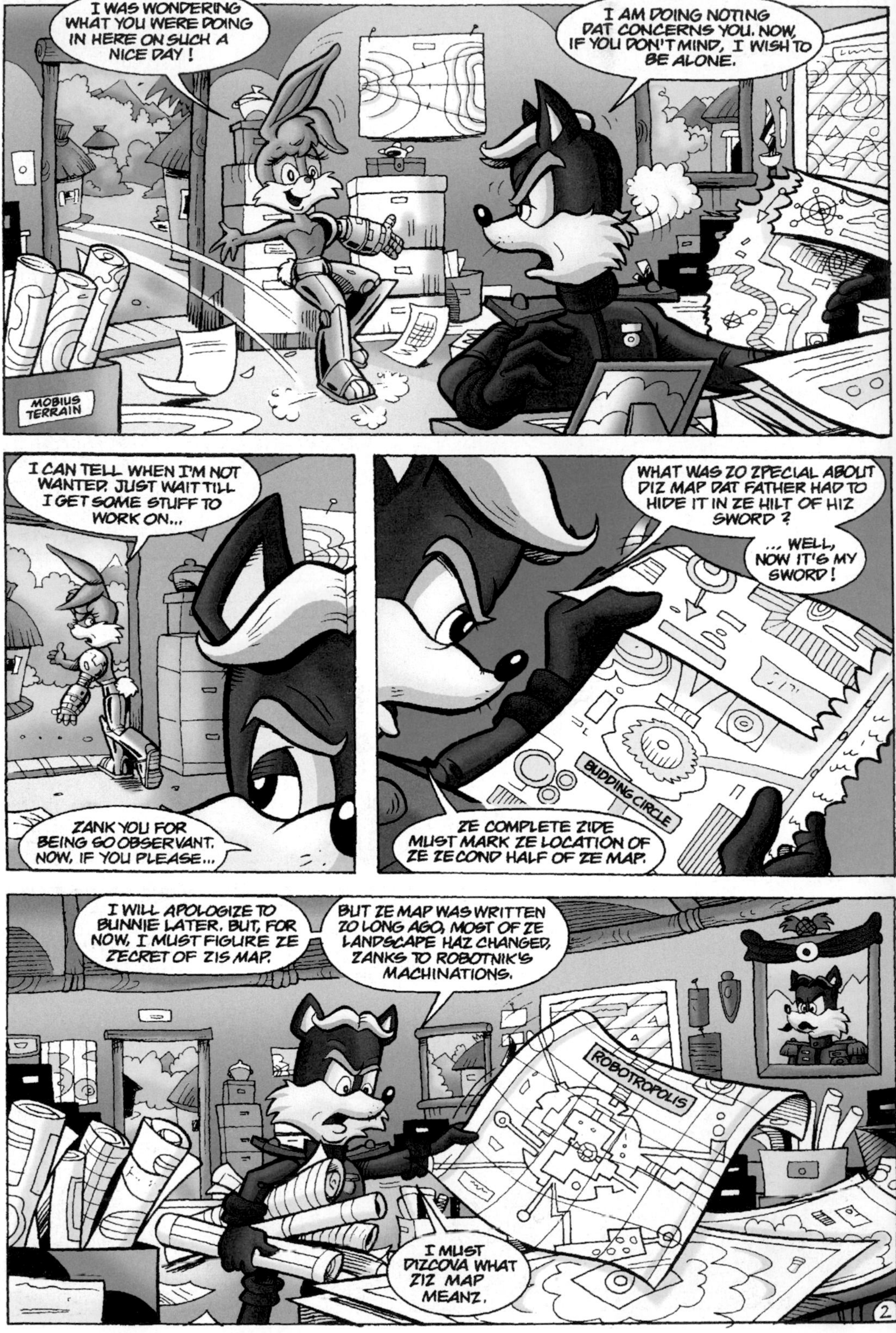
I WAS WONDERING WHAT YOU WERE DOING IN HERE ON SUCH A NICE DAY!
I AM DOING NOTING DAT CONCERNS YOU. NOW, IF YOU DON'T MIND, I WISH TO BE ALONE.
MOBIUS TERRAIN
I CAN TELL WHEN I'M NOT WANTED. JUST WAIT TILL I GET SOME STUFF TO WORK ON...
ZANK YOU FOR BEING SO OBSERVANT. NOW, IF YOU PLEASE...
WHAT WAS ZO ZPECIAL ABOUT DIZ MAP DAT FATHER HAD TO HIDE IT IN ZE HILT OF HIZ SWORD?
... WELL, NOW IT'S MY SWORD!
BUDDING CIRCLE
ZE COMPLETE ZIDE MUST MARK ZE LOCATION OF ZE ZECOND HALF OF ZE MAP.
I WILL APOLOGIZE TO BUNNIE LATER. BUT, FOR NOW, I MUST FIGURE ZE ZECRET OF ZIS MAP.
BUT ZE MAP WAS WRITTEN ZO LONG AGO, MOST OF ZE LANDSCAPE HAZ CHANGED, ZANKS TO ROBOTNIK'S MACHINATIONS.
ROBOTROPOLIS
I MUST DIZCOVA WHAT ZIZ MAP MEANZ.

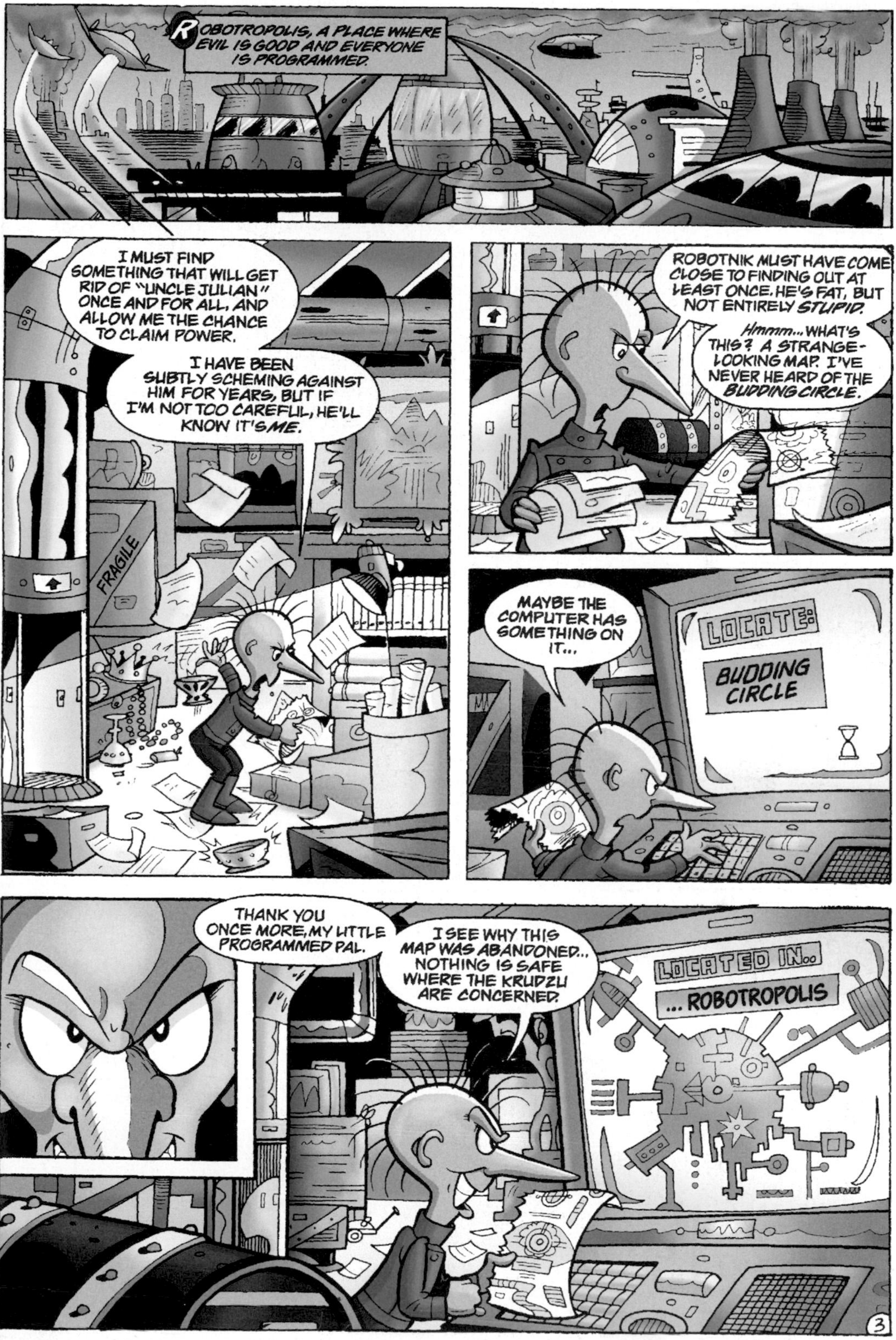
ROBOTROPOLIS, A PLACE WHERE EVIL IS GOOD AND EVERYONE IS PROGRAMMED.
I MUST FIND SOMETHING THAT WILL GET RID OF "UNCLE JULIAN" ONCE AND FOR ALL, AND ALLOW ME THE CHANCE TO CLAIM POWER.
I HAVE BEEN SUBTLY SCHEMING AGAINST HIM FOR YEARS, BUT IF I'M NOT TOO CAREFUL, HE'LL KNOW IT'S ME.
FRAGILE
ROBOTNIK MUST HAVE COME CLOSE TO FINDING OUT AT LEAST ONCE. HE'S FAT, BUT NOT ENTIRELY STUPID.
Hmmm... WHAT'S THIS? A STRANGE-LOOKING MAP. I'VE NEVER HEARD OF THE BUDDING CIRCLE.
MAYBE THE COMPUTER HAS SOMETHING ON IT...
LOCATE:
BUDDING CIRCLE
THANK YOU ONCE MORE, MY LITTLE PROGRAMMED PAL.
I SEE WHY THIS MAP WAS ABANDONED... NOTHING IS SAFE WHERE THE KRUDZU ARE CONCERNED.
LOCATED IN..
... ROBOTROPOLIS

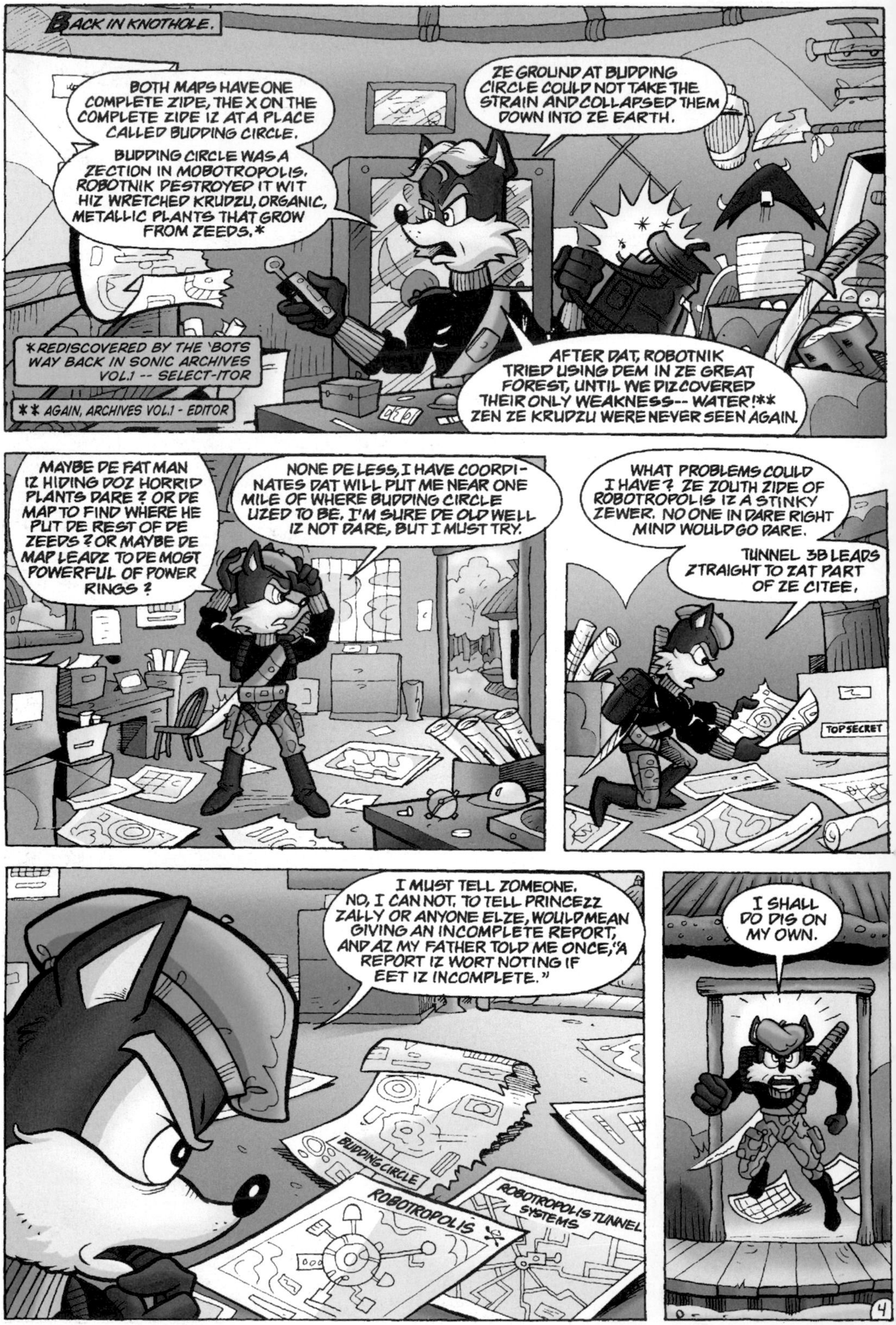
BACK IN KNOTHOLE.
BOTH MAPS HAVE ONE COMPLETE ZIDE, THE X ON THE COMPLETE ZIDE IZ AT A PLACE CALLED BUDDING CIRCLE.
BUDDING CIRCLE WAS A ZECTION IN MOBOTROPOLIS. ROBOTNIK DESTROYED IT WIT HIZ WRETCHED KRUDZU, ORGANIC, METALLIC PLANTS THAT GROW FROM ZEEDS.*
ZE GROUND AT BUDDING CIRCLE COULD NOT TAKE THE STRAIN AND COLLAPSED THEM DOWN INTO ZE EARTH.
*REDISCOVERED BY THE 'BOTS WAY BACK IN SONIC ARCHIVES VOL.1 -- SELECT-ITOR
** AGAIN, ARCHIVES VOL.1 - EDITOR
AFTER DAT, ROBOTNIK TRIED USING DEM IN ZE GREAT FOREST, UNTIL WE DIZCOVERED THEIR ONLY WEAKNESS-- WATER!** ZEN ZE KRUDZU WERE NEVER SEEN AGAIN.
MAYBE DE FAT MAN IZ HIDING DOZ HORRID PLANTS DARE? OR DE MAP TO FIND WHERE HE PUT DE REST OF DE ZEEDS? OR MAYBE DE MAP LEADZ TO DE MOST POWERFUL OF POWER RINGS?
NONE DE LESS, I HAVE COORDINATES DAT WILL PUT ME NEAR ONE MILE OF WHERE BUDDING CIRCLE UZED TO BE. I'M SURE DE OLD WELL IZ NOT DARE, BUT I MUST TRY.
WHAT PROBLEMS COULD I HAVE? ZE ZOUTH ZIDE OF ROBOTROPOLIS IZ A STINKY ZEWER. NO ONE IN DARE RIGHT MIND WOULD GO DARE.
TUNNEL 3B LEADS ZTRAIGHT TO ZAT PART OF ZE CITEE.
TOP SECRET
I MUST TELL ZOMEONE. NO, I CAN NOT. TO TELL PRINCEZZ ZALLY OR ANYONE ELZE, WOULD MEAN GIVING AN INCOMPLETE REPORT, AND AZ MY FATHER TOLD ME ONCE, "A REPORT IZ WORT NOTING IF EET IZ INCOMPLETE."
BUDDING CIRCLE
ROBOTROPOLIS
ROBOTROPOLIS TUNNEL SYSTEMS
I SHALL DO DIS ON MY OWN.

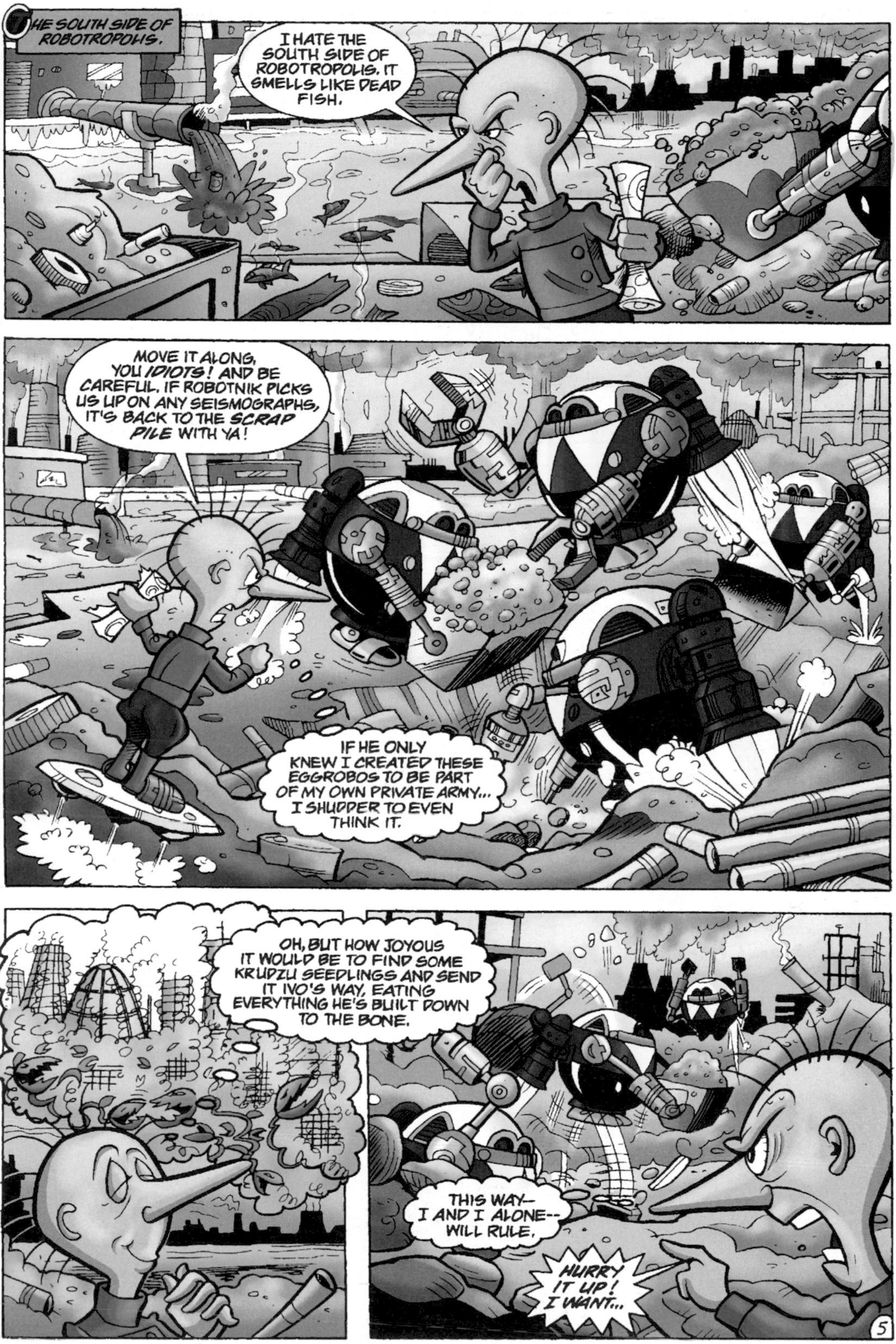
THE SOUTH SIDE OF ROBOTROPOLIS.
I HATE THE SOUTH SIDE OF ROBOTROPOLIS. IT SMELLS LIKE DEAD FISH.
MOVE IT ALONG, YOU IDIOTS! AND BE CAREFUL. IF ROBOTNIK PICKS US UP ON ANY SEISMOGRAPHS, IT'S BACK TO THE SCRAP PILE WITH YA!
IF HE ONLY KNEW I CREATED THESE EGGROBOS TO BE PART OF MY OWN PRIVATE ARMY... I SHUDDER TO EVEN THINK IT.
OH, BUT HOW JOYOUS IT WOULD BE TO FIND SOME KRUDZU SEEDLINGS AND SEND IT IVO'S WAY, EATING EVERYTHING HE'S BUILT DOWN TO THE BONE.
THIS WAY-- I AND I ALONE-- WILL RULE.
HURRY IT UP! I WANT...

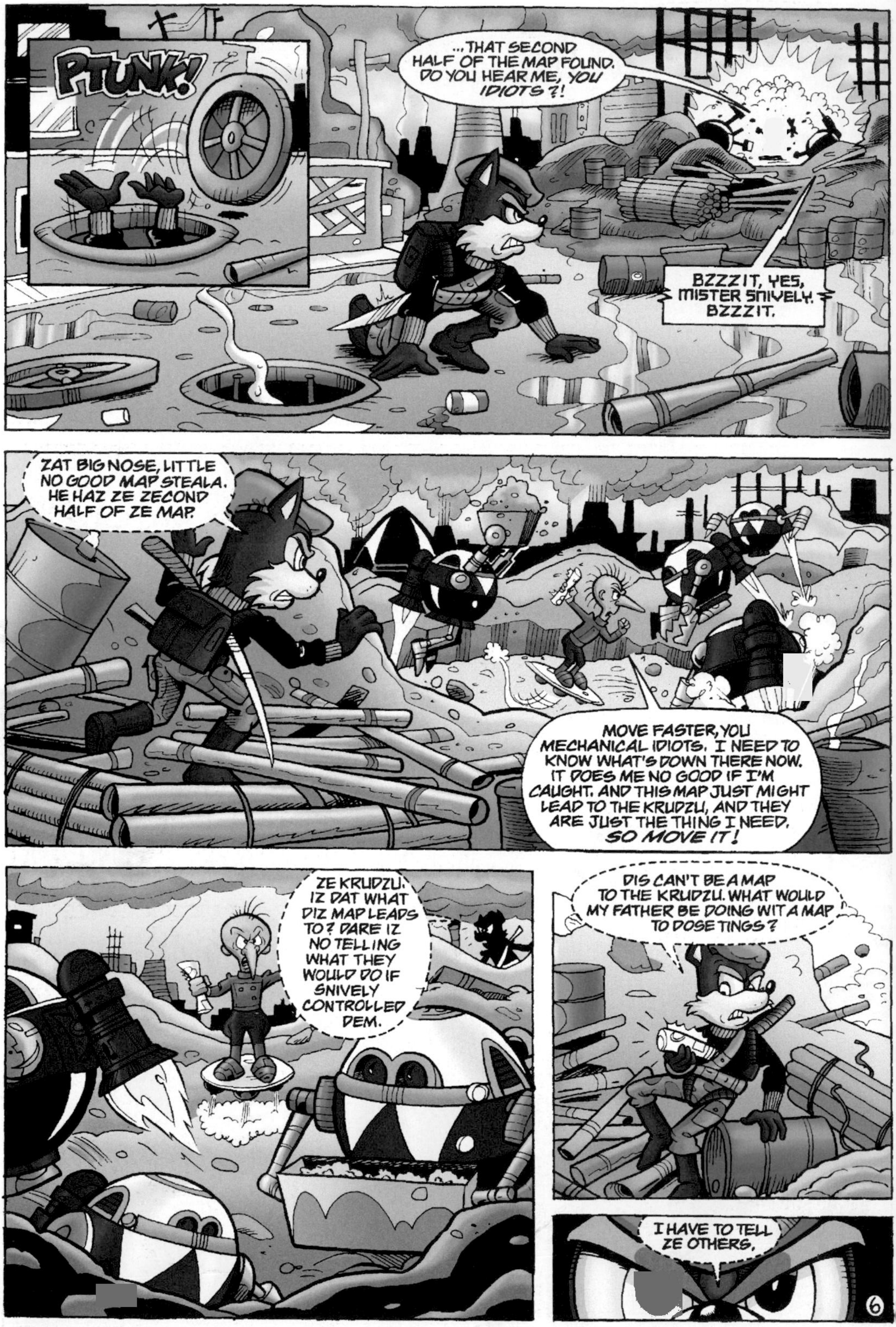
PTUNK!
...THAT SECOND HALF OF THE MAP FOUND. DO YOU HEAR ME, YOU IDIOTS?!
BZZZIT, YES, MISTER SNIVELY. BZZZIT.
ZAT BIG NOSE, LITTLE NO GOOD MAP STEALA. HE HAZ ZE ZECOND HALF OF ZE MAP.
MOVE FASTER, YOU MECHANICAL IDIOTS. I NEED TO KNOW WHAT'S DOWN THERE NOW. IT DOES ME NO GOOD IF I'M CAUGHT. AND THIS MAP JUST MIGHT LEAD TO THE KRUDZU, AND THEY ARE JUST THE THING I NEED. SO MOVE IT!
ZE KRUDZU. IZ DAT WHAT DIZ MAP LEADS TO? DARE IZ NO TELLING WHAT THEY WOULD DO IF SNIVELY CONTROLLED DEM.
DIS CAN'T BE A MAP TO THE KRUDZU. WHAT WOULD MY FATHER BE DOING WIT A MAP TO DOSE TINGS?
I HAVE TO TELL ZE OTHERS.

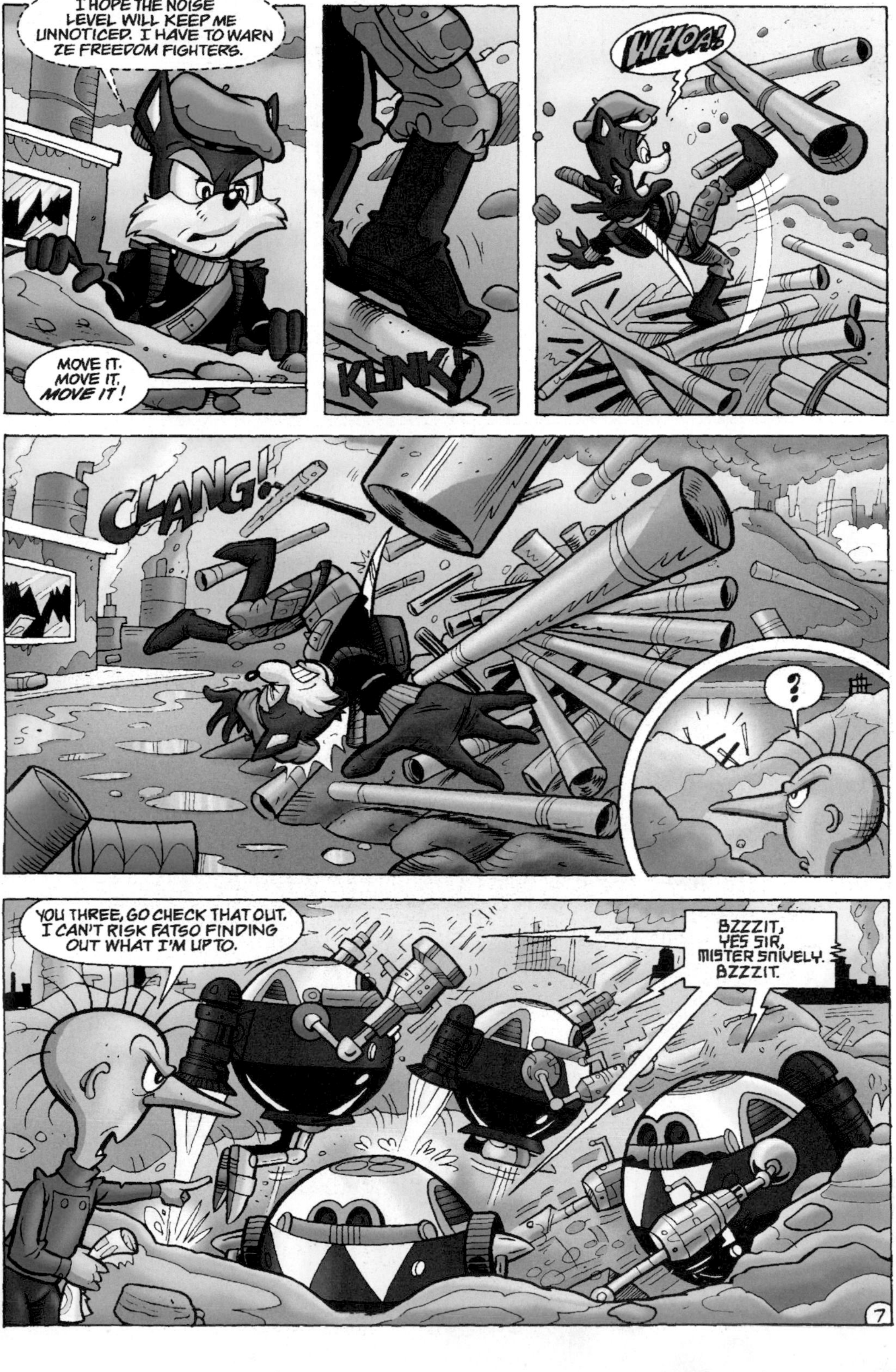
I HOPE THE NOISE LEVEL WILL KEEP ME UNNOTICED. I HAVE TO WARN ZE FREEDOM FIGHTERS.
MOVE IT. MOVE IT, *MOVE IT*!
KLINK!
WHOA!
CLANG!
?
YOU THREE, GO CHECK THAT OUT. I CAN'T RISK FATSO FINDING OUT WHAT I'M UP TO.
BZZZIT, YES SIR, MISTER SNIVELY. BZZZIT.

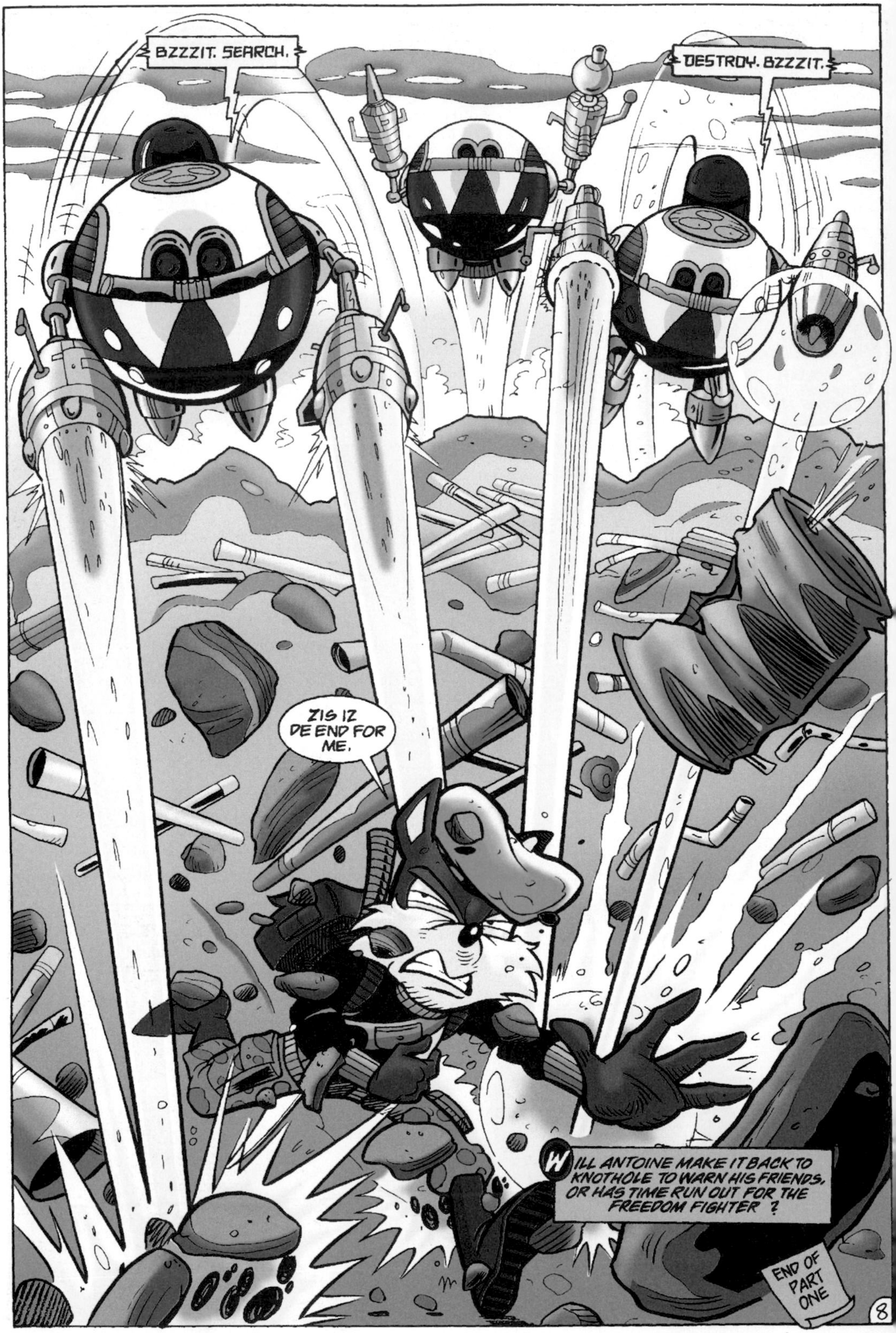
BZZZIT. SEARCH.
DESTROY. BZZZIT.
ZIS IZ DE END FOR ME.
WILL ANTOINE MAKE IT BACK TO KNOTHOLE TO WARN HIS FRIENDS, OR HAS TIME RUN OUT FOR THE FREEDOM FIGHTER ?
END OF PART ONE
8

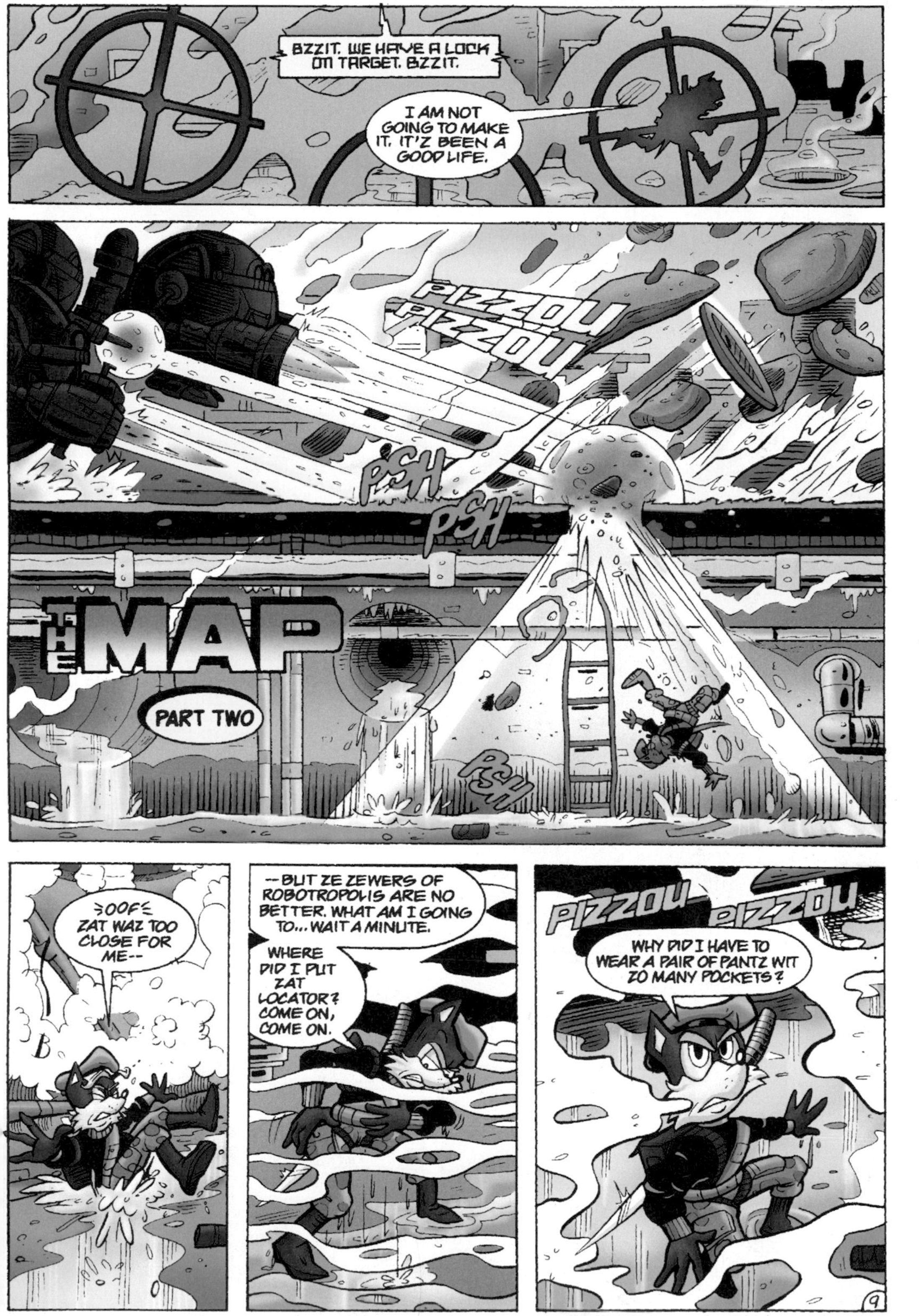

BZZIT. WE HAVE A LOCK ON TARGET. BZZIT.
I AM NOT GOING TO MAKE IT. IT'Z BEEN A GOOD LIFE.
PIZZOU PIZZOU
PSH PSH
THE MAP
PART TWO
PSH
OOF ZAT WAZ TOO CLOSE FOR ME--
--BUT ZE ZEWERS OF ROBOTROPOLIS ARE NO BETTER. WHAT AM I GOING TO... WAIT A MINUTE.
WHERE DID I PUT ZAT LOCATOR? COME ON, COME ON.
PIZZOU PIZZOU
WHY DID I HAVE TO WEAR A PAIR OF PANTZ WIT ZO MANY POCKETS?

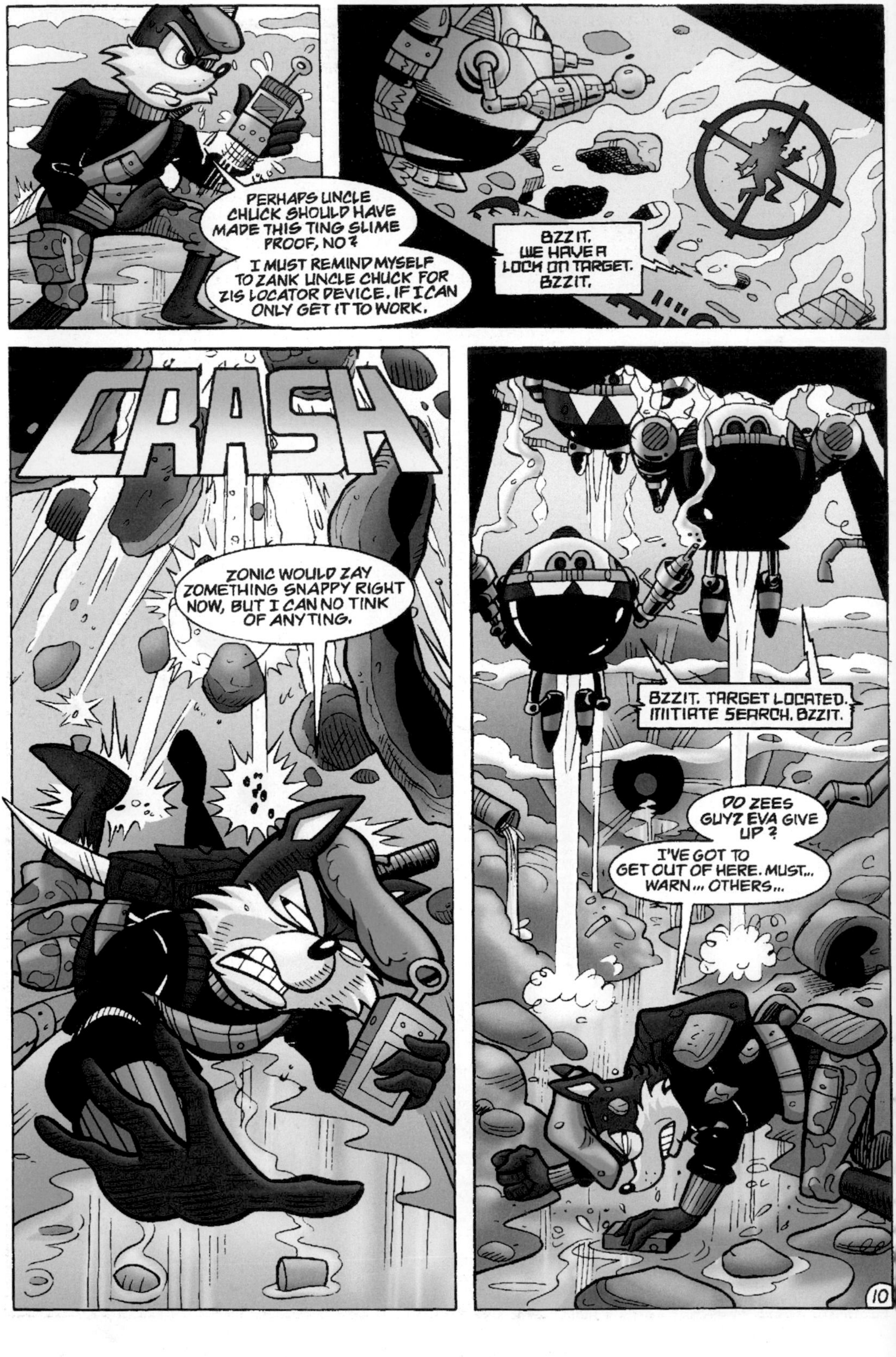
PERHAPS UNCLE CHUCK SHOULD HAVE MADE THIS TING SLIME PROOF, NO?
I MUST REMIND MYSELF TO ZANK UNCLE CHUCK FOR ZIS LOCATOR DEVICE. IF I CAN ONLY GET IT TO WORK.
BZZIT. WE HAVE A LOCK ON TARGET. BZZIT.
CRASH
ZONIC WOULD ZAY ZOMETHING SNAPPY RIGHT NOW, BUT I CAN NO TINK OF ANYTING.
BZZIT. TARGET LOCATED. INITIATE SEARCH. BZZIT.
DO ZEES GUYZ EVA GIVE UP?
I'VE GOT TO GET OUT OF HERE. MUST... WARN... OTHERS...

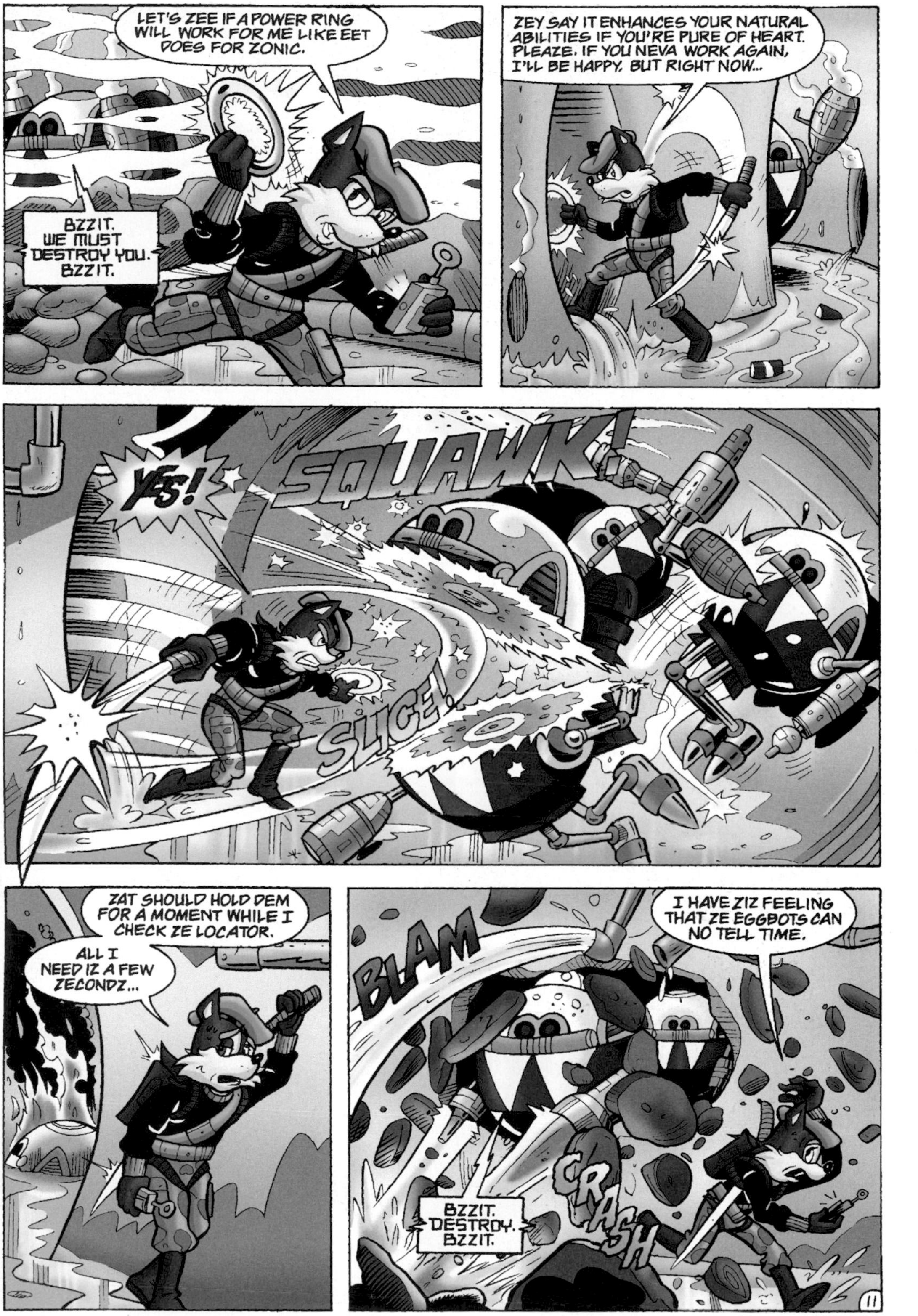
LET'S ZEE IF A POWER RING WILL WORK FOR ME LIKE EET DOES FOR ZONIC.
BZZIT. WE MUST DESTROY YOU. BZZIT.
ZEY SAY IT ENHANCES YOUR NATURAL ABILITIES IF YOU'RE PURE OF HEART. PLEAZE. IF YOU NEVA WORK AGAIN, I'LL BE HAPPY. BUT RIGHT NOW...
YES!
SQUAWK!
SLICE!
ZAT SHOULD HOLD DEM FOR A MOMENT WHILE I CHECK ZE LOCATOR.
ALL I NEED IZ A FEW ZECONDZ...
BLAM
I HAVE ZIZ FEELING THAT ZE EGGBOTS CAN NO TELL TIME.
BZZIT. DESTROY. BZZIT.
CRASH

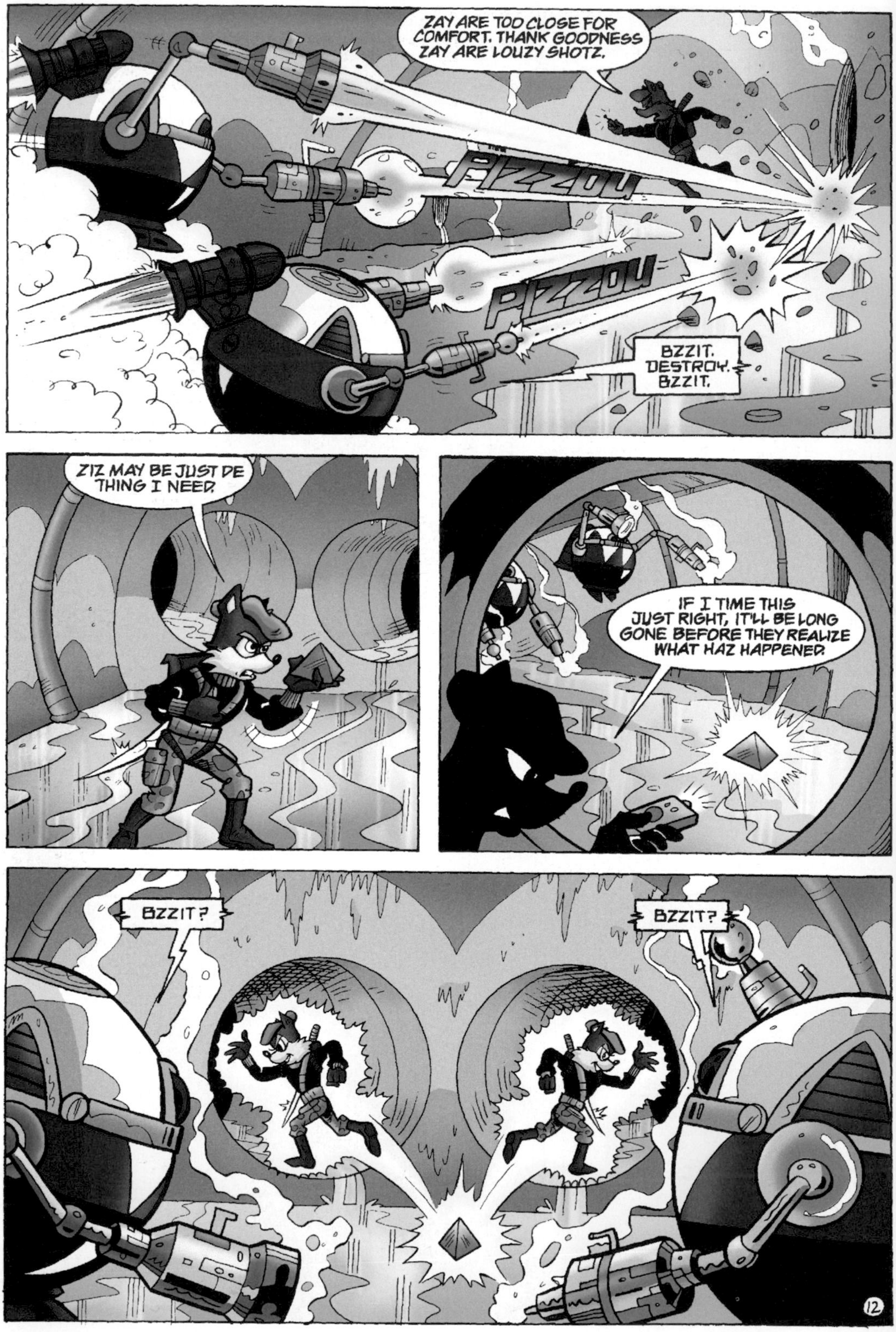
ZAY ARE TOO CLOSE FOR COMFORT. THANK GOODNESS ZAY ARE LOUZY SHOTZ.
PIZZOU
PIZZOU
BZZIT. DESTROY. BZZIT.
ZIZ MAY BE JUST DE THING I NEED.
IF I TIME THIS JUST RIGHT, IT'LL BE LONG GONE BEFORE THEY REALIZE WHAT HAZ HAPPENED.
BZZIT?
BZZIT?

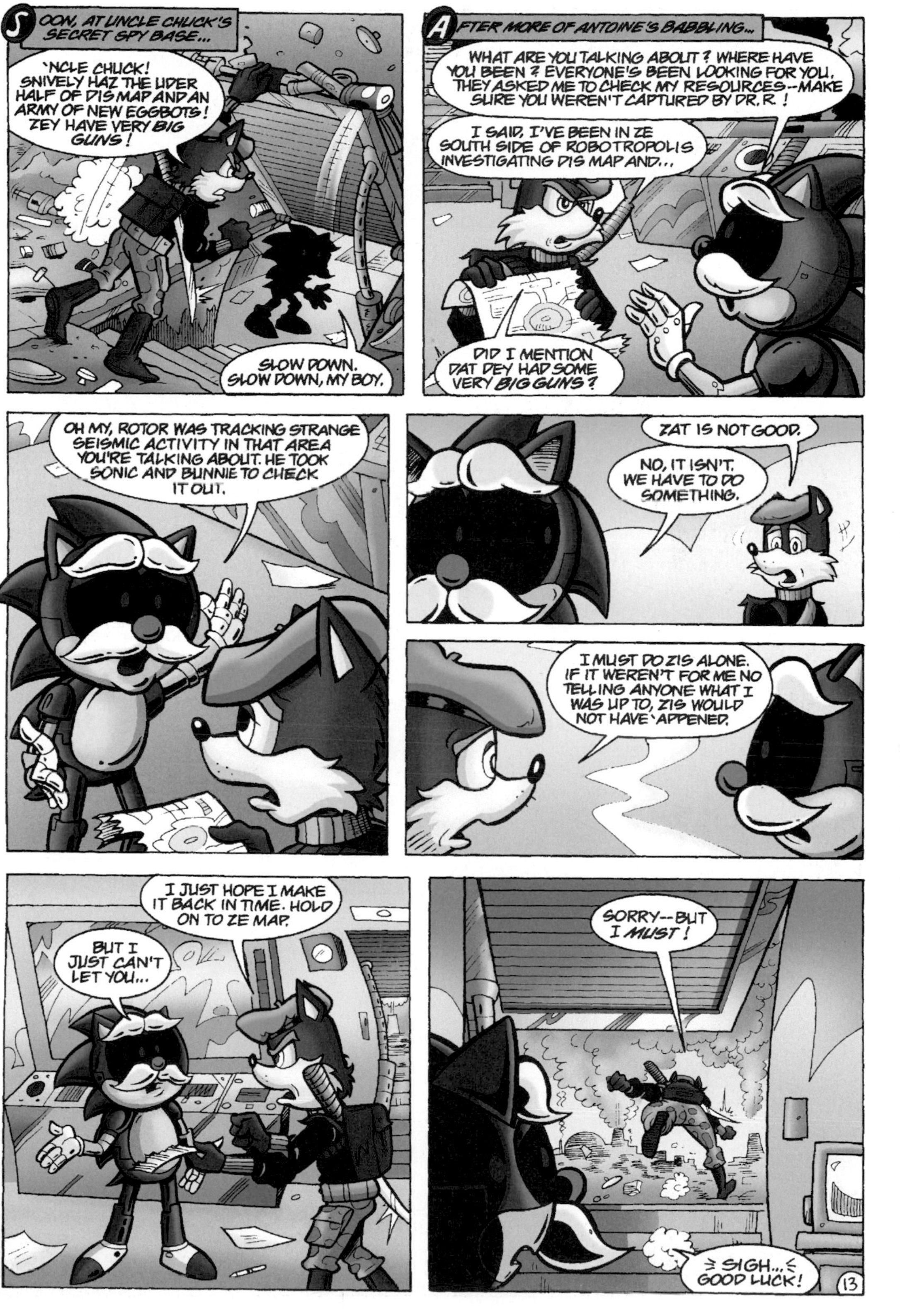
SOON, AT UNCLE CHUCK'S SECRET SPY BASE...
'NCLE CHUCK! SNIVELY HAZ THE UDER HALF OF DIS MAP AND AN ARMY OF NEW EGGBOTS! ZEY HAVE VERY BIG GUNS!
SLOW DOWN. SLOW DOWN, MY BOY.
AFTER MORE OF ANTOINE'S BABBLING...
WHAT ARE YOU TALKING ABOUT? WHERE HAVE YOU BEEN? EVERYONE'S BEEN LOOKING FOR YOU. THEY ASKED ME TO CHECK MY RESOURCES--MAKE SURE YOU WEREN'T CAPTURED BY DR. R.!
I SAID, I'VE BEEN IN ZE SOUTH SIDE OF ROBOTROPOLIS INVESTIGATING DIS MAP AND...
DID I MENTION DAT DEY HAD SOME VERY BIG GUNS?
OH MY, ROTOR WAS TRACKING STRANGE SEISMIC ACTIVITY IN THAT AREA YOU'RE TALKING ABOUT. HE TOOK SONIC AND BUNNIE TO CHECK IT OUT.
ZAT IS NOT GOOD.
NO, IT ISN'T. WE HAVE TO DO SOMETHING.
I MUST DO ZIS ALONE. IF IT WEREN'T FOR ME NO TELLING ANYONE WHAT I WAS UP TO, ZIS WOULD NOT HAVE 'APPENED.
I JUST HOPE I MAKE IT BACK IN TIME. HOLD ON TO ZE MAP.
BUT I JUST CAN'T LET YOU...
SORRY--BUT I MUST!
SIGH... GOOD LUCK!

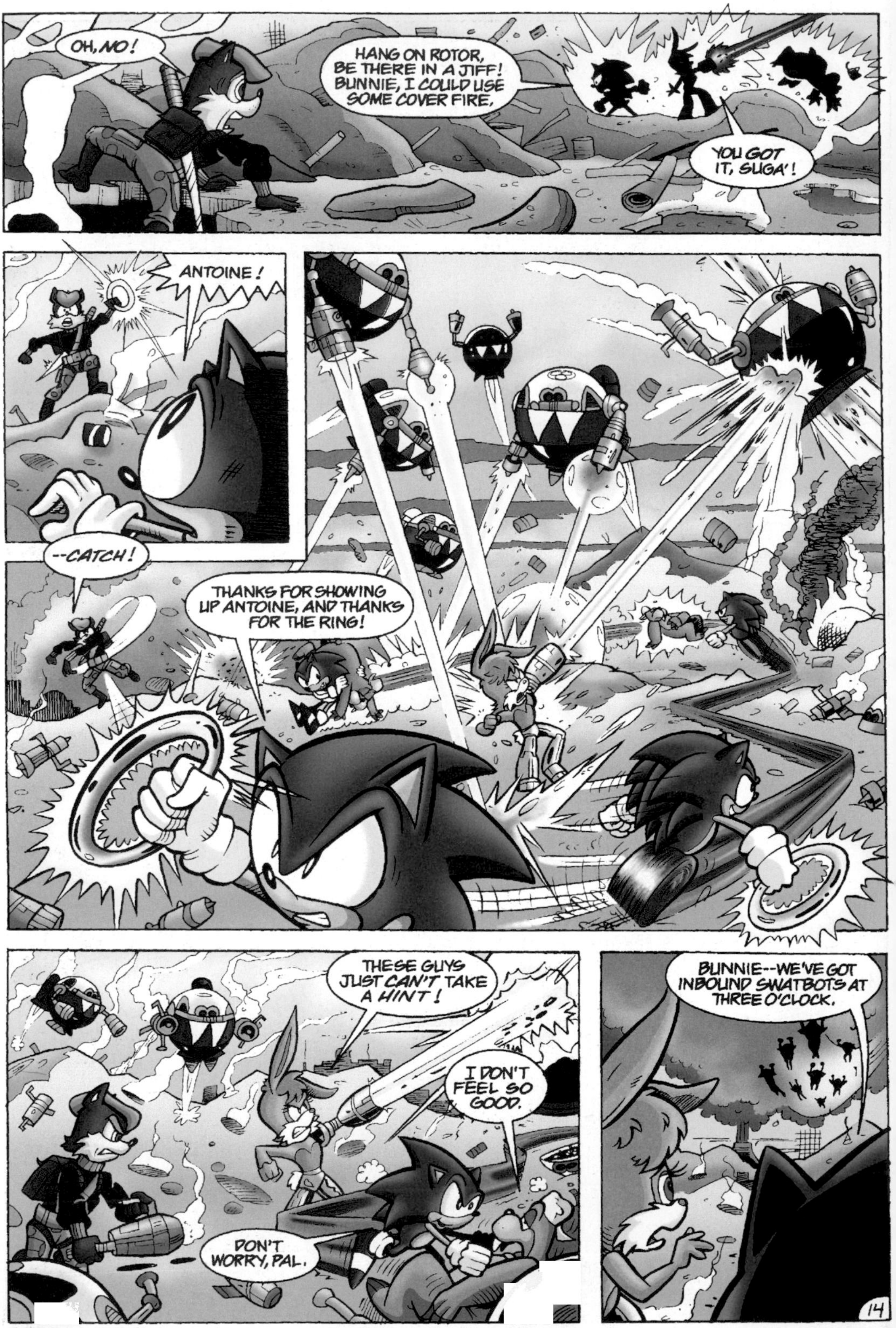

OH, NO!
HANG ON ROTOR, BE THERE IN A JIFF! BUNNIE, I COULD USE SOME COVER FIRE.
YOU GOT IT, SUGA'!
ANTOINE!
--CATCH!
THANKS FOR SHOWING UP ANTOINE, AND THANKS FOR THE RING!
THESE GUYS JUST CAN'T TAKE A HINT!
I DON'T FEEL SO GOOD.
DON'T WORRY, PAL.
BUNNIE--WE'VE GOT INBOUND SWATBOTS AT THREE O'CLOCK.

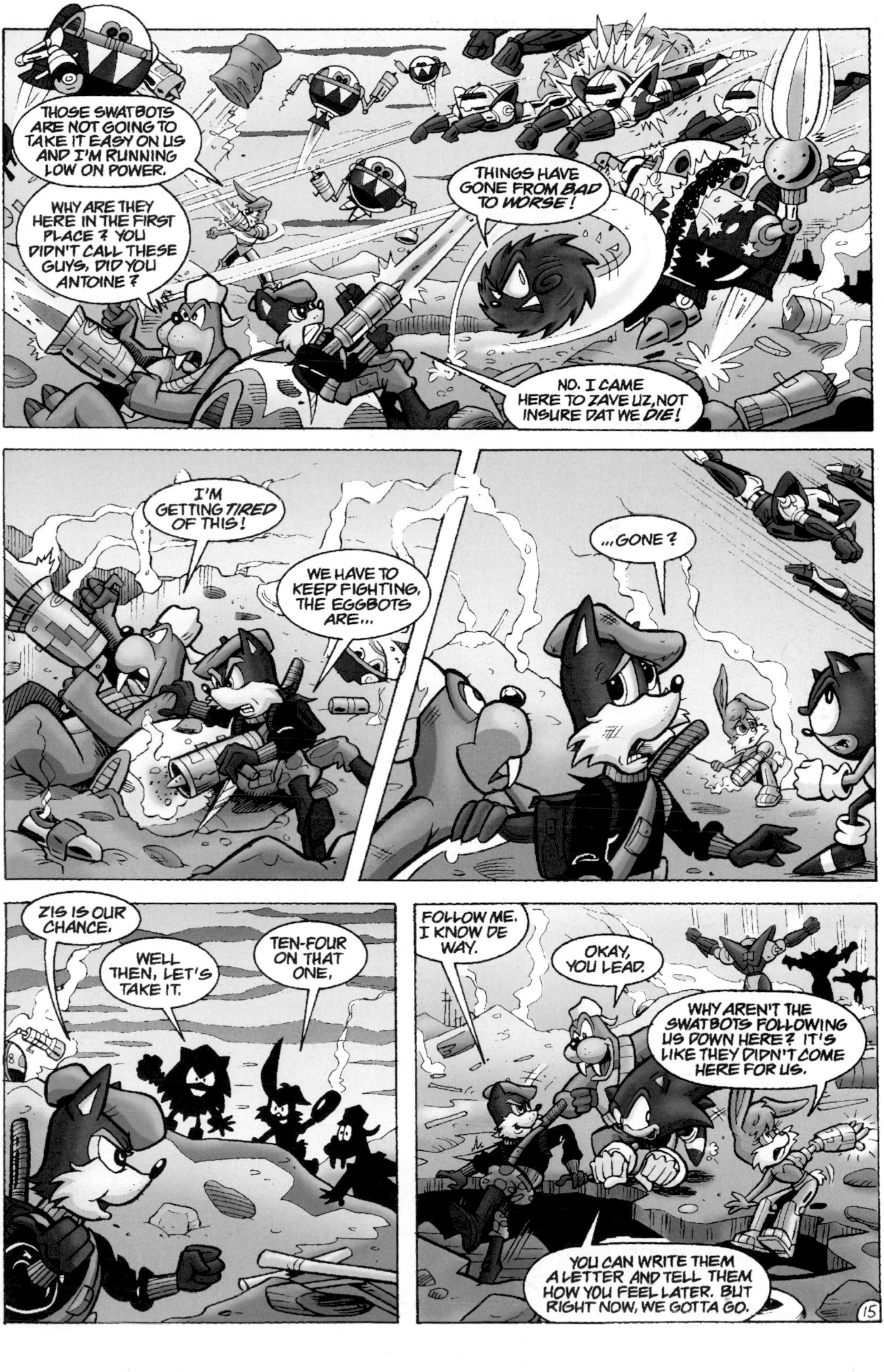
THOSE SWATBOTS ARE NOT GOING TO TAKE IT EASY ON US AND I'M RUNNING LOW ON POWER.
WHY ARE THEY HERE IN THE FIRST PLACE ? YOU DIDN'T CALL THESE GUYS, DID YOU ANTOINE ?
THINGS HAVE GONE FROM BAD TO WORSE !
NO. I CAME HERE TO ZAVE UZ, NOT INSURE DAT WE DIE!
I'M GETTING TIRED OF THIS!
WE HAVE TO KEEP FIGHTING, THE EGGBOTS ARE...
...GONE ?
ZIS IS OUR CHANCE.
WELL THEN, LET'S TAKE IT.
TEN-FOUR ON THAT ONE.
FOLLOW ME. I KNOW DE WAY.
OKAY, YOU LEAD.
WHY AREN'T THE SWATBOTS FOLLOWING US DOWN HERE? IT'S LIKE THEY DIDN'T COME HERE FOR US.
YOU CAN WRITE THEM A LETTER AND TELL THEM HOW YOU FEEL LATER. BUT RIGHT NOW, WE GOTTA GO.

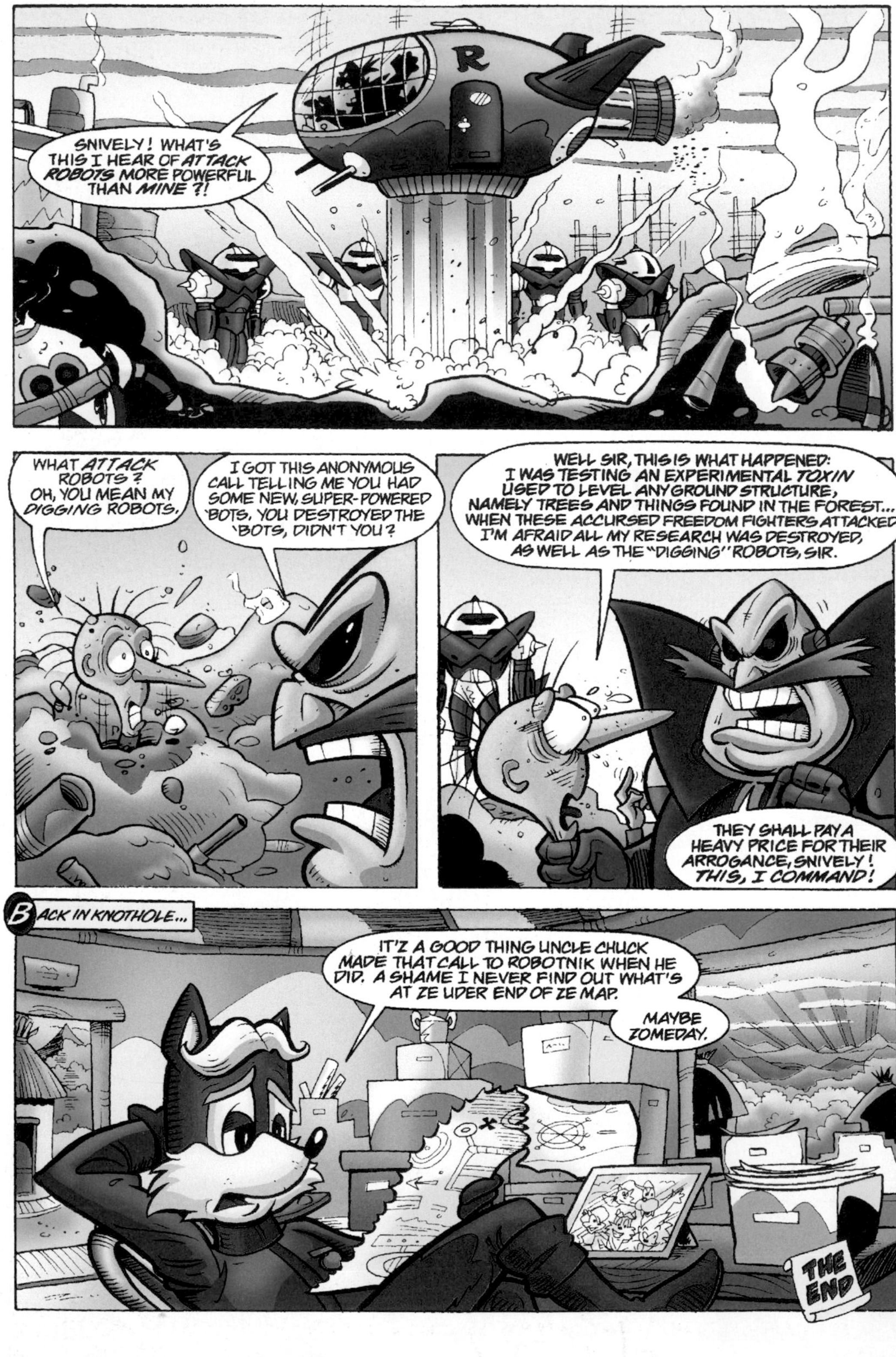
SNIVELY! WHAT'S THIS I HEAR OF ATTACK ROBOTS MORE POWERFUL THAN MINE ?!
WHAT ATTACK ROBOTS ? OH, YOU MEAN MY DIGGING ROBOTS.
I GOT THIS ANONYMOUS CALL TELLING ME YOU HAD SOME NEW, SUPER-POWERED 'BOTS. YOU DESTROYED THE 'BOTS, DIDN'T YOU ?
WELL SIR, THIS IS WHAT HAPPENED: I WAS TESTING AN EXPERIMENTAL TOXIN USED TO LEVEL ANY GROUND STRUCTURE, NAMELY TREES AND THINGS FOUND IN THE FOREST... WHEN THESE ACCURSED FREEDOM FIGHTERS ATTACKED. I'M AFRAID ALL MY RESEARCH WAS DESTROYED, AS WELL AS THE "DIGGING" ROBOTS, SIR.
THEY SHALL PAY A HEAVY PRICE FOR THEIR ARROGANCE, SNIVELY! THIS, I COMMAND!
BACK IN KNOTHOLE...
IT'Z A GOOD THING UNCLE CHUCK MADE THAT CALL TO ROBOTNIK WHEN HE DID. A SHAME I NEVER FIND OUT WHAT'S AT ZE UDER END OF ZE MAP.
MAYBE ZOMEDAY.
THE END

SONIC™ vs. KNUCKLES™

BATTLE ROYAL

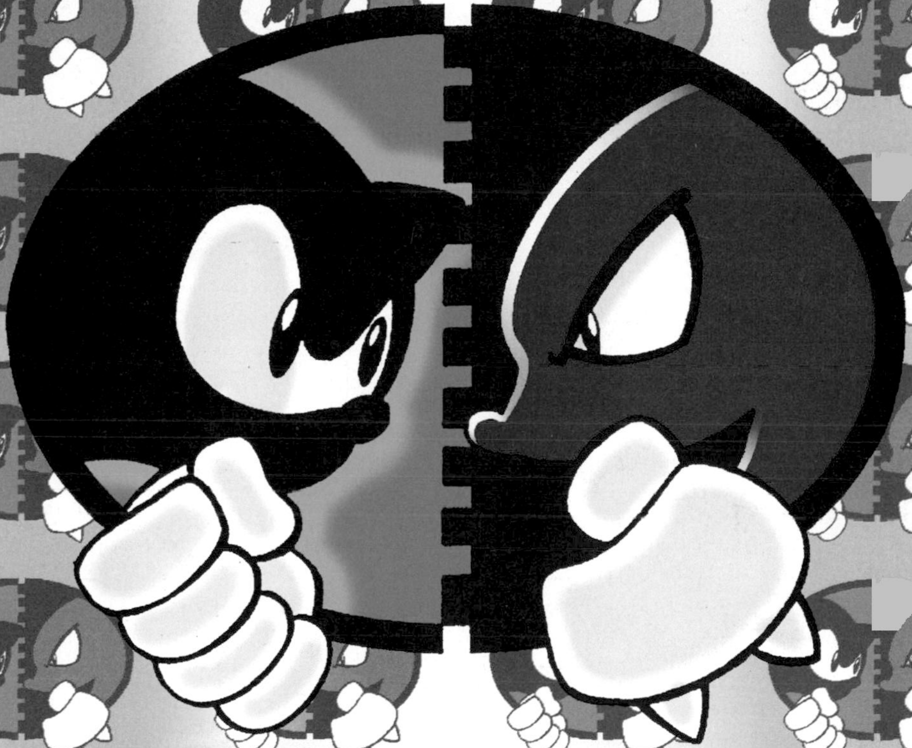

"BATTLE ROYAL!"

Kent Taylor & Ken Pender-Writers, Sam Maxwell-Penciler
Jim Amash-Inker, Karl Bollers-Colorist, Jeff Powell-Letterer

"THE MAP"

Tom Rolston-Writer, Dave Manak-Penciler, Rich Koslowski-In[illegible]er
Barry Grossman-Colorist, Vickie Williams-Letterer

J. Freddy Gabrie-Editor, Victor Gorelick-Managing Editor
Richard Goldwater-Editor-In-Chief

SPECIAL THANKS to Susan Sua[illegible]z and Helen Ball

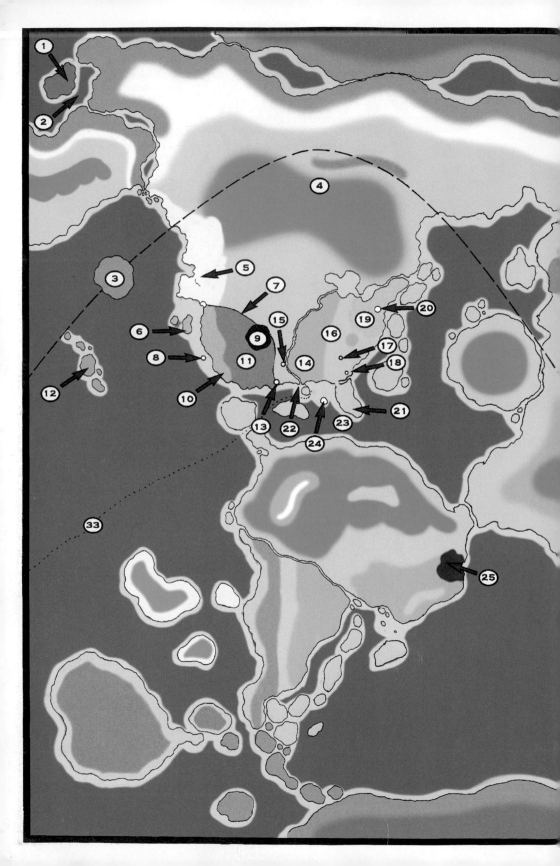

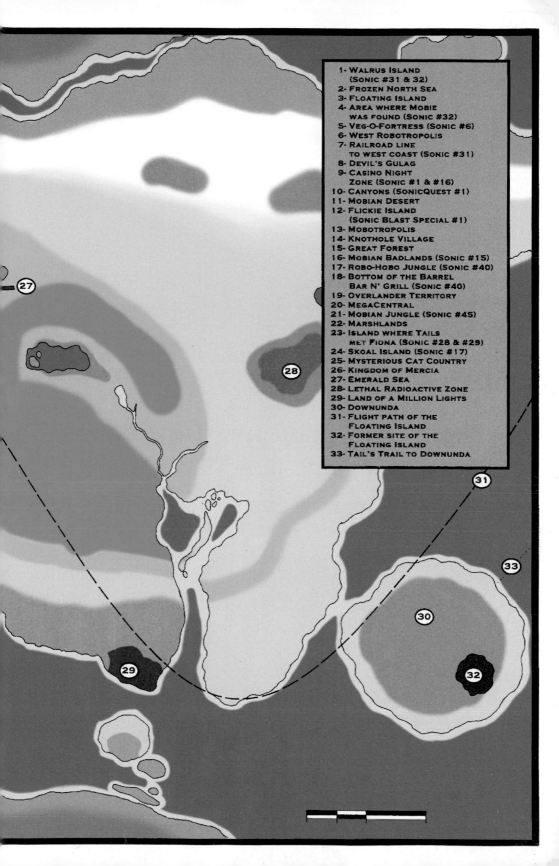

1- Walrus Island
   (Sonic #31 & 32)
2- Frozen North Sea
3- Floating Island
4- Area where Mobie
   was found (Sonic #32)
5- Veg-O-Fortress (Sonic #6)
6- West Robotropolis
7- Railroad line
   to west coast (Sonic #31)
8- Devil's Gulag
9- Casino Night
   Zone (Sonic #1 & #16)
10- Canyons (SonicQuest #1)
11- Mobian Desert
12- Flickie Island
    (Sonic Blast Special #1)
13- Mobotropolis
14- Knothole Village
15- Great Forest
16- Mobian Badlands (Sonic #15)
17- Robo-Hobo Jungle (Sonic #40)
18- Bottom of the Barrel
    Bar N' Grill (Sonic #40)
19- Overlander Territory
20- MegaCentral
21- Mobian Jungle (Sonic #45)
22- Marshlands
23- Island where Tails
    met Fiona (Sonic #28 & #29)
24- Skoal Island (Sonic #17)
25- Mysterious Cat Country
26- Kingdom of Mercia
27- Emerald Sea
28- Lethal Radioactive Zone
29- Land of a Million Lights
30- Downunda
31- Flight path of the
    Floating Island
32- Former site of the
    Floating Island
33- Tail's Trail to Downunda

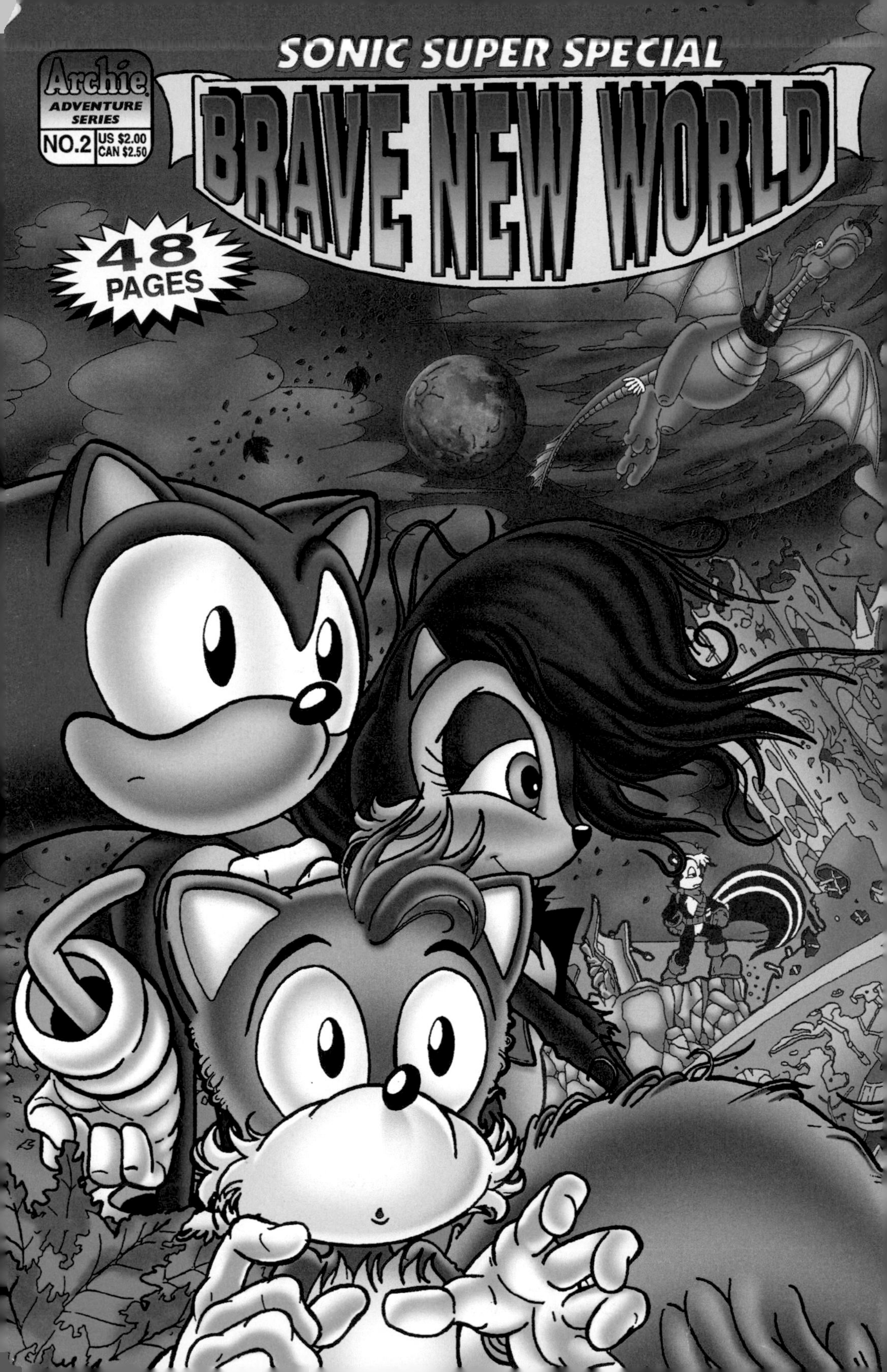
SONIC SUPER SPECIAL
Archie
ADVENTURE SERIES
NO.2
US $2.00
CAN $2.50
BRAVE NEW WORLD
48 PAGES

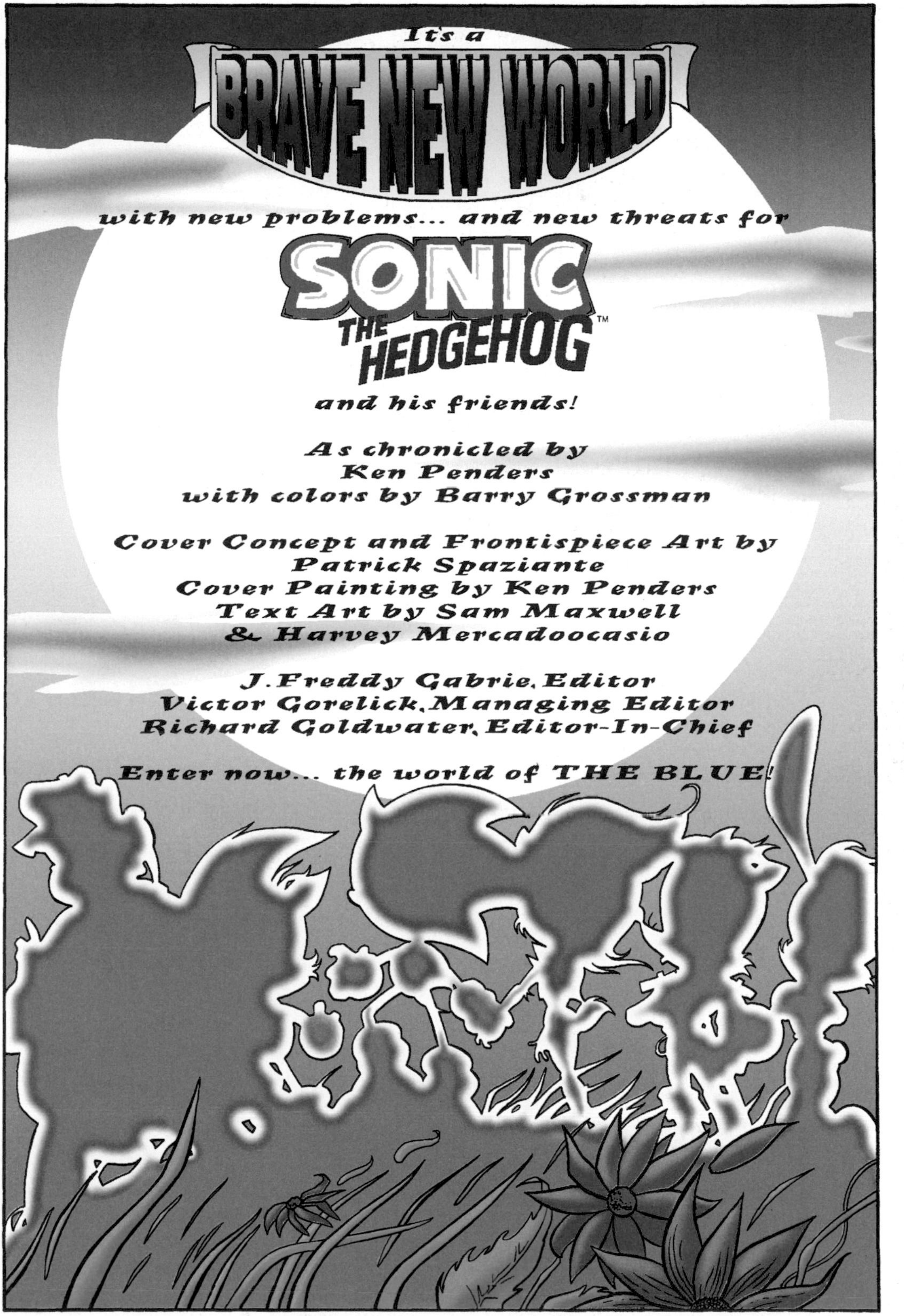
It's a
BRAVE NEW WORLD
with new problems... and new threats for
SONIC THE HEDGEHOG™
and his friends!
As chronicled by
Ken Penders
with colors by Barry Grossman
Cover Concept and Frontispiece Art by
Patrick Spaziante
Cover Painting by Ken Penders
Text Art by Sam Maxwell
& Harvey Mercadoocasio
J.Freddy Gabrie,Editor
Victor Gorelick,Managing Editor
Richard Goldwater,Editor-In-Chief
Enter now... the world of THE BLUE!

It had been more than a decade since the inhabitants of what used to be called Mobotropolis had known peace. Since that time, they were betrayed by an enemy they once thought of as one of their own. He had sought to enslave them through his nefarious schemes, with ultimate domination overall he surveyed his final goal.

But the inhabitants created a beachhead they called Knothole Village and fought back, hoping to overcome and reclaim what was rightfully theirs. As the struggle grew, it became apparent that victory would not be won without a price.

And so the final battle between the evil despot and the courageous freedom fighters was fought, with the cause for freedom prevailing in the end. Though Doctor Robotnik had been vanquished, that victory didn't necessarily mean the end of their hardships.

In fact, it was only the beginning...

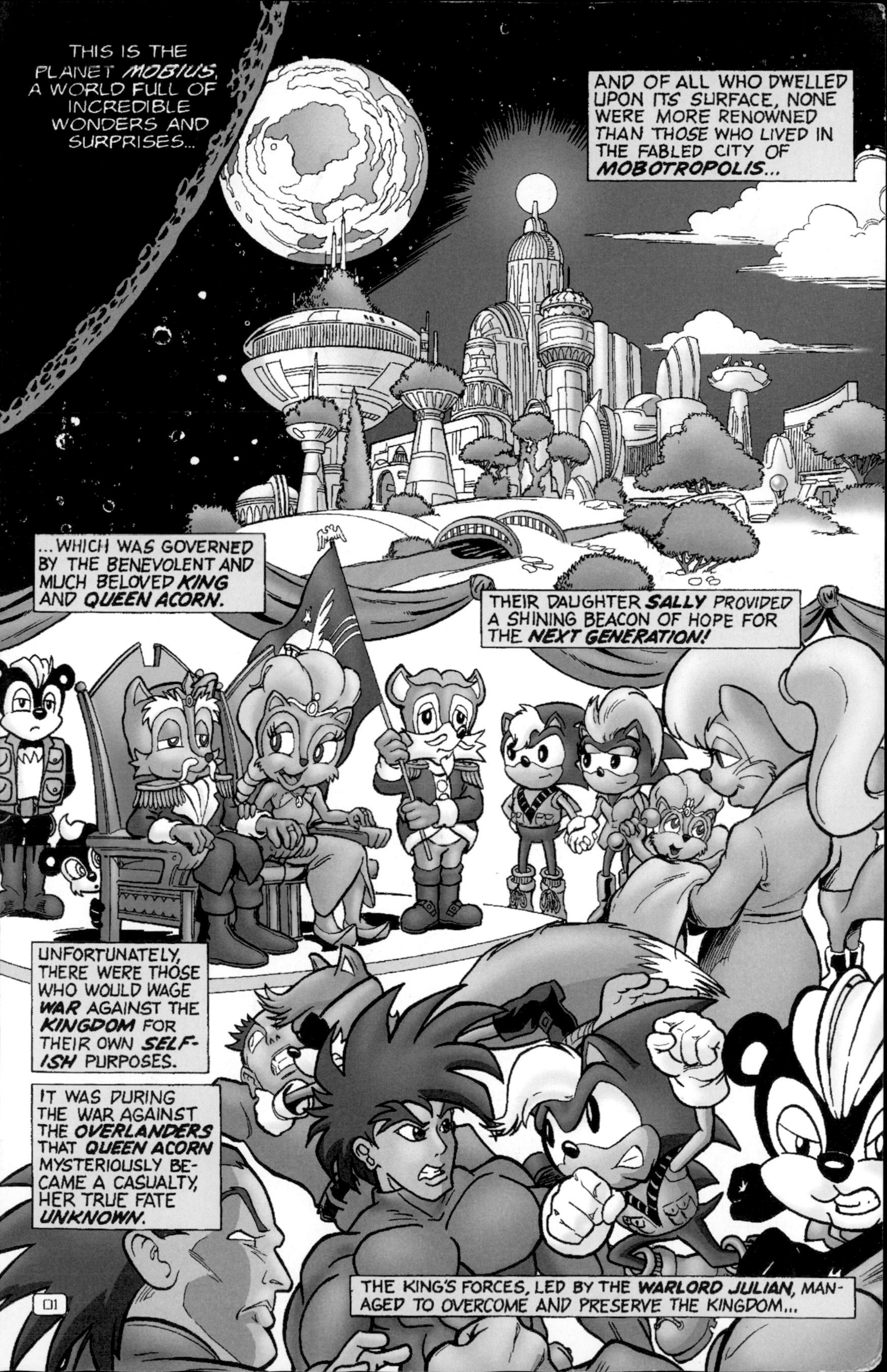
THIS IS THE PLANET MOBIUS, A WORLD FULL OF INCREDIBLE WONDERS AND SURPRISES...
AND OF ALL WHO DWELLED UPON ITS SURFACE, NONE WERE MORE RENOWNED THAN THOSE WHO LIVED IN THE FABLED CITY OF MOBOTROPOLIS...
...WHICH WAS GOVERNED BY THE BENEVOLENT AND MUCH BELOVED KING AND QUEEN ACORN.
THEIR DAUGHTER SALLY PROVIDED A SHINING BEACON OF HOPE FOR THE NEXT GENERATION!
UNFORTUNATELY, THERE WERE THOSE WHO WOULD WAGE WAR AGAINST THE KINGDOM FOR THEIR OWN SELF-ISH PURPOSES.
IT WAS DURING THE WAR AGAINST THE OVERLANDERS THAT QUEEN ACORN MYSTERIOUSLY BE-CAME A CASUALTY, HER TRUE FATE UNKNOWN.
THE KING'S FORCES, LED BY THE WARLORD JULIAN, MAN-AGED TO OVERCOME AND PRESERVE THE KINGDOM...

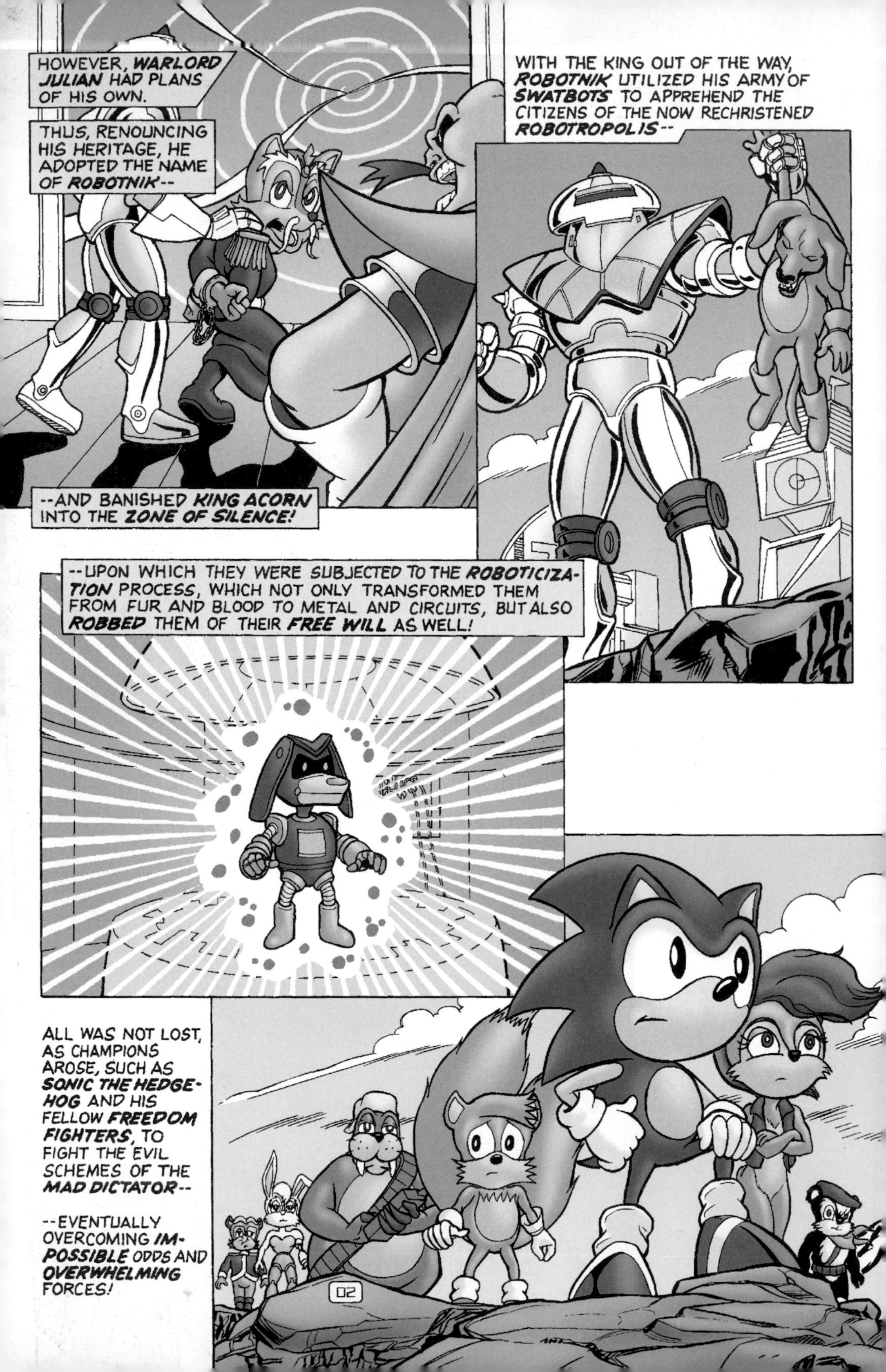
HOWEVER, WARLORD JULIAN HAD PLANS OF HIS OWN.
THUS, RENOUNCING HIS HERITAGE, HE ADOPTED THE NAME OF ROBOTNIK--
--AND BANISHED KING ACORN INTO THE ZONE OF SILENCE!
WITH THE KING OUT OF THE WAY, ROBOTNIK UTILIZED HIS ARMY OF SWATBOTS TO APPREHEND THE CITIZENS OF THE NOW RECHRISTENED ROBOTROPOLIS--
--UPON WHICH THEY WERE SUBJECTED TO THE ROBOTICIZATION PROCESS, WHICH NOT ONLY TRANSFORMED THEM FROM FUR AND BLOOD TO METAL AND CIRCUITS, BUT ALSO ROBBED THEM OF THEIR FREE WILL AS WELL!
ALL WAS NOT LOST, AS CHAMPIONS AROSE, SUCH AS SONIC THE HEDGEHOG AND HIS FELLOW FREEDOM FIGHTERS, TO FIGHT THE EVIL SCHEMES OF THE MAD DICTATOR--
--EVENTUALLY OVERCOMING IMPOSSIBLE ODDS AND OVERWHELMING FORCES!

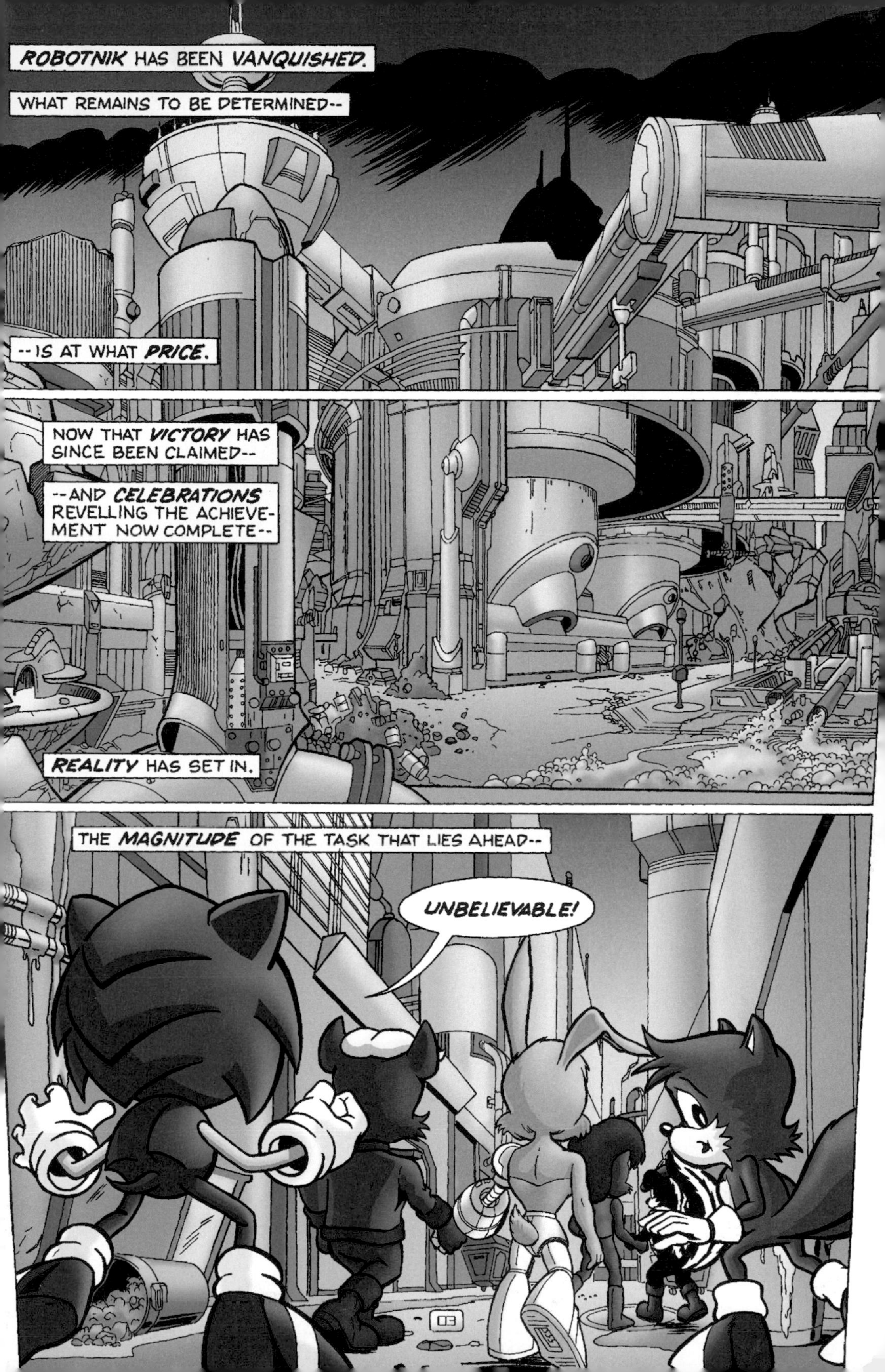

ROBOTNIK HAS BEEN VANQUISHED.
WHAT REMAINS TO BE DETERMINED--
--IS AT WHAT PRICE.
NOW THAT VICTORY HAS SINCE BEEN CLAIMED--
--AND CELEBRATIONS REVELLING THE ACHIEVEMENT NOW COMPLETE--
REALITY HAS SET IN.
THE MAGNITUDE OF THE TASK THAT LIES AHEAD--
UNBELIEVABLE!

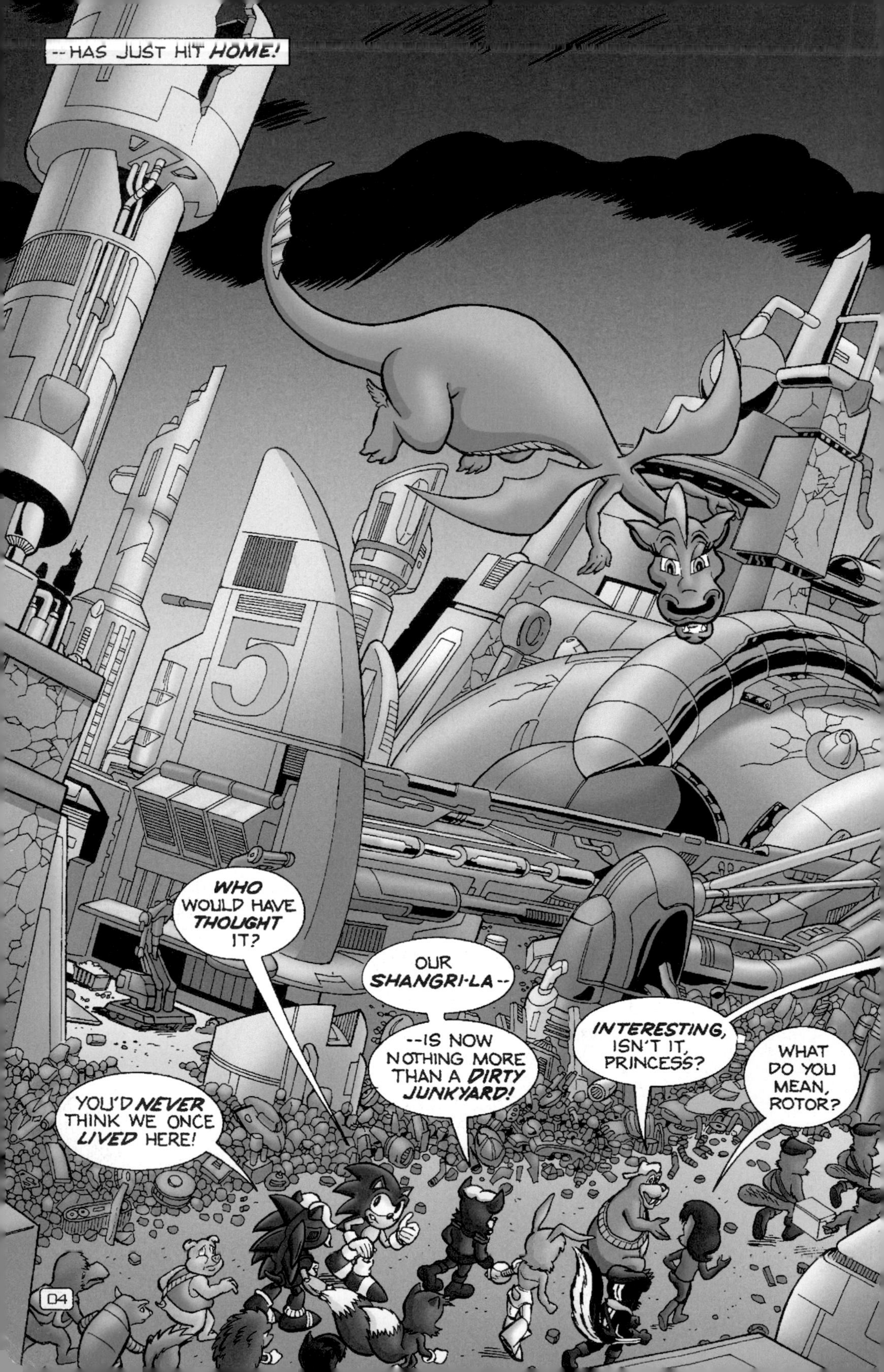
--HAS JUST HIT HOME!
YOU'D NEVER THINK WE ONCE LIVED HERE!
WHO WOULD HAVE THOUGHT IT?
OUR SHANGRI-LA--
--IS NOW NOTHING MORE THAN A DIRTY JUNKYARD!
INTERESTING, ISN'T IT, PRINCESS?
WHAT DO YOU MEAN, ROTOR?
5
04

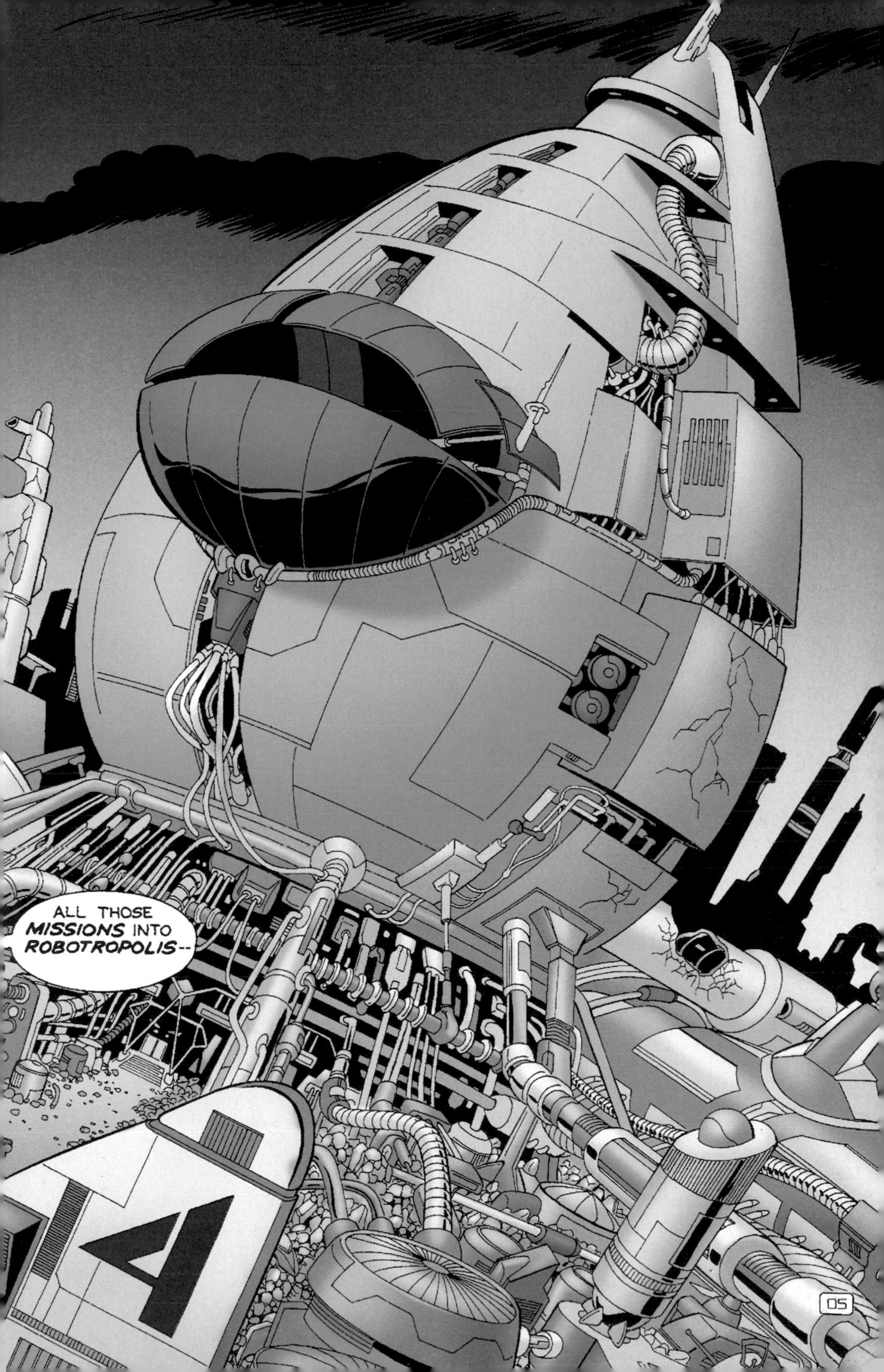
ALL THOSE MISSIONS INTO ROBOTROPOLIS--

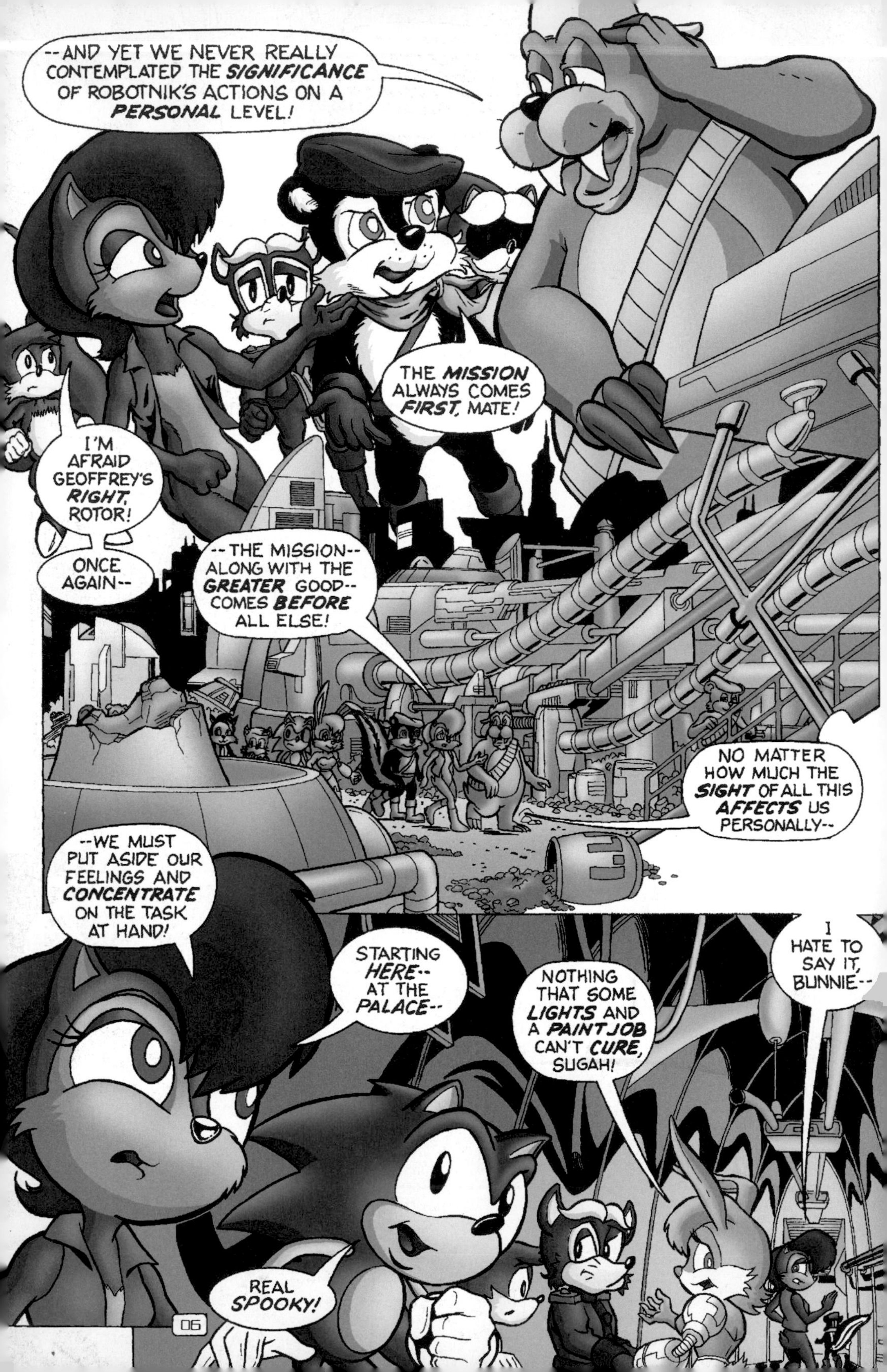
--AND YET WE NEVER REALLY CONTEMPLATED THE SIGNIFICANCE OF ROBOTNIK'S ACTIONS ON A PERSONAL LEVEL!
THE MISSION ALWAYS COMES FIRST, MATE!
I'M AFRAID GEOFFREY'S RIGHT, ROTOR!
ONCE AGAIN--
--THE MISSION-- ALONG WITH THE GREATER GOOD-- COMES BEFORE ALL ELSE!
NO MATTER HOW MUCH THE SIGHT OF ALL THIS AFFECTS US PERSONALLY--
--WE MUST PUT ASIDE OUR FEELINGS AND CONCENTRATE ON THE TASK AT HAND!
STARTING HERE-- AT THE PALACE--
NOTHING THAT SOME LIGHTS AND A PAINT JOB CAN'T CURE, SUGAH!
I HATE TO SAY IT, BUNNIE--
REAL SPOOKY!
06

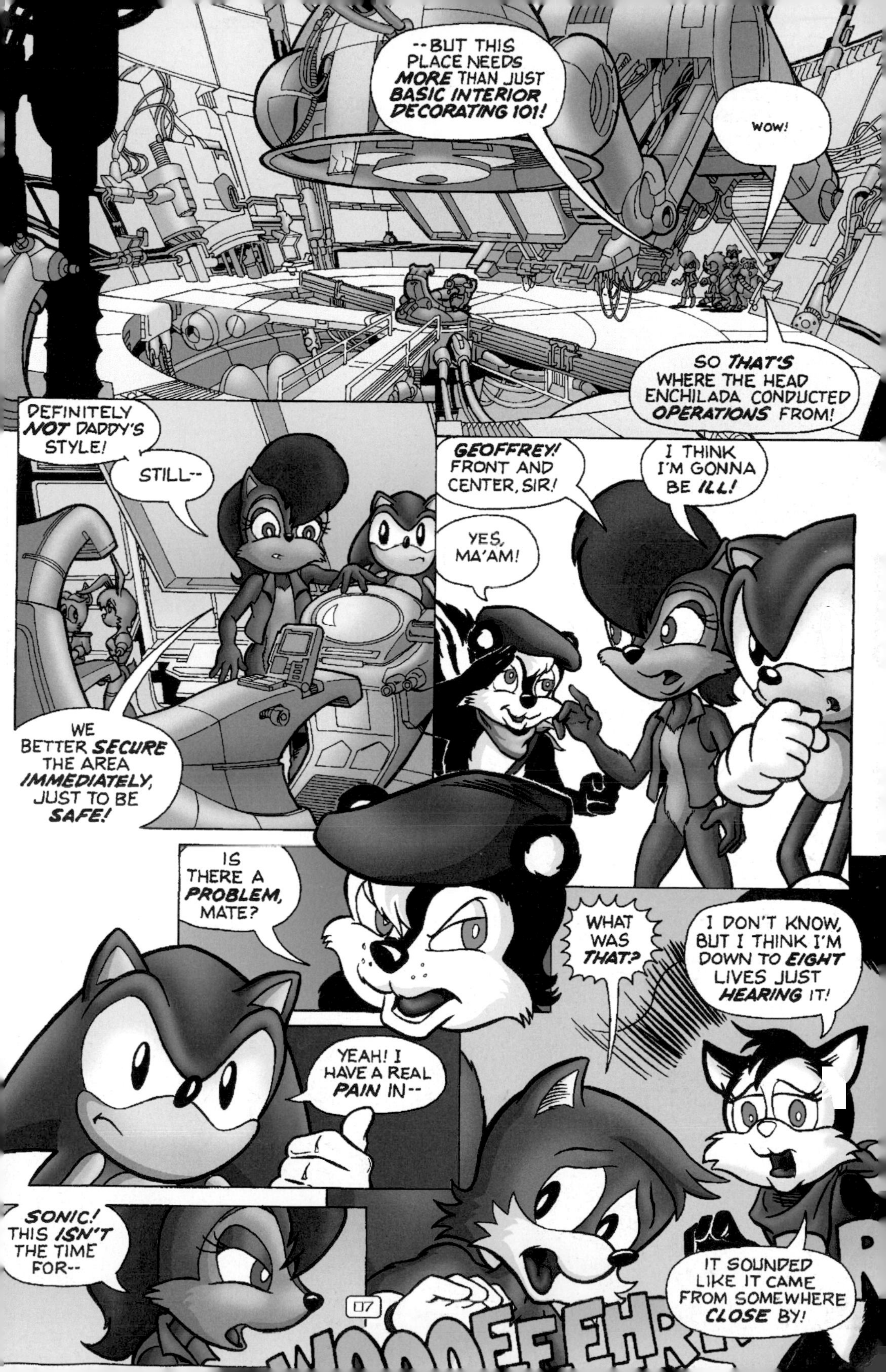
--BUT THIS PLACE NEEDS MORE THAN JUST BASIC INTERIOR DECORATING 101!
WOW!
SO THAT'S WHERE THE HEAD ENCHILADA CONDUCTED OPERATIONS FROM!
DEFINITELY NOT DADDY'S STYLE!
STILL--
WE BETTER SECURE THE AREA IMMEDIATELY, JUST TO BE SAFE!
GEOFFREY! FRONT AND CENTER, SIR!
I THINK I'M GONNA BE ILL!
YES, MA'AM!
IS THERE A PROBLEM, MATE?
YEAH! I HAVE A REAL PAIN IN--
WHAT WAS THAT?
I DON'T KNOW, BUT I THINK I'M DOWN TO EIGHT LIVES JUST HEARING IT!
SONIC! THIS ISN'T THE TIME FOR--
IT SOUNDED LIKE IT CAME FROM SOMEWHERE CLOSE BY!
WOOOEEEHR

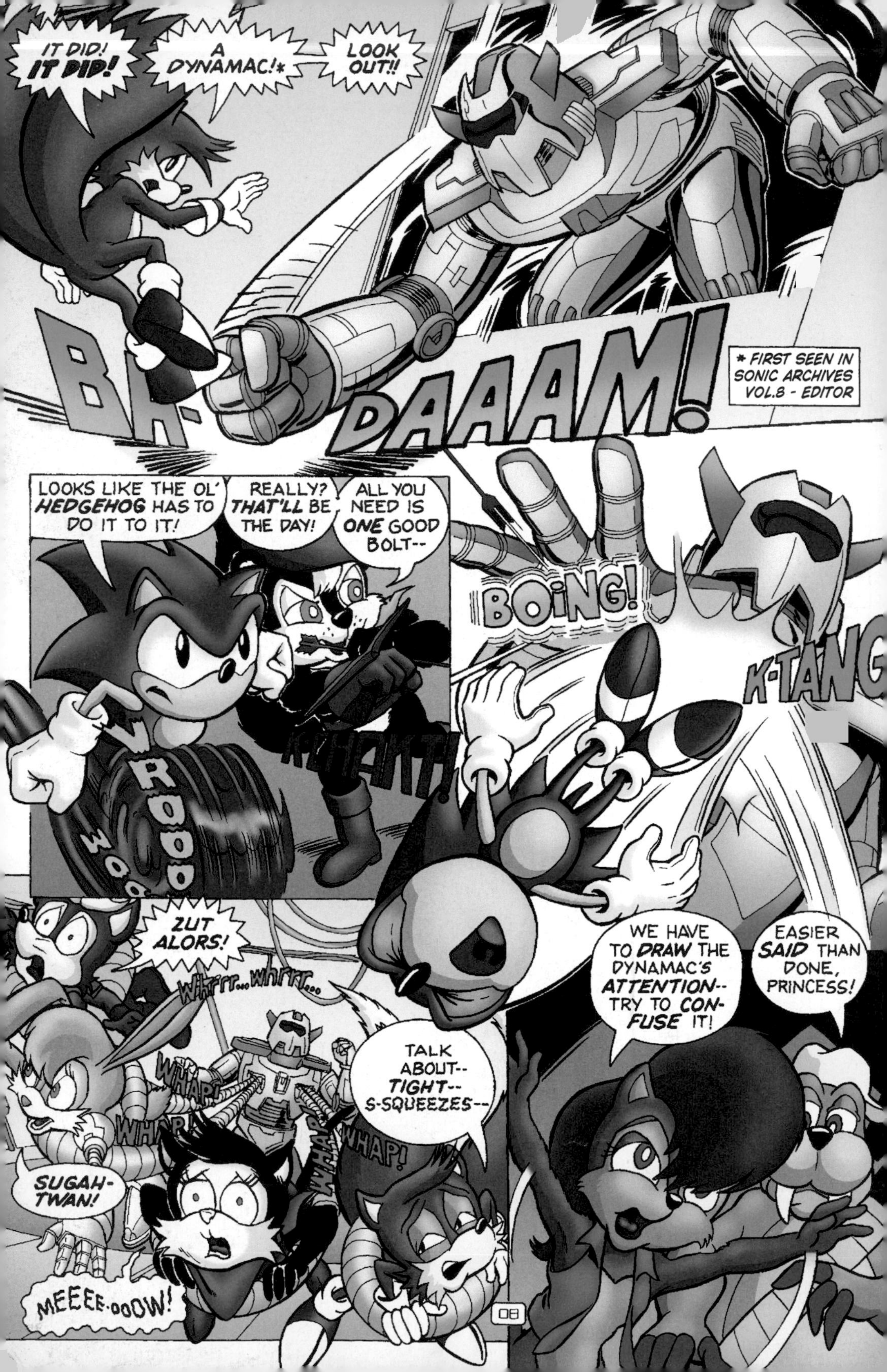
IT DID! IT DID!
A DYNAMAC!*
LOOK OUT!!
BA-DAAAM!
* FIRST SEEN IN SONIC ARCHIVES VOL.8 - EDITOR
LOOKS LIKE THE OL' HEDGEHOG HAS TO DO IT TO IT!
REALLY? THAT'LL BE THE DAY!
ALL YOU NEED IS ONE GOOD BOLT--
VRRROOOOM
BOING!
K-TANG
ZUT ALORS!
whrrr...whrrr...
WHAP!
WHAP!
WHAP!
WHAP!
TALK ABOUT-- TIGHT-- S-SQUEEZES--
WE HAVE TO DRAW THE DYNAMAC'S ATTENTION-- TRY TO CONFUSE IT!
EASIER SAID THAN DONE, PRINCESS!
SUGAH-TWAN!
MEEEE-OOOW!

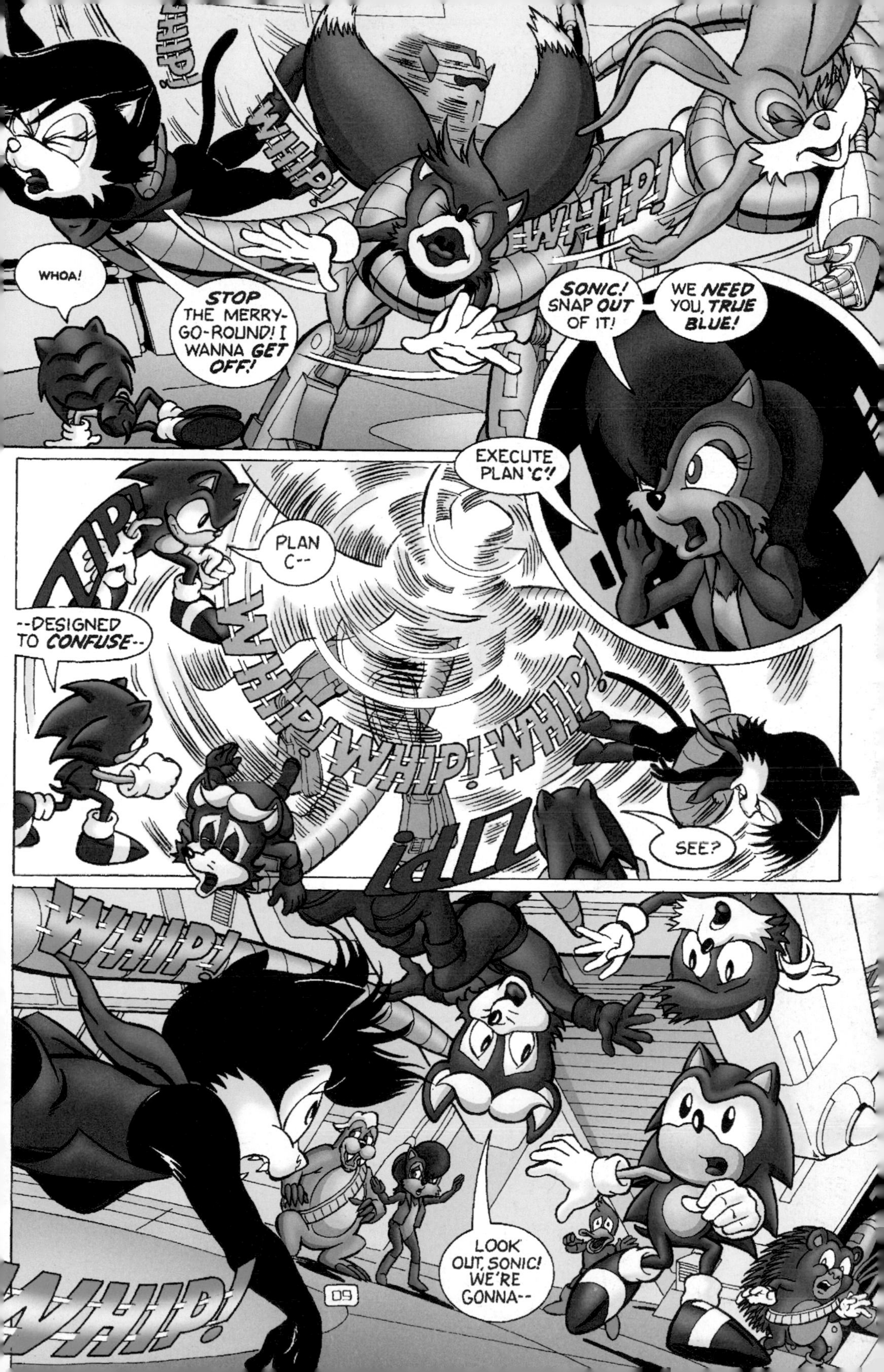

WHIP!
WHIP!
WHIP!
WHOA!
STOP THE MERRY-GO-ROUND! I WANNA GET OFF!
SONIC! SNAP OUT OF IT!
WE NEED YOU, TRUE BLUE!
EXECUTE PLAN 'C'!
ZIP!
PLAN C--
--DESIGNED TO CONFUSE--
WHIP! WHIP! WHIP!
SEE?
ZIP!
WHIP!
LOOK OUT, SONIC! WE'RE GONNA--
WHIP!

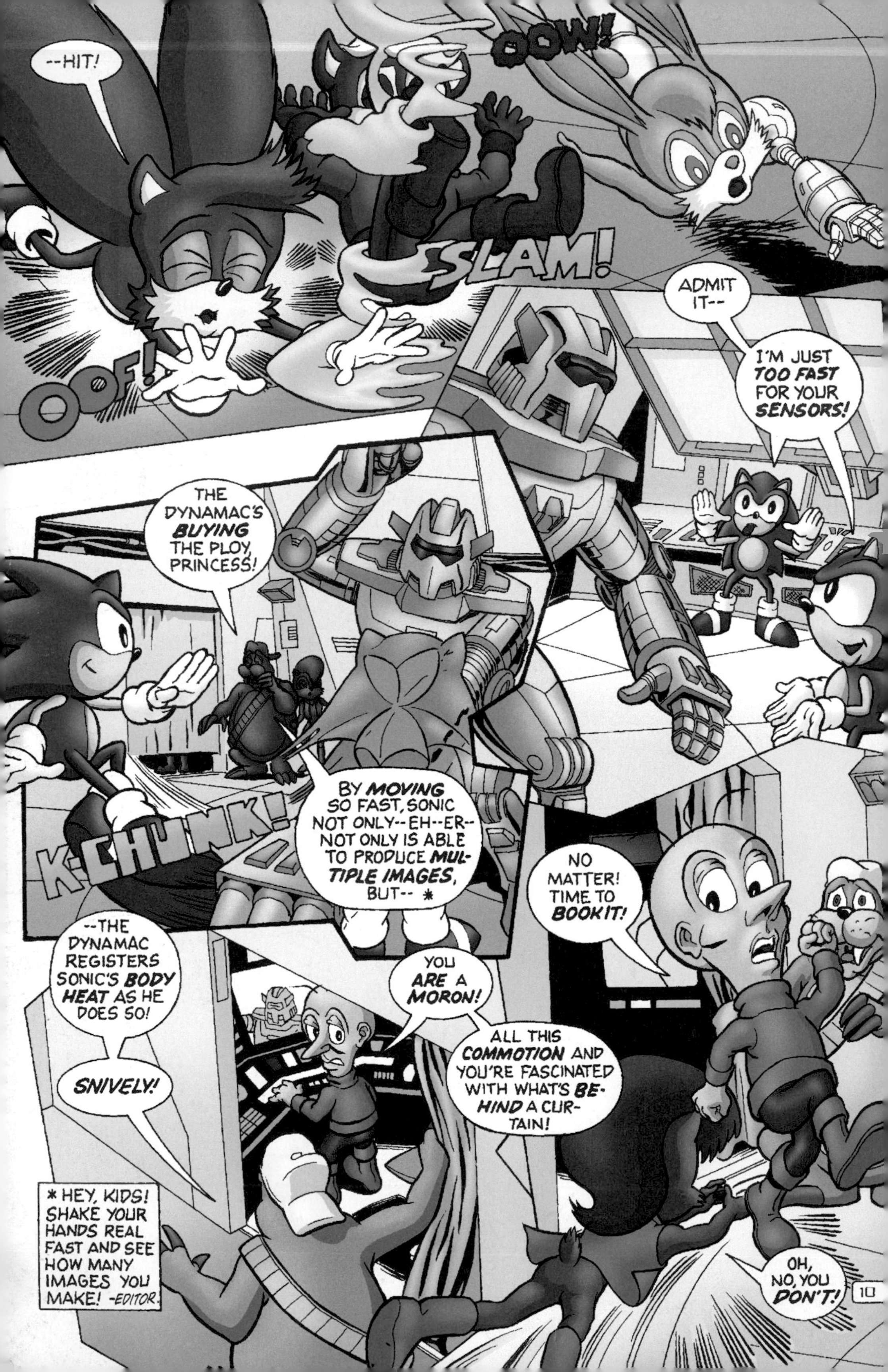
--HIT!
OOW!
SLAM!
OOF!
ADMIT IT--
I'M JUST TOO FAST FOR YOUR SENSORS!
THE DYNAMAC'S BUYING THE PLOY, PRINCESS!
K-CHUNK!
BY MOVING SO FAST, SONIC NOT ONLY--EH--ER-- NOT ONLY IS ABLE TO PRODUCE MULTIPLE IMAGES, BUT-- *
--THE DYNAMAC REGISTERS SONIC'S BODY HEAT AS HE DOES SO!
SNIVELY!
NO MATTER! TIME TO BOOK IT!
YOU ARE A MORON!
ALL THIS COMMOTION AND YOU'RE FASCINATED WITH WHAT'S BEHIND A CURTAIN!
* HEY, KIDS! SHAKE YOUR HANDS REAL FAST AND SEE HOW MANY IMAGES YOU MAKE! -EDITOR
OH, NO, YOU DON'T!

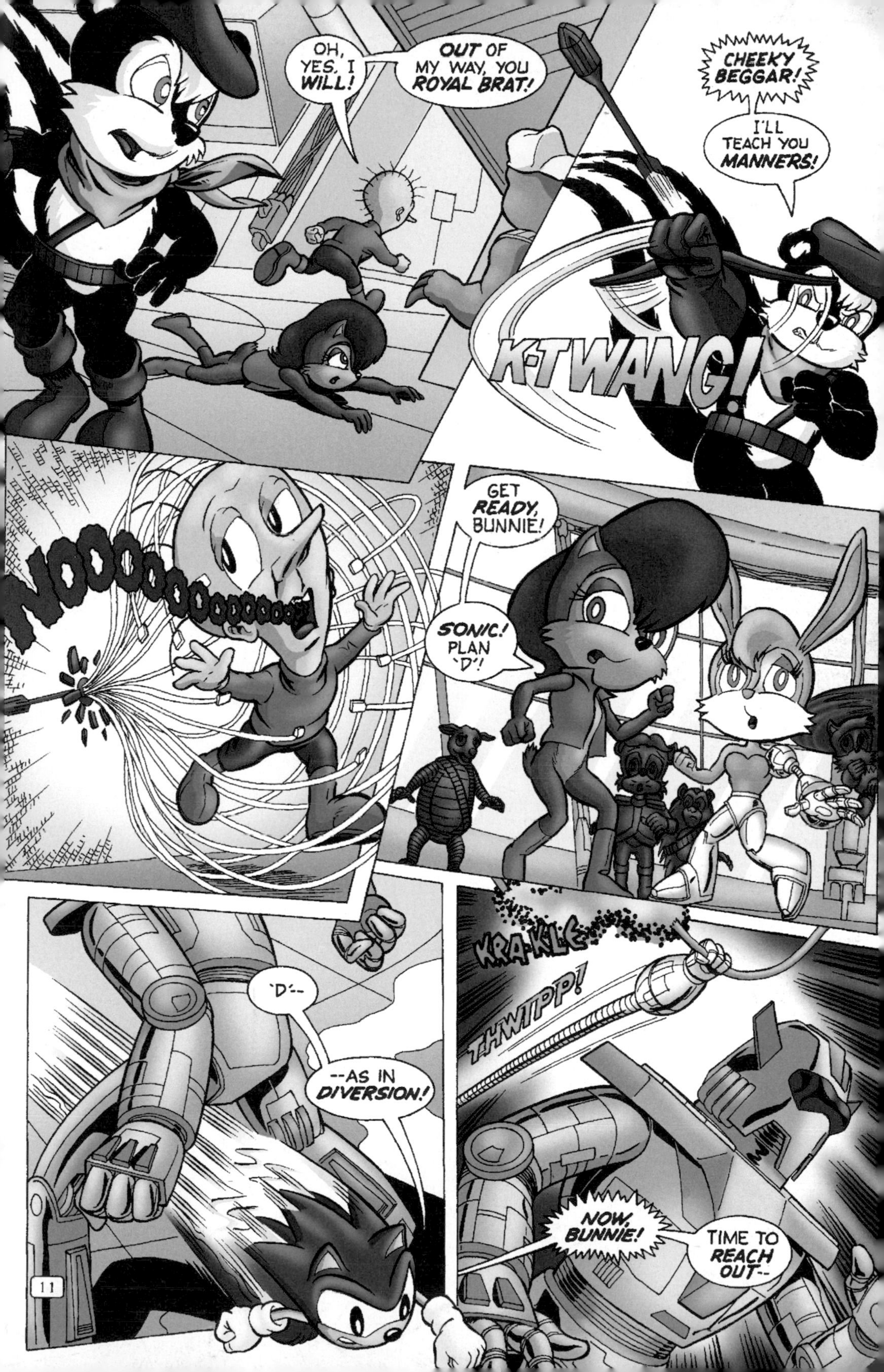

OH, YES, I WILL!
OUT OF MY WAY, YOU ROYAL BRAT!
CHEEKY BEGGAR!
I'LL TEACH YOU MANNERS!
K-TWANG!
NOOOOOOOOOOOOOO
GET READY, BUNNIE!
SONIC! PLAN 'D'!
'D'--
--AS IN DIVERSION!
KRA-KLE
THWIPP!
NOW, BUNNIE!
TIME TO REACH OUT--

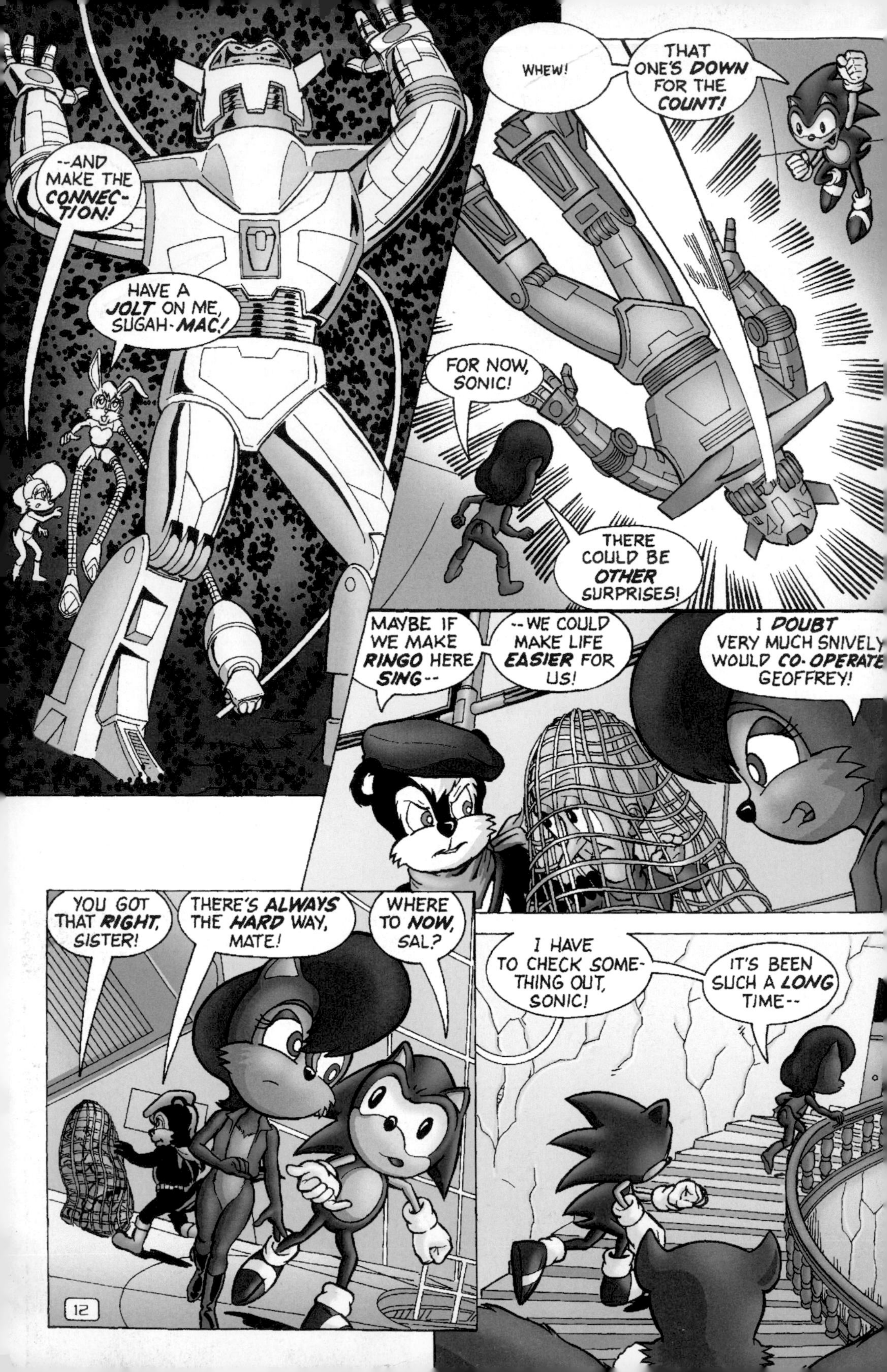
--AND MAKE THE CONNEC-TION!
HAVE A JOLT ON ME, SUGAH-MAC!
WHEW!
THAT ONE'S DOWN FOR THE COUNT!
FOR NOW, SONIC!
THERE COULD BE OTHER SURPRISES!
MAYBE IF WE MAKE RINGO HERE SING--
--WE COULD MAKE LIFE EASIER FOR US!
I DOUBT VERY MUCH SNIVELY WOULD CO-OPERATE GEOFFREY!
YOU GOT THAT RIGHT, SISTER!
THERE'S ALWAYS THE HARD WAY, MATE!
WHERE TO NOW, SAL?
I HAVE TO CHECK SOME-THING OUT, SONIC!
IT'S BEEN SUCH A LONG TIME--
12

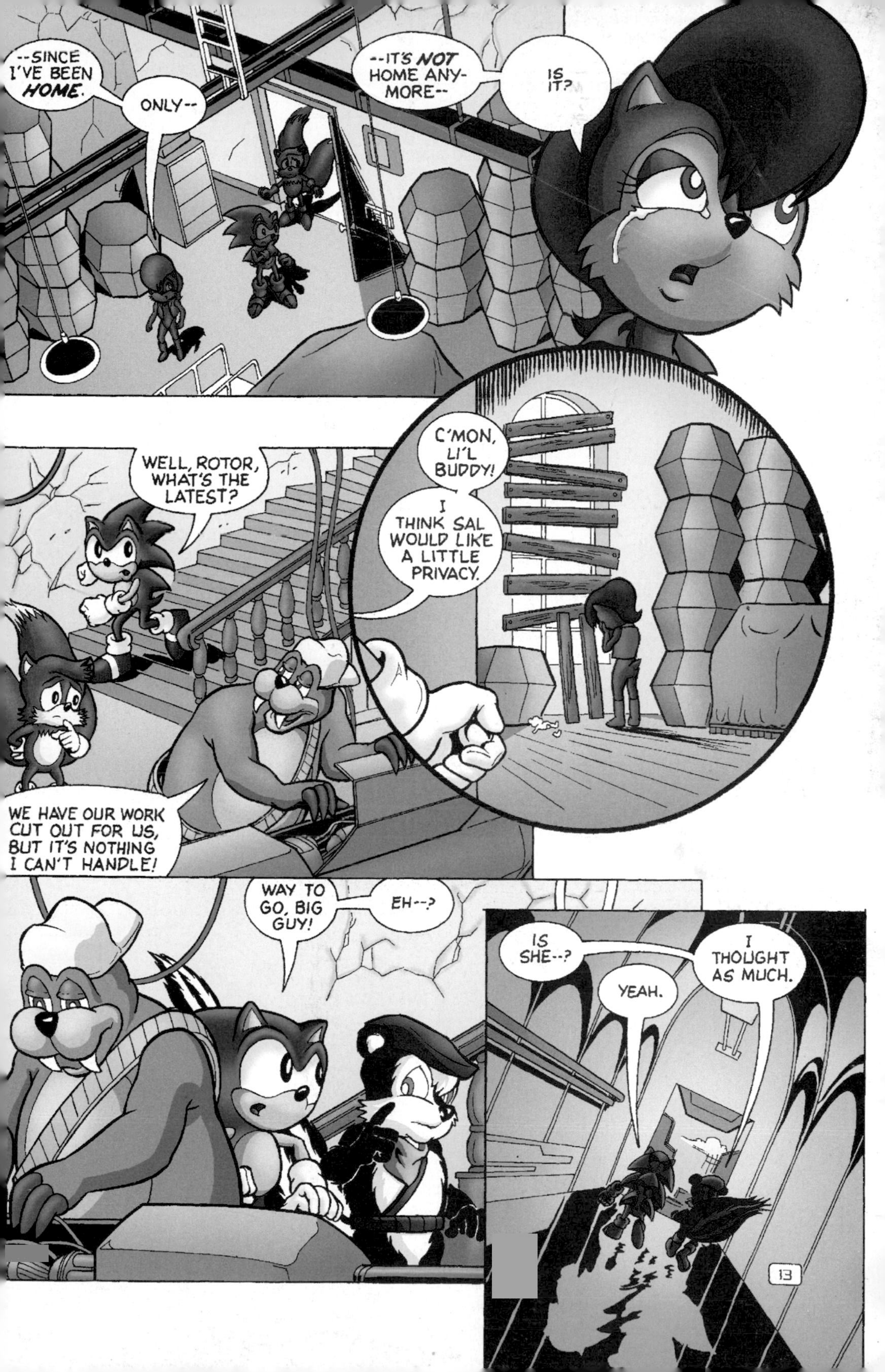
--SINCE I'VE BEEN *HOME*.
ONLY--
--IT'S *NOT* HOME ANY-MORE--
IS IT?
WELL, ROTOR, WHAT'S THE LATEST?
C'MON, LI'L BUDDY!
I THINK SAL WOULD LIKE A LITTLE PRIVACY.
WE HAVE OUR WORK CUT OUT FOR US, BUT IT'S NOTHING I CAN'T HANDLE!
WAY TO GO, BIG GUY!
EH--?
IS SHE--?
YEAH.
I THOUGHT AS MUCH.
13

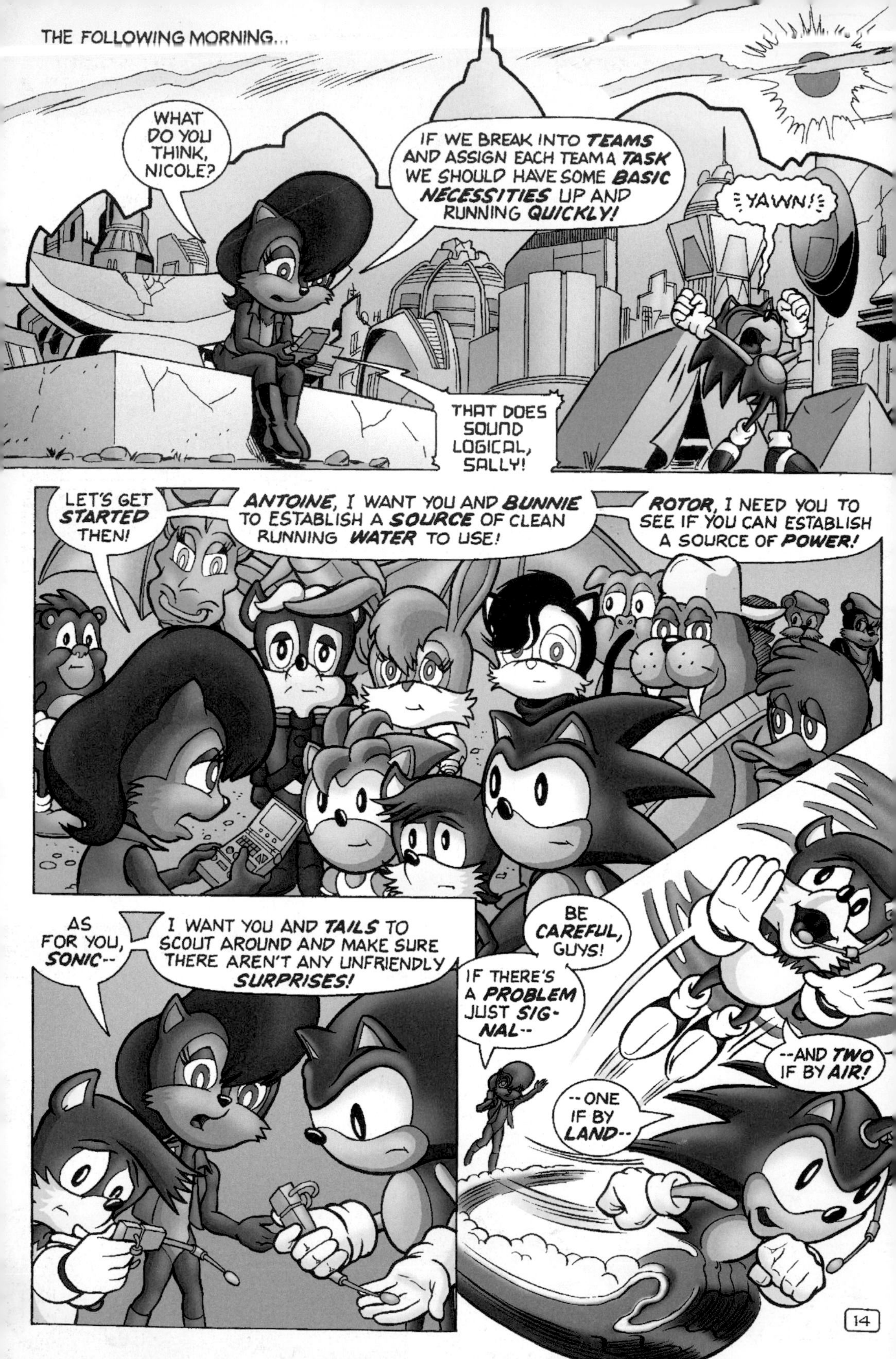
THE FOLLOWING MORNING...
WHAT DO YOU THINK, NICOLE?
IF WE BREAK INTO TEAMS AND ASSIGN EACH TEAM A TASK WE SHOULD HAVE SOME BASIC NECESSITIES UP AND RUNNING QUICKLY!
YAWN!
THAT DOES SOUND LOGICAL, SALLY!
LET'S GET STARTED THEN!
ANTOINE, I WANT YOU AND BUNNIE TO ESTABLISH A SOURCE OF CLEAN RUNNING WATER TO USE!
ROTOR, I NEED YOU TO SEE IF YOU CAN ESTABLISH A SOURCE OF POWER!
AS FOR YOU, SONIC--
I WANT YOU AND TAILS TO SCOUT AROUND AND MAKE SURE THERE AREN'T ANY UNFRIENDLY SURPRISES!
BE CAREFUL, GUYS!
IF THERE'S A PROBLEM JUST SIG-NAL--
--ONE IF BY LAND--
--AND TWO IF BY AIR!

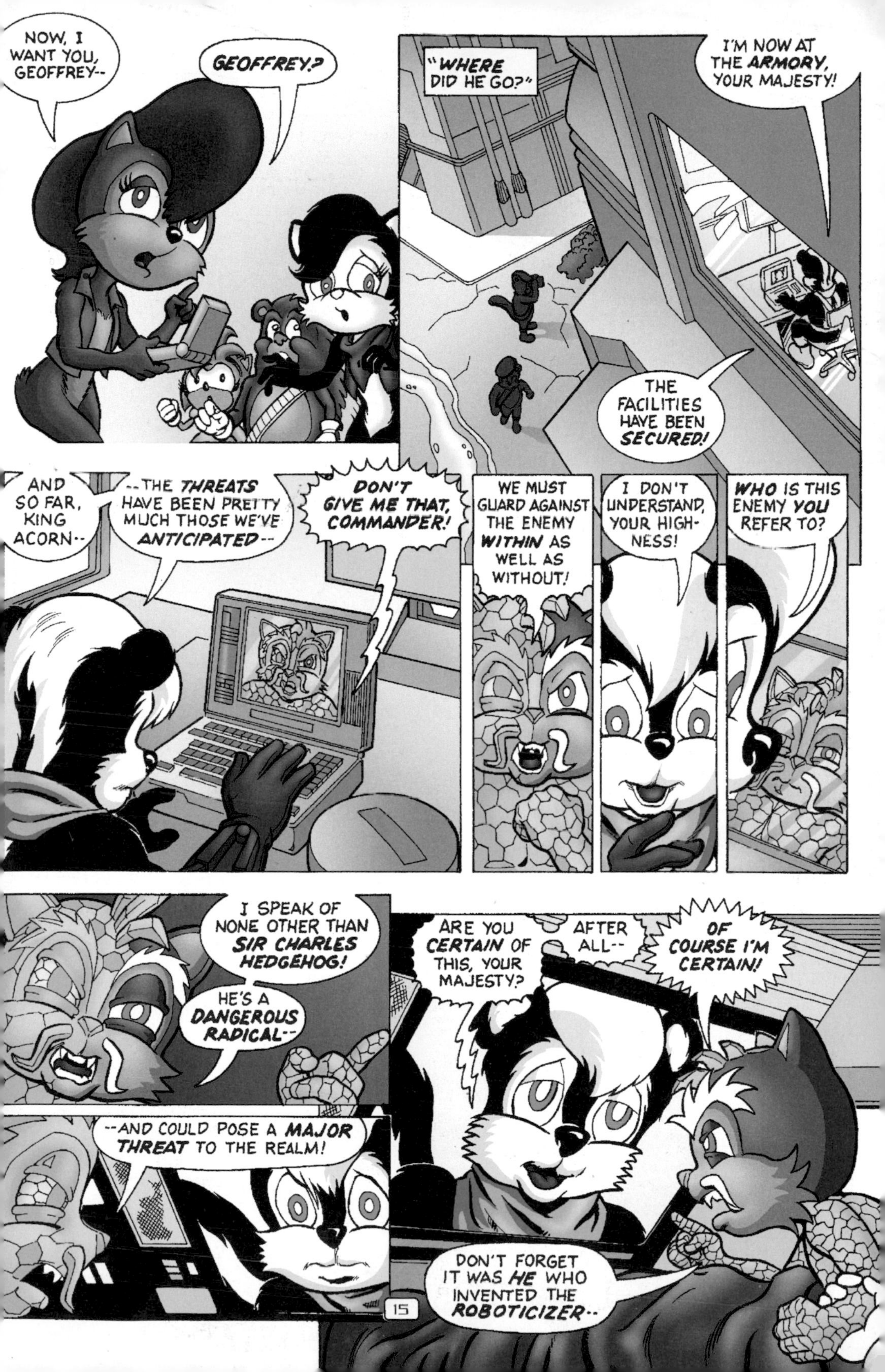
NOW, I WANT YOU, GEOFFREY--
GEOFFREY?
"WHERE DID HE GO?"
I'M NOW AT THE ARMORY, YOUR MAJESTY!
THE FACILITIES HAVE BEEN SECURED!
AND SO FAR, KING ACORN--
--THE THREATS HAVE BEEN PRETTY MUCH THOSE WE'VE ANTICIPATED--
DON'T GIVE ME THAT, COMMANDER!
WE MUST GUARD AGAINST THE ENEMY WITHIN AS WELL AS WITHOUT!
I DON'T UNDERSTAND, YOUR HIGH-NESS!
WHO IS THIS ENEMY YOU REFER TO?
I SPEAK OF NONE OTHER THAN SIR CHARLES HEDGEHOG!
HE'S A DANGEROUS RADICAL--
--AND COULD POSE A MAJOR THREAT TO THE REALM!
ARE YOU CERTAIN OF THIS, YOUR MAJESTY?
AFTER ALL--
OF COURSE I'M CERTAIN!
DON'T FORGET IT WAS HE WHO INVENTED THE ROBOTICIZER--

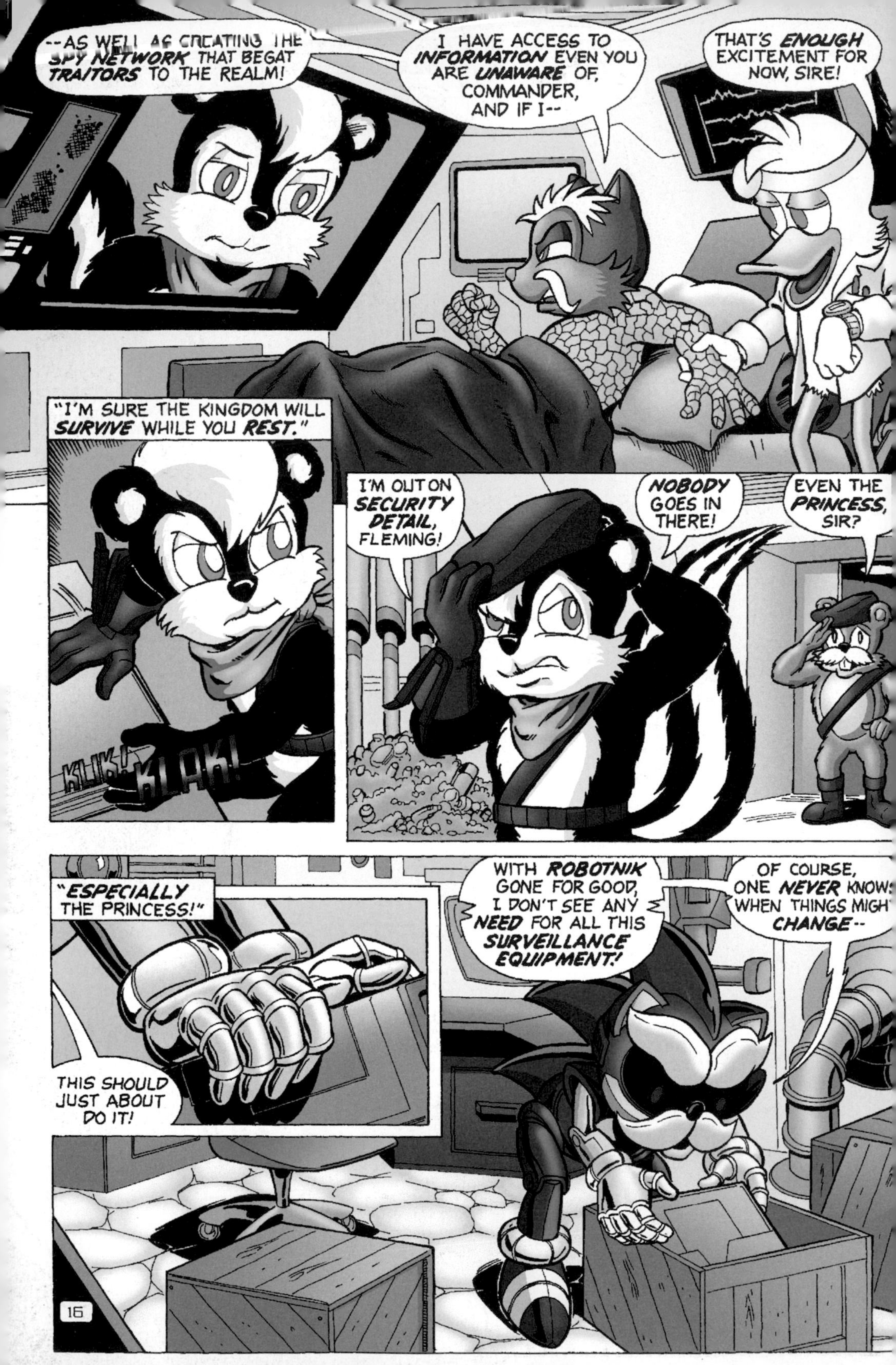
--AS WELL AS CREATING THE SPY NETWORK THAT BEGAT TRAITORS TO THE REALM!
I HAVE ACCESS TO INFORMATION EVEN YOU ARE UNAWARE OF, COMMANDER, AND IF I--
THAT'S ENOUGH EXCITEMENT FOR NOW, SIRE!
"I'M SURE THE KINGDOM WILL SURVIVE WHILE YOU REST."
KLIK! KLAK!
I'M OUT ON SECURITY DETAIL, FLEMING!
NOBODY GOES IN THERE!
EVEN THE PRINCESS, SIR?
"ESPECIALLY THE PRINCESS!"
THIS SHOULD JUST ABOUT DO IT!
WITH ROBOTNIK GONE FOR GOOD, I DON'T SEE ANY NEED FOR ALL THIS SURVEILLANCE EQUIPMENT!
OF COURSE, ONE NEVER KNOWS WHEN THINGS MIGHT CHANGE--

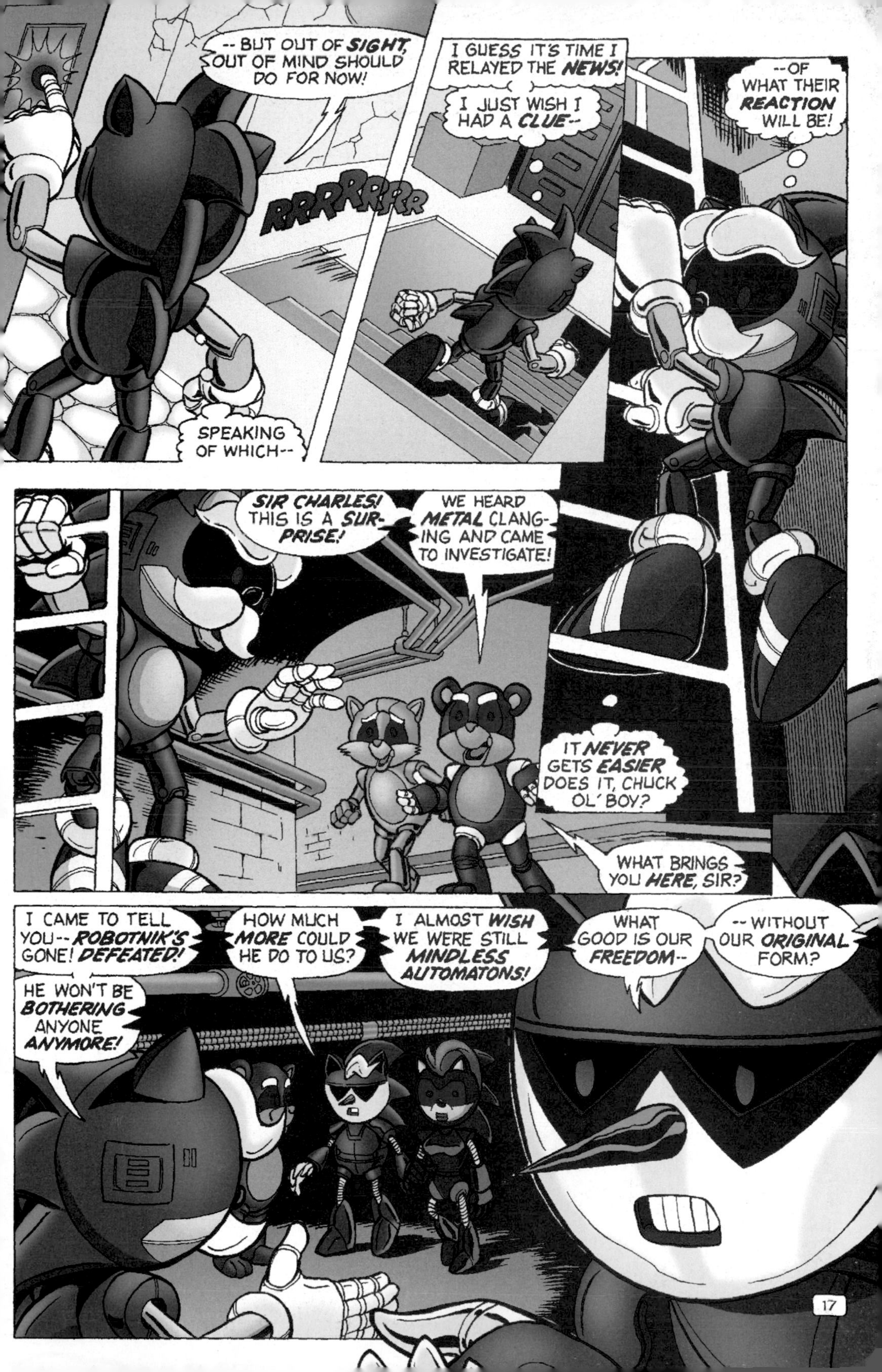
-- BUT OUT OF SIGHT, OUT OF MIND SHOULD DO FOR NOW!
RRRRRRRR
SPEAKING OF WHICH--
I GUESS IT'S TIME I RELAYED THE NEWS!
I JUST WISH I HAD A CLUE--
--OF WHAT THEIR REACTION WILL BE!
SIR CHARLES! THIS IS A SURPRISE!
WE HEARD METAL CLANGING AND CAME TO INVESTIGATE!
IT NEVER GETS EASIER DOES IT, CHUCK OL' BOY?
WHAT BRINGS YOU HERE, SIR?
I CAME TO TELL YOU-- ROBOTNIK'S GONE! DEFEATED!
HE WON'T BE BOTHERING ANYONE ANYMORE!
HOW MUCH MORE COULD HE DO TO US?
I ALMOST WISH WE WERE STILL MINDLESS AUTOMATONS!
WHAT GOOD IS OUR FREEDOM--
-- WITHOUT OUR ORIGINAL FORM?

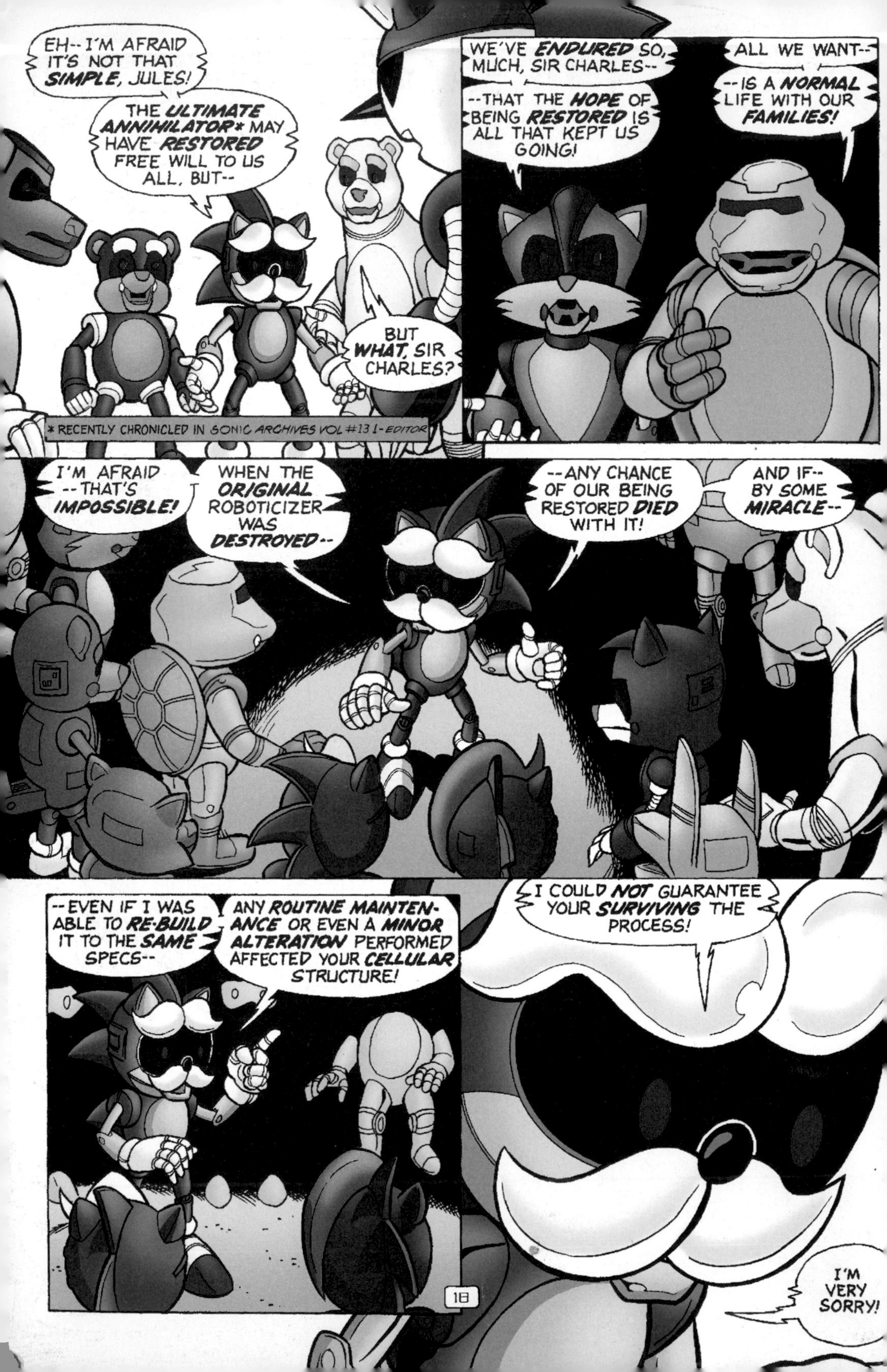
EH-- I'M AFRAID IT'S NOT THAT SIMPLE, JULES!
THE ULTIMATE ANNIHILATOR* MAY HAVE RESTORED FREE WILL TO US ALL, BUT--
BUT WHAT, SIR CHARLES?
* RECENTLY CHRONICLED IN SONIC ARCHIVES VOL #13 !-EDITOR
WE'VE ENDURED SO, MUCH, SIR CHARLES--
--THAT THE HOPE OF BEING RESTORED IS ALL THAT KEPT US GOING!
ALL WE WANT--
--IS A NORMAL LIFE WITH OUR FAMILIES!
I'M AFRAID --THAT'S IMPOSSIBLE!
WHEN THE ORIGINAL ROBOTICIZER WAS DESTROYED--
--ANY CHANCE OF OUR BEING RESTORED DIED WITH IT!
AND IF-- BY SOME MIRACLE--
--EVEN IF I WAS ABLE TO RE-BUILD IT TO THE SAME SPECS--
ANY ROUTINE MAINTEN-ANCE OR EVEN A MINOR ALTERATION PERFORMED AFFECTED YOUR CELLULAR STRUCTURE!
I COULD NOT GUARANTEE YOUR SURVIVING THE PROCESS!
I'M VERY SORRY!

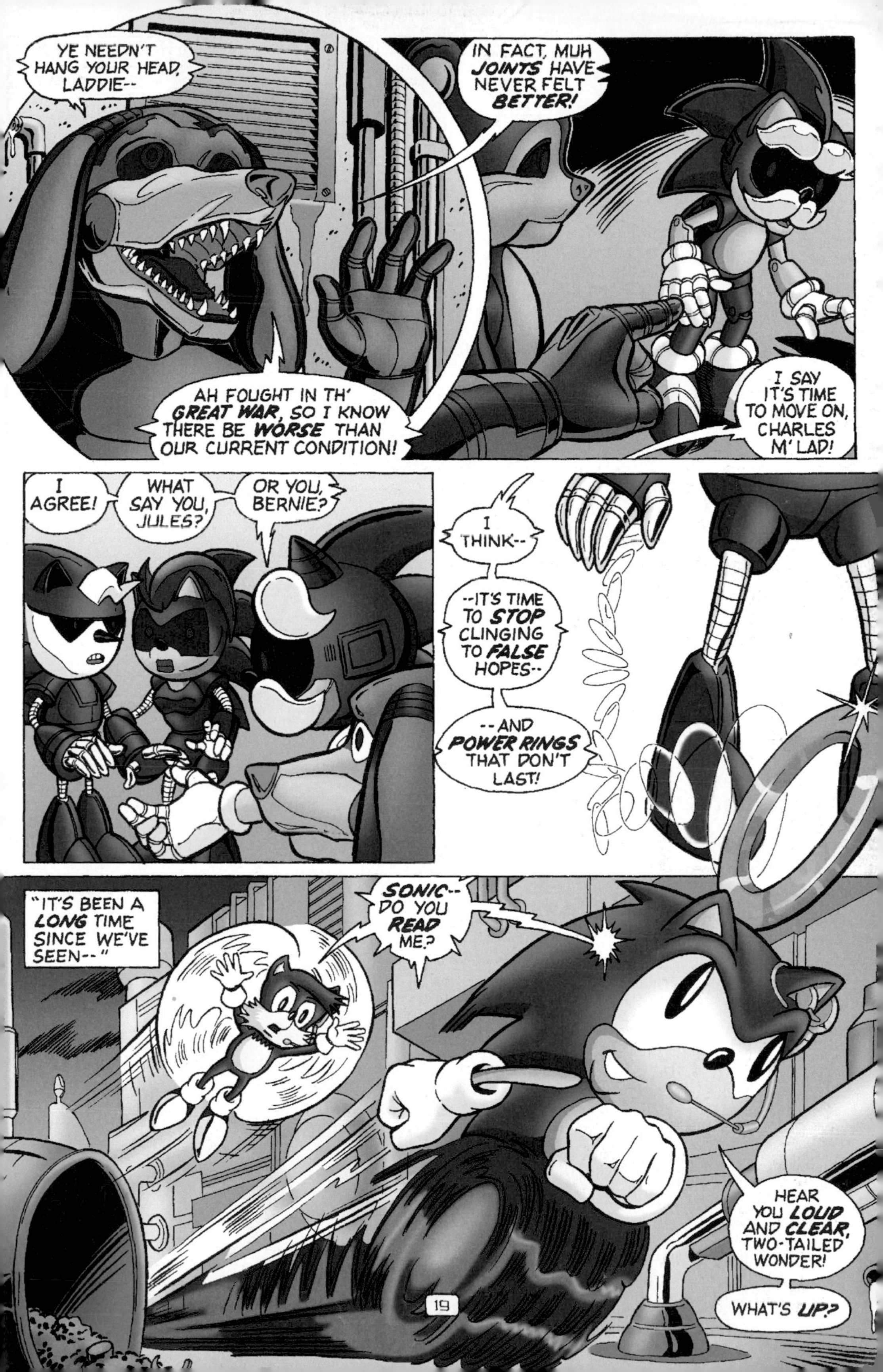
YE NEEDN'T HANG YOUR HEAD, LADDIE--
IN FACT, MUH JOINTS HAVE NEVER FELT BETTER!
AH FOUGHT IN TH' GREAT WAR, SO I KNOW THERE BE WORSE THAN OUR CURRENT CONDITION!
I SAY IT'S TIME TO MOVE ON, CHARLES M' LAD!
I AGREE!
WHAT SAY YOU, JULES?
OR YOU, BERNIE?
I THINK--
--IT'S TIME TO STOP CLINGING TO FALSE HOPES--
--AND POWER RINGS THAT DON'T LAST!
"IT'S BEEN A LONG TIME SINCE WE'VE SEEN--"
SONIC-- DO YOU READ ME?
HEAR YOU LOUD AND CLEAR, TWO-TAILED WONDER!
WHAT'S UP?

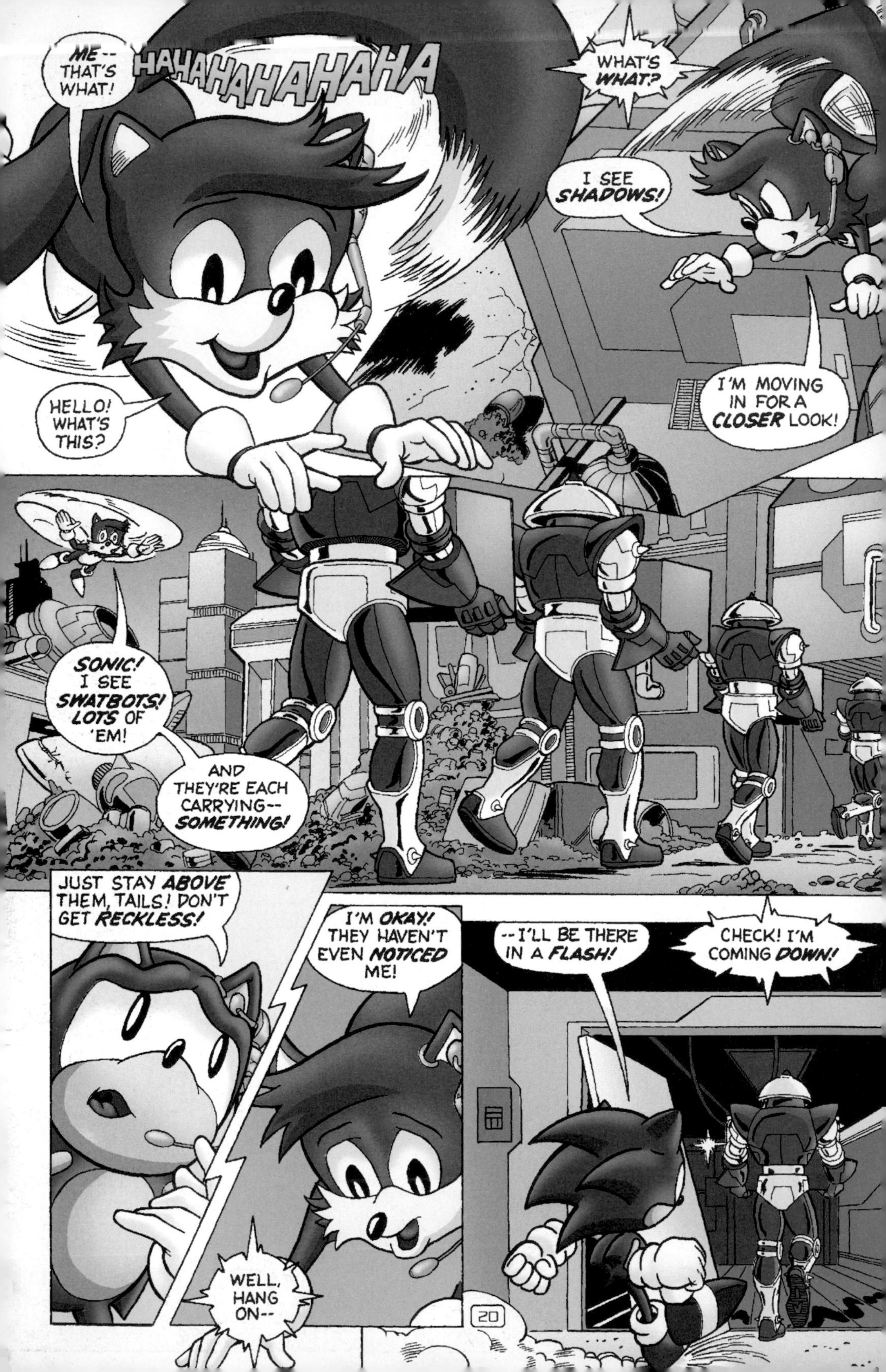

ME-- THAT'S WHAT!
HAHAHAHAHAHAHA
WHAT'S WHAT?
I SEE SHADOWS!
HELLO! WHAT'S THIS?
I'M MOVING IN FOR A CLOSER LOOK!
SONIC! I SEE SWATBOTS! LOTS OF 'EM!
AND THEY'RE EACH CARRYING-- SOMETHING!
JUST STAY ABOVE THEM, TAILS! DON'T GET RECKLESS!
I'M OKAY! THEY HAVEN'T EVEN NOTICED ME!
WELL, HANG ON--
--I'LL BE THERE IN A FLASH!
CHECK! I'M COMING DOWN!

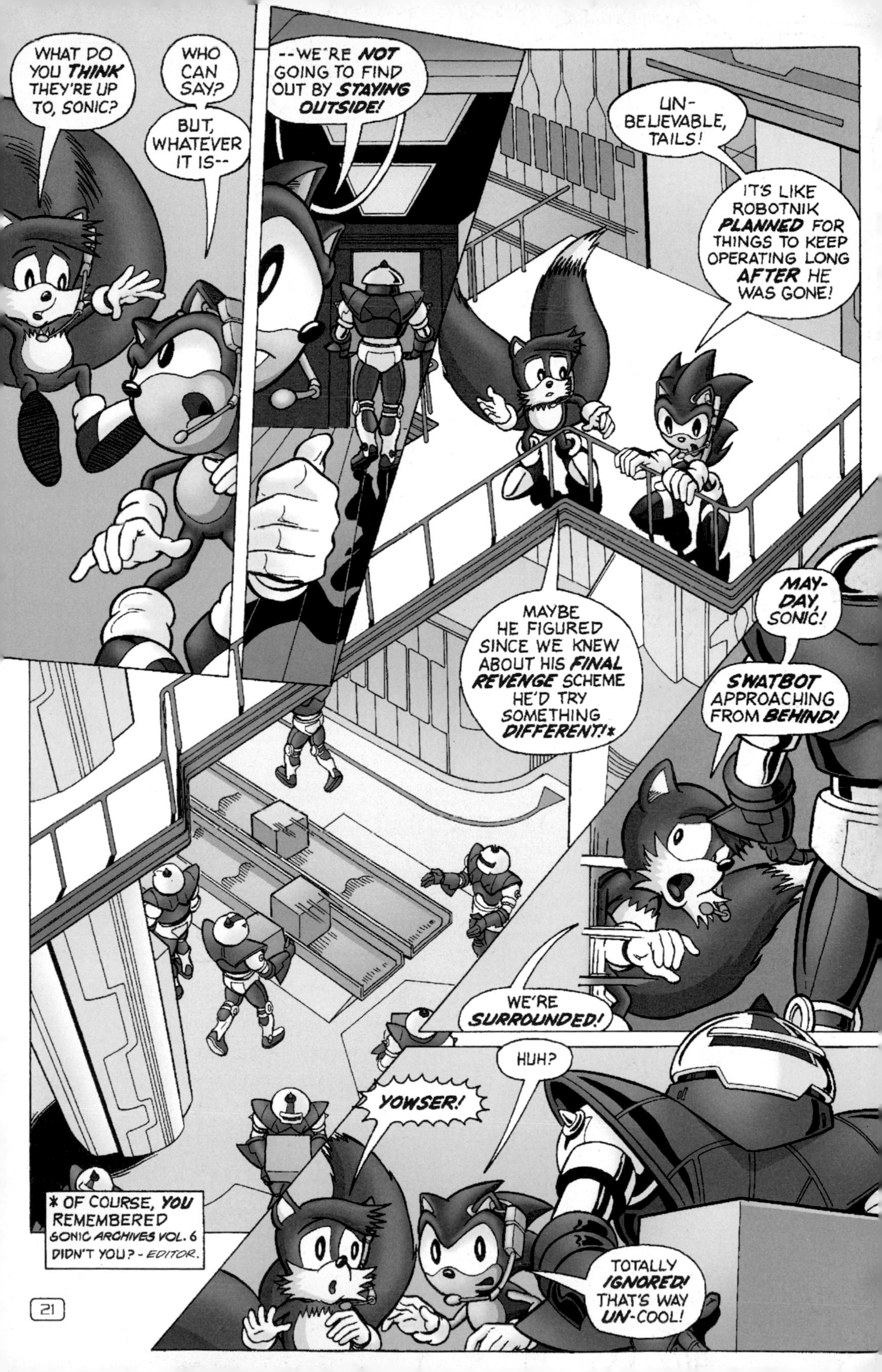
WHAT DO YOU THINK THEY'RE UP TO, SONIC?
WHO CAN SAY?
BUT, WHATEVER IT IS--
--WE'RE NOT GOING TO FIND OUT BY STAYING OUTSIDE!
UN-BELIEVABLE, TAILS!
IT'S LIKE ROBOTNIK PLANNED FOR THINGS TO KEEP OPERATING LONG AFTER HE WAS GONE!
MAYBE HE FIGURED SINCE WE KNEW ABOUT HIS FINAL REVENGE SCHEME HE'D TRY SOMETHING DIFFERENT!*
MAY-DAY, SONIC!
SWATBOT APPROACHING FROM BEHIND!
WE'RE SURROUNDED!
HUH?
YOWSER!
TOTALLY IGNORED! THAT'S WAY UN-COOL!
* OF COURSE, YOU REMEMBERED SONIC ARCHIVES VOL. 6 DIDN'T YOU? - EDITOR.

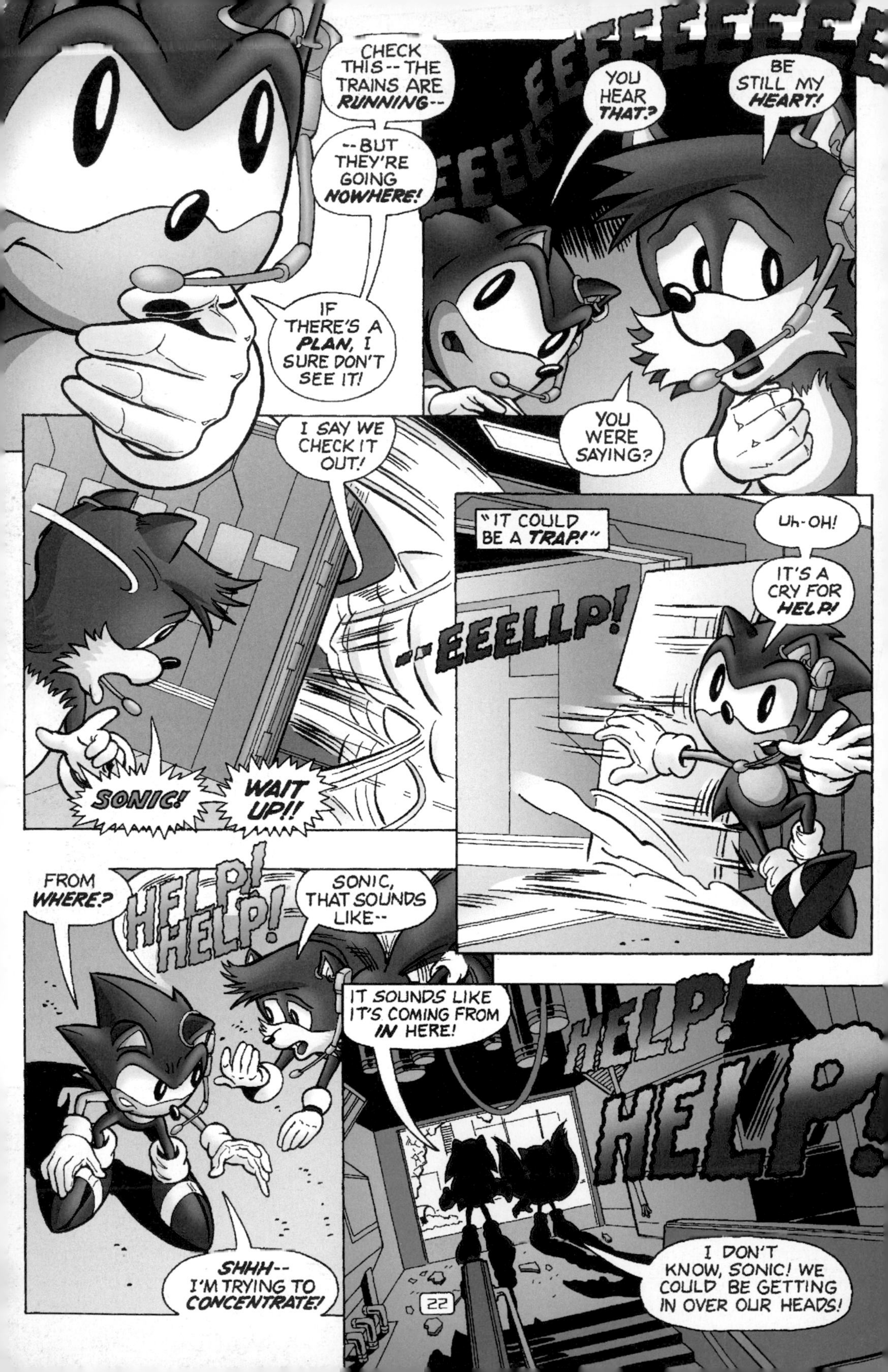
CHECK THIS -- THE TRAINS ARE RUNNING --
-- BUT THEY'RE GOING NOWHERE!
IF THERE'S A PLAN, I SURE DON'T SEE IT!
EEEEEEEEEEEEEEEE
YOU HEAR THAT?
BE STILL MY HEART!
YOU WERE SAYING?
I SAY WE CHECK IT OUT!
SONIC!
WAIT UP!!
"IT COULD BE A TRAP!"
UH-OH!
IT'S A CRY FOR HELP!
--EEELLP!
FROM WHERE?
HELP! HELP!
SONIC, THAT SOUNDS LIKE--
SHHH-- I'M TRYING TO CONCENTRATE!
IT SOUNDS LIKE IT'S COMING FROM IN HERE!
HELP! HELP!
I DON'T KNOW, SONIC! WE COULD BE GETTING IN OVER OUR HEADS!
22

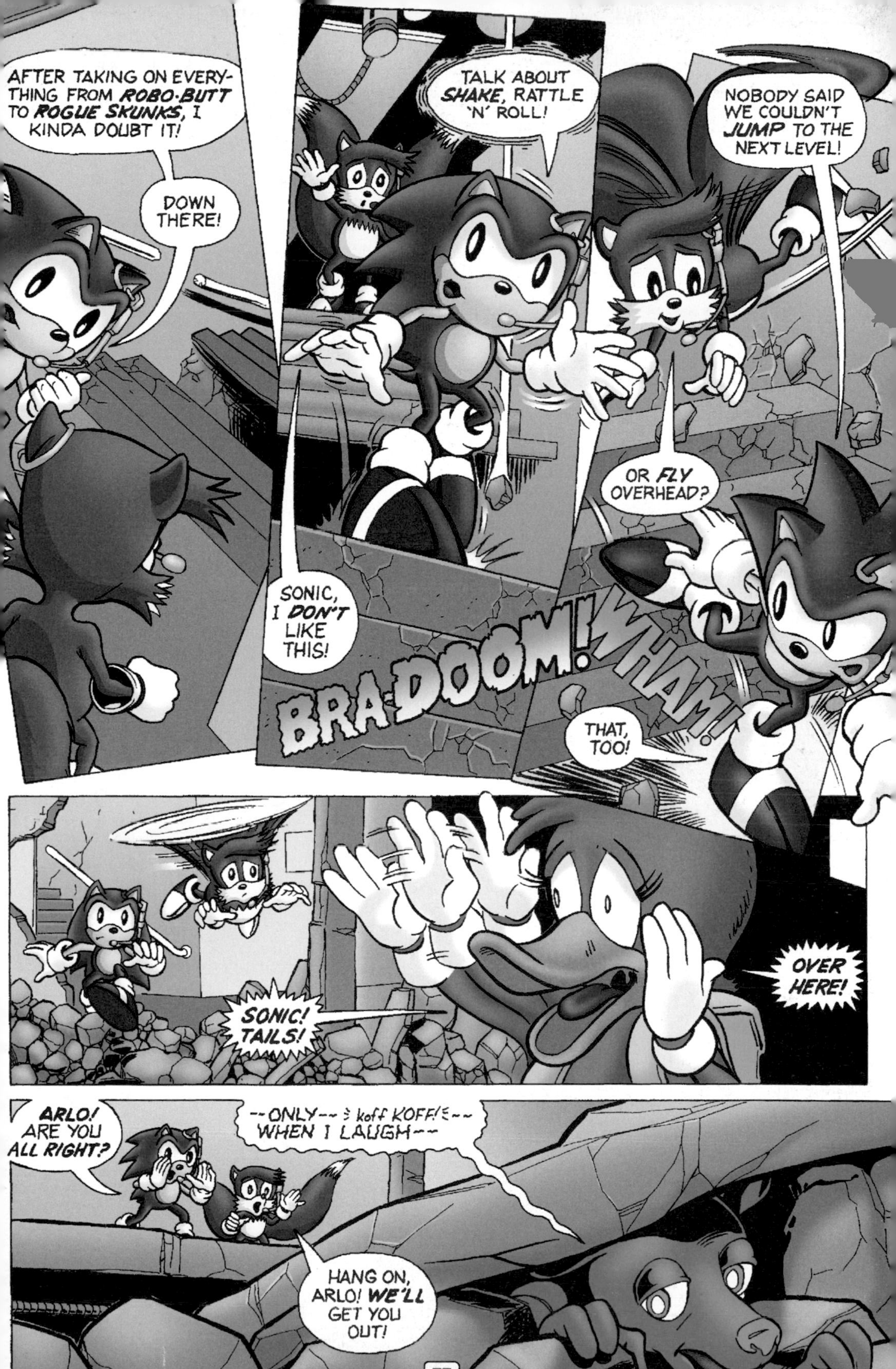
AFTER TAKING ON EVERYTHING FROM ROBO-BUTT TO ROGUE SKUNKS, I KINDA DOUBT IT!
DOWN THERE!
TALK ABOUT SHAKE, RATTLE 'N' ROLL!
SONIC, I DON'T LIKE THIS!
BRA-DOOM!
NOBODY SAID WE COULDN'T JUMP TO THE NEXT LEVEL!
OR FLY OVERHEAD?
WHAM!
THAT, TOO!
SONIC! TAILS!
OVER HERE!
ARLO! ARE YOU ALL RIGHT?
--ONLY-- koff KOFF! --WHEN I LAUGH--
HANG ON, ARLO! WE'LL GET YOU OUT!

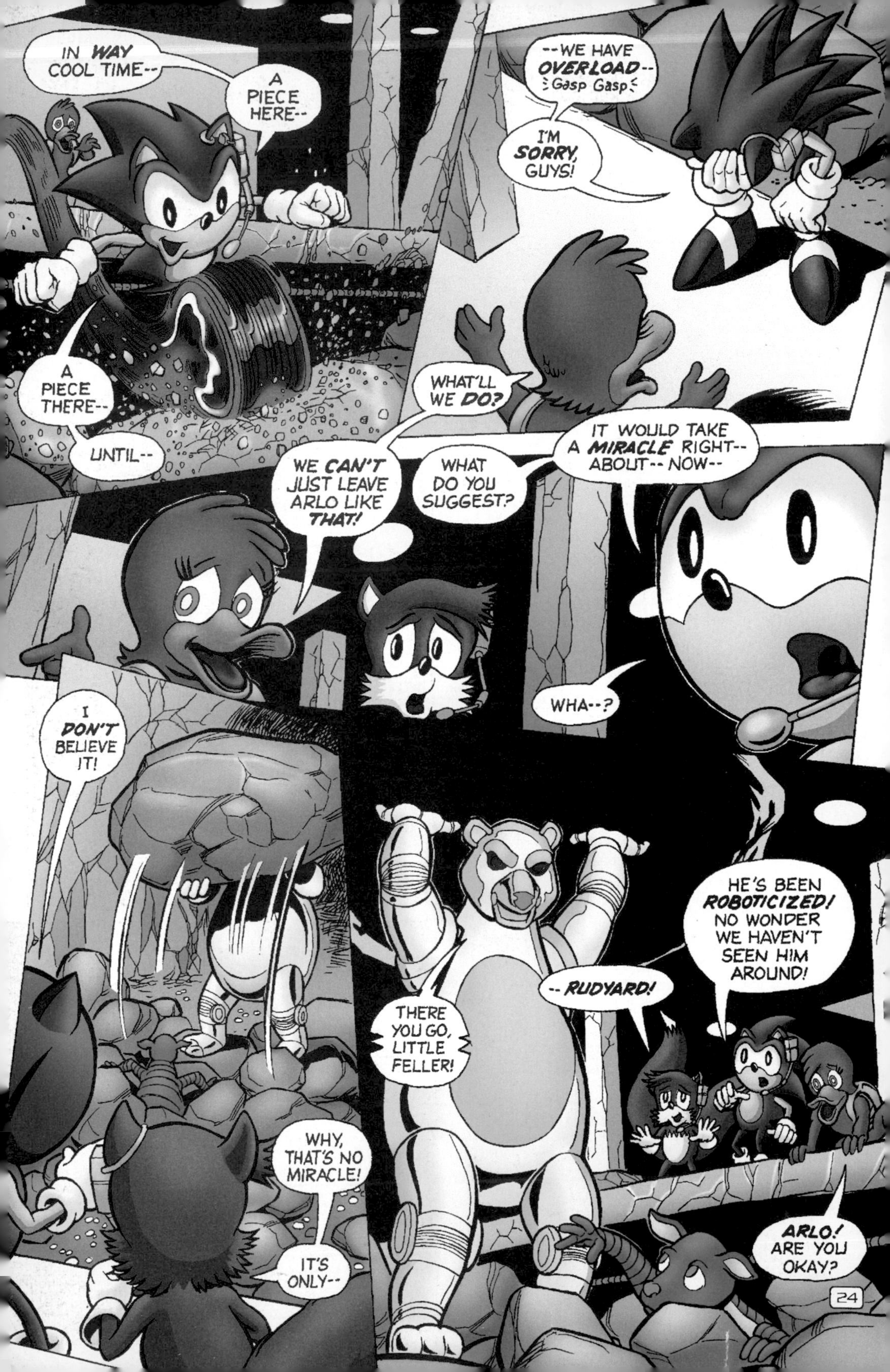

IN **WAY** COOL TIME--
A PIECE HERE--
A PIECE THERE--
UNTIL--
--WE HAVE **OVERLOAD**--
Gasp Gasp
I'M **SORRY**, GUYS!
WHAT'LL WE **DO?**
WE **CAN'T** JUST LEAVE ARLO LIKE **THAT!**
WHAT DO YOU SUGGEST?
IT WOULD TAKE A **MIRACLE** RIGHT-- ABOUT-- NOW--
WHA--?
I **DON'T** BELIEVE IT!
WHY, THAT'S NO MIRACLE!
IT'S ONLY--
-- **RUDYARD!**
HE'S BEEN **ROBOTICIZED!** NO WONDER WE HAVEN'T SEEN HIM AROUND!
THERE YOU GO, LITTLE FELLER!
ARLO! ARE YOU OKAY?

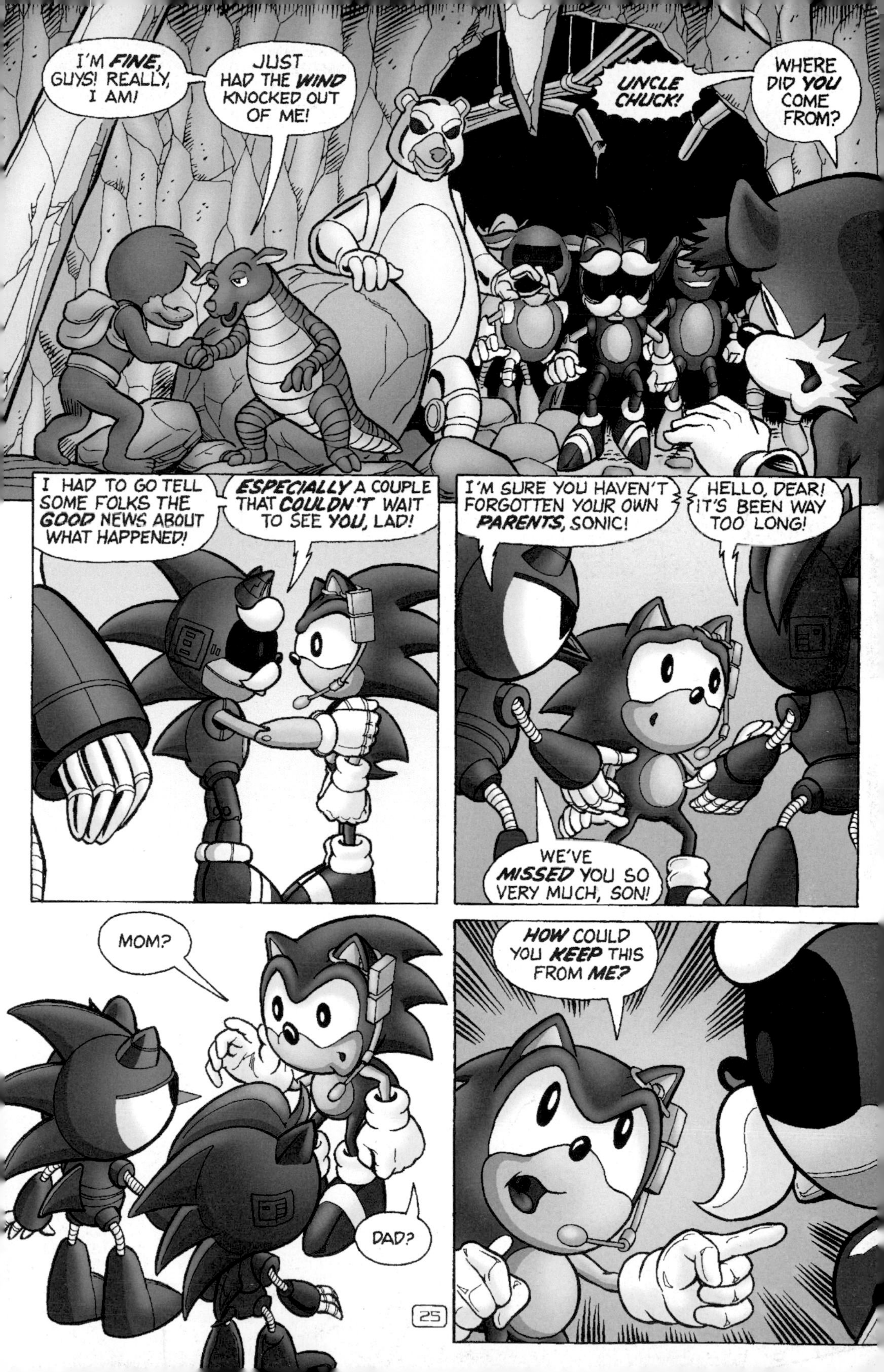
I'M FINE, GUYS! REALLY, I AM!
JUST HAD THE WIND KNOCKED OUT OF ME!
UNCLE CHUCK!
WHERE DID YOU COME FROM?
I HAD TO GO TELL SOME FOLKS THE GOOD NEWS ABOUT WHAT HAPPENED!
ESPECIALLY A COUPLE THAT COULDN'T WAIT TO SEE YOU, LAD!
I'M SURE YOU HAVEN'T FORGOTTEN YOUR OWN PARENTS, SONIC!
HELLO, DEAR! IT'S BEEN WAY TOO LONG!
WE'VE MISSED YOU SO VERY MUCH, SON!
MOM?
DAD?
HOW COULD YOU KEEP THIS FROM ME?
25

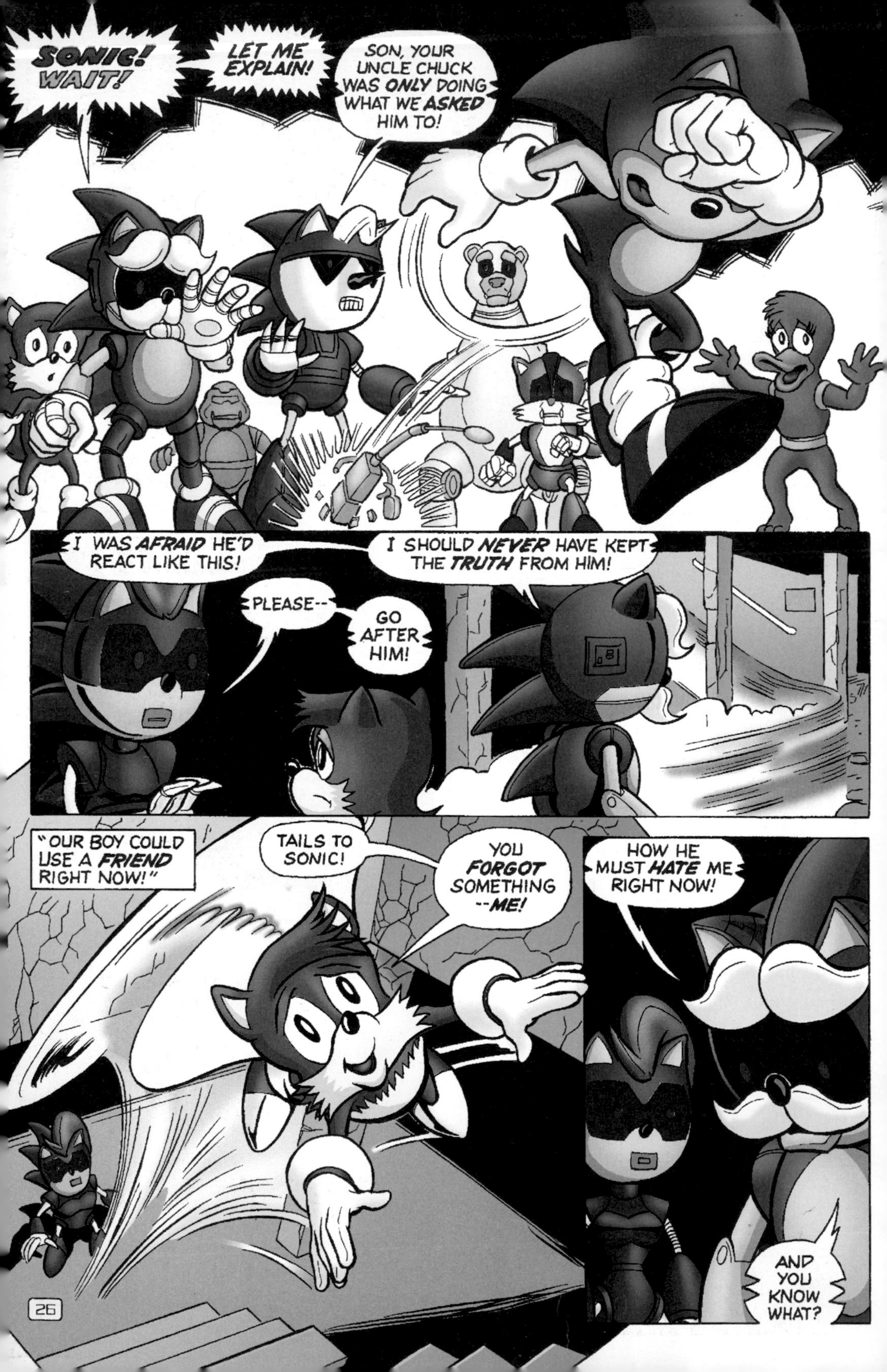
SONIC! WAIT!
LET ME EXPLAIN!
SON, YOUR UNCLE CHUCK WAS ONLY DOING WHAT WE ASKED HIM TO!
I WAS AFRAID HE'D REACT LIKE THIS!
I SHOULD NEVER HAVE KEPT THE TRUTH FROM HIM!
PLEASE--
GO AFTER HIM!
"OUR BOY COULD USE A FRIEND RIGHT NOW!"
TAILS TO SONIC!
YOU FORGOT SOMETHING --ME!
HOW HE MUST HATE ME RIGHT NOW!
AND YOU KNOW WHAT?

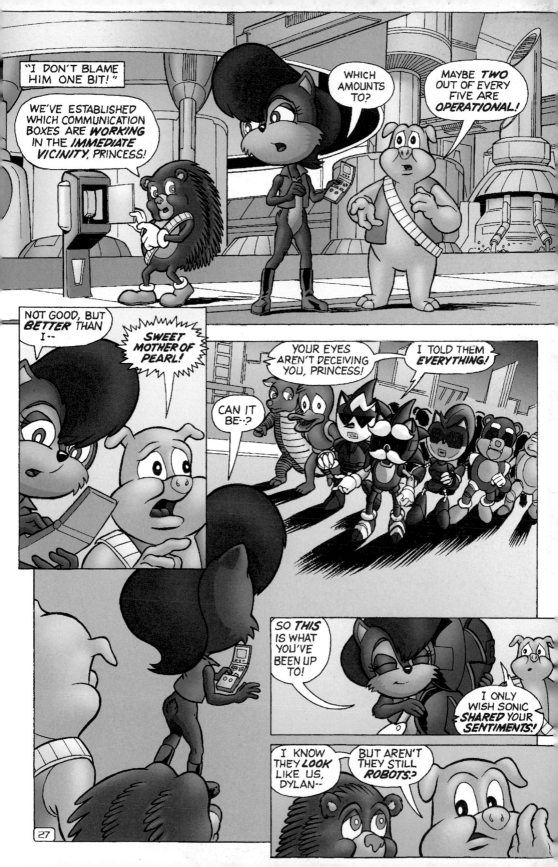

"I DON'T BLAME HIM ONE BIT!"

WE'VE ESTABLISHED WHICH COMMUNICATION BOXES ARE *WORKING* IN THE *IMMEDIATE VICINITY*, PRINCESS!

WHICH AMOUNTS TO?

MAYBE *TWO* OUT OF EVERY FIVE ARE *OPERATIONAL!*

NOT GOOD, BUT *BETTER* THAN I--

SWEET MOTHER OF PEARL!

YOUR EYES AREN'T DECEIVING YOU, PRINCESS!

I TOLD THEM *EVERYTHING!*

CAN IT BE--?

SO *THIS* IS WHAT YOU'VE BEEN UP TO!

I ONLY WISH SONIC *SHARED* YOUR SENTIMENTS!

I KNOW THEY *LOOK* LIKE US, DYLAN--

BUT AREN'T THEY STILL *ROBOTS?*

27

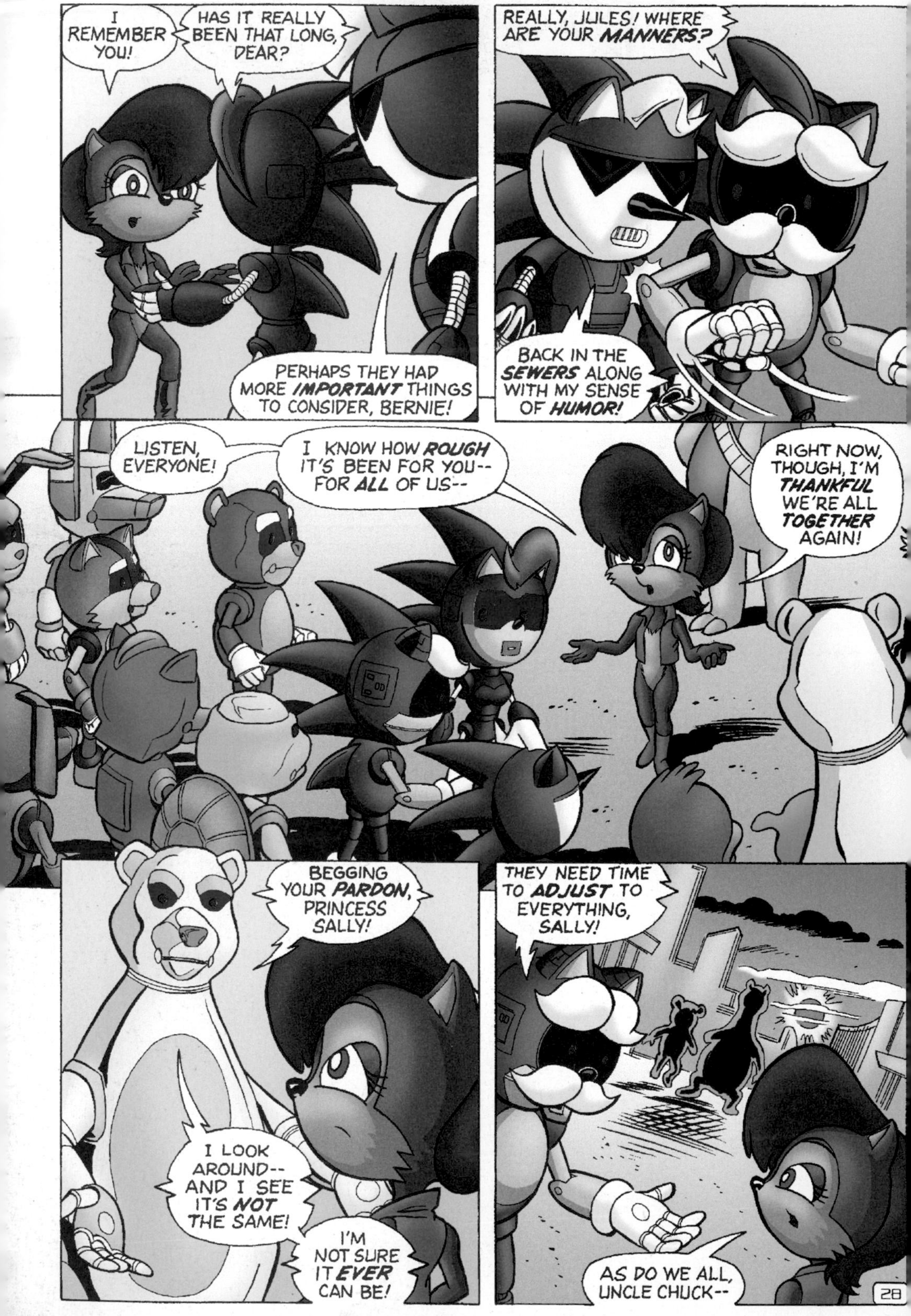
I REMEMBER YOU!
HAS IT REALLY BEEN THAT LONG, DEAR?
PERHAPS THEY HAD MORE *IMPORTANT* THINGS TO CONSIDER, BERNIE!
REALLY, JULES! WHERE ARE YOUR *MANNERS?*
BACK IN THE *SEWERS* ALONG WITH MY SENSE OF *HUMOR!*
LISTEN, EVERYONE!
I KNOW HOW *ROUGH* IT'S BEEN FOR YOU-- FOR *ALL* OF US--
RIGHT NOW, THOUGH, I'M *THANKFUL* WE'RE ALL *TOGETHER* AGAIN!
BEGGING YOUR *PARDON*, PRINCESS SALLY!
I LOOK AROUND-- AND I SEE IT'S *NOT* THE SAME!
I'M NOT SURE IT *EVER* CAN BE!
THEY NEED TIME TO *ADJUST* TO EVERYTHING, SALLY!
AS DO WE ALL, UNCLE CHUCK--

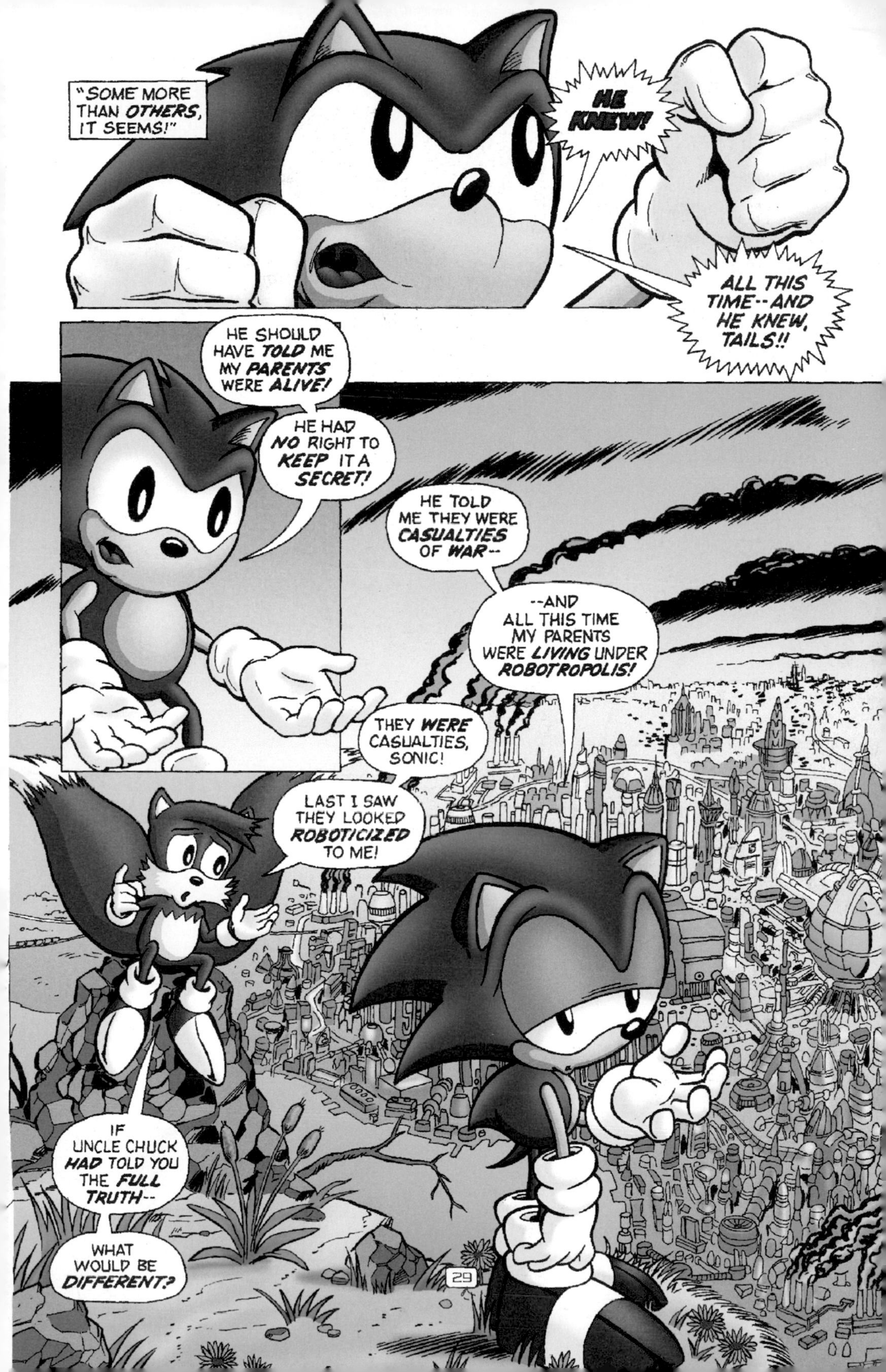
"SOME MORE THAN OTHERS, IT SEEMS!"
HE KNEW!
ALL THIS TIME--AND HE KNEW, TAILS!!
HE SHOULD HAVE TOLD ME MY PARENTS WERE ALIVE!
HE HAD NO RIGHT TO KEEP IT A SECRET!
HE TOLD ME THEY WERE CASUALTIES OF WAR--
--AND ALL THIS TIME MY PARENTS WERE LIVING UNDER ROBOTROPOLIS!
THEY WERE CASUALTIES, SONIC!
LAST I SAW THEY LOOKED ROBOTICIZED TO ME!
IF UNCLE CHUCK HAD TOLD YOU THE FULL TRUTH--
WHAT WOULD BE DIFFERENT?

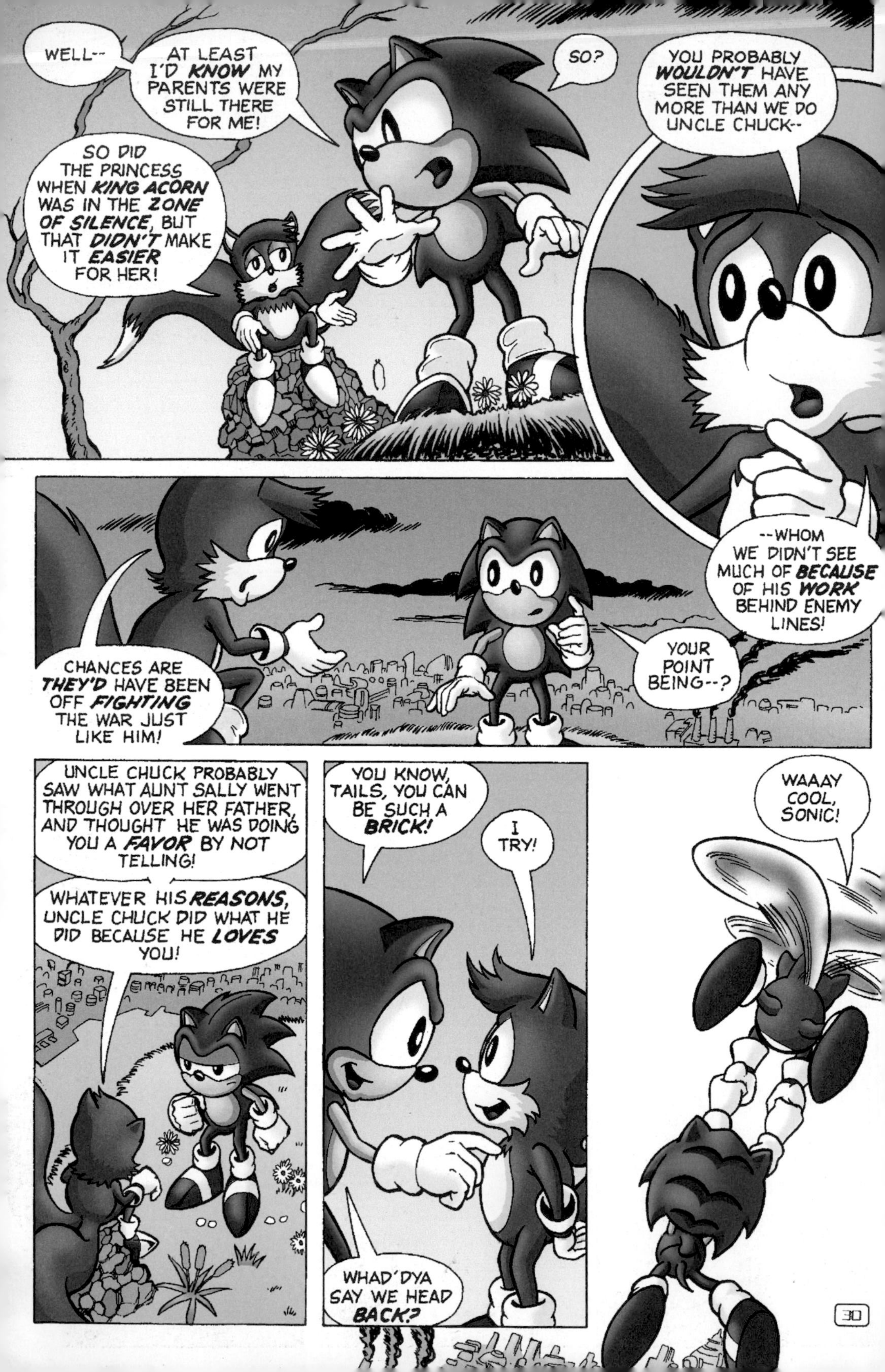
WELL--
AT LEAST I'D KNOW MY PARENTS WERE STILL THERE FOR ME!
SO?
SO DID THE PRINCESS WHEN KING ACORN WAS IN THE ZONE OF SILENCE, BUT THAT DIDN'T MAKE IT EASIER FOR HER!
YOU PROBABLY WOULDN'T HAVE SEEN THEM ANY MORE THAN WE DO UNCLE CHUCK--
--WHOM WE DIDN'T SEE MUCH OF BECAUSE OF HIS WORK BEHIND ENEMY LINES!
YOUR POINT BEING--?
CHANCES ARE THEY'D HAVE BEEN OFF FIGHTING THE WAR JUST LIKE HIM!
UNCLE CHUCK PROBABLY SAW WHAT AUNT SALLY WENT THROUGH OVER HER FATHER, AND THOUGHT HE WAS DOING YOU A FAVOR BY NOT TELLING!
WHATEVER HIS REASONS, UNCLE CHUCK DID WHAT HE DID BECAUSE HE LOVES YOU!
YOU KNOW, TAILS, YOU CAN BE SUCH A BRICK!
I TRY!
WHAD'DYA SAY WE HEAD BACK?
WAAAY COOL, SONIC!

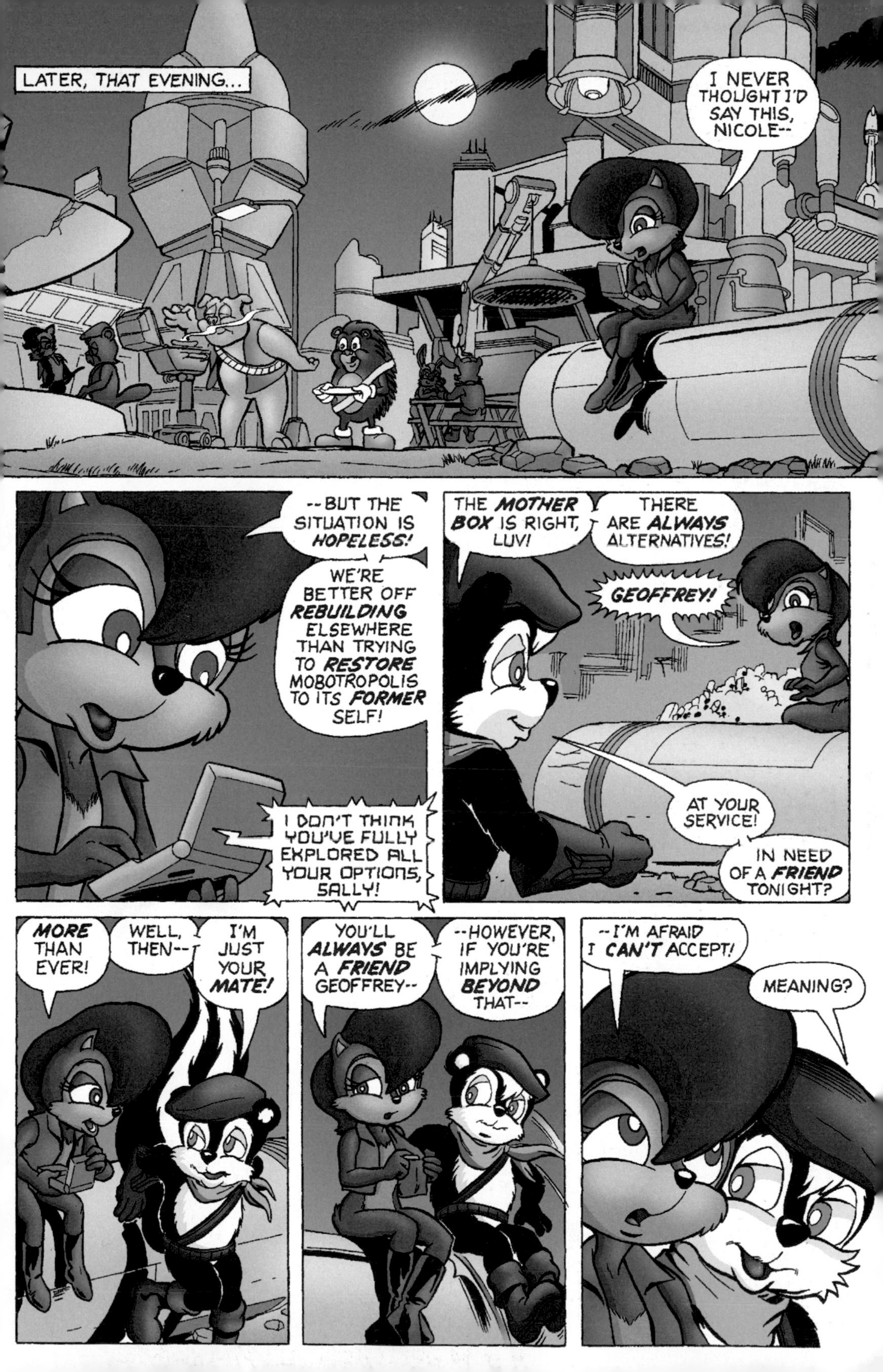
LATER, THAT EVENING...
I NEVER THOUGHT I'D SAY THIS, NICOLE--
--BUT THE SITUATION IS HOPELESS!
WE'RE BETTER OFF REBUILDING ELSEWHERE THAN TRYING TO RESTORE MOBOTROPOLIS TO ITS FORMER SELF!
I DON'T THINK YOU'VE FULLY EXPLORED ALL YOUR OPTIONS, SALLY!
THE MOTHER BOX IS RIGHT, LUV!
THERE ARE ALWAYS ALTERNATIVES!
GEOFFREY!
AT YOUR SERVICE!
IN NEED OF A FRIEND TONIGHT?
MORE THAN EVER!
WELL, THEN--
I'M JUST YOUR MATE!
YOU'LL ALWAYS BE A FRIEND GEOFFREY--
--HOWEVER, IF YOU'RE IMPLYING BEYOND THAT--
--I'M AFRAID I CAN'T ACCEPT!
MEANING?

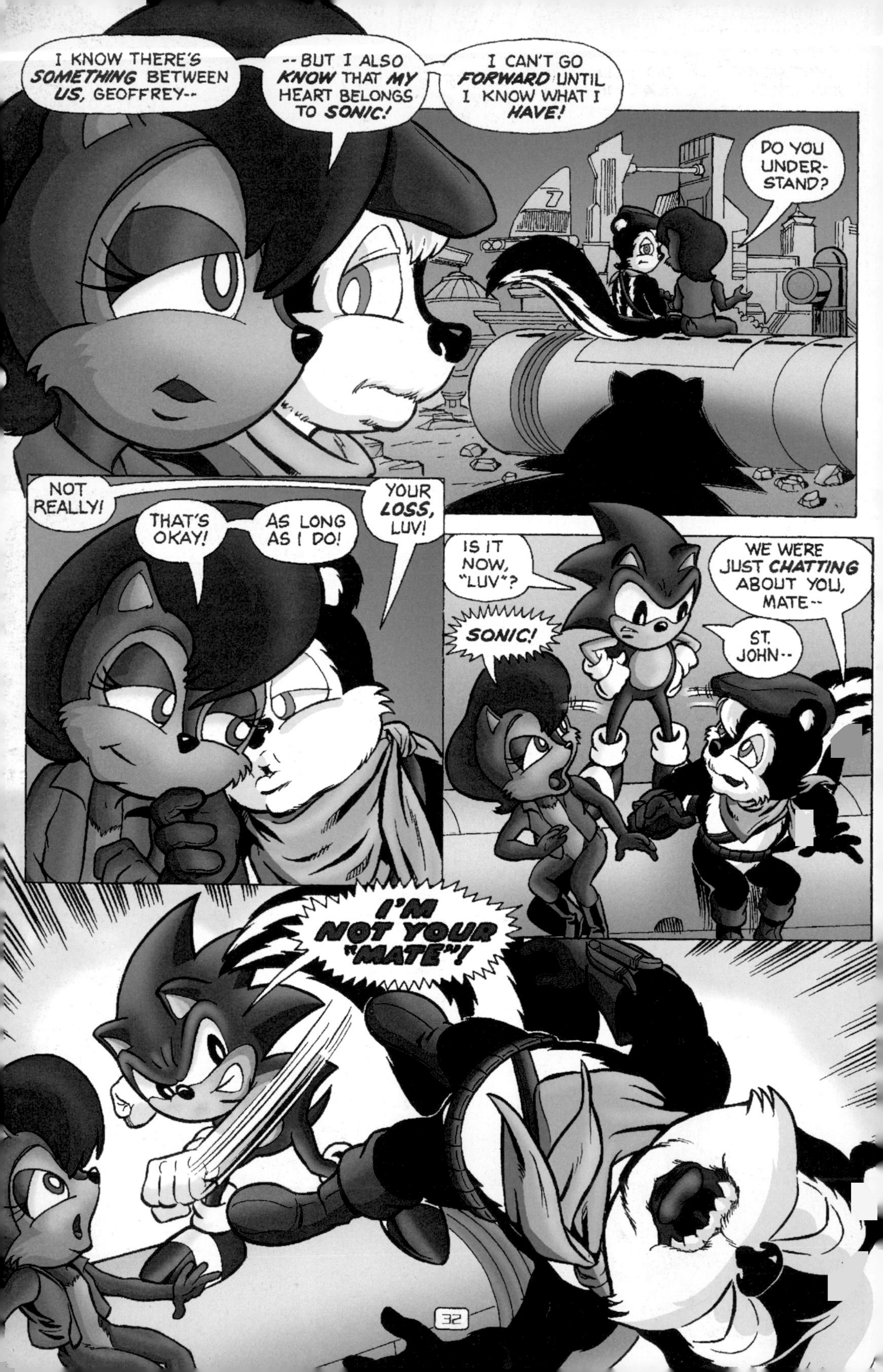
I KNOW THERE'S SOMETHING BETWEEN US, GEOFFREY--
-- BUT I ALSO KNOW THAT MY HEART BELONGS TO SONIC!
I CAN'T GO FORWARD UNTIL I KNOW WHAT I HAVE!
DO YOU UNDER-STAND?
NOT REALLY!
THAT'S OKAY!
AS LONG AS I DO!
YOUR LOSS, LUV!
IS IT NOW, "LUV"?
SONIC!
WE WERE JUST CHATTING ABOUT YOU, MATE--
ST. JOHN--
I'M NOT YOUR "MATE"!

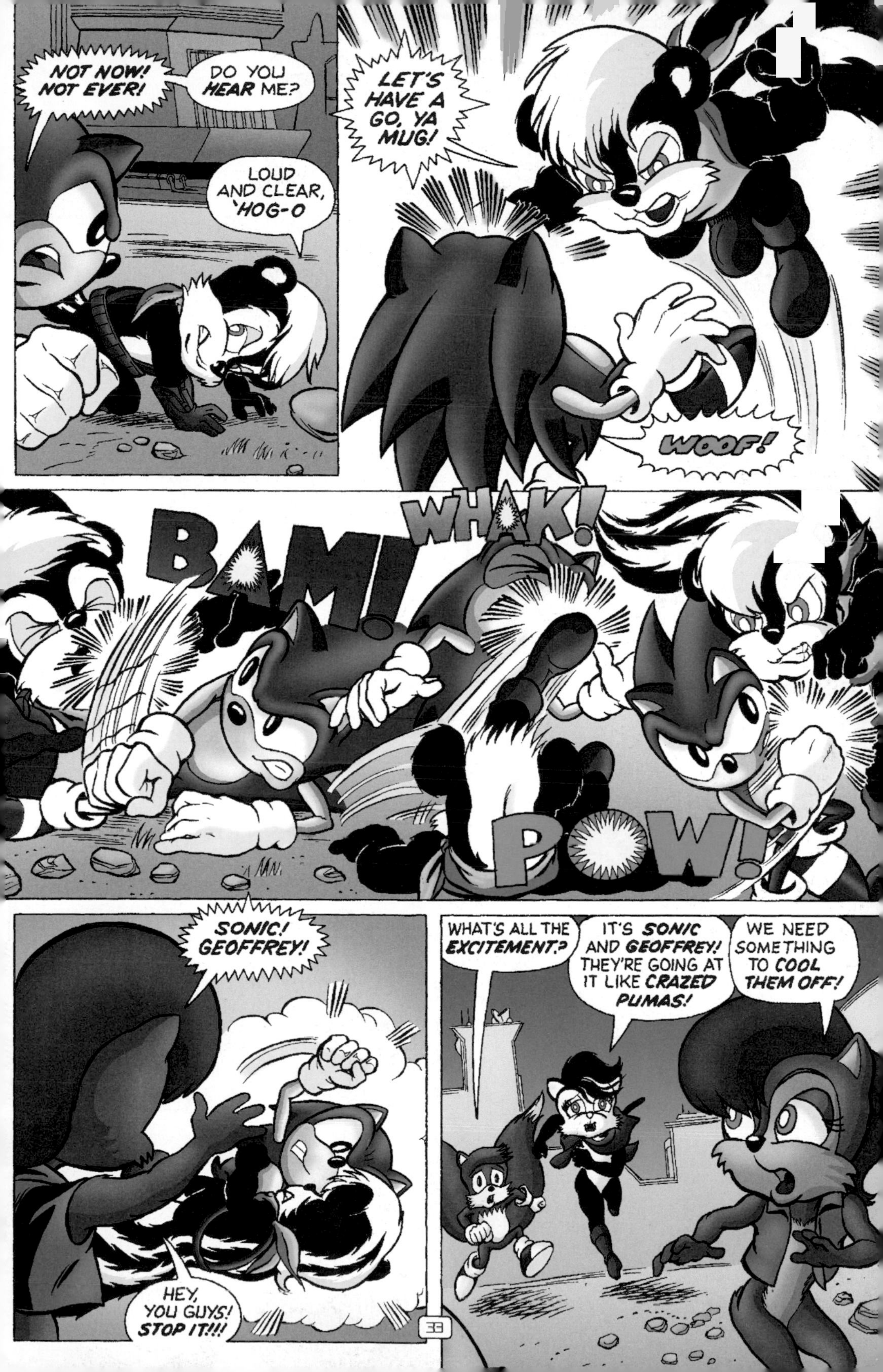
NOT NOW! NOT EVER!
DO YOU HEAR ME?
LOUD AND CLEAR, 'HOG-O
LET'S HAVE A GO, YA MUG!
WOOF!
BAM!
WHAK!
POW!
SONIC! GEOFFREY!
HEY, YOU GUYS! STOP IT!!!
WHAT'S ALL THE EXCITEMENT?
IT'S SONIC AND GEOFFREY! THEY'RE GOING AT IT LIKE CRAZED PUMAS!
WE NEED SOMETHING TO COOL THEM OFF!

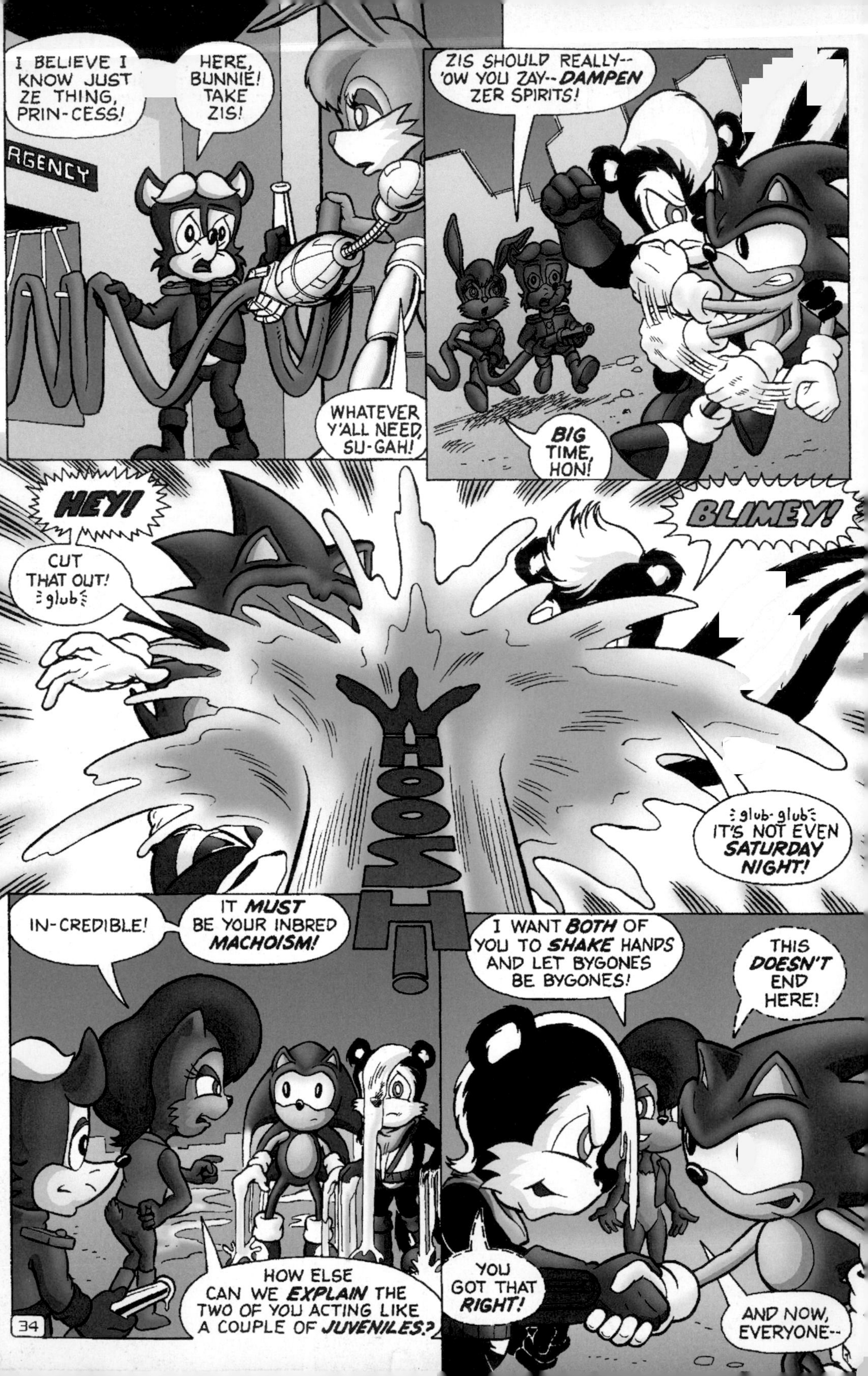
I BELIEVE I KNOW JUST ZE THING, PRIN-CESS!
HERE, BUNNIE! TAKE ZIS!
AGENCY
WHATEVER Y'ALL NEED, SU-GAH!
ZIS SHOULD REALLY-- 'OW YOU ZAY--DAMPEN ZER SPIRITS!
BIG TIME, HON!
HEY!
CUT THAT OUT! glub
BLIMEY!
WHOOSH
glub-glub IT'S NOT EVEN SATURDAY NIGHT!
IN-CREDIBLE!
IT MUST BE YOUR INBRED MACHOISM!
HOW ELSE CAN WE EXPLAIN THE TWO OF YOU ACTING LIKE A COUPLE OF JUVENILES?
I WANT BOTH OF YOU TO SHAKE HANDS AND LET BYGONES BE BYGONES!
THIS DOESN'T END HERE!
YOU GOT THAT RIGHT!
AND NOW, EVERYONE--

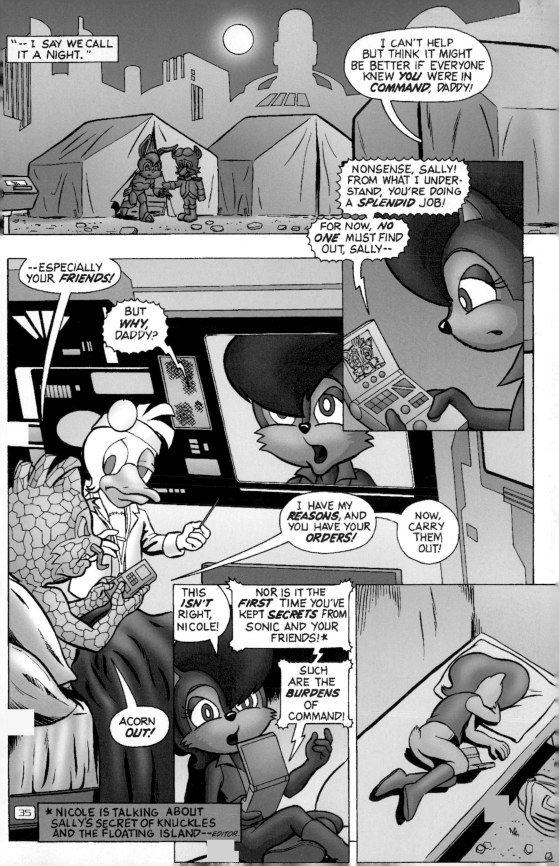

"-- I SAY WE CALL IT A NIGHT."

I CAN'T HELP BUT THINK IT MIGHT BE BETTER IF EVERYONE KNEW *YOU* WERE IN *COMMAND,* DADDY!

NONSENSE, SALLY! FROM WHAT I UNDER-STAND, YOU'RE DOING A *SPLENDID* JOB!

FOR NOW, *NO ONE* MUST FIND OUT, SALLY--

--ESPECIALLY YOUR *FRIENDS!*

BUT *WHY,* DADDY?

I HAVE MY *REASONS,* AND YOU HAVE YOUR *ORDERS!*

NOW, CARRY THEM OUT!

THIS *ISN'T* RIGHT, NICOLE!

NOR IS IT THE *FIRST* TIME YOU'VE KEPT *SECRETS* FROM SONIC AND YOUR FRIENDS! *

SUCH ARE THE *BURDENS* OF COMMAND!

ACORN *OUT!*

* NICOLE IS TALKING ABOUT SALLY'S SECRET OF KNUCKLES AND THE FLOATING ISLAND--*EDITOR*

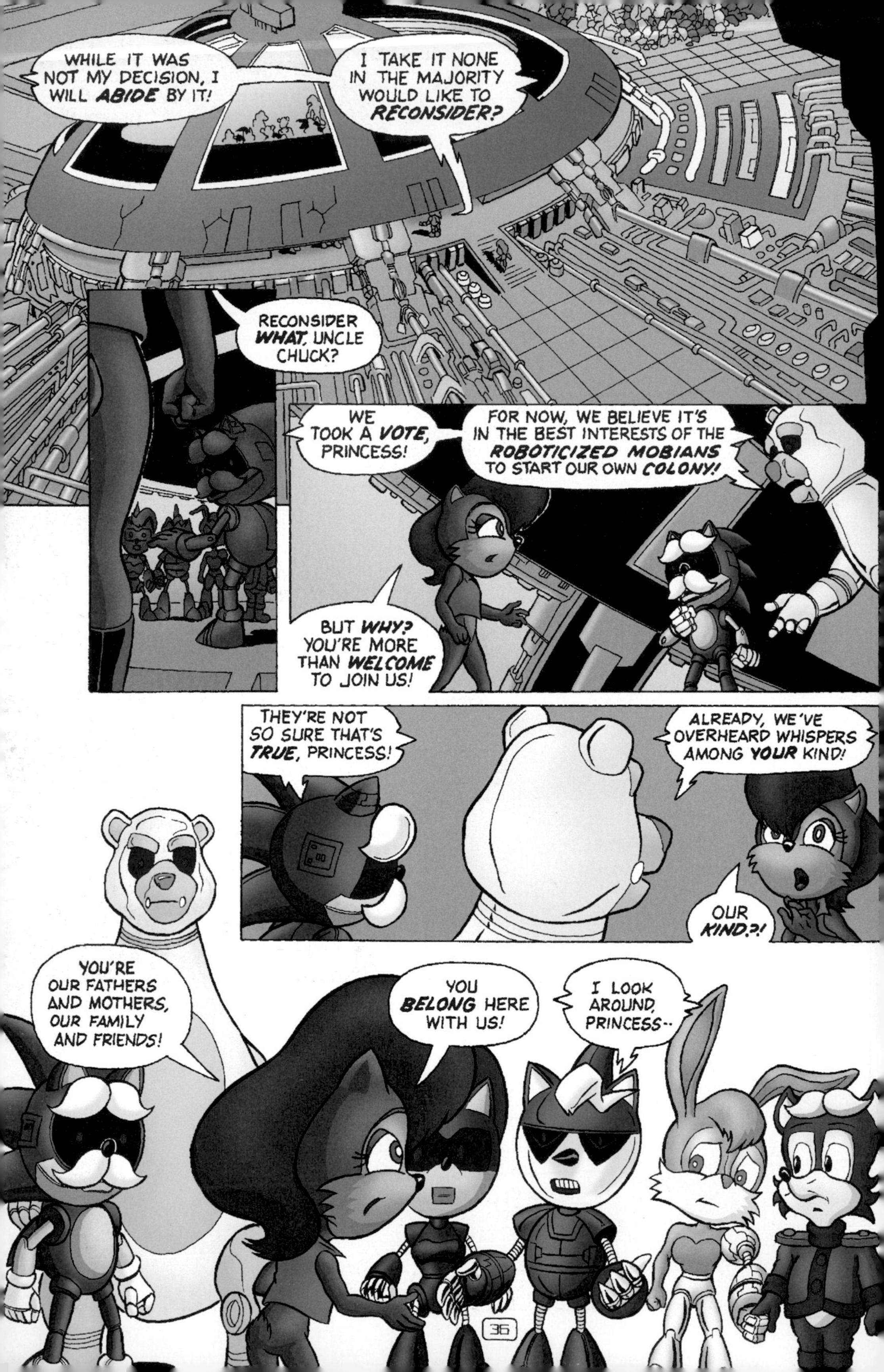
WHILE IT WAS NOT MY DECISION, I WILL ABIDE BY IT!
I TAKE IT NONE IN THE MAJORITY WOULD LIKE TO RECONSIDER?
RECONSIDER WHAT, UNCLE CHUCK?
WE TOOK A VOTE, PRINCESS!
FOR NOW, WE BELIEVE IT'S IN THE BEST INTERESTS OF THE ROBOTICIZED MOBIANS TO START OUR OWN COLONY!
BUT WHY? YOU'RE MORE THAN WELCOME TO JOIN US!
THEY'RE NOT SO SURE THAT'S TRUE, PRINCESS!
ALREADY, WE'VE OVERHEARD WHISPERS AMONG YOUR KIND!
OUR KIND?!
YOU'RE OUR FATHERS AND MOTHERS, OUR FAMILY AND FRIENDS!
YOU BELONG HERE WITH US!
I LOOK AROUND, PRINCESS--

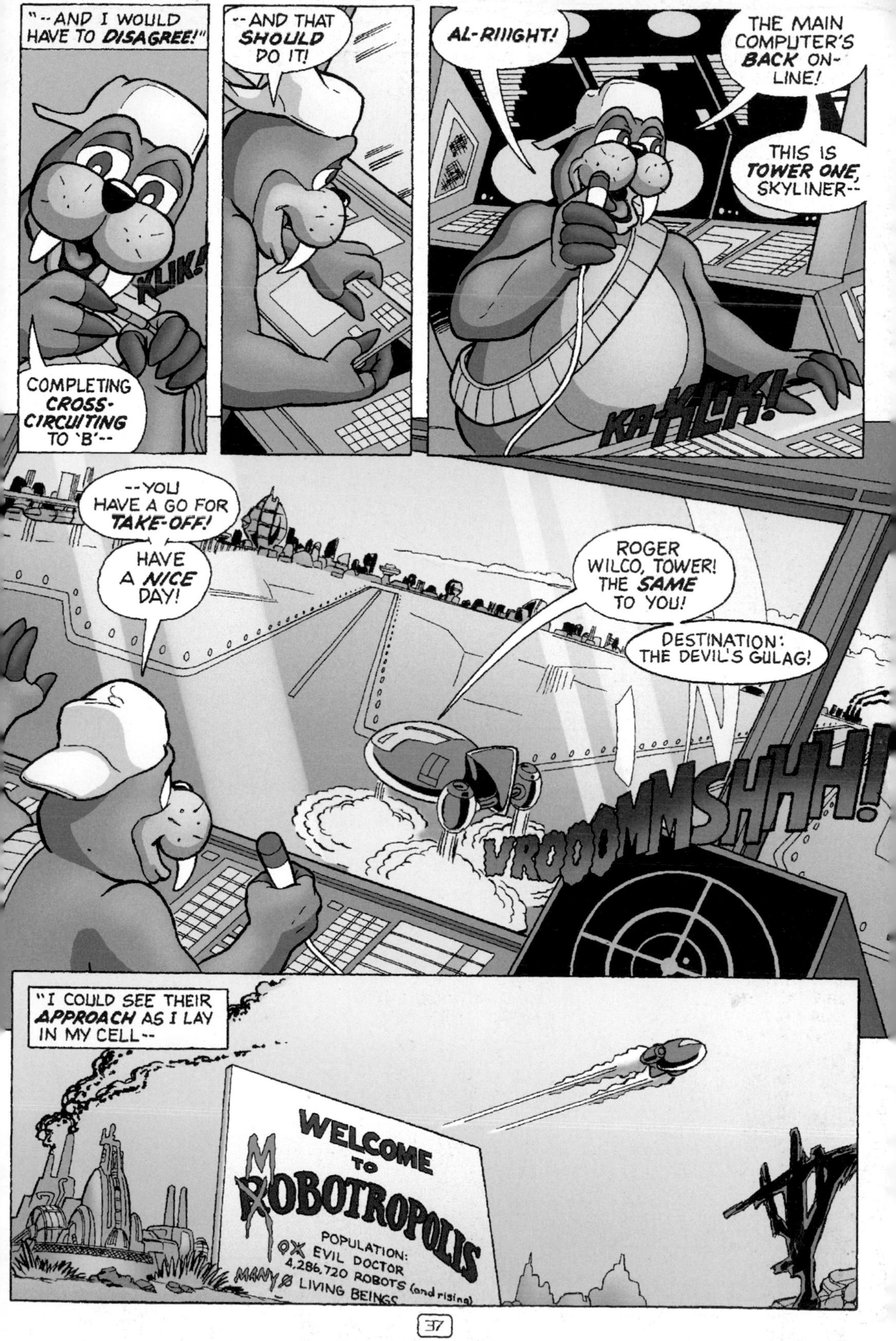
"--AND I WOULD HAVE TO DISAGREE!"
KLIK!
COMPLETING CROSS-CIRCUITING TO 'B'--
--AND THAT SHOULD DO IT!
AL-RIIIGHT!
THE MAIN COMPUTER'S BACK ON-LINE!
THIS IS TOWER ONE, SKYLINER--
KA-KLIK!
--YOU HAVE A GO FOR TAKE-OFF!
HAVE A NICE DAY!
ROGER WILCO, TOWER! THE SAME TO YOU!
DESTINATION: THE DEVIL'S GULAG!
VROOOMMSHHH!
"I COULD SEE THEIR APPROACH AS I LAY IN MY CELL--
WELCOME TO MOBOTROPOLIS
POPULATION:
0X EVIL DOCTOR
4,286,720 ROBOTS (and rising)
MANY Ø LIVING BEINGS

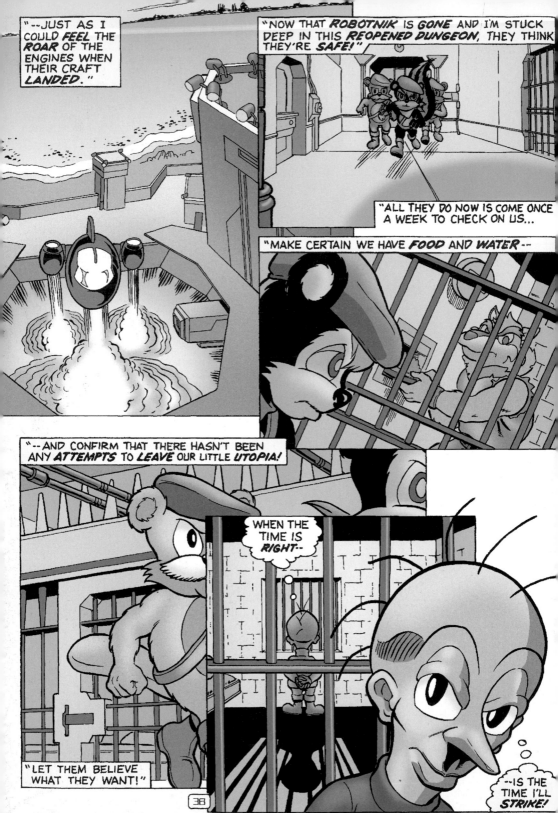

"--JUST AS I COULD *FEEL* THE *ROAR* OF THE ENGINES WHEN THEIR CRAFT *LANDED*."

"NOW THAT *ROBOTNIK* IS *GONE* AND I'M STUCK DEEP IN THIS *REOPENED DUNGEON*, THEY THINK THEY'RE *SAFE!*"

"ALL THEY DO NOW IS COME ONCE A WEEK TO CHECK ON US...

"MAKE CERTAIN WE HAVE *FOOD* AND *WATER--*

"--AND CONFIRM THAT THERE HASN'T BEEN ANY *ATTEMPTS* TO *LEAVE* OUR LITTLE *UTOPIA!*

WHEN THE TIME IS *RIGHT--*

"LET THEM BELIEVE WHAT THEY WANT!"

--IS THE TIME I'LL *STRIKE!*

THE STAGE HAS BEEN SET. THE CURTAIN HAS RISEN. NOW THAT YOU HAVE ENTERED *SONIC'S BRAVE NEW WORLD*, CONTINUE THE JOURNEY IN *SONIC ARCHIVES VOL. 14*, AS THINGS GET WILDER STILL!

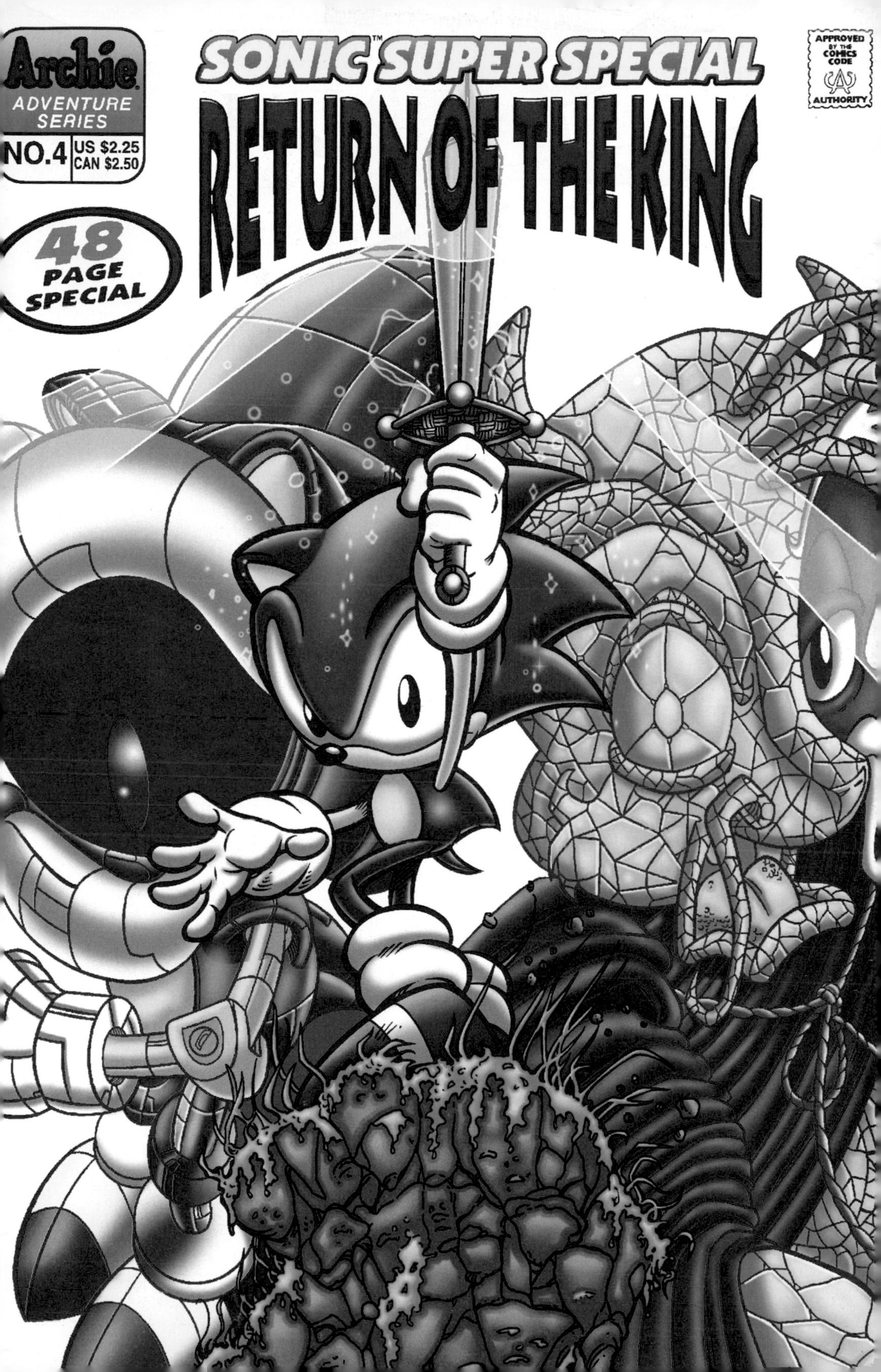
Archie
ADVENTURE SERIES
NO.4
US $2.25
CAN $2.50
SONIC™ SUPER SPECIAL
RETURN OF THE KING
APPROVED BY THE COMICS CODE AUTHORITY
48 PAGE SPECIAL

Once a virtual paradise, the planet **Mobius** was enslaved when conquered by the techno-evil of **Doctor Robotnik.** In the aftermath, a **courageous group of "Freedom Fighters"** has risen to restore the order and beauty that was once theirs. The greatest among them is the **fastest and way-coolest dude on two feet... SONIC THE HEDGEHOG!**

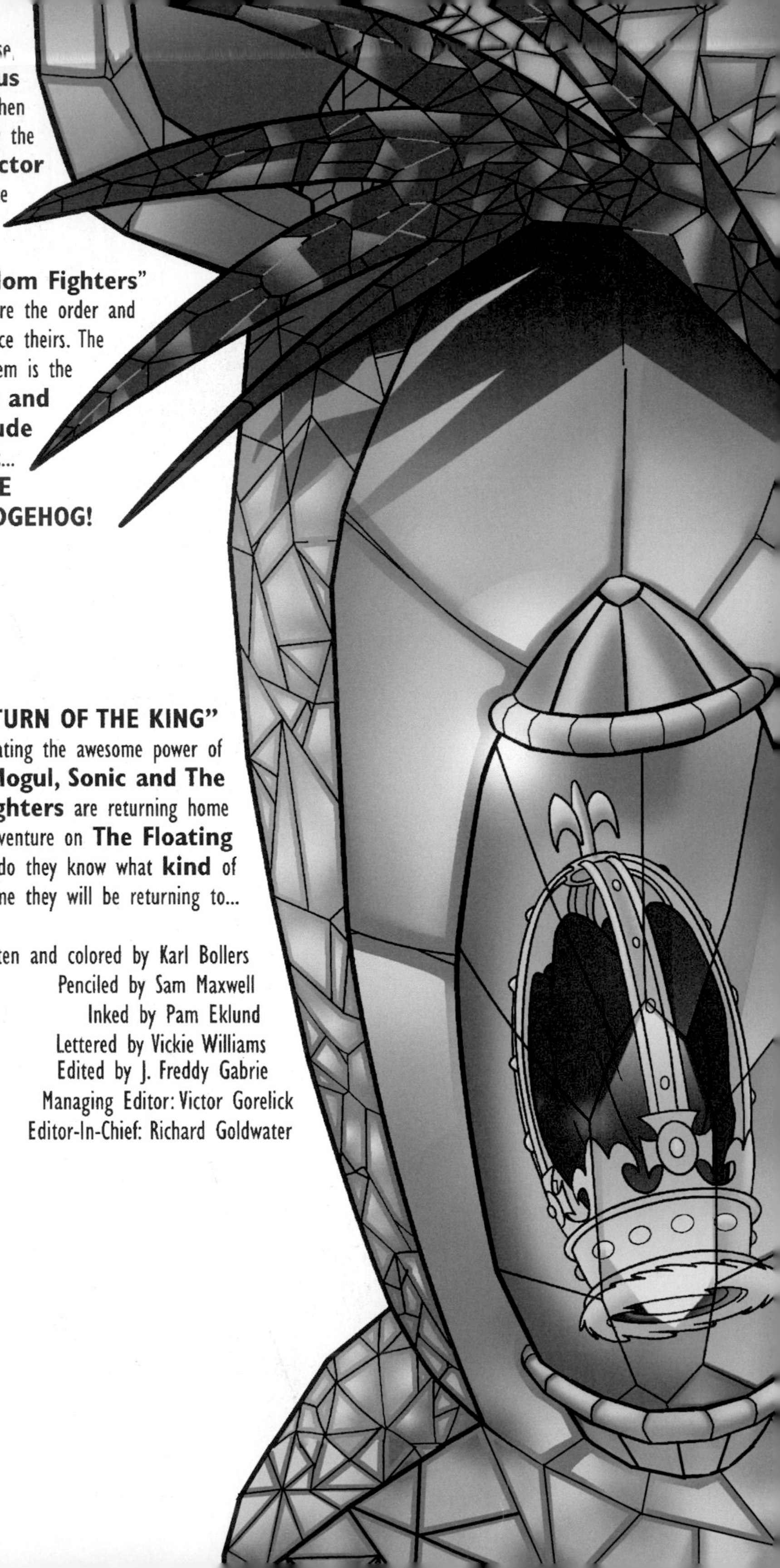

"THE RETURN OF THE KING"

After defeating the awesome power of **Mammoth Mogul, Sonic and The Freedom Fighters** are returning home from their adventure on **The Floating Island.** Little do they know what **kind** of home they will be returning to...

Written and colored by Karl Bollers
Penciled by Sam Maxwell
Inked by Pam Eklund
Lettered by Vickie Williams
Edited by J. Freddy Gabrie
Managing Editor: Victor Gorelick
Editor-In-Chief: Richard Goldwater

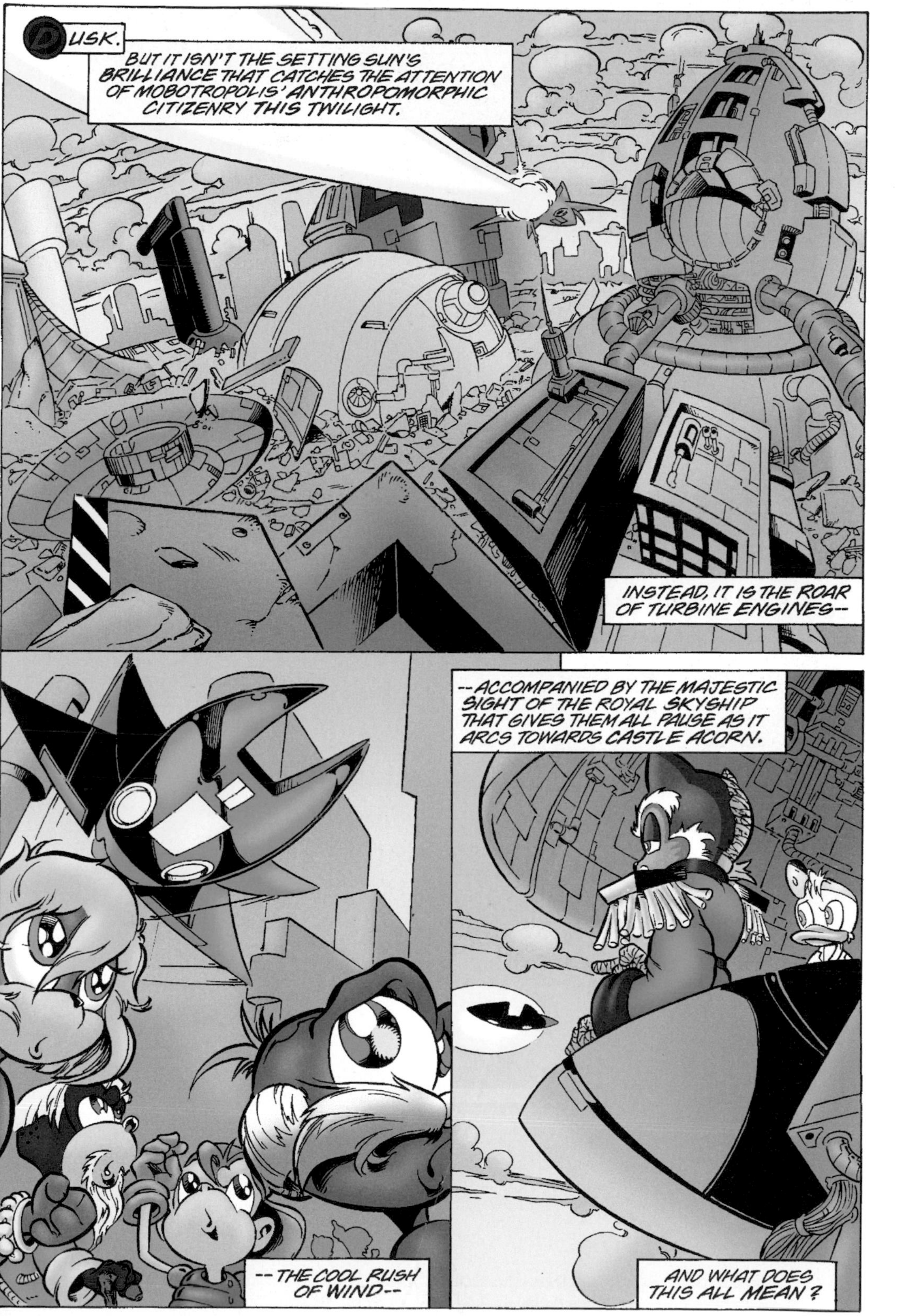
DUSK.
BUT IT ISN'T THE SETTING SUN'S BRILLIANCE THAT CATCHES THE ATTENTION OF MOBOTROPOLIS' ANTHROPOMORPHIC CITIZENRY THIS TWILIGHT.
INSTEAD, IT IS THE ROAR OF TURBINE ENGINES--
--THE COOL RUSH OF WIND--
--ACCOMPANIED BY THE MAJESTIC SIGHT OF THE ROYAL SKYSHIP THAT GIVES THEM ALL PAUSE AS IT ARCS TOWARDS CASTLE ACORN.
AND WHAT DOES THIS ALL MEAN?

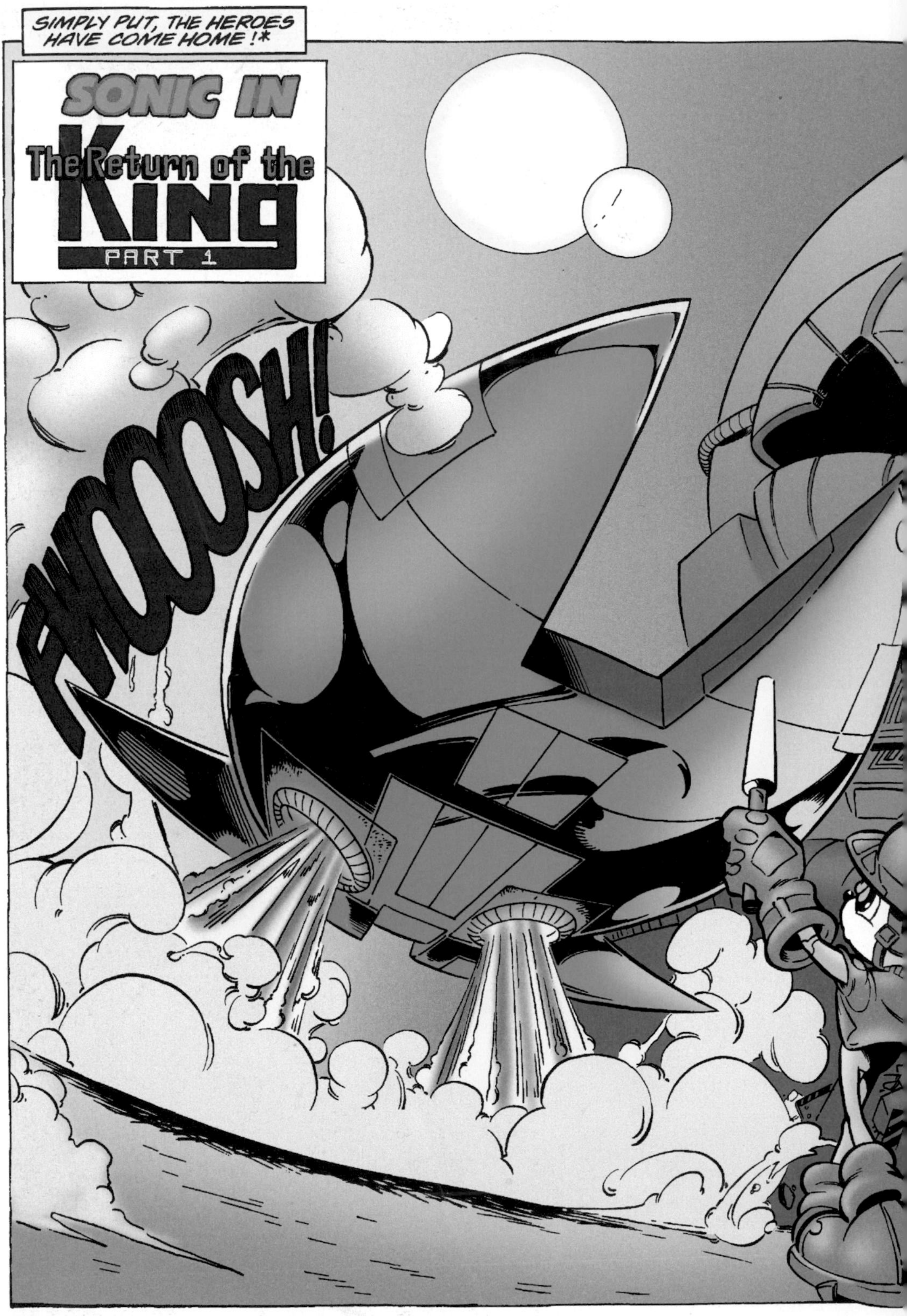
SIMPLY PUT, THE HEROES HAVE COME HOME !*
SONIC IN
The Return of the
KING
PART 1
FWOOOSH!

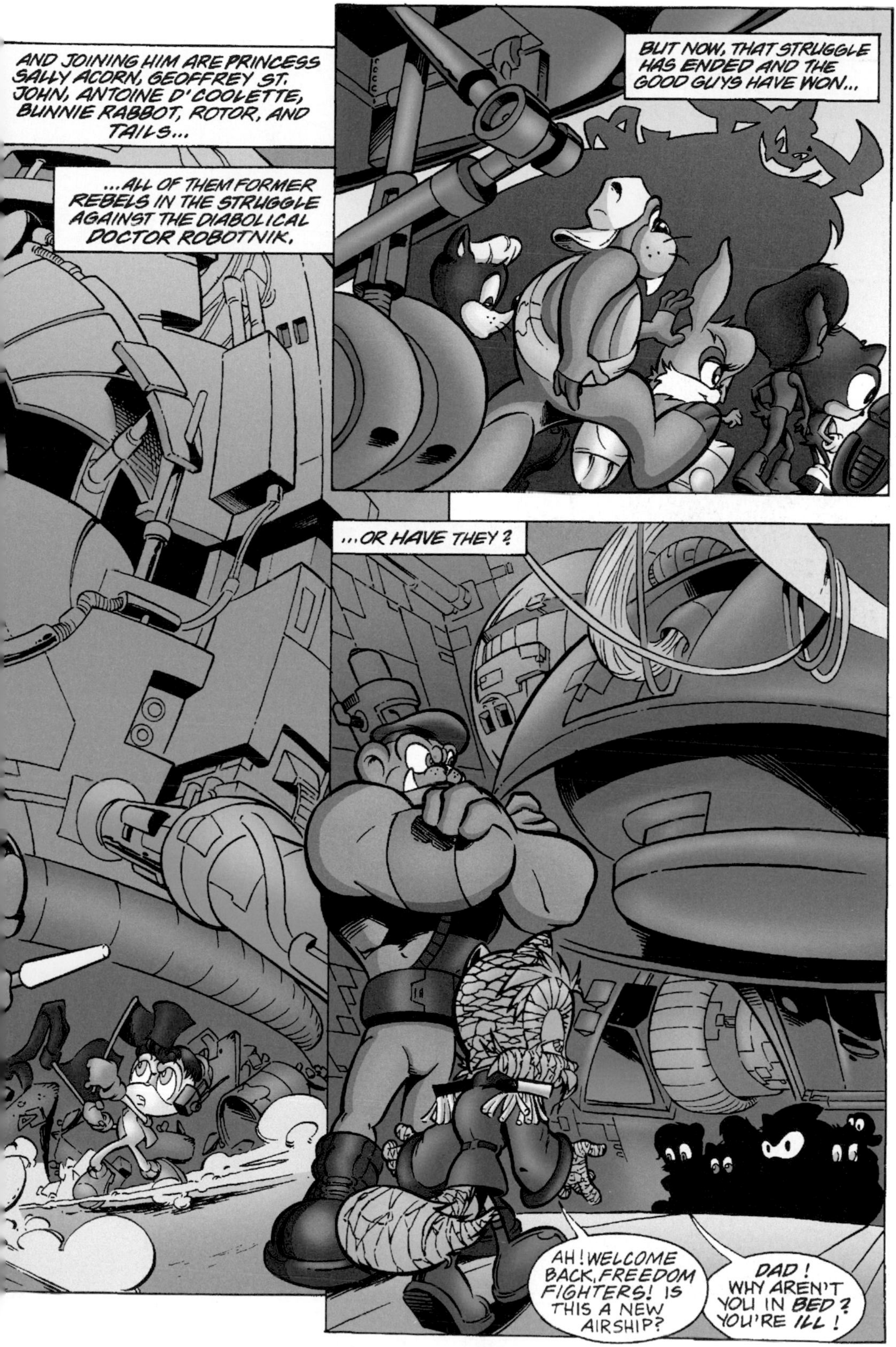
AND JOINING HIM ARE PRINCESS SALLY ACORN, GEOFFREY ST. JOHN, ANTOINE D'COOLETTE, BUNNIE RABBOT, ROTOR, AND TAILS...
...ALL OF THEM FORMER REBELS IN THE STRUGGLE AGAINST THE DIABOLICAL DOCTOR ROBOTNIK.
BUT NOW, THAT STRUGGLE HAS ENDED AND THE GOOD GUYS HAVE WON...
...OR HAVE THEY?
AH! WELCOME BACK, FREEDOM FIGHTERS! IS THIS A NEW AIRSHIP?
DAD! WHY AREN'T YOU IN BED? YOU'RE ILL!

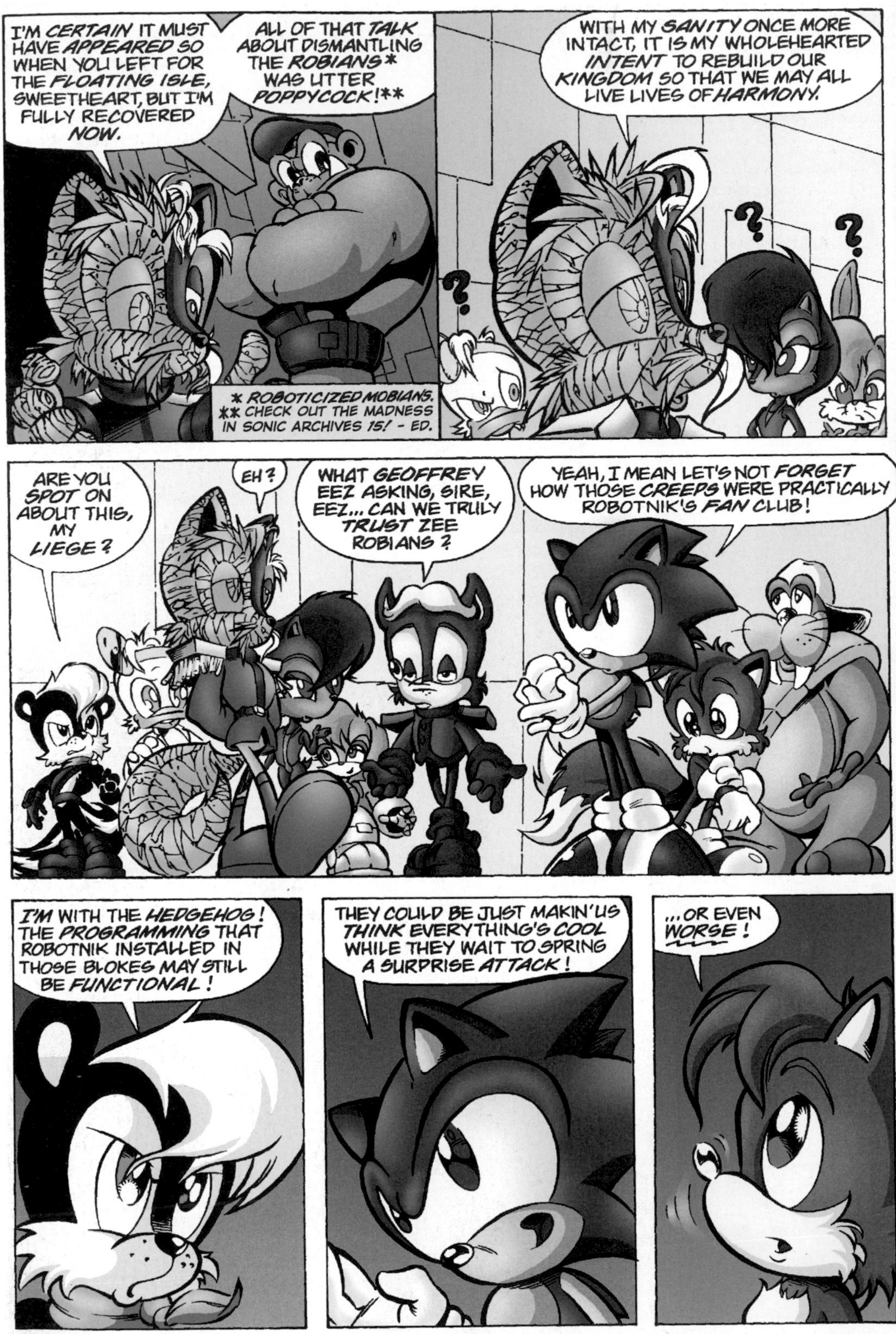
I'M CERTAIN IT MUST HAVE APPEARED SO WHEN YOU LEFT FOR THE FLOATING ISLE, SWEETHEART, BUT I'M FULLY RECOVERED NOW.
ALL OF THAT TALK ABOUT DISMANTLING THE ROBIANS* WAS UTTER POPPYCOCK!**
* ROBOTICIZED MOBIANS.
** CHECK OUT THE MADNESS IN SONIC ARCHIVES 15! - ED.
WITH MY SANITY ONCE MORE INTACT, IT IS MY WHOLEHEARTED INTENT TO REBUILD OUR KINGDOM SO THAT WE MAY ALL LIVE LIVES OF HARMONY.
?
?
?
ARE YOU SPOT ON ABOUT THIS, MY LIEGE?
EH?
WHAT GEOFFREY EEZ ASKING, SIRE, EEZ... CAN WE TRULY TRUST ZEE ROBIANS?
YEAH, I MEAN LET'S NOT FORGET HOW THOSE CREEPS WERE PRACTICALLY ROBOTNIK'S FAN CLUB!
I'M WITH THE HEDGEHOG! THE PROGRAMMING THAT ROBOTNIK INSTALLED IN THOSE BLOKES MAY STILL BE FUNCTIONAL!
THEY COULD BE JUST MAKIN' US THINK EVERYTHING'S COOL WHILE THEY WAIT TO SPRING A SURPRISE ATTACK!
...OR EVEN WORSE!

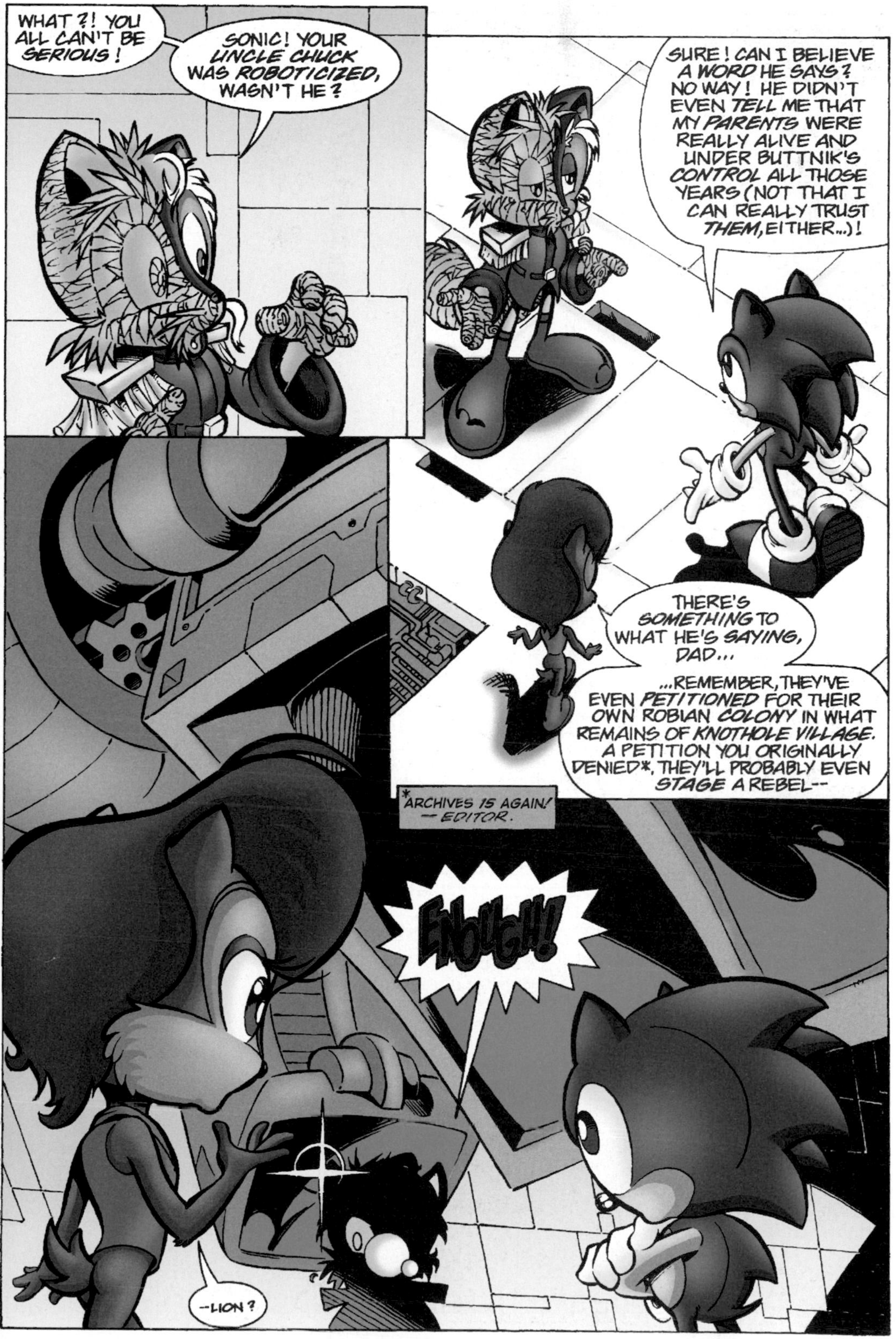
WHAT ?! YOU ALL CAN'T BE SERIOUS !
SONIC! YOUR UNCLE CHUCK WAS ROBOTICIZED, WASN'T HE ?
SURE! CAN I BELIEVE A WORD HE SAYS ? NO WAY! HE DIDN'T EVEN TELL ME THAT MY PARENTS WERE REALLY ALIVE AND UNDER BUTTNIK'S CONTROL ALL THOSE YEARS (NOT THAT I CAN REALLY TRUST THEM, EITHER...)!
THERE'S SOMETHING TO WHAT HE'S SAYING, DAD...
...REMEMBER, THEY'VE EVEN PETITIONED FOR THEIR OWN ROBIAN COLONY IN WHAT REMAINS OF KNOTHOLE VILLAGE. A PETITION YOU ORIGINALLY DENIED*. THEY'LL PROBABLY EVEN STAGE A REBEL--
*ARCHIVES IS AGAIN! — EDITOR.
ENOUGH!
--LION ?

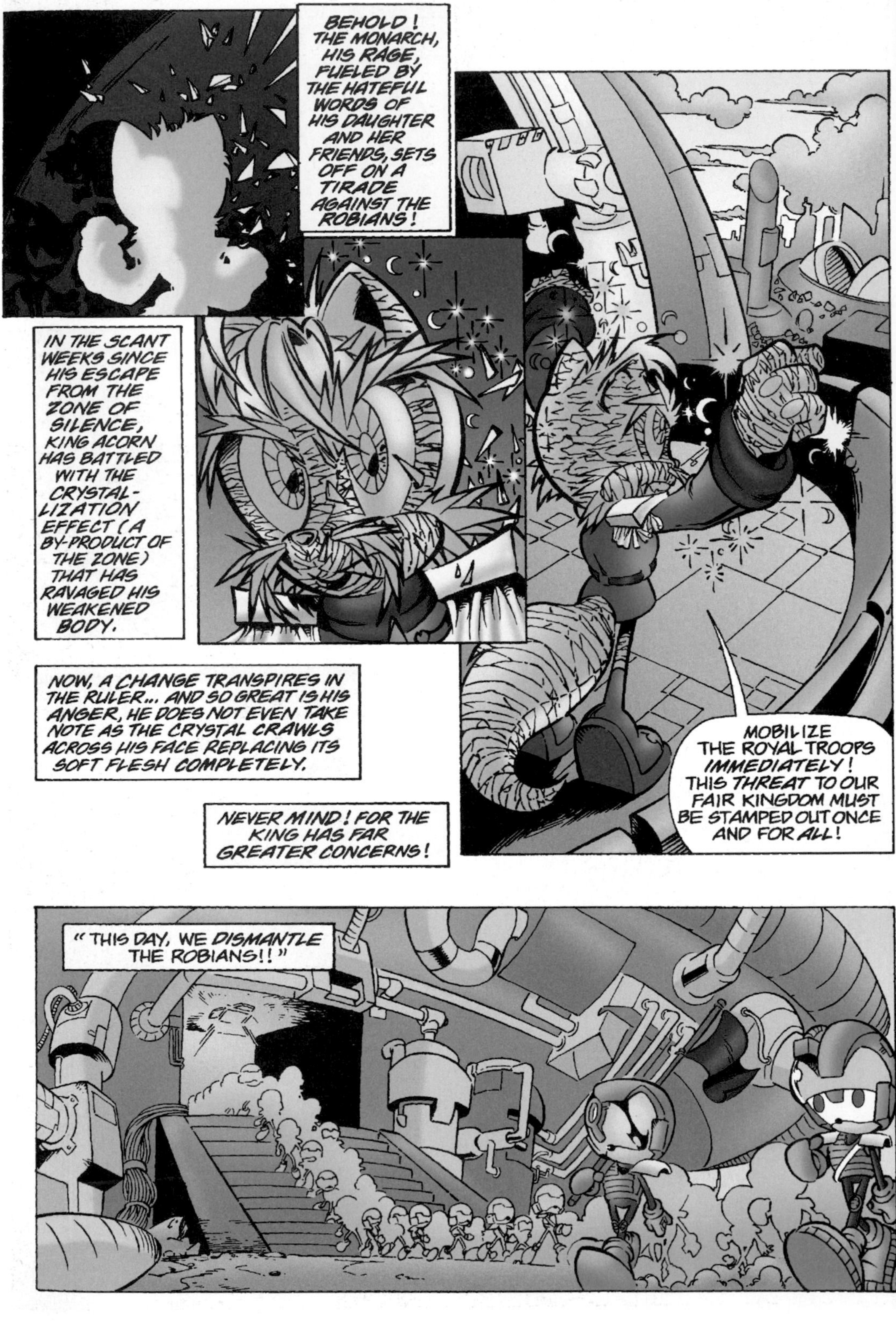
BEHOLD! THE MONARCH, HIS RAGE, FUELED BY THE HATEFUL WORDS OF HIS DAUGHTER AND HER FRIENDS, SETS OFF ON A TIRADE AGAINST THE ROBIANS!
IN THE SCANT WEEKS SINCE HIS ESCAPE FROM THE ZONE OF SILENCE, KING ACORN HAS BATTLED WITH THE CRYSTAL-LIZATION EFFECT (A BY-PRODUCT OF THE ZONE) THAT HAS RAVAGED HIS WEAKENED BODY.
NOW, A CHANGE TRANSPIRES IN THE RULER... AND SO GREAT IS HIS ANGER, HE DOES NOT EVEN TAKE NOTE AS THE CRYSTAL CRAWLS ACROSS HIS FACE REPLACING ITS SOFT FLESH COMPLETELY.
NEVER MIND! FOR THE KING HAS FAR GREATER CONCERNS!
MOBILIZE THE ROYAL TROOPS IMMEDIATELY! THIS THREAT TO OUR FAIR KINGDOM MUST BE STAMPED OUT ONCE AND FOR ALL!
"THIS DAY, WE DISMANTLE THE ROBIANS!!"

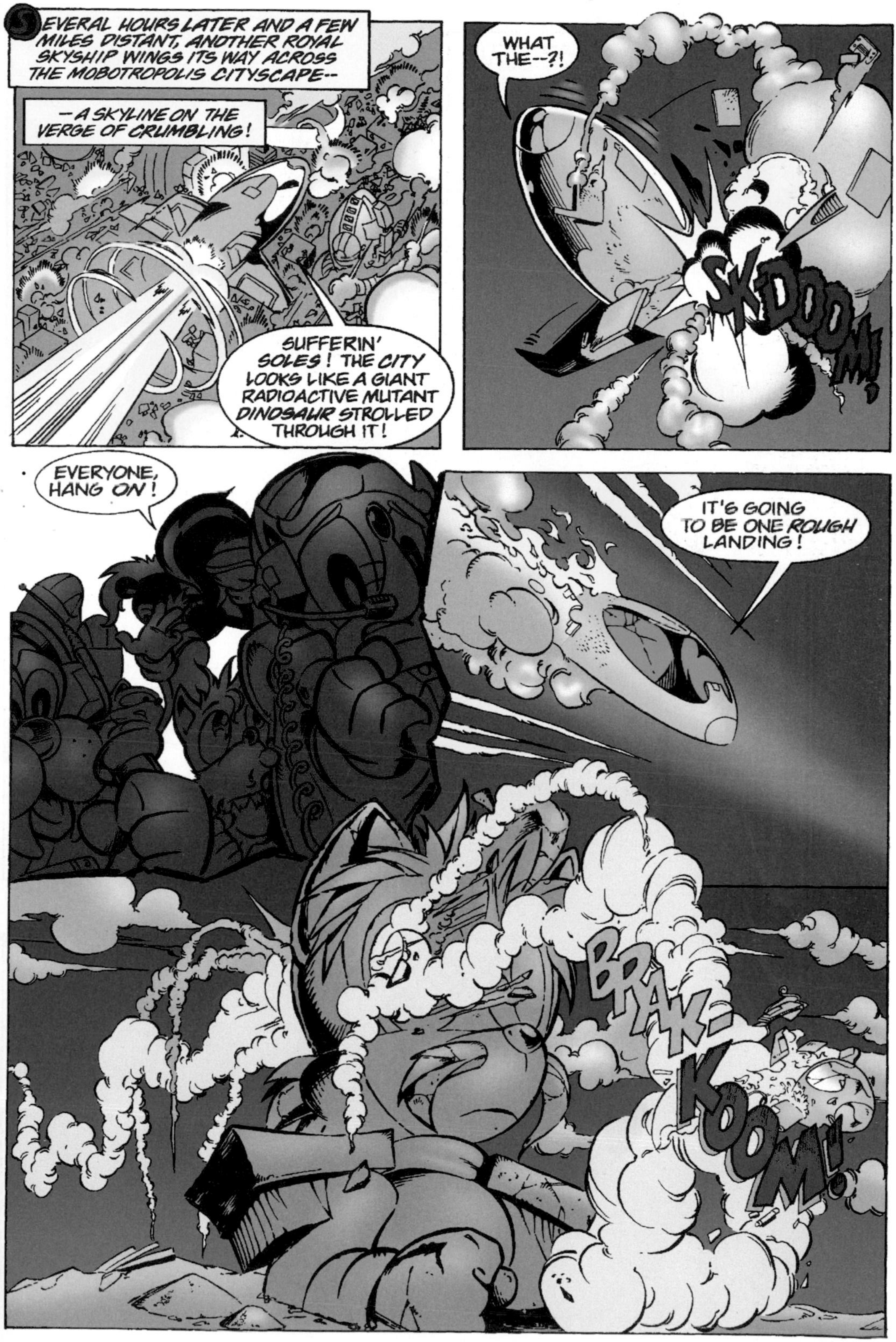
SEVERAL HOURS LATER AND A FEW MILES DISTANT, ANOTHER ROYAL SKYSHIP WINGS ITS WAY ACROSS THE MOBOTROPOLIS CITYSCAPE--
--A SKYLINE ON THE VERGE OF CRUMBLING!
SUFFERIN' SOLES! THE CITY LOOKS LIKE A GIANT RADIOACTIVE MUTANT DINOSAUR STROLLED THROUGH IT!
WHAT THE--?!
SKDOOM!
EVERYONE, HANG ON!
IT'S GOING TO BE ONE ROUGH LANDING!
BRAK-KOOM!

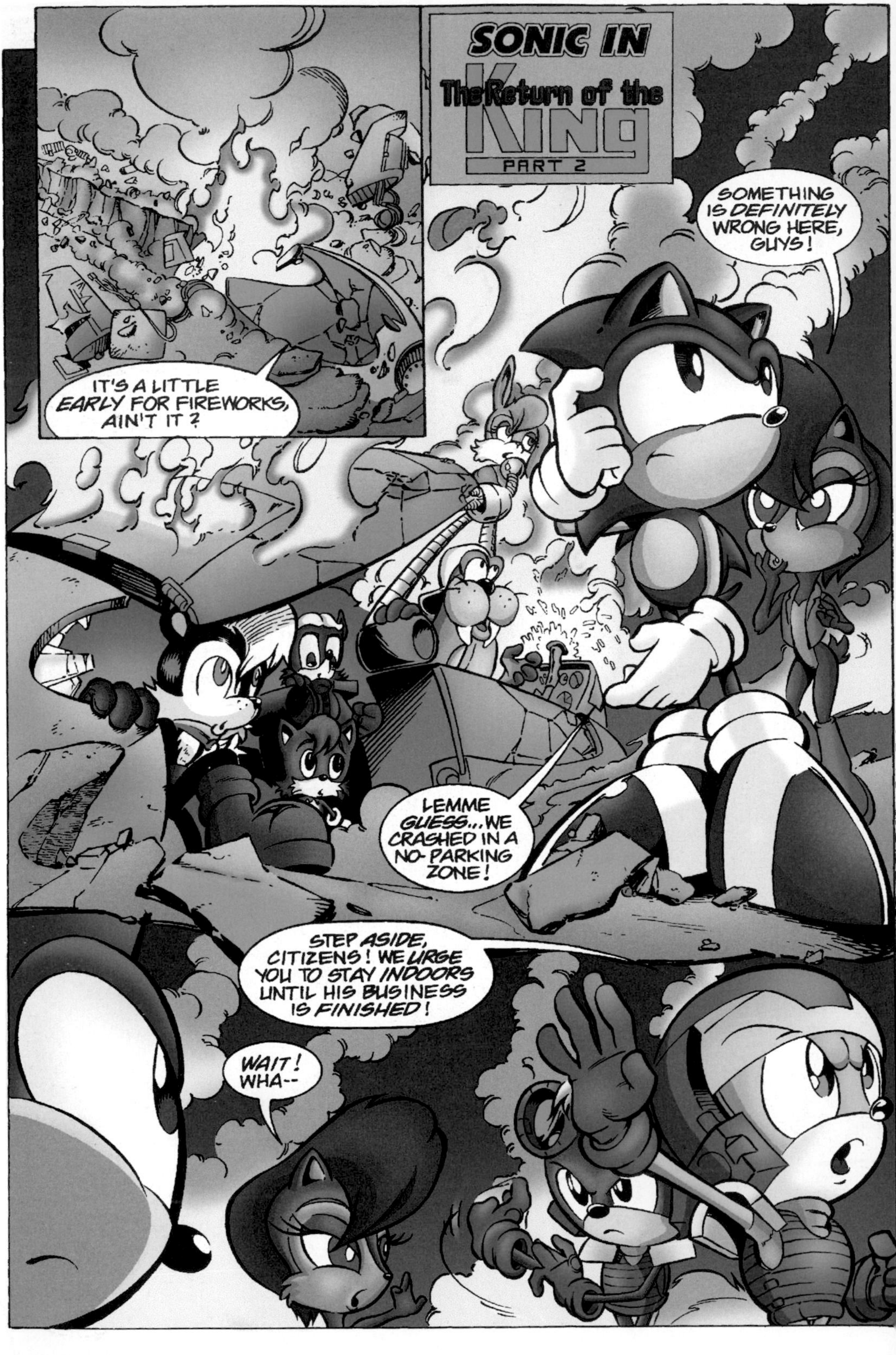
SONIC IN
The Return of the King
PART 2
IT'S A LITTLE EARLY FOR FIREWORKS, AIN'T IT?
SOMETHING IS DEFINITELY WRONG HERE, GUYS!
LEMME GUESS... WE CRASHED IN A NO-PARKING ZONE!
STEP ASIDE, CITIZENS! WE URGE YOU TO STAY INDOORS UNTIL HIS BUSINESS IS FINISHED!
WAIT! WHA--

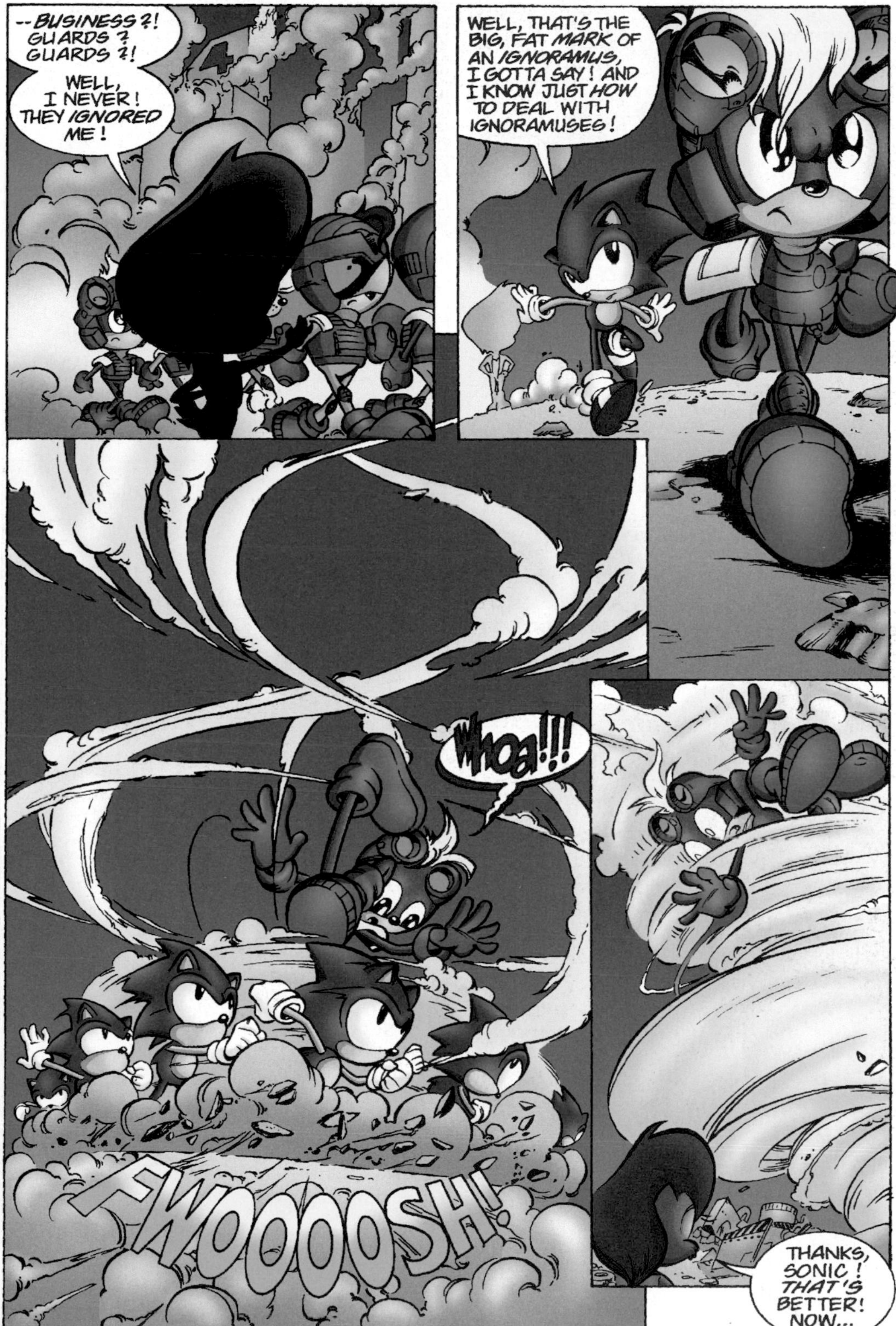
--BUSINESS?! GUARDS? GUARDS?!
WELL, I NEVER! THEY IGNORED ME!
WELL, THAT'S THE BIG, FAT MARK OF AN IGNORAMUS, I GOTTA SAY! AND I KNOW JUST HOW TO DEAL WITH IGNORAMUSES!
WHOA!!!
FWOOOOSH!
THANKS, SONIC! THAT'S BETTER! NOW...

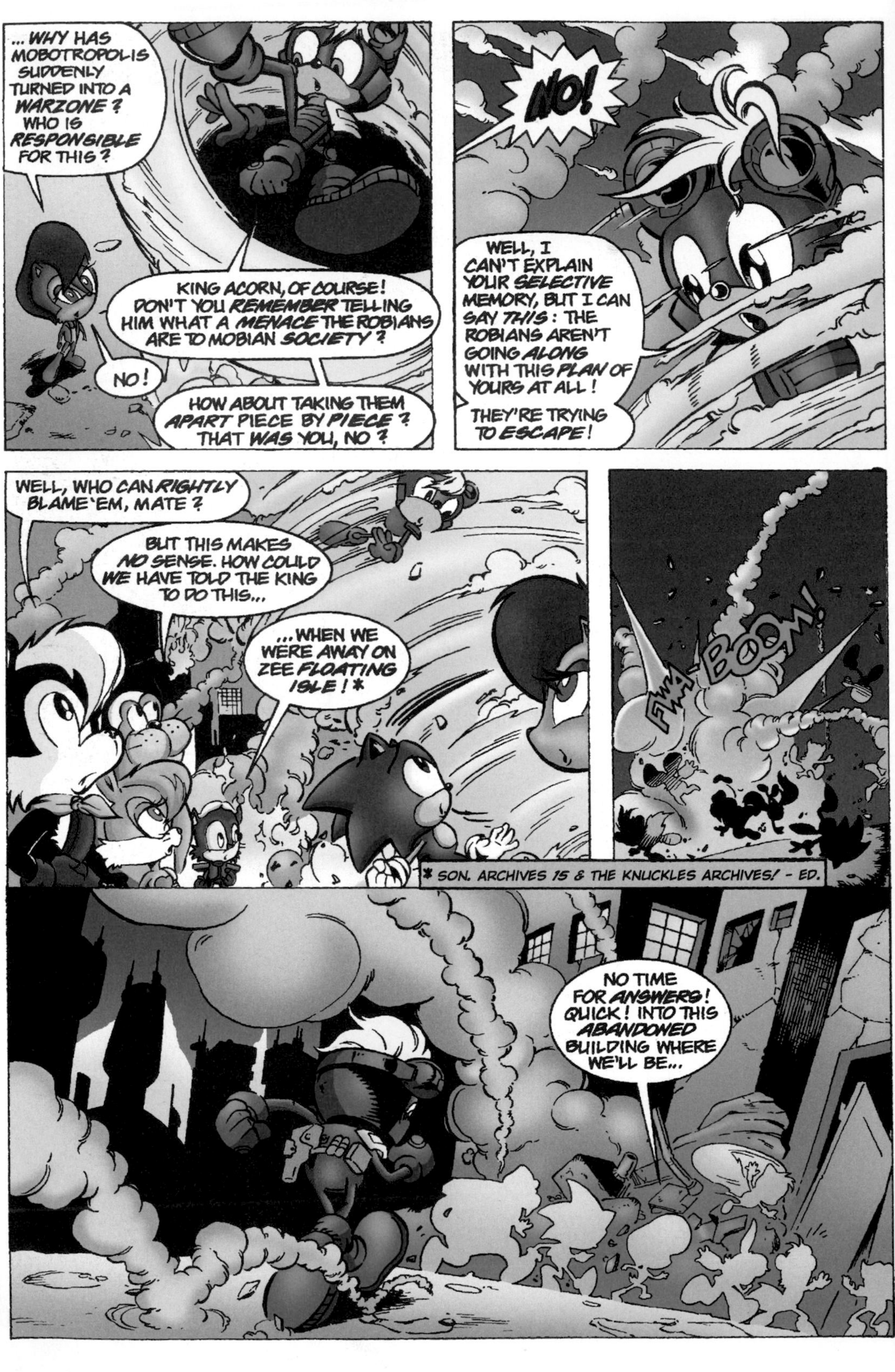
...WHY HAS MOBOTROPOLIS SUDDENLY TURNED INTO A WARZONE? WHO IS RESPONSIBLE FOR THIS?
KING ACORN, OF COURSE! DON'T YOU REMEMBER TELLING HIM WHAT A MENACE THE ROBIANS ARE TO MOBIAN SOCIETY?
NO!
HOW ABOUT TAKING THEM APART PIECE BY PIECE? THAT WAS YOU, NO?
NO!
WELL, I CAN'T EXPLAIN YOUR SELECTIVE MEMORY, BUT I CAN SAY THIS: THE ROBIANS AREN'T GOING ALONG WITH THIS PLAN OF YOURS AT ALL!
THEY'RE TRYING TO ESCAPE!
WELL, WHO CAN RIGHTLY BLAME 'EM, MATE?
BUT THIS MAKES NO SENSE. HOW COULD WE HAVE TOLD THE KING TO DO THIS...
...WHEN WE WERE AWAY ON ZEE FLOATING ISLE! *
* SON. ARCHIVES 15 & THE KNUCKLES ARCHIVES! - ED.
FWA-BOOM!
NO TIME FOR ANSWERS! QUICK! INTO THIS ABANDONED BUILDING WHERE WE'LL BE...

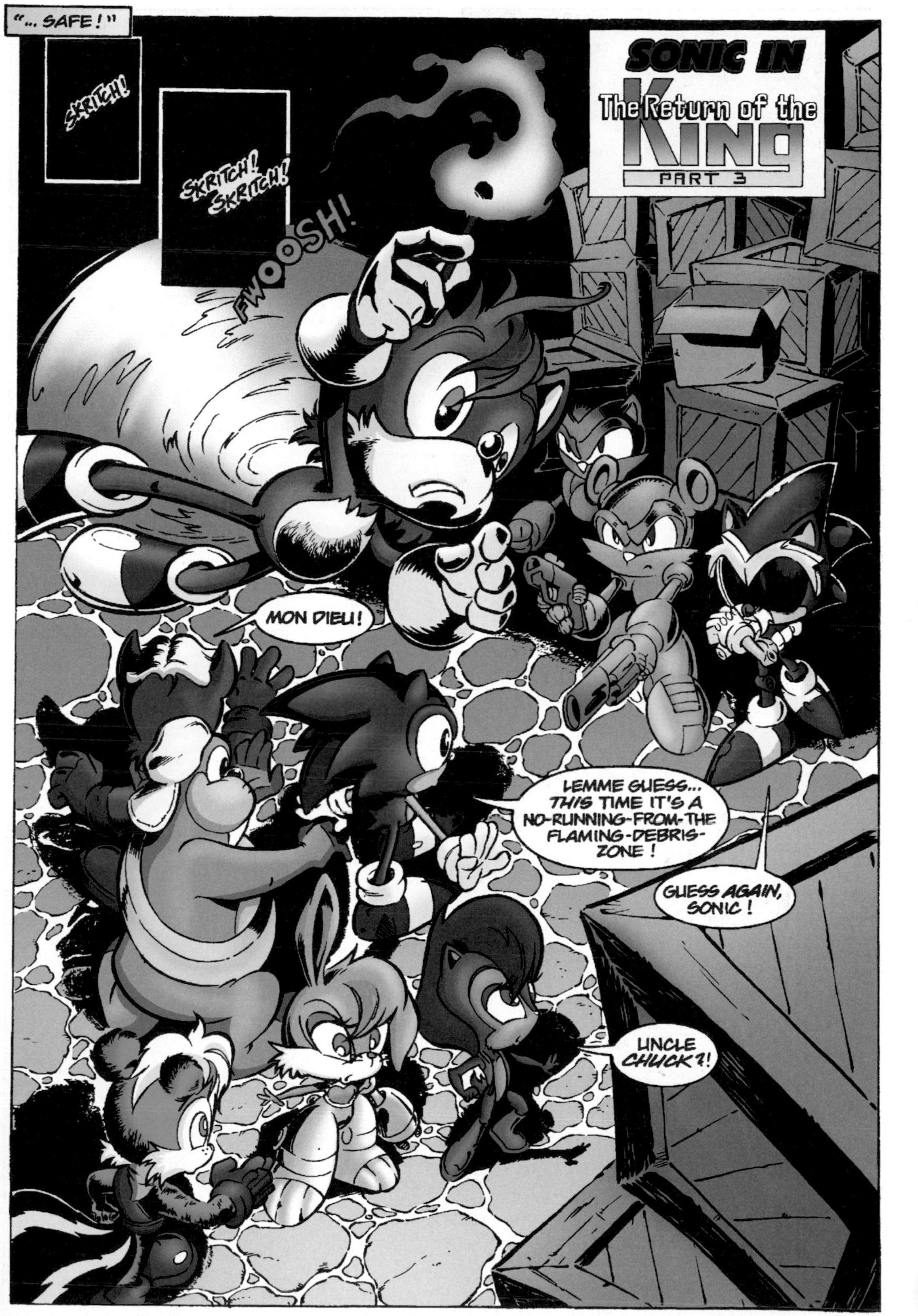
"... SAFE!"
SKRITCH!
SKRITCH! SKRITCH!
SONIC IN
The Return of the King
PART 3
FWOOSH!
MON DIEU!
LEMME GUESS... THIS TIME IT'S A NO-RUNNING-FROM-THE FLAMING-DEBRIS-ZONE!
GUESS AGAIN, SONIC!
UNCLE CHUCK?!

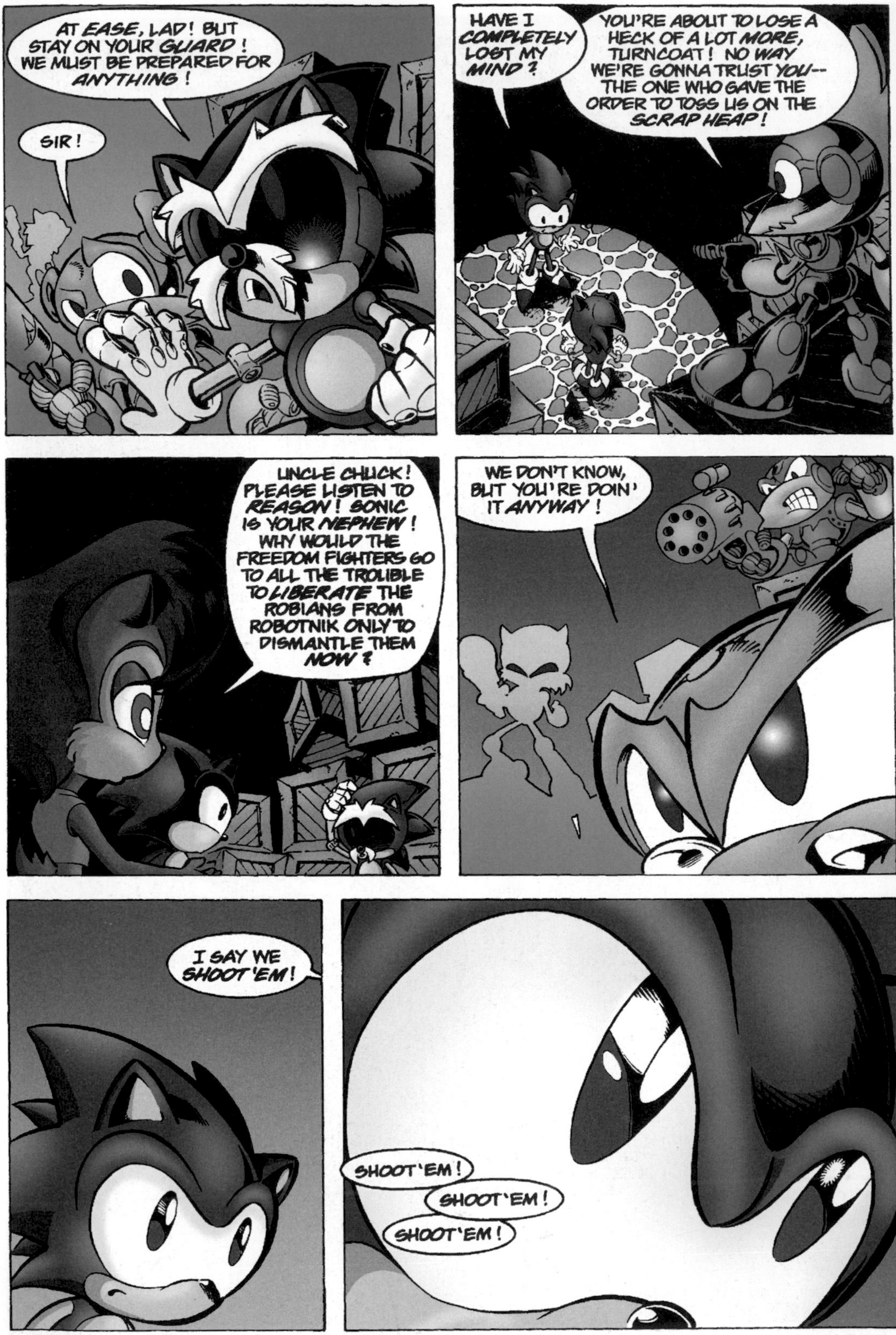
AT EASE, LAD! BUT STAY ON YOUR GUARD! WE MUST BE PREPARED FOR ANYTHING!
SIR!
HAVE I COMPLETELY LOST MY MIND?
YOU'RE ABOUT TO LOSE A HECK OF A LOT MORE, TURNCOAT! NO WAY WE'RE GONNA TRUST YOU-- THE ONE WHO GAVE THE ORDER TO TOSS US ON THE SCRAP HEAP!
UNCLE CHUCK! PLEASE LISTEN TO REASON! SONIC IS YOUR NEPHEW! WHY WOULD THE FREEDOM FIGHTERS GO TO ALL THE TROUBLE TO LIBERATE THE ROBIANS FROM ROBOTNIK ONLY TO DISMANTLE THEM NOW?
WE DON'T KNOW, BUT YOU'RE DOIN' IT ANYWAY!
I SAY WE SHOOT 'EM!
SHOOT 'EM!
SHOOT 'EM!
SHOOT 'EM!

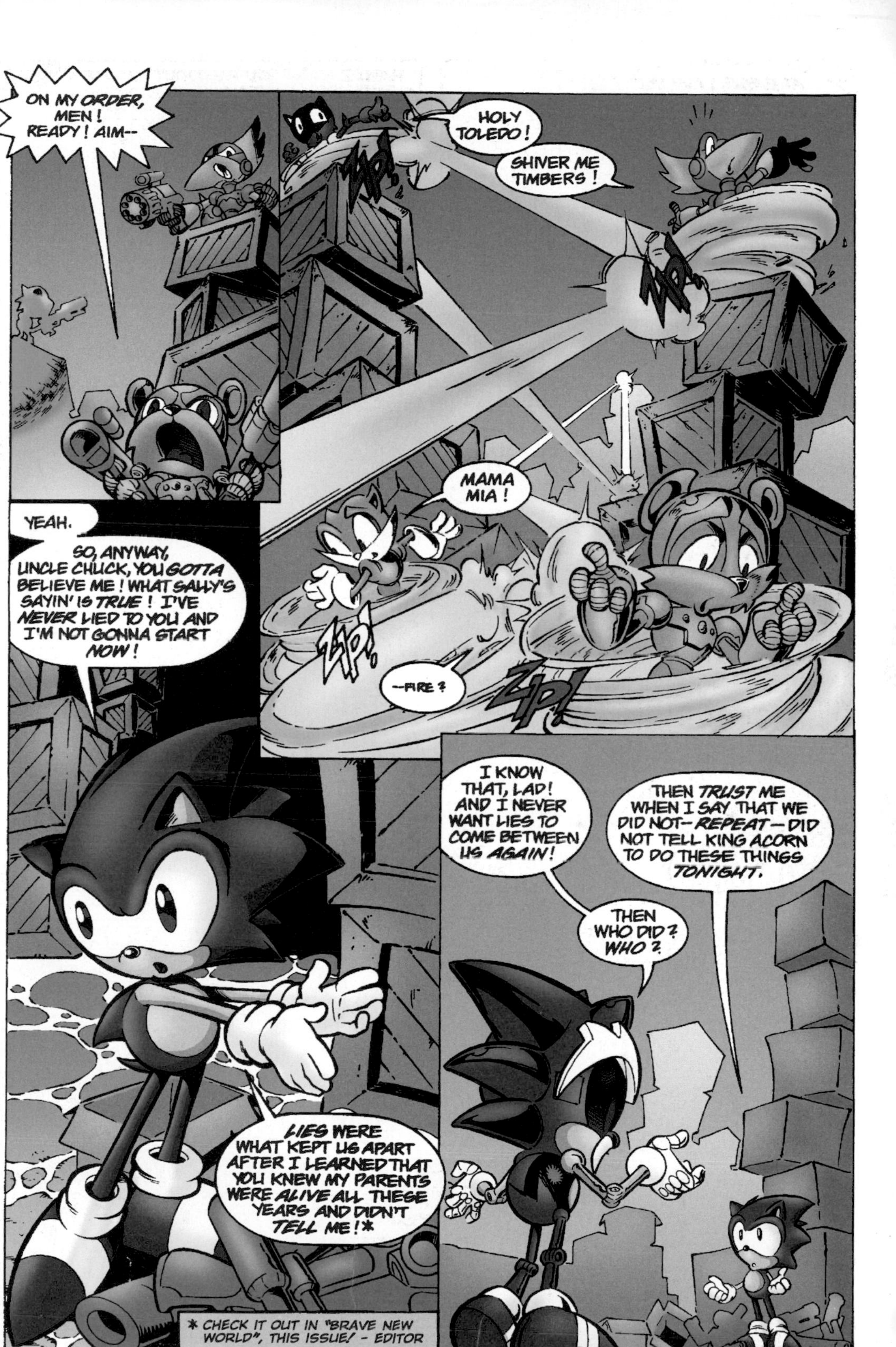
ON MY ORDER, MEN! READY! AIM--
HOLY TOLEDO!
SHIVER ME TIMBERS!
ZAP!
ZAP!
MAMA MIA!
ZAP!
--FIRE?
ZAP!
YEAH.
SO, ANYWAY, UNCLE CHUCK, YOU GOTTA BELIEVE ME! WHAT SALLY'S SAYIN' IS TRUE! I'VE NEVER LIED TO YOU AND I'M NOT GONNA START NOW!
LIES WERE WHAT KEPT US APART AFTER I LEARNED THAT YOU KNEW MY PARENTS WERE ALIVE ALL THESE YEARS AND DIDN'T TELL ME!*
* CHECK IT OUT IN "BRAVE NEW WORLD", THIS ISSUE! - EDITOR
I KNOW THAT, LAD! AND I NEVER WANT LIES TO COME BETWEEN US AGAIN!
THEN TRUST ME WHEN I SAY THAT WE DID NOT--REPEAT--DID NOT TELL KING ACORN TO DO THESE THINGS TONIGHT.
THEN WHO DID? WHO?

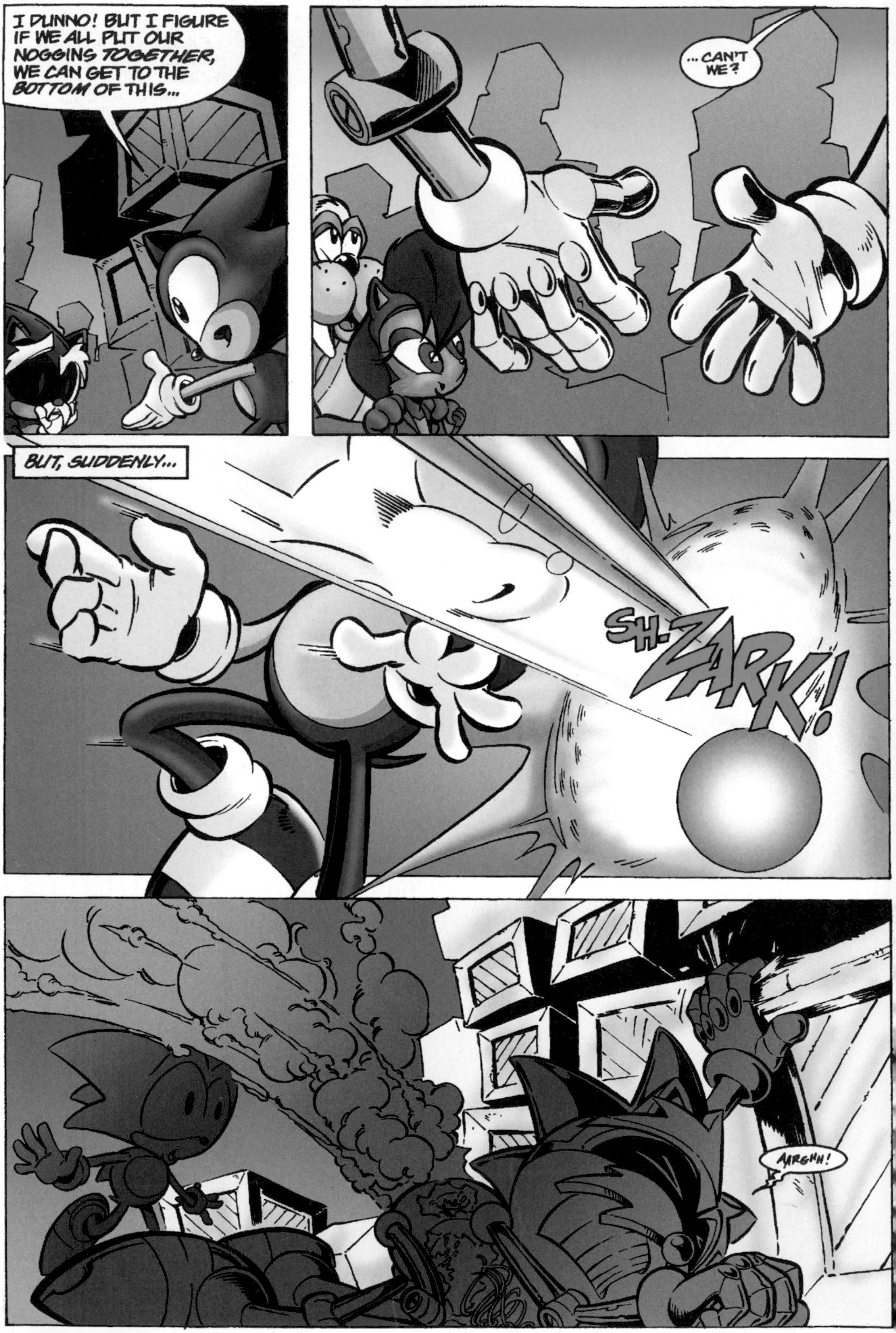
I DUNNO! BUT I FIGURE IF WE ALL PUT OUR NOGGINS TOGETHER, WE CAN GET TO THE BOTTOM OF THIS...
...CAN'T WE?
BUT, SUDDENLY...
SH-ZARK!
AARGHH!

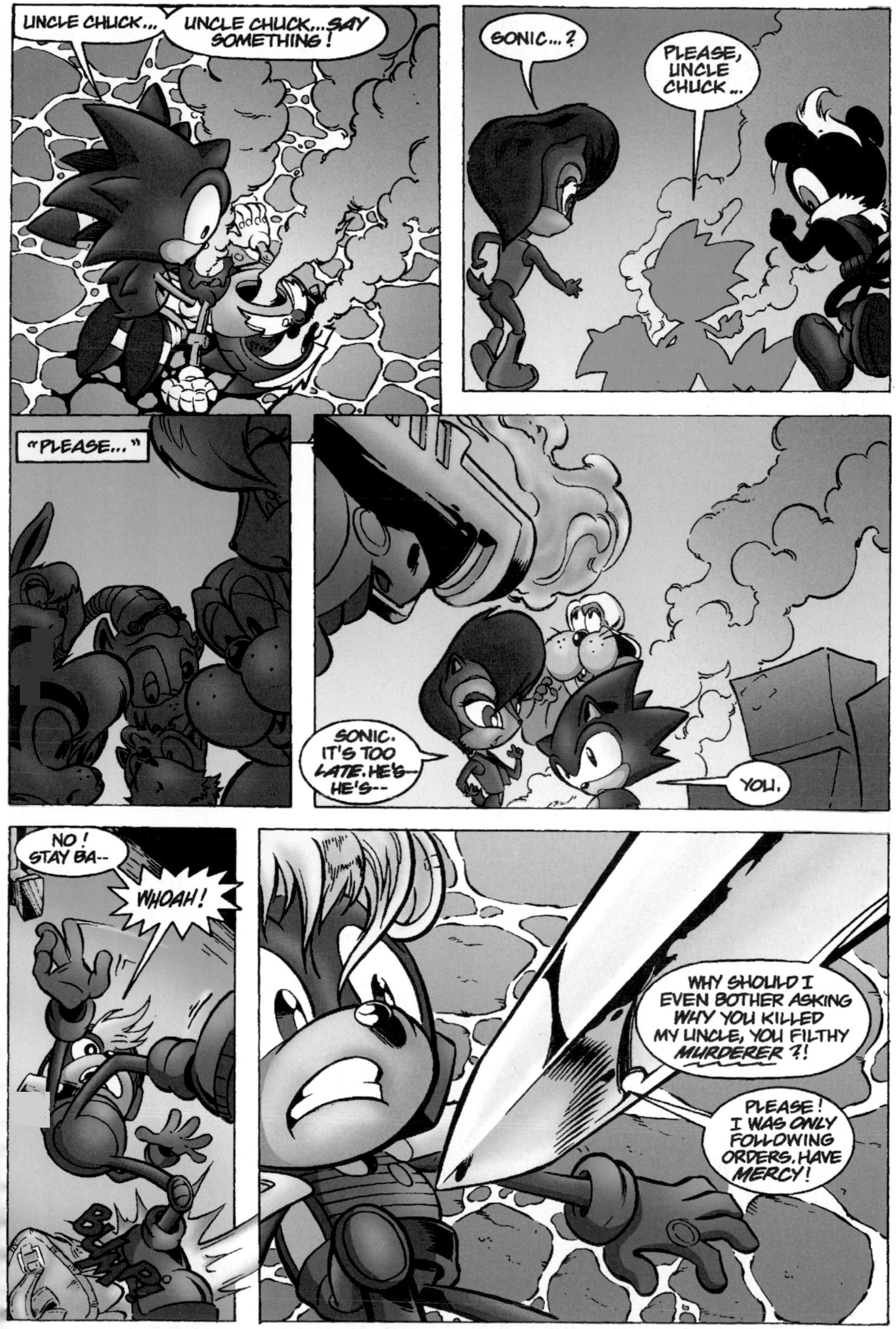
UNCLE CHUCK...
UNCLE CHUCK...SAY SOMETHING!
SONIC...?
PLEASE, UNCLE CHUCK...
"PLEASE..."
SONIC. IT'S TOO LATE. HE'S-- HE'S--
YOU.
NO! STAY BA--
WHOAH!
WHY SHOULD I EVEN BOTHER ASKING WHY YOU KILLED MY UNCLE, YOU FILTHY MURDERER ?!
PLEASE! I WAS ONLY FOLLOWING ORDERS. HAVE MERCY!

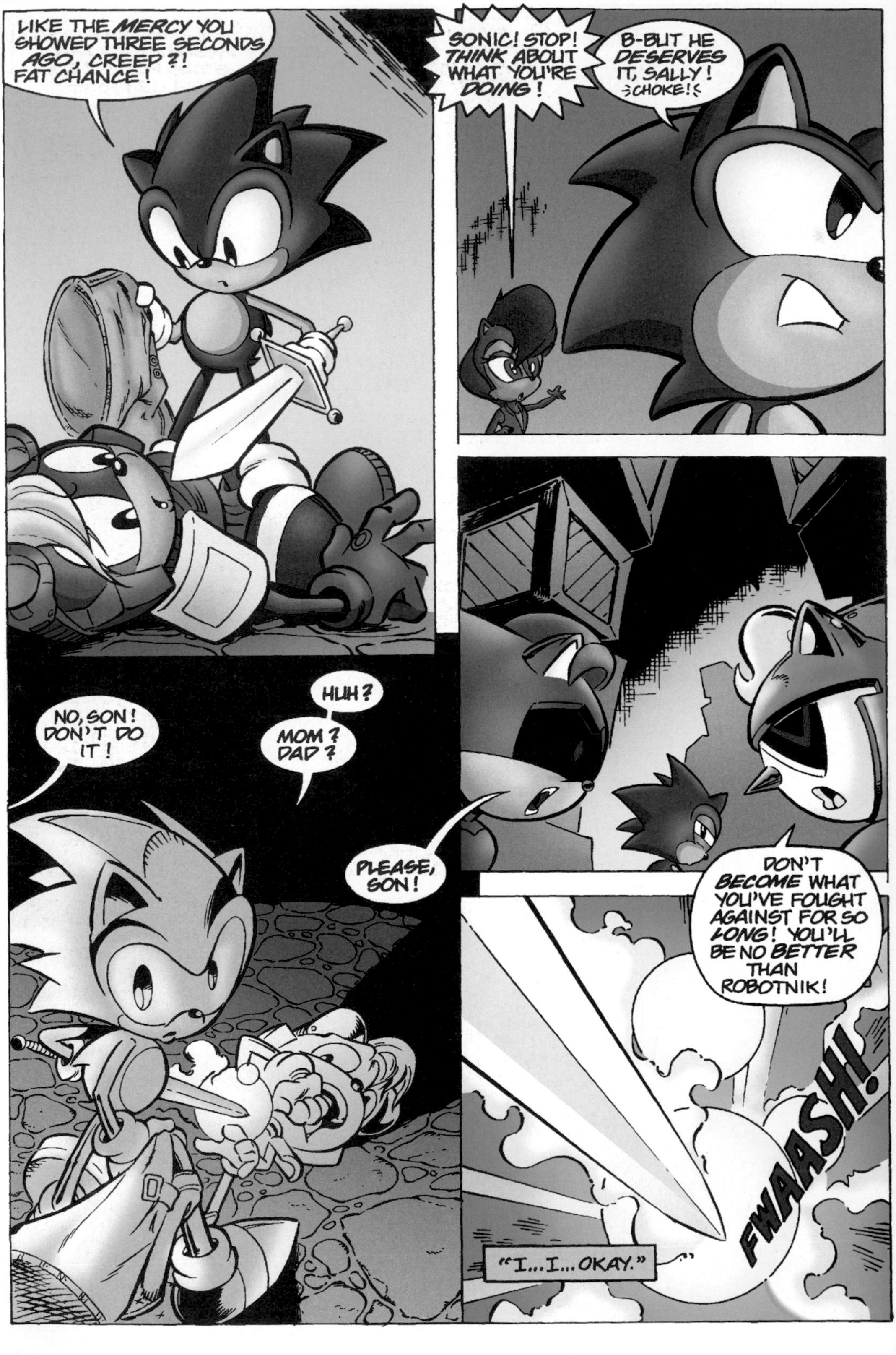
LIKE THE MERCY YOU SHOWED THREE SECONDS AGO, CREEP?! FAT CHANCE!
SONIC! STOP! THINK ABOUT WHAT YOU'RE DOING!
B-BUT HE DESERVES IT, SALLY! CHOKE!
NO, SON! DON'T DO IT!
HUH?
MOM? DAD?
PLEASE, SON!
DON'T BECOME WHAT YOU'VE FOUGHT AGAINST FOR SO LONG! YOU'LL BE NO BETTER THAN ROBOTNIK!
FWAASH!
"I...I...OKAY."

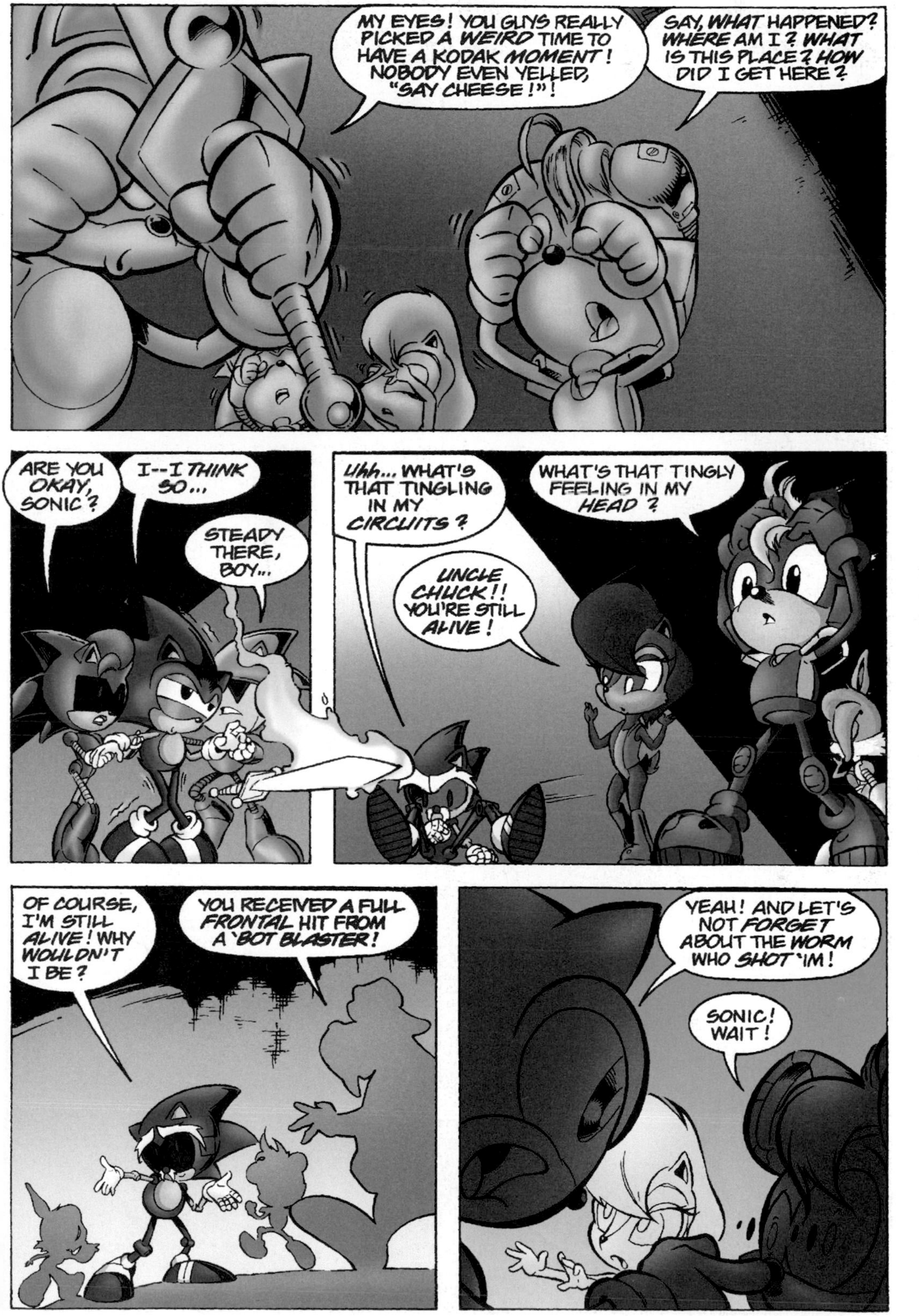

MY EYES! YOU GUYS REALLY PICKED A WEIRD TIME TO HAVE A KODAK MOMENT! NOBODY EVEN YELLED, "SAY CHEESE!"!
SAY, WHAT HAPPENED? WHERE AM I? WHAT IS THIS PLACE? HOW DID I GET HERE?
ARE YOU OKAY, SONIC?
I--I THINK SO...
STEADY THERE, BOY...
Uhh... WHAT'S THAT TINGLING IN MY CIRCUITS?
WHAT'S THAT TINGLY FEELING IN MY HEAD?
UNCLE CHUCK!! YOU'RE STILL ALIVE!
OF COURSE, I'M STILL ALIVE! WHY WOULDN'T I BE?
YOU RECEIVED A FULL FRONTAL HIT FROM A 'BOT BLASTER!
YEAH! AND LET'S NOT FORGET ABOUT THE WORM WHO SHOT 'IM!
SONIC! WAIT!

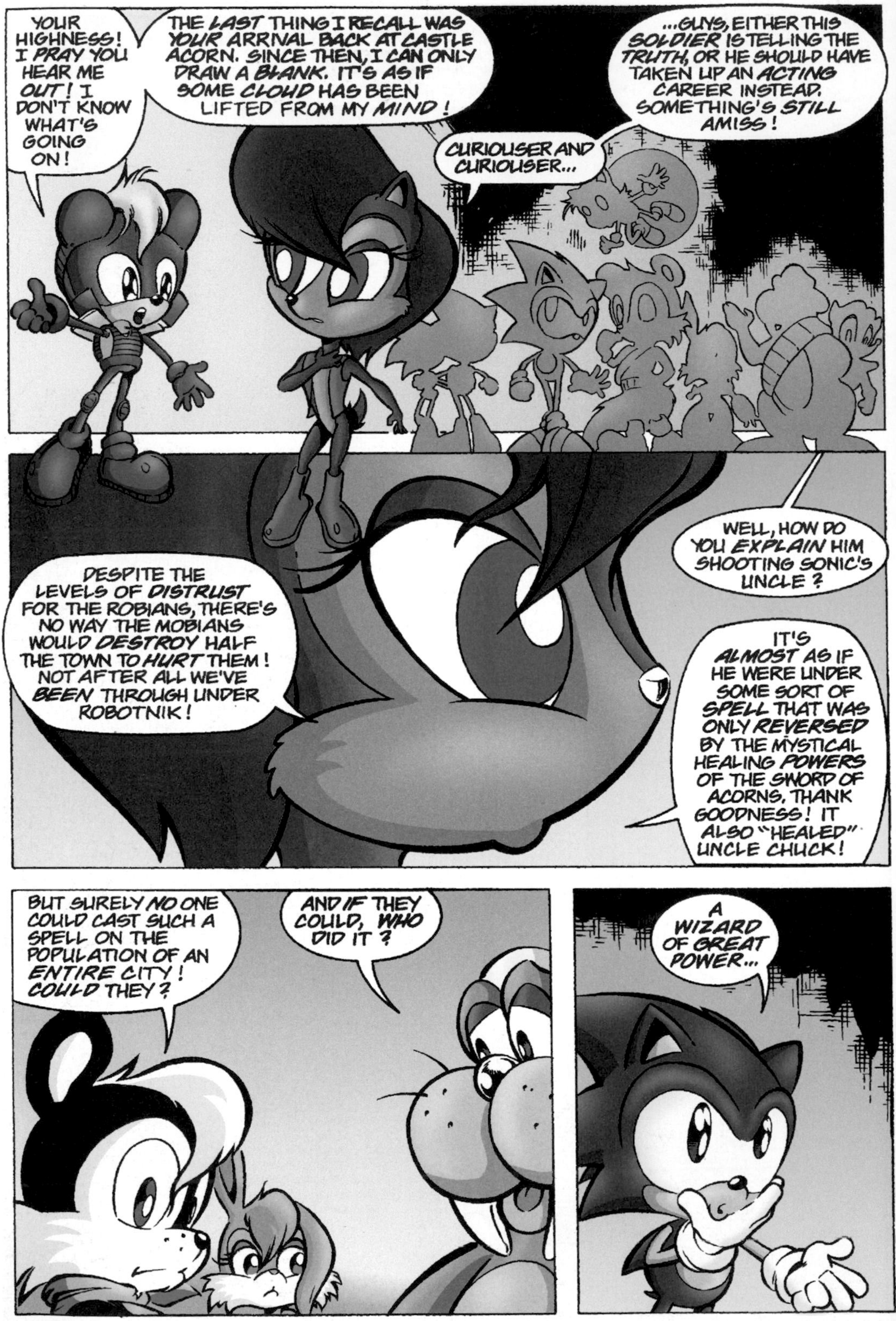
YOUR HIGHNESS! I PRAY YOU HEAR ME OUT! I DON'T KNOW WHAT'S GOING ON!
THE LAST THING I RECALL WAS YOUR ARRIVAL BACK AT CASTLE ACORN. SINCE THEN, I CAN ONLY DRAW A BLANK. IT'S AS IF SOME CLOUD HAS BEEN LIFTED FROM MY MIND!
CURIOUSER AND CURIOUSER...
...GUYS, EITHER THIS SOLDIER IS TELLING THE TRUTH, OR HE SHOULD HAVE TAKEN UP AN ACTING CAREER INSTEAD. SOMETHING'S STILL AMISS!
WELL, HOW DO YOU EXPLAIN HIM SHOOTING SONIC'S UNCLE?
DESPITE THE LEVELS OF DISTRUST FOR THE ROBIANS, THERE'S NO WAY THE MOBIANS WOULD DESTROY HALF THE TOWN TO HURT THEM! NOT AFTER ALL WE'VE BEEN THROUGH UNDER ROBOTNIK!
IT'S ALMOST AS IF HE WERE UNDER SOME SORT OF SPELL THAT WAS ONLY REVERSED BY THE MYSTICAL HEALING POWERS OF THE SWORD OF ACORNS. THANK GOODNESS! IT ALSO "HEALED" UNCLE CHUCK!
BUT SURELY NO ONE COULD CAST SUCH A SPELL ON THE POPULATION OF AN ENTIRE CITY! COULD THEY?
AND IF THEY COULD, WHO DID IT?
A WIZARD OF GREAT POWER...

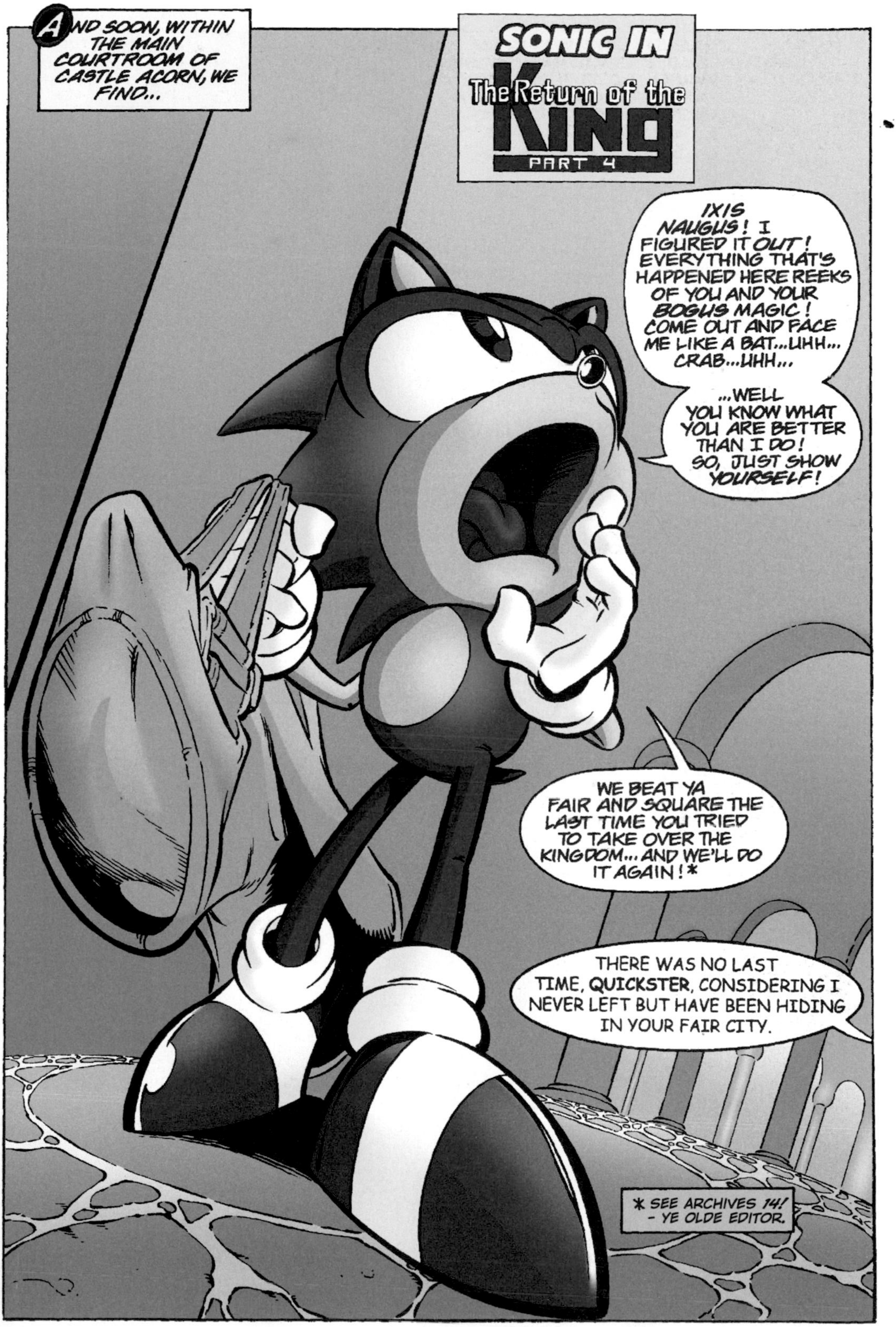
AND SOON, WITHIN THE MAIN COURTROOM OF CASTLE ACORN, WE FIND...
SONIC IN
The Return of the King
PART 4
IXIS NAUGUS! I FIGURED IT OUT! EVERYTHING THAT'S HAPPENED HERE REEKS OF YOU AND YOUR BOGUS MAGIC! COME OUT AND FACE ME LIKE A BAT...UHH... CRAB...UHH...
...WELL YOU KNOW WHAT YOU ARE BETTER THAN I DO! SO, JUST SHOW YOURSELF!
WE BEAT YA FAIR AND SQUARE THE LAST TIME YOU TRIED TO TAKE OVER THE KINGDOM... AND WE'LL DO IT AGAIN!*
THERE WAS NO LAST TIME, QUICKSTER, CONSIDERING I NEVER LEFT BUT HAVE BEEN HIDING IN YOUR FAIR CITY.
* SEE ARCHIVES 14! - YE OLDE EDITOR.

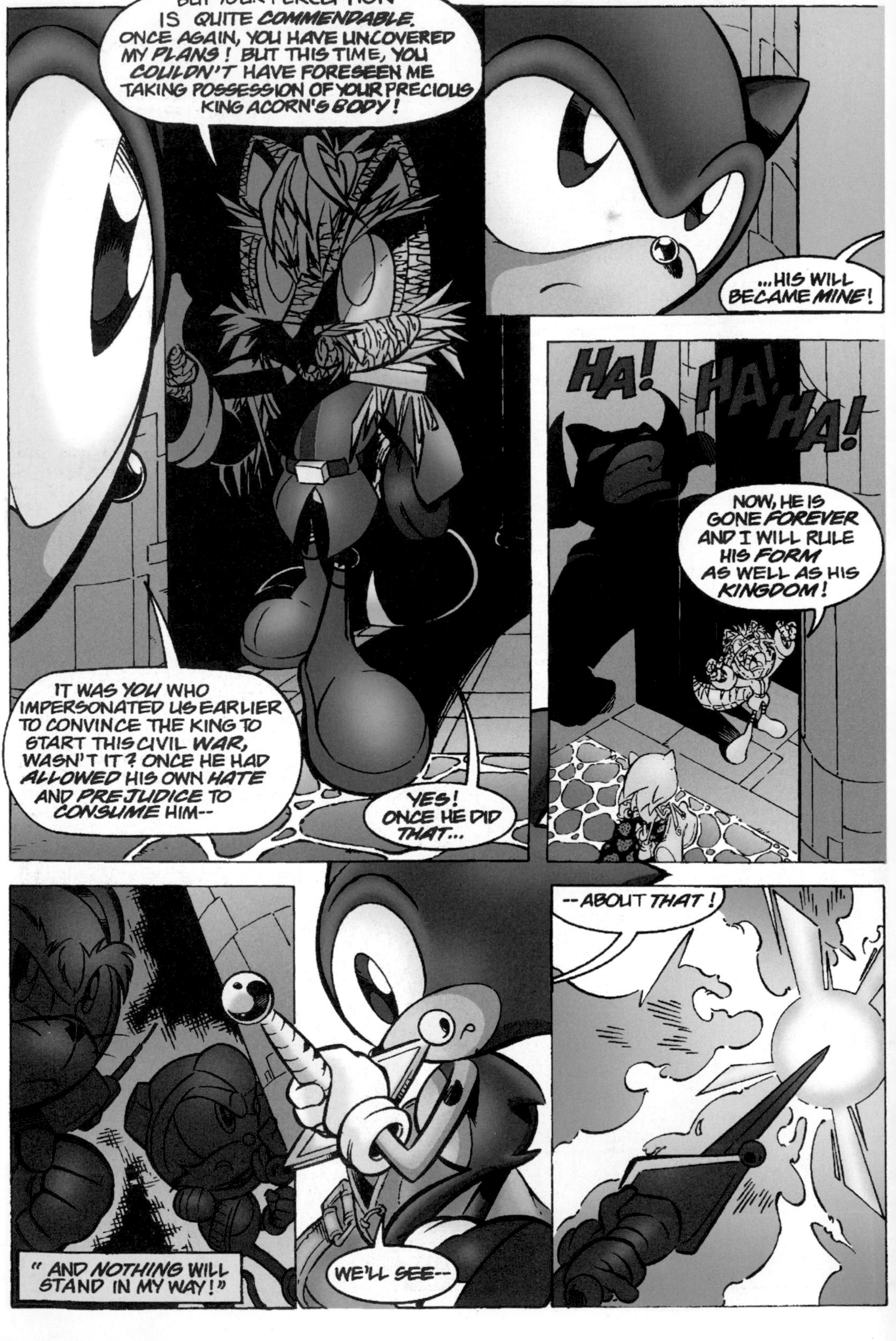

BUT YOUR PERCEPTION IS QUITE COMMENDABLE. ONCE AGAIN, YOU HAVE UNCOVERED MY PLANS! BUT THIS TIME, YOU COULDN'T HAVE FORESEEN ME TAKING POSSESSION OF YOUR PRECIOUS KING ACORN'S BODY!
IT WAS YOU WHO IMPERSONATED US EARLIER TO CONVINCE THE KING TO START THIS CIVIL WAR, WASN'T IT? ONCE HE HAD ALLOWED HIS OWN HATE AND PREJUDICE TO CONSUME HIM--
YES! ONCE HE DID THAT...
...HIS WILL BECAME MINE!
HA! HA! HA!
NOW, HE IS GONE FOREVER AND I WILL RULE HIS FORM AS WELL AS HIS KINGDOM!
" AND NOTHING WILL STAND IN MY WAY!"
WE'LL SEE--
--ABOUT THAT!

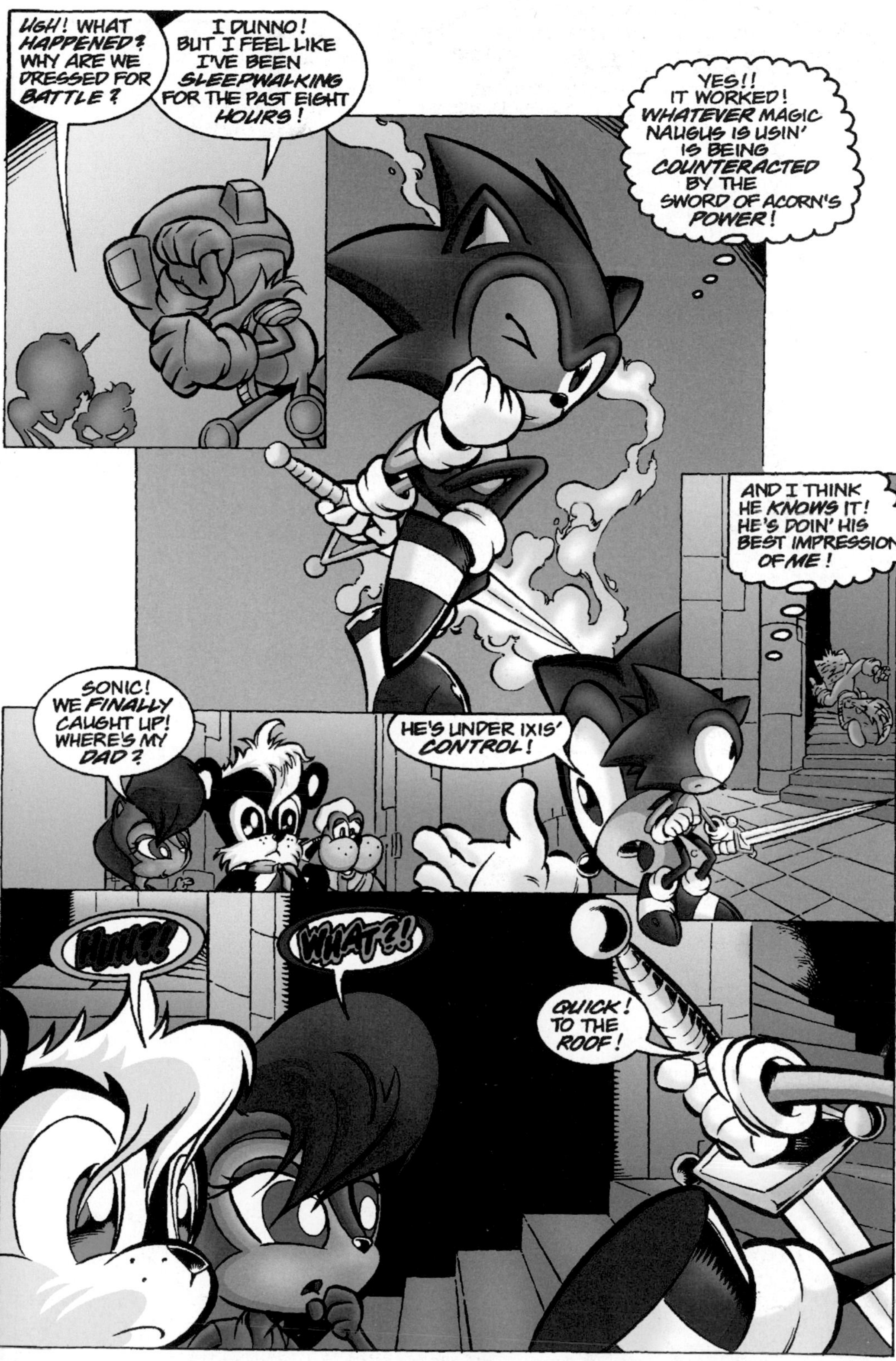

UGH! WHAT HAPPENED? WHY ARE WE DRESSED FOR BATTLE?
I DUNNO! BUT I FEEL LIKE I'VE BEEN SLEEPWALKING FOR THE PAST EIGHT HOURS!
YES!! IT WORKED! WHATEVER MAGIC NAUGUS IS USIN' IS BEING COUNTERACTED BY THE SWORD OF ACORN'S POWER!
AND I THINK HE KNOWS IT! HE'S DOIN' HIS BEST IMPRESSION OF ME!
SONIC! WE FINALLY CAUGHT UP! WHERE'S MY DAD?
HE'S UNDER IXIS' CONTROL!
HUH?!
WHAT?!
QUICK! TO THE ROOF!

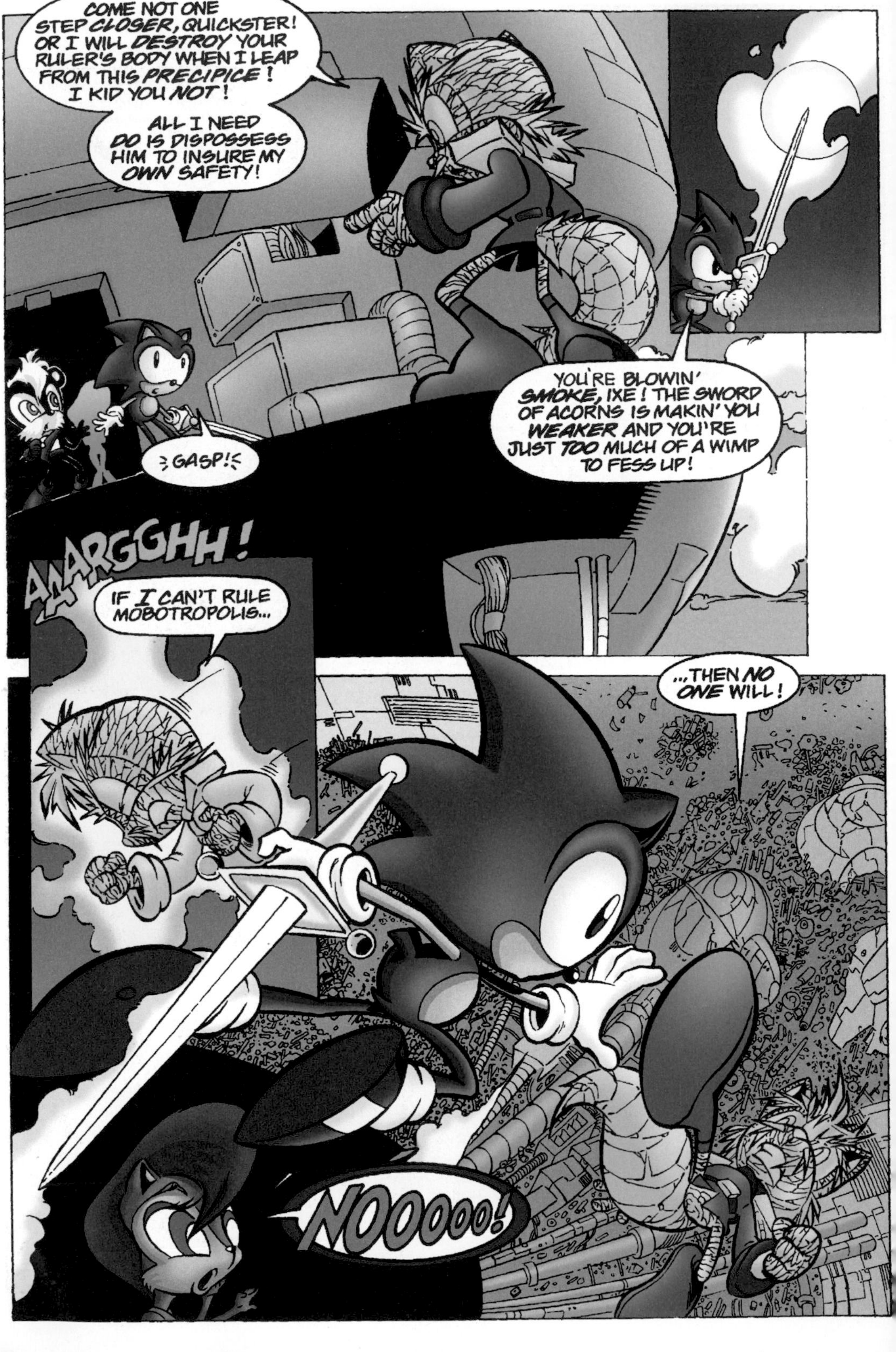
COME NOT ONE STEP CLOSER, QUICKSTER! OR I WILL DESTROY YOUR RULER'S BODY WHEN I LEAP FROM THIS PRECIPICE! I KID YOU NOT!
ALL I NEED DO IS DISPOSSESS HIM TO INSURE MY OWN SAFETY!
GASP!
YOU'RE BLOWIN' SMOKE, IXE! THE SWORD OF ACORNS IS MAKIN' YOU WEAKER AND YOU'RE JUST TOO MUCH OF A WIMP TO FESS UP!
AAARGGHH!
IF I CAN'T RULE MOBOTROPOLIS...
...THEN NO ONE WILL!
NOOOOO!

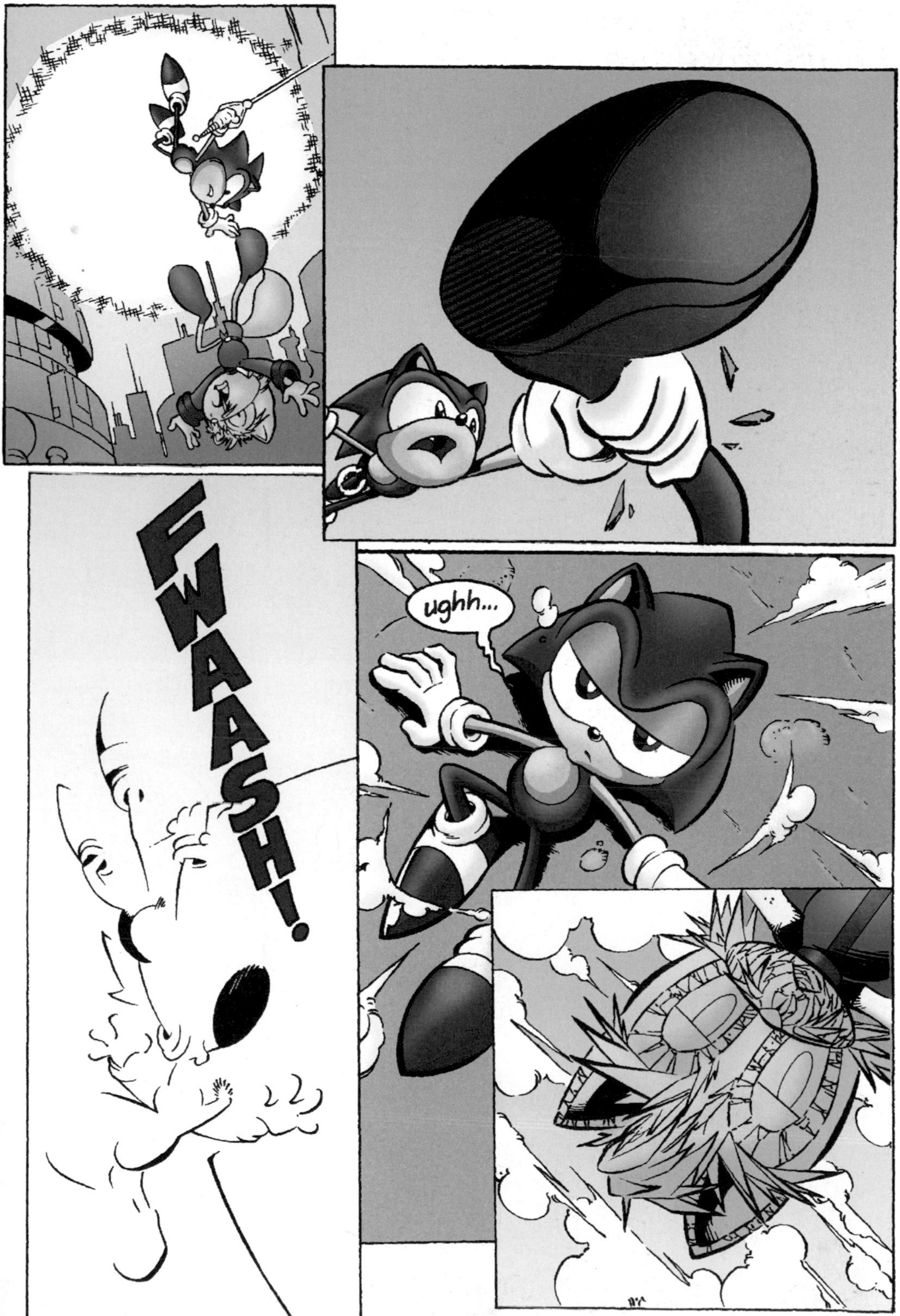
FWAASH!
ughh...

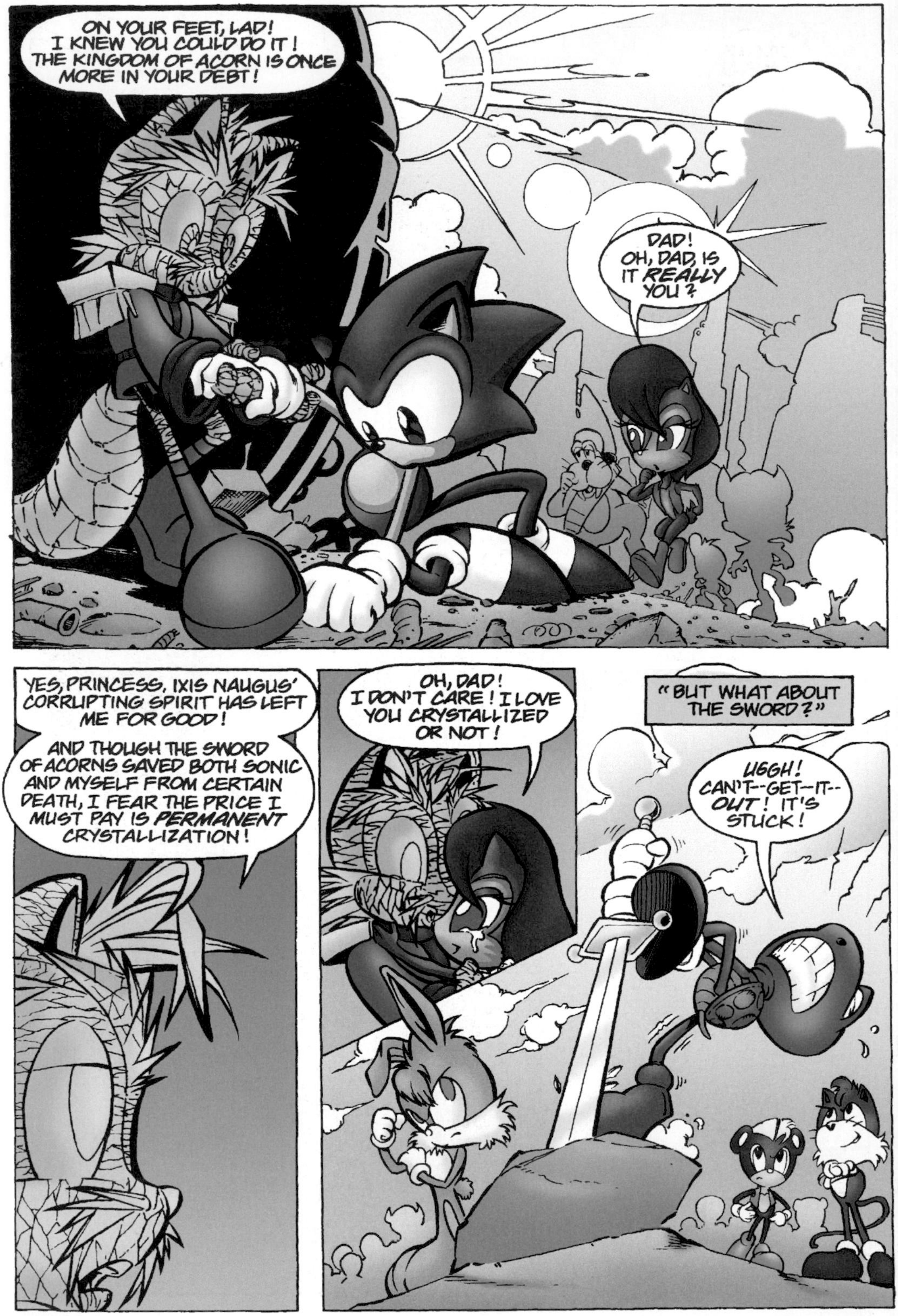
ON YOUR FEET, LAD! I KNEW YOU COULD DO IT! THE KINGDOM OF ACORN IS ONCE MORE IN YOUR DEBT!
DAD! OH, DAD, IS IT REALLY YOU?
YES, PRINCESS, IXIS NAUGUS' CORRUPTING SPIRIT HAS LEFT ME FOR GOOD!
AND THOUGH THE SWORD OF ACORNS SAVED BOTH SONIC AND MYSELF FROM CERTAIN DEATH, I FEAR THE PRICE I MUST PAY IS PERMANENT CRYSTALLIZATION!
OH, DAD! I DON'T CARE! I LOVE YOU CRYSTALLIZED OR NOT!
"BUT WHAT ABOUT THE SWORD?"
UGGH! CAN'T--GET--IT--OUT! IT'S STUCK!

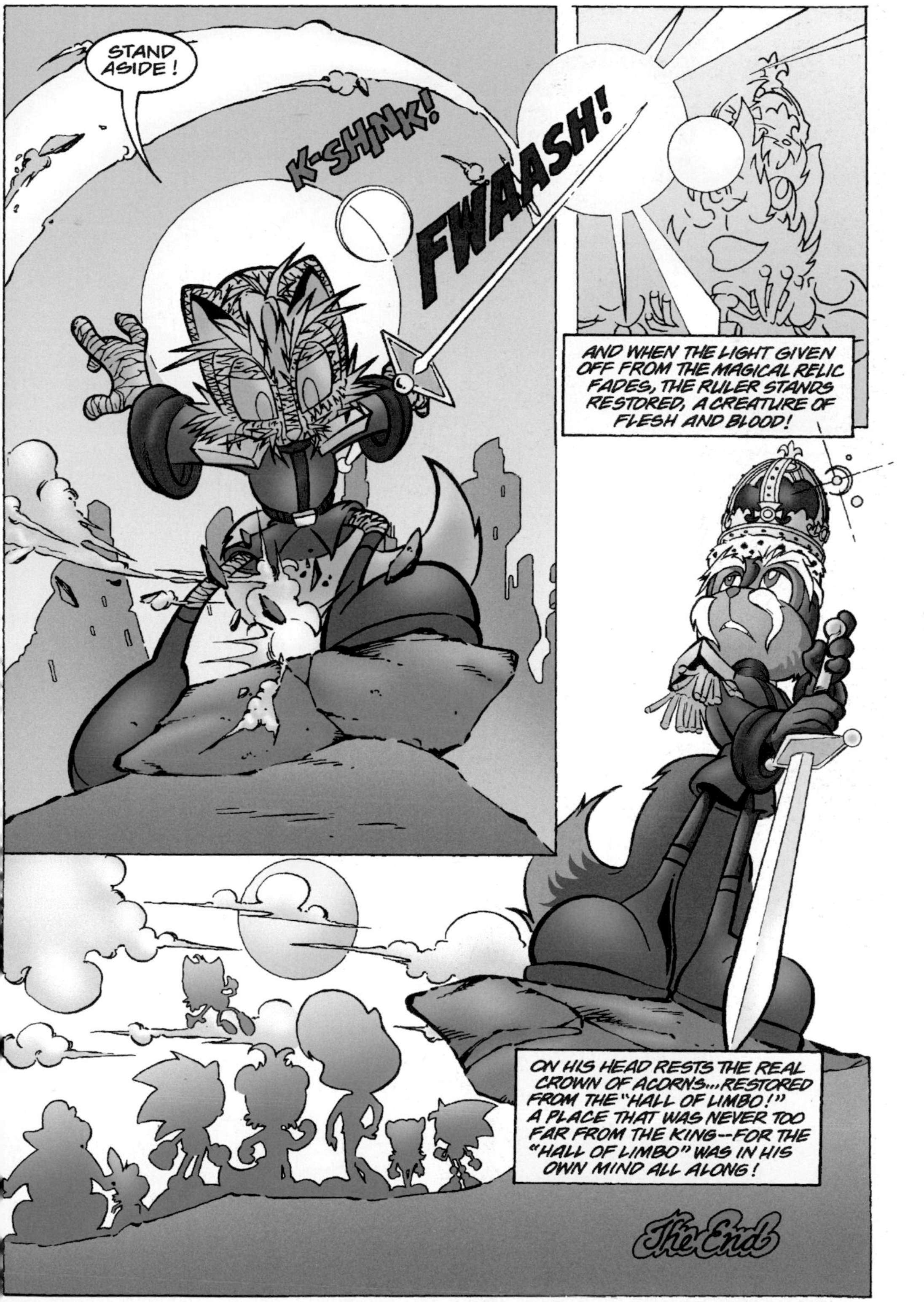
STAND ASIDE!
K-SHINK!
FWAASH!
AND WHEN THE LIGHT GIVEN OFF FROM THE MAGICAL RELIC FADES, THE RULER STANDS RESTORED, A CREATURE OF FLESH AND BLOOD!
ON HIS HEAD RESTS THE REAL CROWN OF ACORNS... RESTORED FROM THE "HALL OF LIMBO!" A PLACE THAT WAS NEVER TOO FAR FROM THE KING--FOR THE "HALL OF LIMBO" WAS IN HIS OWN MIND ALL ALONG!
The End

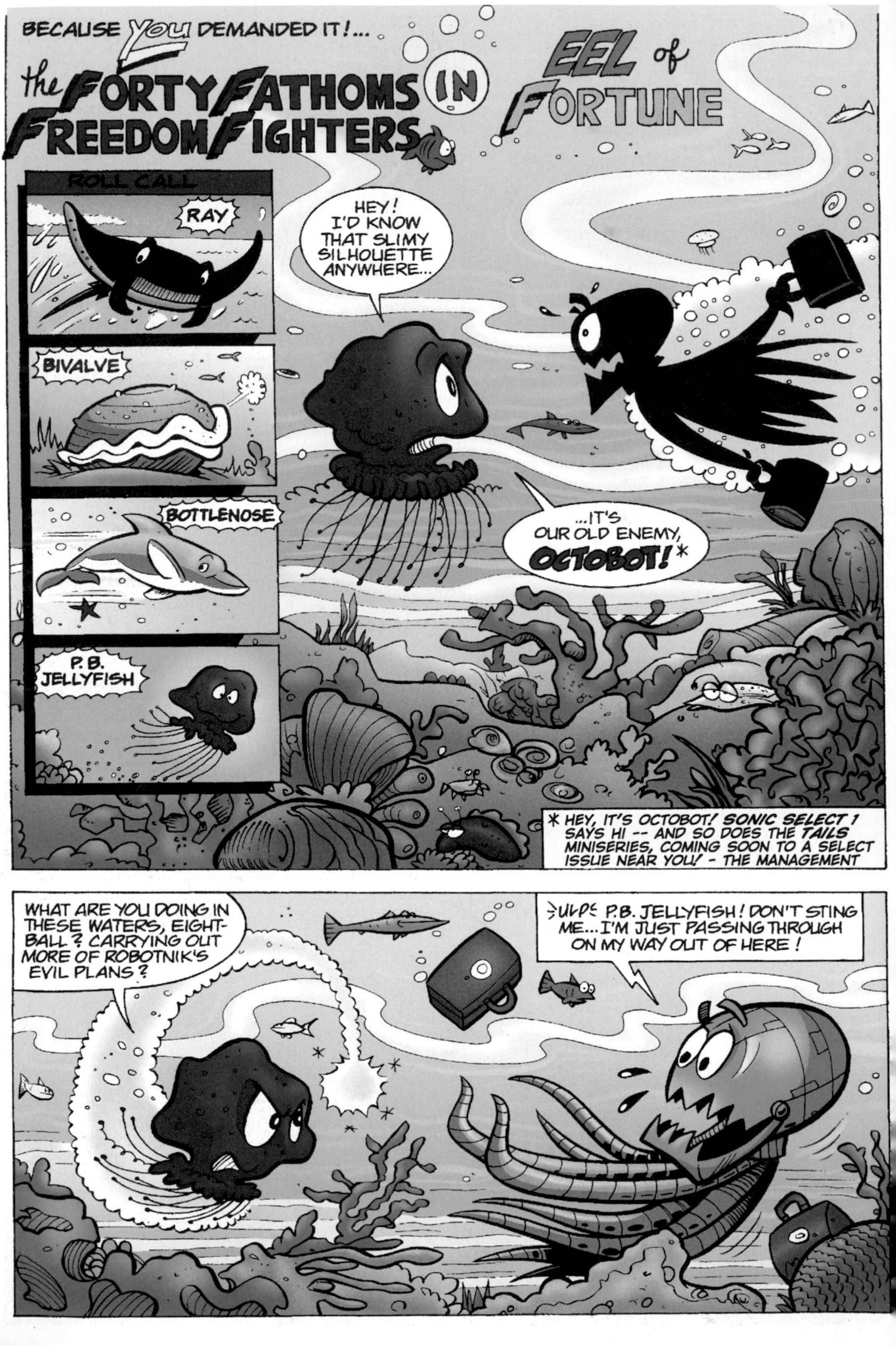
BECAUSE YOU DEMANDED IT!...
the FORTY FATHOMS FREEDOM FIGHTERS IN
EEL of FORTUNE
ROLL CALL
RAY
BIVALVE
BOTTLENOSE
P.B. JELLYFISH
HEY! I'D KNOW THAT SLIMY SILHOUETTE ANYWHERE...
...IT'S OUR OLD ENEMY, OCTOBOT!*
* HEY, IT'S OCTOBOT! SONIC SELECT 1 SAYS HI -- AND SO DOES THE TAILS MINISERIES, COMING SOON TO A SELECT ISSUE NEAR YOU! - THE MANAGEMENT
WHAT ARE YOU DOING IN THESE WATERS, EIGHT-BALL? CARRYING OUT MORE OF ROBOTNIK'S EVIL PLANS?
GULP! P.B. JELLYFISH! DON'T STING ME...I'M JUST PASSING THROUGH ON MY WAY OUT OF HERE!

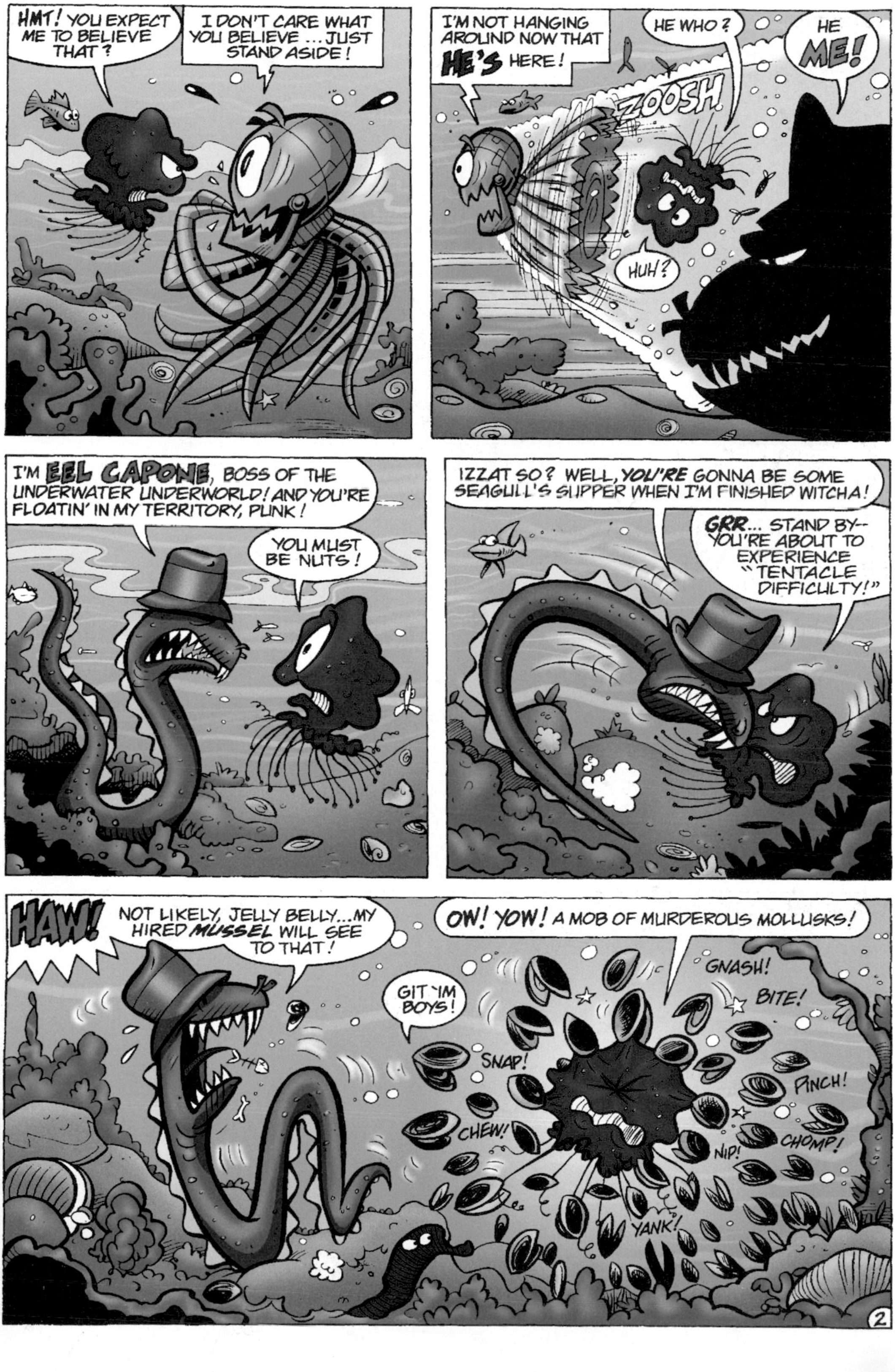
HMT! YOU EXPECT ME TO BELIEVE THAT?
I DON'T CARE WHAT YOU BELIEVE ... JUST STAND ASIDE!
I'M NOT HANGING AROUND NOW THAT HE'S HERE!
HE WHO?
HE ME!
ZOOSH
HUH?
I'M EEL CAPONE, BOSS OF THE UNDERWATER UNDERWORLD! AND YOU'RE FLOATIN' IN MY TERRITORY, PUNK!
YOU MUST BE NUTS!
IZZAT SO? WELL, YOU'RE GONNA BE SOME SEAGULL'S SUPPER WHEN I'M FINISHED WITCHA!
GRR... STAND BY-- YOU'RE ABOUT TO EXPERIENCE "TENTACLE DIFFICULTY!"
HAW!
NOT LIKELY, JELLY BELLY...MY HIRED MUSSEL WILL SEE TO THAT!
OW! YOW! A MOB OF MURDEROUS MOLLUSKS!
GIT 'IM BOYS!
GNASH!
BITE!
SNAP!
PINCH!
CHEW!
CHOMP!
NIP!
YANK!

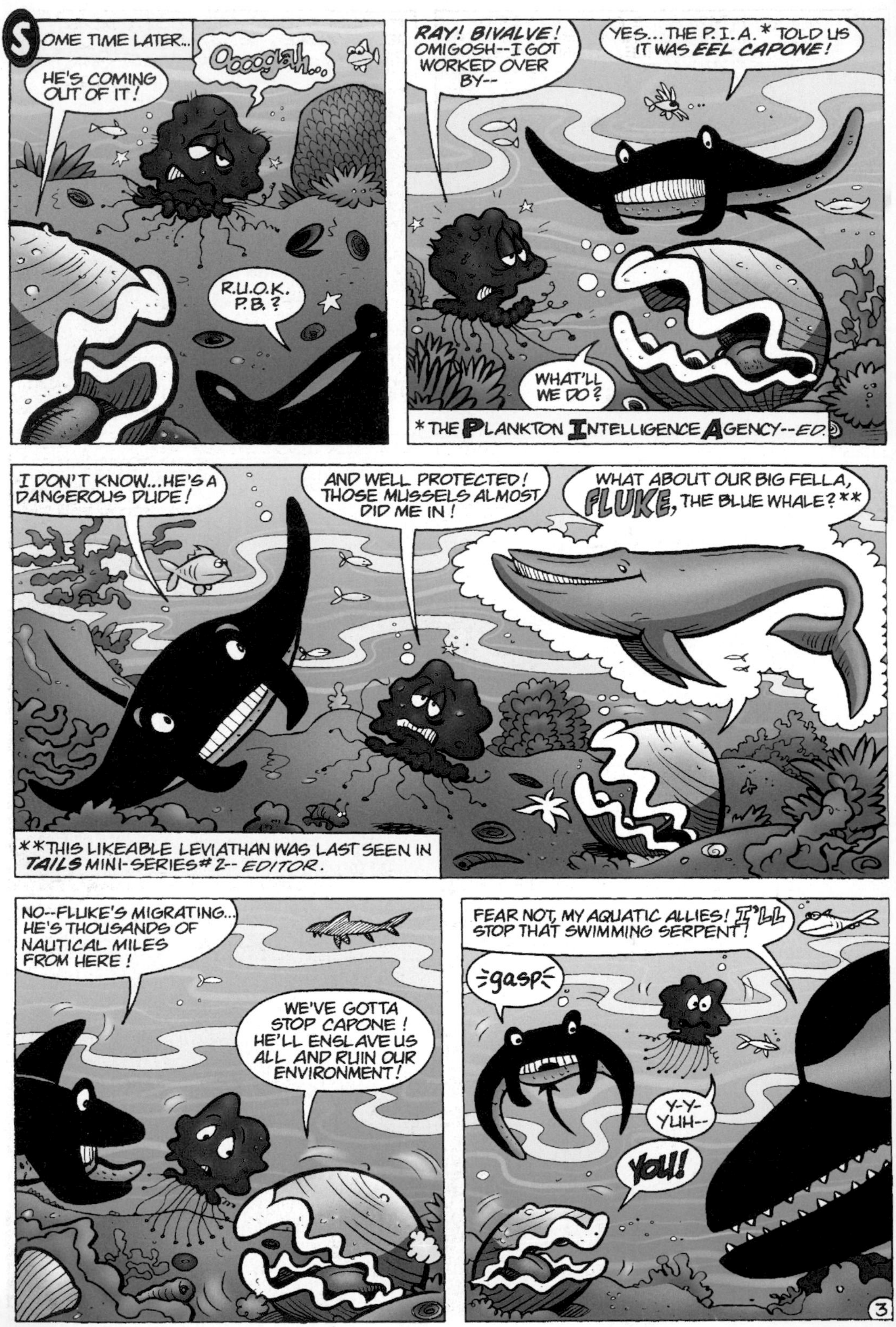
SOME TIME LATER...
Ooooglah...
HE'S COMING OUT OF IT!
R.U.O.K. P.B.?
RAY! BIVALVE! OMIGOSH--I GOT WORKED OVER BY--
YES...THE P.I.A.* TOLD US IT WAS EEL CAPONE!
WHAT'LL WE DO?
* THE PLANKTON INTELLIGENCE AGENCY--ED.
I DON'T KNOW...HE'S A DANGEROUS DUDE!
AND WELL PROTECTED! THOSE MUSSELS ALMOST DID ME IN!
WHAT ABOUT OUR BIG FELLA, FLUKE, THE BLUE WHALE?**
**THIS LIKEABLE LEVIATHAN WAS LAST SEEN IN TAILS MINI-SERIES #2-- EDITOR.
NO--FLUKE'S MIGRATING... HE'S THOUSANDS OF NAUTICAL MILES FROM HERE!
WE'VE GOTTA STOP CAPONE! HE'LL ENSLAVE US ALL AND RUIN OUR ENVIRONMENT!
FEAR NOT, MY AQUATIC ALLIES! I'LL STOP THAT SWIMMING SERPENT!
gasp
Y-Y-YUH--
YOU!
3

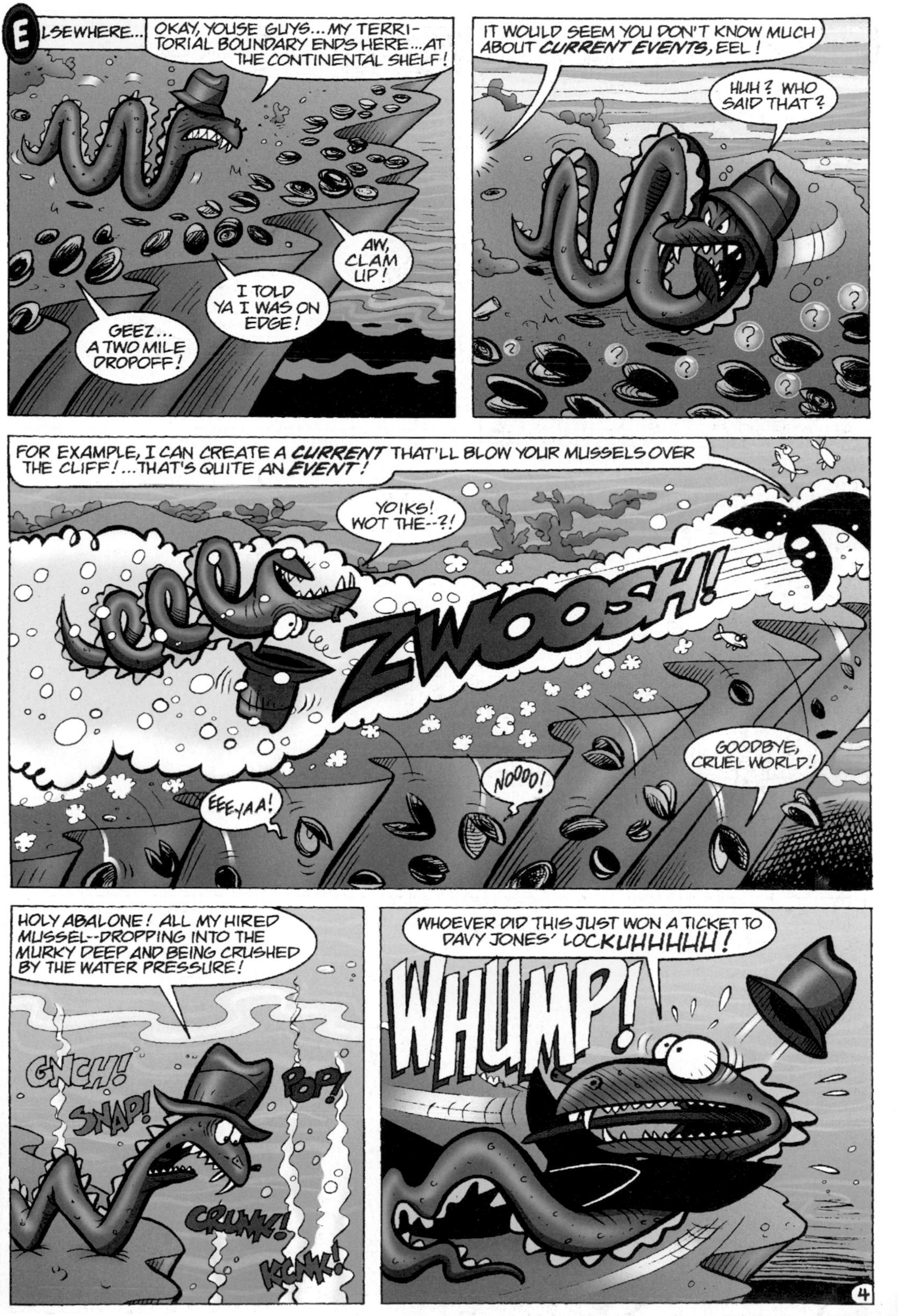
ELSEWHERE...
OKAY, YOUSE GUYS... MY TERRITORIAL BOUNDARY ENDS HERE... AT THE CONTINENTAL SHELF!
AW, CLAM UP!
I TOLD YA I WAS ON EDGE!
GEEZ... A TWO MILE DROPOFF!
IT WOULD SEEM YOU DON'T KNOW MUCH ABOUT CURRENT EVENTS, EEL!
HUH? WHO SAID THAT?
FOR EXAMPLE, I CAN CREATE A CURRENT THAT'LL BLOW YOUR MUSSELS OVER THE CLIFF! ...THAT'S QUITE AN EVENT!
YOIKS! WOT THE--?!
ZWOOSH!
GOODBYE, CRUEL WORLD!
NOOOO!
EEEYAA!
HOLY ABALONE! ALL MY HIRED MUSSEL--DROPPING INTO THE MURKY DEEP AND BEING CRUSHED BY THE WATER PRESSURE!
GNCH!
SNAP!
POP!
CRUNK!
KNK!
WHOEVER DID THIS JUST WON A TICKET TO DAVY JONES' LOCKUHHHHH!
WHUMP!

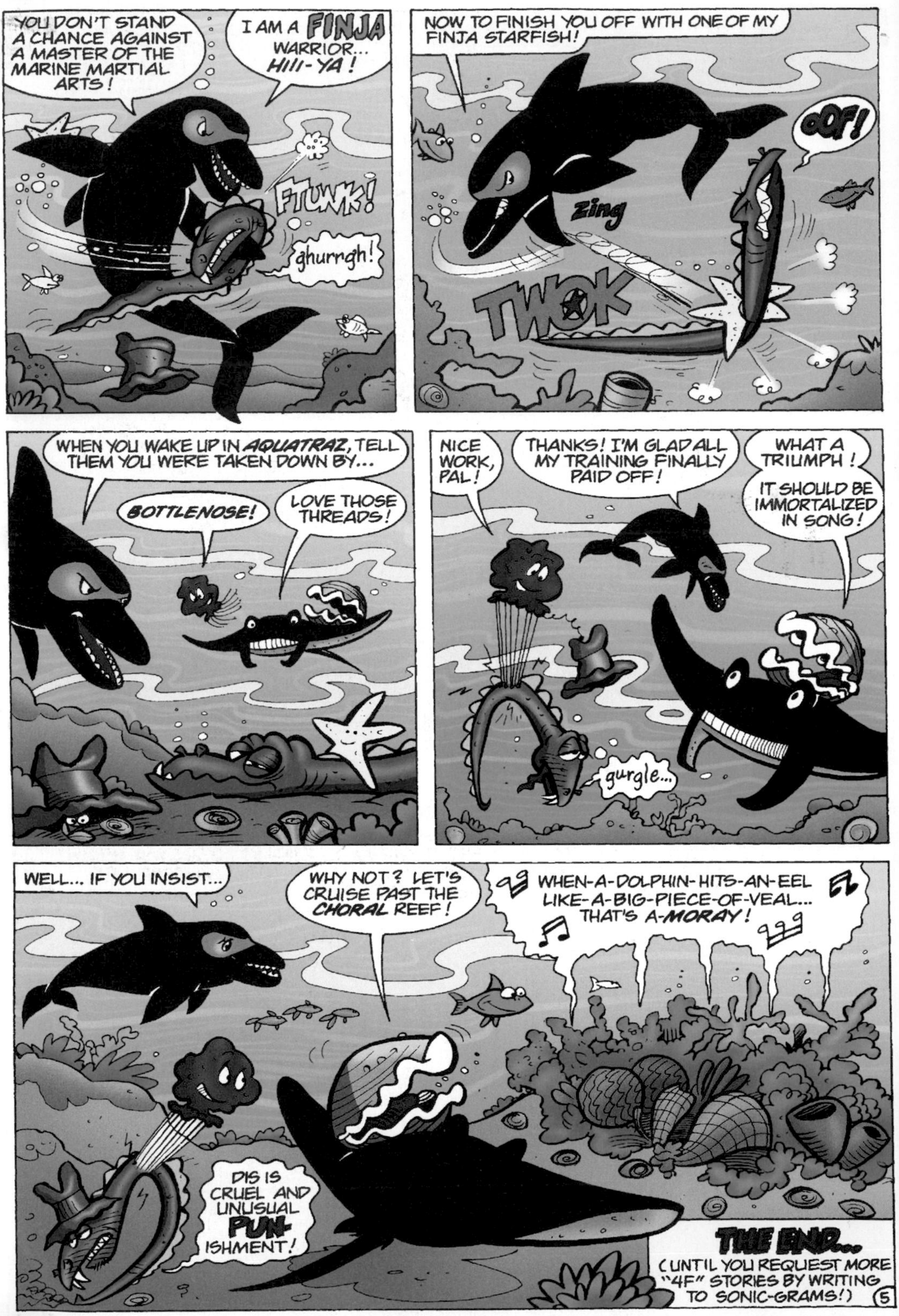
YOU DON'T STAND A CHANCE AGAINST A MASTER OF THE MARINE MARTIAL ARTS!
I AM A FINJA WARRIOR... HIII-YA!
FTUNK!
ghurrgh!
NOW TO FINISH YOU OFF WITH ONE OF MY FINJA STARFISH!
OOF!
Zing
TWOK
WHEN YOU WAKE UP IN AQUATRAZ, TELL THEM YOU WERE TAKEN DOWN BY...
BOTTLENOSE!
LOVE THOSE THREADS!
NICE WORK, PAL!
THANKS! I'M GLAD ALL MY TRAINING FINALLY PAID OFF!
WHAT A TRIUMPH!
IT SHOULD BE IMMORTALIZED IN SONG!
gurgle...
WELL... IF YOU INSIST...
WHY NOT? LET'S CRUISE PAST THE CHORAL REEF!
WHEN-A-DOLPHIN-HITS-AN-EEL LIKE-A-BIG-PIECE-OF-VEAL... THAT'S A-MORAY!
DIS IS CRUEL AND UNUSUAL PUN-ISHMENT!
THE END...
(UNTIL YOU REQUEST MORE "4F" STORIES BY WRITING TO SONIC-GRAMS!)
5

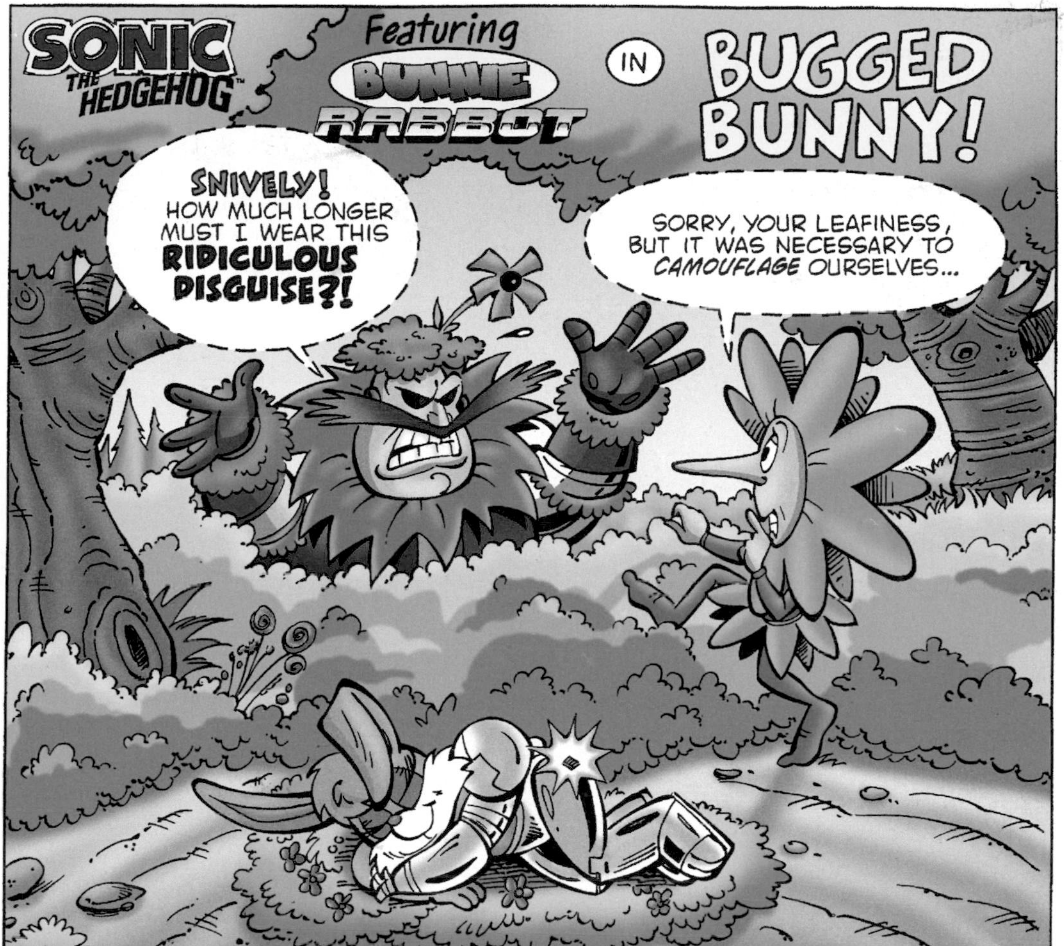
SONIC THE HEDGEHOG
Featuring BUNNIE RABBOT IN BUGGED BUNNY!
SNIVELY! HOW MUCH LONGER MUST I WEAR THIS RIDICULOUS DISGUISE?!
SORRY, YOUR LEAFINESS, BUT IT WAS NECESSARY TO CAMOUFLAGE OURSELVES...

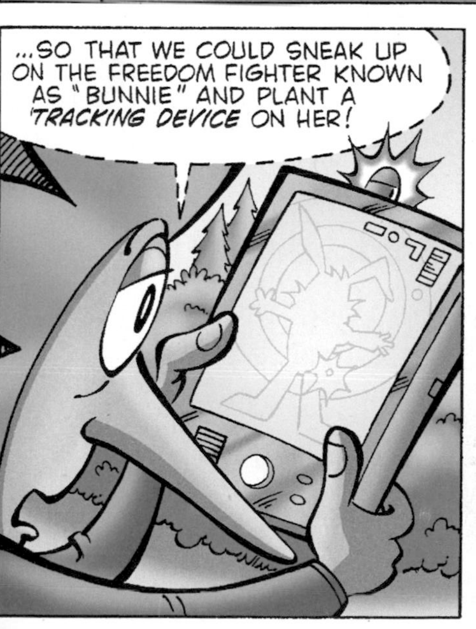
...SO THAT WE COULD SNEAK UP ON THE FREEDOM FIGHTER KNOWN AS "BUNNIE" AND PLANT A TRACKING DEVICE ON HER!

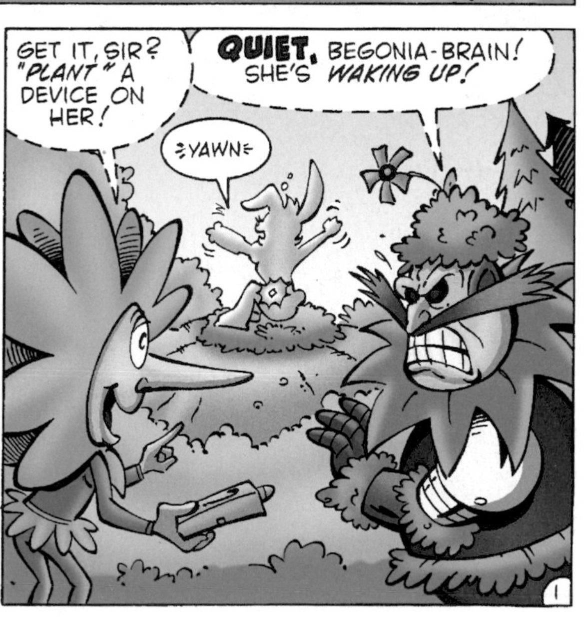
GET IT, SIR? "PLANT" A DEVICE ON HER!
QUIET, BEGONIA-BRAIN! SHE'S WAKING UP!
YAWN
1

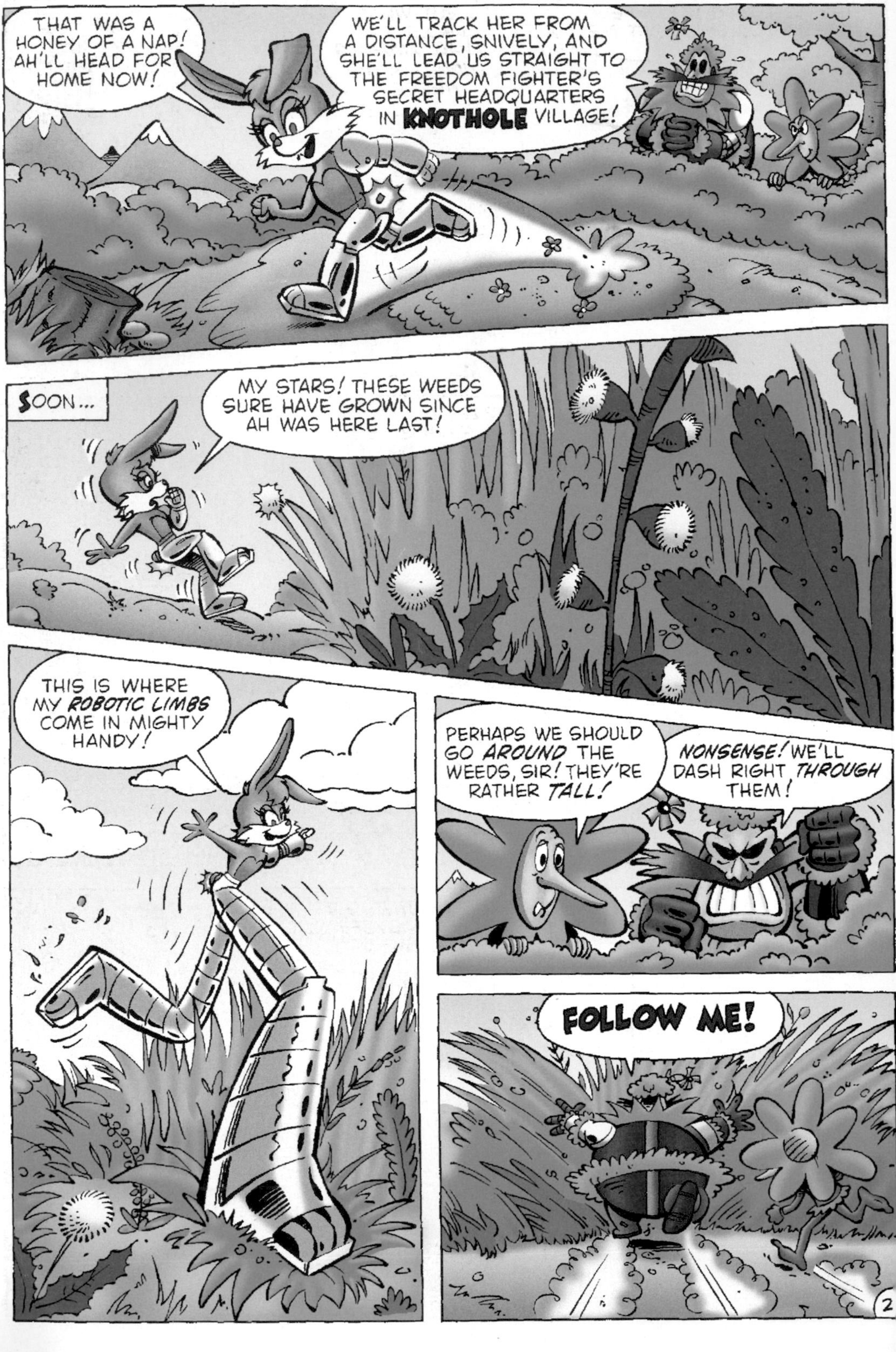
THAT WAS A HONEY OF A NAP! AH'LL HEAD FOR HOME NOW!
WE'LL TRACK HER FROM A DISTANCE, SNIVELY, AND SHE'LL LEAD US STRAIGHT TO THE FREEDOM FIGHTER'S SECRET HEADQUARTERS IN KNOTHOLE VILLAGE!
SOON...
MY STARS! THESE WEEDS SURE HAVE GROWN SINCE AH WAS HERE LAST!
THIS IS WHERE MY ROBOTIC LIMBS COME IN MIGHTY HANDY!
PERHAPS WE SHOULD GO AROUND THE WEEDS, SIR! THEY'RE RATHER TALL!
NONSENSE! WE'LL DASH RIGHT THROUGH THEM!
FOLLOW ME!

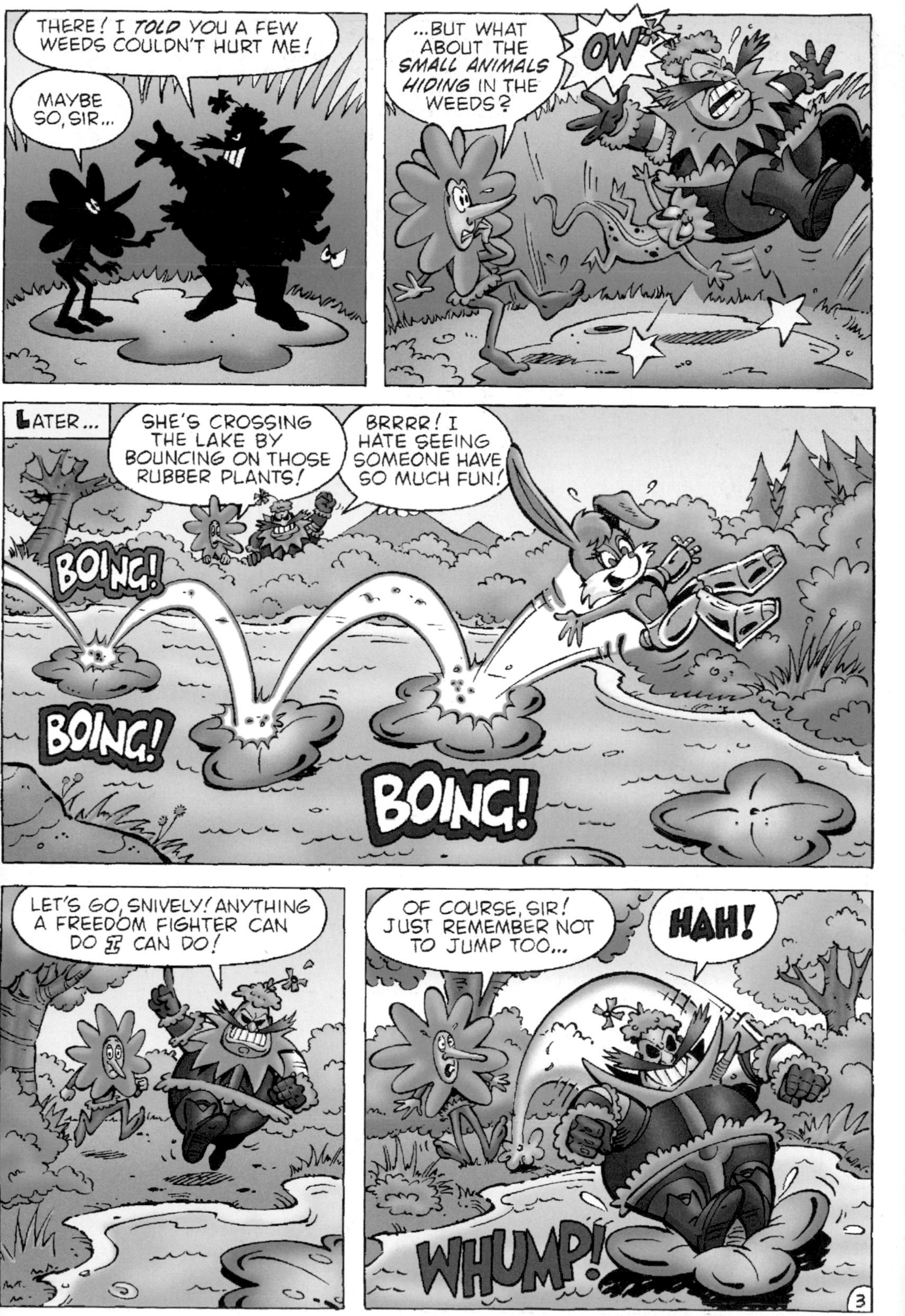
THERE! I TOLD YOU A FEW WEEDS COULDN'T HURT ME!
MAYBE SO, SIR...
...BUT WHAT ABOUT THE SMALL ANIMALS HIDING IN THE WEEDS?
OW
LATER...
SHE'S CROSSING THE LAKE BY BOUNCING ON THOSE RUBBER PLANTS!
BRRRR! I HATE SEEING SOMEONE HAVE SO MUCH FUN!
BOING!
BOING!
BOING!
LET'S GO, SNIVELY! ANYTHING A FREEDOM FIGHTER CAN DO I CAN DO!
OF COURSE, SIR! JUST REMEMBER NOT TO JUMP TOO...
HAH!
WHUMP!

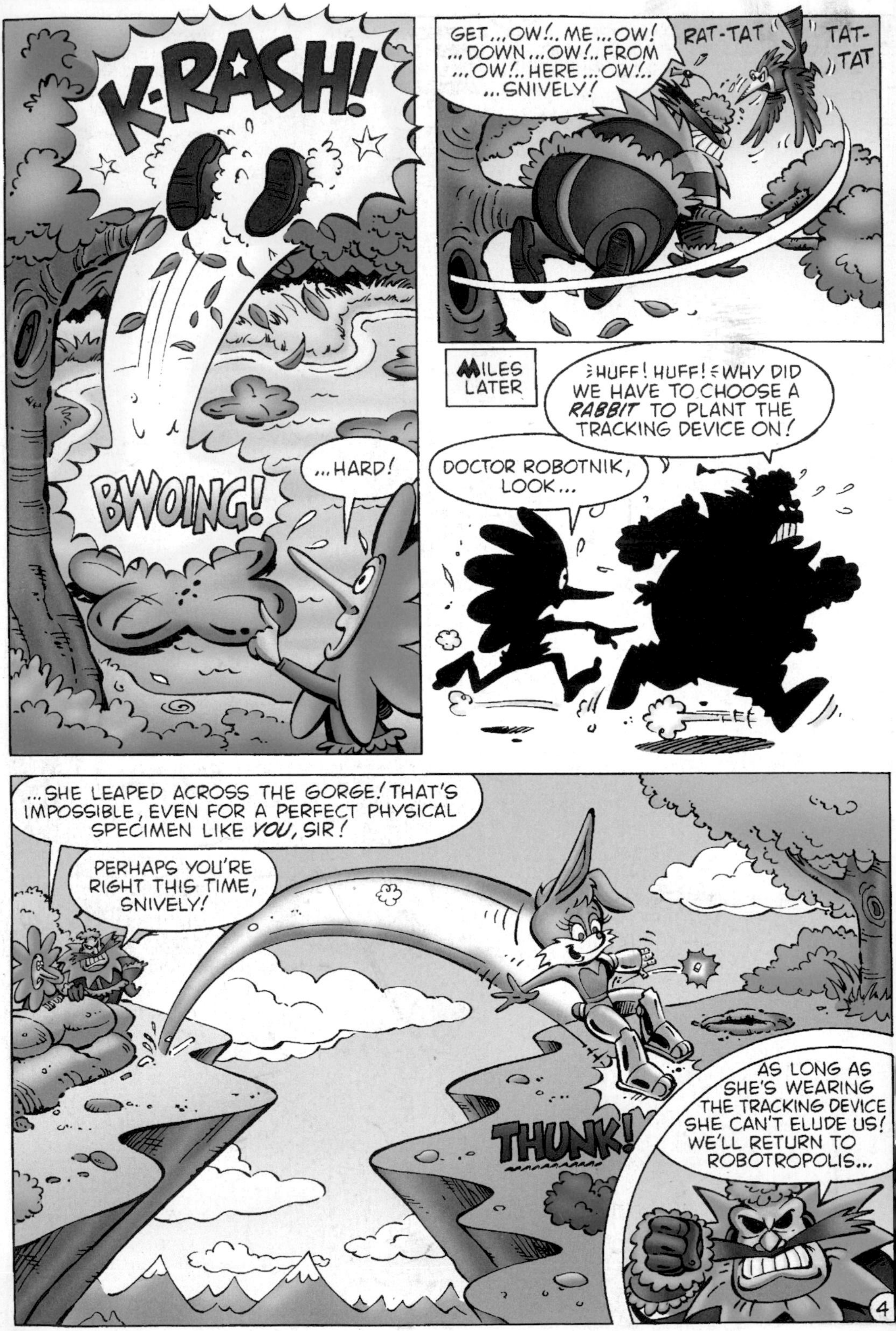
K-RASH!
BWOING!
...HARD!
GET...OW!.. ME...OW! ...DOWN...OW!.. FROM ...OW!.. HERE...OW!.. ...SNIVELY!
RAT-TAT
TAT-TAT
MILES LATER
HUFF! HUFF! WHY DID WE HAVE TO CHOOSE A RABBIT TO PLANT THE TRACKING DEVICE ON!
DOCTOR ROBOTNIK, LOOK...
...SHE LEAPED ACROSS THE GORGE! THAT'S IMPOSSIBLE, EVEN FOR A PERFECT PHYSICAL SPECIMEN LIKE YOU, SIR!
PERHAPS YOU'RE RIGHT THIS TIME, SNIVELY!
THUNK!
AS LONG AS SHE'S WEARING THE TRACKING DEVICE SHE CAN'T ELUDE US! WE'LL RETURN TO ROBOTROPOLIS...
4

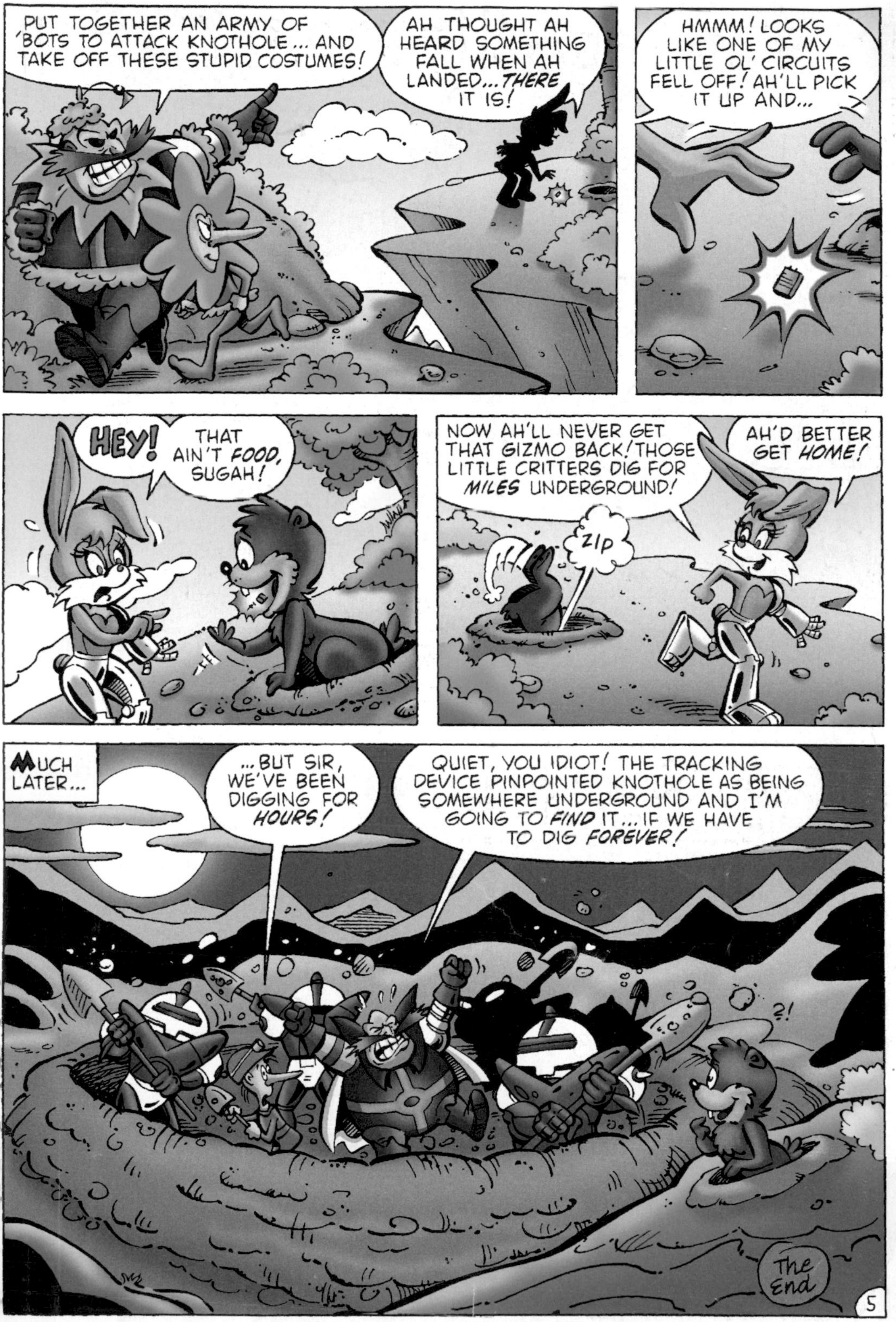
PUT TOGETHER AN ARMY OF 'BOTS TO ATTACK KNOTHOLE... AND TAKE OFF THESE STUPID COSTUMES!
AH THOUGHT AH HEARD SOMETHING FALL WHEN AH LANDED... THERE IT IS!
HMMM! LOOKS LIKE ONE OF MY LITTLE OL' CIRCUITS FELL OFF! AH'LL PICK IT UP AND...
HEY!
THAT AIN'T FOOD, SUGAH!
NOW AH'LL NEVER GET THAT GIZMO BACK! THOSE LITTLE CRITTERS DIG FOR MILES UNDERGROUND!
ZIP
AH'D BETTER GET HOME!
MUCH LATER...
...BUT SIR, WE'VE BEEN DIGGING FOR HOURS!
QUIET, YOU IDIOT! THE TRACKING DEVICE PINPOINTED KNOTHOLE AS BEING SOMEWHERE UNDERGROUND AND I'M GOING TO FIND IT... IF WE HAVE TO DIG FOREVER!
?!
The End

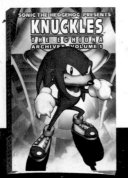